DEVIL'S NIGHT

A NOVEL

GARY REILLY

Running Meter Press

DENVER

Published by
Running Meter Press
2509 Xanthia St.
Denver, CO 80238
Publisher@RunningMeterPress.com
720-328-5488

Cover art by John Sherffius
Composition by D.K. Luraas

ISBN 978-0-9908666-5-7
Library of Congress Control Number: 2016943735

First Edition 2016

Printed in the United States of America

Other Titles in The Asphalt Warrior Series

The Asphalt Warrior

Ticket to Hollywood

Heart of Darkness Club

Home for the Holidays

Doctor Lovebeads

Dark Night of the Soul

Pickup at Union Station

CHAPTER 1

I try not to think about the events that took place during that last weekend in October, but I'm going to piece them together for you anyway. If you don't want to hear this, I'll shut off the meter and you can climb out of my taxi right here. No charge and no tip necessary. You can walk to wherever you're going. In fact, that might not be a bad idea. If you stay put, this could be the worst ride of your life. I know it was for me.

It all started one windy evening a few days before Halloween. Dry leaves were scuttling along the sidewalk. Don't ask me where the leaves came from because I was parked in the middle of a brick city. Some people call it "Denver." I have a handful of affectionate names for the burg that I have lived in for the past twenty years, and 38 percent of them are not fit for polite company—but I'll let you be the judge of who you are.

I was sitting slouched behind the steering wheel of Rocky Mountain Taxicab #123, which was parked at the cabstand outside the Brown Palace Hotel. I was counting my profits before my shift was done in direct violation of the ground rules set by Kenny Rogers when my back door opened and Frankenstein climbed in. It was my third Frankenstein of the day.

I know what you are thinking—"Frankenstein" was the baron, not the monster. But the English language is a malleable substance in a constant state of change in spite of the purists who want to hammer a stake through its heart like Van Helsing shoving a whittled stick between the ribs of Bela Lugosi in order to bring an end to the tyranny of linguistic evolution. But life is not a trivia game. Everybody knows the monster had no name, but it does nowadays, and its name is "Frankenstein." I blame Universal Studios. Face it—the *Bride of Frankenstein* was not stitched together in order to marry Colin Clive, but let's not get into an altercation over the negative impact of movies on *The Chicago Manual of Style*.

"The Center for the Performing Arts," the monster said.

There. Does that satisfy you purists?

"Yes, sir," I said, sitting up and tucking my profits into my T-shirt pocket.

DCPA was only a few blocks away from the Brown. They were having a Halloween bash in the ballroom and I had been dropping off ghosts and ghoulies and things that go bump in the backseat all evening. Wealthy spirits, I assumed. A lot of them came out of the hotels, couples or groups dressed like witches, hobos, princesses. My guess was that the mayor or the governor might be making an appearance. It was a charity event. Politicians lunge at hype. But I didn't know and didn't ask. I try not to mix politics with anything. All I knew was that I was making decent money because the trips were short and fast. Business had been picking up ever since the sun began going down. This happens when a major event takes place in Denver. I know what you're thinking—but major events *do* take place in Denver. I've never seen a city so desperate to be real.

Frankenstein leaned forward and placed his big green hands on the seat-back. "Will I have trouble getting a cab back to the hotel after the party is over?"

I glanced at his hands and experienced an electric thrill. I knew I was in the presence of an out-of-towner. It made me feel intellectually superior. This is a character flaw that I have suffered from ever since I first began talking to people. I really don't know how long I've been talking but every time I meet someone who doesn't know something that I myself know, my sense of decency crumbles and I feel like mocking him mercilessly.

"You won't have any problem sir," I said with a straight face. "There's a taxi-stand right outside the front entrance of the arts center. Cabs will be running all night."

His hands slowly slid off the cushion. I heard his massive torso press against the backseat. It was all padding of course, like most of my unpublished novels, but I don't want to talk about that. His costume was pretty good-looking. Obviously an expensive rental. He was probably out to impress the babes. I knew there were babes at the party because I had already hauled a few of them to DCPA from the Fairmont, the Hilton, etc.

After I dropped the monster off at the stand I hung around for a bit to look at the women arriving with their husbands or dates escorting the female partygoers who were dressed like the kind of women you never saw anywhere in the real world except the Lulu Room, which is farther down 15th Street and around the corner. It had a cover charge but I never let that stop me.

I saw a lady climb out of a Metro Taxi dressed like Wonder Woman. I don't know what her escort was dressed like because I didn't give the lucky bastard a glance. It made me feel guilty, though, to gawk at one of my favorite comic-book characters. I was raised Catholic. Let's move on.

There was one taxi ahead of me at the stand, a Yellow Cab, so I decided to fill out my trip-sheet before the number of fares for the evening piled up and too much paperwork ensued. I had been putting off marking down my trips on the sheet, which happens when the town is jumping and you get one fare right after another in your cab. I had learned to at least jot down the cost of the fare in the proper rectangle on my trip-sheet, and then fill out the pickup and destination and time boxes later when business slowed down.

I like the phrase "time boxes" but I promise not to say it again.

It was getting on toward six p.m. and I had made seventeen short runs in the past two hours. All of the customers had dropped a fiver on me and said, "Keep it," before climbing out at DCPA. Seventeen times five is eighty-five dollars for those of you who are lousy at math too. But I tried not to get excited. It's always great when major events take place, but I never start dreaming about buying a house in the ritzy part of town. The holiday gold rush would subside in a few days and I would be back to netting fifty bucks per shift and dreaming about going home to my apartment and shutting out the entire world. This is one of my rare dreams that actually do come true. It comes true three times a week. I drive a taxi three times a week. You connect the dots.

I was just filling out the Frankenstein rectangle when I heard a tap on my shotgun-seat window. I tried to ignore it. People who want to hire a cab at an officially authorized taxi-stand are required by PUC regulation to go to the first cab in line. In the cloying little world of my brain I was officially invisible to pedestrians, so I started to do what I had seen other taxi drivers do during the past fifteen years and simply point to the Yellow Cab ahead of me without looking to see who was trying to get my attention. This was about as rude as taxi drivers get in Denver, but my cloak of invisibility made me feel "special."

I'll be honest though. I had never incorporated the "rude point" before. It isn't in my nature to be rude to strangers. My friends are another story, but I don't have time to go into that because at the precise moment that I began to raise my hand with my index finger extended I glanced up and realized that the Yellow Cab had driven away while I was busy filling out my trip-sheet.

Good lord. I was first in line and didn't even know it.

The situation had the quality of a painfully excruciating metaphor, but I finessed it by continuing to raise my hand and casually scratching my right earlobe. I looked at the shotgun-window and saw a beautiful princess peering in at me. She was accompanied by a tin-man and a scarecrow. I would like to stop describing her companions right there because the tableau was so dazzlingly trite, but she was also accompanied by a Dracula and a hobo.

I leaned across the seat and cracked the window.

"Can you take us somewhere?" the princess said.

I realized I was in the presence of teenagers. Only a teenager would ask a question like that of a cab driver.

"Yes," I said. I conscientiously speak with clarity around teenagers. It's my only defense.

I had to move a pile of junk from the front seat before anyone could get seated shotgun. This consisted of a plastic briefcase and a small toolbox and some Twinkie wrappers and a couple of empty soda cans. There were other items but I was so embarrassed about being such a slob that I'll end the list there. The thing is though, I am a deliberate slob when I drive a taxi. I have no explanation for the rest of my life but I clutter up my shotgun seat while on cab duty in order to discourage fares from getting into the front seat. I prefer that my customers sit in the backseat where I don't have to look at them while I do a job on their billfolds.

The four "swains," as I instantly thought of them because that's how my mind works, climbed into the backseat and the princess climbed in shotgun. I was going to suggest that two of the kids sit in front, with three in the rear, so that everybody would be comfortable, if not symmetrical, but I reminded myself that I was dealing with teenagers. Anybody who deals with teenagers needs some kind of goddamn therapy.

"Where to?" I said.

"We want to go to a haunted house," the princess said.

"Yeah, man," one of the boys in the backroom chirped. The boys made off-stage remarks like that all during the ride, accompanied by teen snickers, but I won't repeat the remarks unless they are relevant to the main conversation. I learned relevance in creative-writing classes in college where the teachers often admonished me to stop snickering.

"Do you have an address?" I said.

A pasty white hand slithered across the backseat between the princess and me. The pale fingers were clutching a slip of paper. "Here is the address," an adenoidal voice said.

I glanced back. Dracula was gazing at me.

I took the paper and read it, then groaned inwardly. The address was on west 38th Avenue, out toward Golden, a town approximately fifteen miles west of the spot where I was groaning. I had only an hour left of my taxi shift, which meant I would not be able to take the kids to the haunted house and get back to the cab company on time to beat the clock. I would end up paying a five-dollar late fee for my taxi. You have to pay five dollars for every half-hour you're late. This would cause me one minute of embarrassment, the fair market value of ineptitude.

"This house is pretty far away," I said. "Are you kids here at the party with your parents?"

"Yes," the princess said.

"Do they know you're going to this place?"

"Yes. They told us it would be all right if we went to the haunted house and then came back here after we finished the tour."

My mental Univac went into action. There were haunted houses all over Denver. I'm talking commercial haunted houses that moneygrubbers not unlike myself opened every Halloween to profit off people's superstitions. I had taken young people to a number of such places during the past few days, but they were all within Denver city limits. For some reason old people don't go to those things.

"It'll take us at least a half-hour to get there," I said. "And you might have trouble getting a taxi back here. I know of a couple haunted houses that are a lot closer than this if you would rather stay in town."

"We want to go to this one," a voice said from the backseat. "It's supposed to be the best."

"Yeah, it's the best," the chorus chimed.

The white hand slowly reached forward and plucked the piece of paper from my fingers. "This house is supposed to actually be haunted," Dracula said.

I felt deeply troubled. Not by Dracula's asinine statement but by the fact that I had told the princess I could take them somewhere, and now I was trying to take them somewhere else. The police refer to this as "bait-and-switch."

"There's a haunted house on south Broadway that's said to be pretty good, are you sure you want to go all the way out to Golden?" I said.

"Indubitably," Dracula said.

His buddies snickered.

"So … your parents know you guys are going to this haunted house, right?" I said.

"Yes," the princess said. "We have their permission."

"Do you have money for cab fare?"

I had learned to say this long ago in situations that troubled me, mostly involving hobos—real hobos, not fun hobos.

"Of course," the girl replied. She was carrying a small white purse. She started to open it. I glanced at the purse, then let her continue to open it. She pulled out a wad of twenty-dollar bills.

"You don't have to pay me right now," I said, after ascertaining that she could pay me at all. "Wait until we get there."

She slid the money back into the purse and snapped it shut.

It was with a sigh of trepidation that I started the engine, put my taxi into gear, pulled onto 15th Street, and set out on a journey that in the days to come would make me wish I had never heard the mispronounced word "Halloween."

CHAPTER 2

"Halloween."

A variation of "All Hallow E'en"—the evening before All Saints' Day.

You are probably as baffled as I am by the fact that mispronounced words make it into the dictionary. According to my *American Heritage Dictionary* there's a shadowy group of intellectuals who call themselves "The Usage Panel" who apparently are in charge of the English language. But I want to know who shortened "Evening" to "E'en" in the first place—some cockney dockworker? And why did the Usage Panel legitimize it by printing it in the dictionary? What if I shortened "Usage Panel" to "Use'pel"? Would the Usage Panel break their necks rushing to print that abomination above the word "usquebaugh" in the diction'ee? I don't think there is anything on earth that enrages people quite like mispronounced words, and yet the English language itself is little more than a grab-bag of mispronounced Latin, with a bit of mispronounced Spanish, mispronounced German, and mispronounced Italian thrown in, along with a lot of other mispronounced languages that existed prior to the invasion of England by the French in 1066. When I was a kid the Franco/Anglo word "chic" was pronounced "sheik." Today people pronounce it "chick." I don't know why this bothers me since I was an English major in college and not a French major. I have a degree from the University of Colorado at Denver. I keep it in a steamer trunk along with my unpublished novels. I use the diploma as a divider to separate my failed novels from my failed screenplays.

By the way, just so you know, "usquebaugh" is the origin of the word "whiskey." Apparently British dockworkers can't say "usquebaugh" without slurring it and I'll give you one guess why.

The eve of All Saints' Day was three nights off. This was Wednesday, and Halloween was the upcoming Saturday. I never work on Saturdays unless I am forced to do so by the immutable laws of economics, which I pronounce "rent." I never argue with laws, whether economics, physics, or civil. By civil I mean "cops." Given the numerous times I have been questioned by law-enforcement officers you would think that an occasional altercation would occur between myself and John Law, but you would be wrong. Whenever I find myself seated on a chair in a small room being interrogated by detectives, I am the most agreeable person in the annals of crime. I know what you're thinking—what a wimp. But when it comes to grueling interrogations I always have one thing going for me. I call it "innocence." It usually takes awhile for the police to drag it out of me, even when I'm holding it up to them like a truffle on a silver platter. But I have learned that the police cast a jaundiced eye on proclamations of innocence erupting from the mouths of sweaty suspects.

As long as I'm on the subject, I find it interesting that the laws of physics don't have an enforcement agency. They pretty much enforce themselves. Take gravity for instance. Conversely, it would be nice if civil laws made it physically impossible to commit crimes. That would certainly take a load off my shoulders.

"Why does the meter already show a dollar-fifty?" a voice said from the backseat. I glanced around and saw Dracula staring at the meter, which flipped over to a dollar-seventy as I drove toward Speer Boulevard.

"That's called a flag-drop," I said, repeating a lecture that I had given so many times during the past fifteen years that I was barely aware of the words coming out of my mouth. I would make a terrible English professor. My interest in explaining the rules of grammar would die after one minute in the ivy-covered walls. "The Public Utilities Commission sets the rates for taxicabs, and PUC regulation states that it costs a customer a dollar-fifty just to climb into a cab."

"What if you climb in and climb right back out," he said. "Do you still have to pay a dollar-fifty?"

His adenoidal voice possessed the somewhat deep, post-pubescent resonance that you often hear in disk jockeys, even old ones. It was the kind of voice that I associated with pseudo-intellectuals. If you ever took Philosophy 101 in college you know the voice. I figured him as the spokesman for this group. He seemed to be about sixteen years old, although the fangs made him look seventeen. I pegged him as an A-student in school, the type who played with the minds of teachers to let them know he was their intellectual equal. I was a C-student version of him in high school, minus the equality factor, so I knew what I was dealing with.

"No," I said.

I let that bombshell hang in the air.

Dracula finally broke the silence by saying, "Why not? You just said it was a regulation."

I came to a crossroad. Not in the street but in my mind. If an adult hassles me about the flag-drop—which does occasionally happen—I offer to let him climb out and take a bus to wherever he is going. But I was dealing with a young person, and I knew deep down inside that I had a moral obligation to explain the real world to him. High school doesn't cover that subject.

"It's a judgment call," I said, as I turned a corner onto Speer and headed toward north Denver. "If I drop the flag and start the meter, the law kicks in and the customer is obligated to pay me a dollar-fifty. But if he climbs back out, I just shut off the meter and forget about it."

"You let him get away with violating the law?" he said.

"Yup."

"Why?"

"Because it would take too long to track down a policeman and catch the guy and make him pay. Some things in life just aren't worth it."

I could almost hear the gears grinding in Dracula's brain, i.e., How could you let someone break a law? Isn't everybody supposed to obey the rules? What kind of grownup are you? These were the kinds of questions that blossomed in my mind when I was a teenager and wanted to paint a grownup into a corner—except I never had the guts. I didn't start painting people into corners until I discovered scotch.

"How much farther is it?" another voice said.

I glanced in the rearview mirror. It was the hobo talking. I was surprised. I didn't think hobos worried about such things.

"Don't start with that nonsense, Conrad," Dracula said in a droll and disapproving tone of voice before I could reply. "We've only been on the road five minutes."

I saw the hobo raise his shoulders and giggle. I sized him up immediately: Conrad was the designated class clown. Dracula obviously was used to his antics. For some reason Dracula reminded me of a friend of mine named Big Al.

"It'll be another twenty to twenty-five minutes," I said, trying to remain above the fray. "This address isn't close to an interstate so I'll have to take a back road."

"You mean a scenic route?" Dracula said.

It took all of my willpower to contain the bristles that began sprouting on my body like the fur that appears on Larry Talbot's flesh whenever the wolfbane blooms and the autumn moon is bright. For a moment there I had liked young Dracula due to his admonishment of the hobo. But I am not a scenic-router. I do not try to gouge customers by taking them the long way to anywhere. Even if I could increase my profits by doing so I would never do it because my primary goal as a cab driver is to get rid of my fares as quickly as possible. I can't stand to have anybody in the backseat of my taxi. If this doesn't make any sense to you, join the club.

Ergo, I ceased to like Dracula. I didn't care if he was only sixteen, ignorant, and scary looking, I still didn't like him.

"No," I said. "PUC regulations require that all taxi drivers proceed to a customer's destination by the most direct route. So we'll be taking Speer Boulevard to Thirty-eighth, and then heading straight west to Golden."

I don't recall the tone of my voice during this brief lecture but I may have inadvertently sounded like a grownup. A silence filled the taxi, accompanied by a chill in the air. It was the sort of chill that is sometimes described as a "cold-spot" by people who are schooled in paranormal phenomena.

I heard a rustling at my side. I glanced over at the princess who was slowly turning around so she could see into the backseat. "Why don't you grow up, Lester?" she said.

My eyes flickered to the rearview mirror. The vampire's shoulders drooped perceptibly. He turned his pale face toward the side window and began studying the architectural wonders of north Denver. We were just coming up on 38th Avenue.

The girl turned her eyes on me and said, "Boys can be so gauche."

She faced forward and stared out the front window as if mortified by the behavior of the entire male species.

Here's the funny thing though: I couldn't help but feel that I was responsible for the sour turn that the ride had taken, and not just because I was a member of the male species but because I had allowed Lester's smart-aleck remark to get under my skin, which in turn caused me to talk like a grownup, the last thing in the world I am qualified to do. Consequently I decided to try and salvage what was left of the trip. I will admit that "salvaging" is another thing I am not qualified to do but I was grasping at straws as usual.

"That's a pretty costume you're wearing," I said to the girl. "What's your name?"

"Shantel," she replied, smiling at me. "What's yours?"

"Murph," I said. "Short for Murphy." I felt compelled to explain my nickname since she was a princess.

I heard the chorus whisper and snicker in the backseat, but rather than ignore it I tried to "go with the flow" and become a part of it by making a concerted effort to recall what it was like to be a teenager making fun of people's names. That didn't take much effort. I know a cop named Artie Argyle.

"Are you supposed to be any one princess in particular?" I said, as I gazed at the road ahead.

"Try Ariella," Dracula said quietly from the backseat.

I looked at the girl. I saw her jawline harden. Believe me, I know my hardened female jawlines. She continued to stare out the front window. A peculiar silence emanated from the backseat. I had the feeling Dracula had touched a raw nerve.

Fer the luvva Christ.

I decided it might be best to keep my mouth shut for the rest of the ride. I should decide that more often.

But my decision was abrogated when Dracula leaned forward with a rustle of his black cape and said, "Tell me something, Mr. Murphy. Do you believe in the afterlife?"

The world began to spin. Suddenly I was back in school. High school or college, it didn't make any difference, except I wasn't drinking beer. I'll admit it. I drank a few beers in high school. During the summer between my junior and senior year I puked my first—well I'm getting off the subject here—which was exactly what I wanted to do on the night Dracula asked me if I believed there was life after death. But it was no-go. He had placed me on the hot seat, and as a cab driver, a Baby Boomer, and a grownup, I had to pretend to be something I wasn't. I'll let you speculate as to what I wasn't.

"My general attitude is that the concept of belief is for children," I said. "I try to deal in what passes for knowledge on this planet. But I do like the idea of an afterlife."

He paused a moment before replying. I assumed he was trying to make sense out of what I had just said. Articulating seemingly contradictory statements was a debating technique that I had utilized as a teenager to baffle my opponents while I cracked another brewski.

"Why?" he finally said, a feeble comeback if I ever heard one.

"The idea of flying around like a ghost appeals to me," I said.

"Does that mean you believe in ghosts?" he said.

"Well, I'll tell ya …" I said, as I pulled around the corner onto 38th and began heading west toward the haunted house, "… the problem that I have with ghosts is gravity."

"What do you mean by that?" he said querulously. He was beginning to lose his cool, I could tell. This happens to people who talk to me even when I don't intend it to happen, which isn't often.

"I don't understand why the gravitational pull of the earth would affect ghosts," I said. "It seems to me that if there was such things as ghosts they would remain at the same point in space where they were floating when they came into existence. I mean, given the fact that millions of people die every year, it seems to me that the earth would leave a jet stream of ghosts all across the cosmos."

The hobo, the tin-man, and the scarecrow began giggling.

"Could we talk about something else?" the girl said, turning around and giving Lester a smile/frown. She was probably used to his antics. This was the first time I ever had two Big Als in my taxi.

"For a dollar-fifty per mile I can talk about anything you like," I interjected.

Dracula sat back and glared at me. I know because I saw his sunken eyes burning a hole in my rearview mirror. He seemed miffed that I had made his friends laugh at him, although I was merely interpreting his re-action. But I based my speculation on how I reacted as a teenager when-ever my friends mocked a subject I had brought up. The world of my youth was filled with laughter.

Ergo, I could not help but feel that I had made an enemy.

A silence ensued, but it did not have the edge of the previous silence. When you drive a cab for a living, you hear a lot of silences, and certainly never enough.

But it didn't last long. Kids and silence have the quality of an oxy-moron. The boys in the back began whispering and snickering again. I felt that they were snickering at me, but that was okay. I wouldn't trust a kid who didn't snicker at grownups. I had my share of gym coaches in high school, too.

We passed out of the western city limits of Denver and entered a magic realm called "Wheat Ridge." For some reason suburbs make me wistful. Most of Denver's suburbs blossomed after World War II and are filled with one-story tan-brick ranch houses that must have seemed cutting-edge in their time, dream houses built by veterans returning from Europe and the Pacific, a unique breed of architecture running neck-and-neck with the wonders of the space age. But the burst of modern growth seemed to have ground to a halt during the sixties, and now had the rundown look of wilted lettuce.

Then came condos.

Condos don't make me feel like anything except stepping on the gas. Pretty soon we were beyond Wheat Ridge and heading out into the countryside that borders the foothills of the Rocky Mountains. There were no stoplights and traffic was thin on the two-lane blacktop. The flora in that part of the metro area had not changed much since I had ar-rived in Denver twenty years earlier. Sparsely populated landscapes with old wooden two-story houses were set back from the road here and there, camouflaged by old-growth oak and cottonwoods. According to a Den-ver history class I took at UCD, when the pioneers arrived in Colorado Territory there weren't nary a tree in sight for miles. Colorado was a part of The Great American Desert back in those days. Kansas still is. This motivated the Denver city government to encourage people to plant trees. Arbor Day might have had something to do with that but I didn't listen very closely in class. I think Arbor Day was actually invented by Nebraska, which seems odd because there are no trees in Nebraska. End result: the Denverites overdid it. There are a hell of a lot of trees between Denver and Golden. This got me to thinking about an agricultural fiction movie called *The Day of the Triffids*, which in turn made me think of writing a horror novel about trees that reproduced in unexpected profusion. In my novel the earth would be saved by termites—possibly bionic.

If I haven't mentioned this to you, I might as well admit that I am an unpublished novelist, and practically anything can start me thinking about writing a novel. If I get lucky though, something distracts me, and in this case it was a traffic jam that seemed to appear out of nowhere. Scores of taillights glowed up ahead like fireflies. At first I thought it might be caused by a speed trap. If you know anything about suburban cops, then you probably know what I'm talking about. Suburban cops can be reeeeeeal efficient. But it turned out to be a line of cars headed for the haunted house.

CHAPTER 3

I slowed down and began making quick calculations. We were a good two hundred feet from the entrance to the property. There was a dirt drive that led up to the house itself, and cars were parked on it as well as on what would have been the front lawn back in the cowboy days. People were walking along the shoulders of the road where a few cars were parked, probably illegally. Think *Woodstock*. I saw a couple of young men wearing orange day-glo vests and waving flashlights. They were directing traffic on the property and guiding cars into parking spaces vacated by people who had already made the scene. The young men were like parking attendants at a dog track. I have always been impressed by the efficiency of dog-track parking attendants. I got my fill of them during the summer I descended into the opium den of gambling addiction. It lasted a week. My "cure" was closely related to financial losses, combined with a lecture from Big Al, but don't get me started on my inability to strike it rich. I've never been cured of that.

I judged that it could take another five minutes before we would arrive at the entrance to the gate, which consisted of two stone pillars on either side of the dirt driveway. We were stuck in your standard traffic jam. I had been there plenty of times as a cab driver and as a human being, i.e., as you travel closer to your goal, your velocity slows proportionately, so that it seems like you are never going to get there. It's like that halfway-point conundrum that drives mathematicians insane. If you don't know what I'm talking about, it doesn't matter.

As I sized up the situation, a Yellow Cab came from the opposite direction, headed toward Denver. I craned my neck and saw two more cabs close to the house dropping people off.

"It could take a while to get up to the gate," I said, glancing over at

Shantel. "If you guys would prefer, you could get out here and walk the rest of the way. We could be sitting here for another five minutes."

I was taking a cabbie risk. On the one hand, they might think I was trying to pull a fast one by not taking them all the way to their destination. On the other hand, if they remained in the cab, the interminable ticking of the meter might make them think I was gouging them. The meter switches to a time clock when a cab is standing still. Either way, they might think I was trying to rip them off. People frequently think this about cab drivers. But I was used to it. When you drive a taxi for a living, suspicion reigns eternal. It never seems to occur to impatient people that cab drivers also try to move things along efficiently.

"Good idea," the tin-man said.

I was glad the scarecrow hadn't agreed with me. I think we all know the story of the scarecrow's inability to think without the aid of a diploma.

"Let's hoof it, dudes," the hobo said. That's my kind of hobo.

The meter came to twenty-one dollars. The princess opened her purse and pulled out a Jackson and a five. She handed both of them to me and said, "Keep the change, Mr. Murphy."

I said thanks. I wasn't surprised that she had tipped me. Females of all ages know how to tip. Young males think the tip is a rip.

"You shouldn't have any trouble getting a cab back to DCPA," I said, as the kids opened their doors and began piling out. "After you finish the tour you can hail one of the cabs that are dropping people off here."

"Okay, Mr. Murphy, thanks," Shantel said, as she shut the shotgun door.

I kept my eye on the white purse in her hand as she joined her friends. The reason I did this was because a white purse had played a key role in a dicey situation that entangled me awhile back. It was nothing really. I was just suspected of kidnapping, robbing, and murdering a young actress who owned a similar purse. But it turned out that she was neither kidnapped nor robbed nor murdered. She wasn't even roughed up. She goes to Denver University nowadays.

I glanced into the backseat to make certain none of the boys had left behind an oilcan or a set of fangs. People were always leaving things in my backseat, like purses or combs or hundreds of thousands of dollars. But I had learned my lesson—*always* check the backseat. When I was trained to become a taxi driver I had been told to do that by my teachers, which included Big Al. But like most lessons it eventually faded from my mind. End result? I had gotten into a number of ridiculous jams, which involved detectives. To date though, I have never gotten into a jam caused by my inability to multiply 2x(a-b). I left those jams in high school. Some people call them "tests."

I waited until traffic coming from the opposite direction was clear, then I made an illegal U-turn on the road and tried not to think about it. Like most people who commit petty crimes I try not to think about my actions beyond calculating the odds of getting nabbed by the police. In this way I think I am human. The majority of the other automobile drivers who saw me do this probably thought I was just a cab driver. Ergo, I used their misconception as a shield, in the sense that people see cab drivers doing peculiar things all the time, such as double parking or parking in no-parking zones. But they just write it off as the zany nature of cabbies, a characterization promulgated by Hollywood movies and real cab drivers. But I have never considered myself a real cab driver. I just hack part-time for a living while waiting to sell a novel, although the Internal Revenue Service views me as a real cab driver—and I think we all have a good idea of the government's grasp of reality.

I will admit that taking advantage of a cliché might qualify as a sleazy trick but it was an effective method of getting me back to Denver on time in order to avoid a double late fee, and when you drive a taxi for a living you rarely get the opportunity to use effective methods.

It was getting on toward seven p.m. and I had a half-hour to get back to the Rocky Mountain Taxicab Company, pay my late fee, be embarrassed for one minute, and then roll on home. It was dark and cold outside, I was hungry, and I hadn't had a beer in so long I couldn't remember when. My guess was twenty-four hours but I try not to dwell on the past.

I went as far as Kipling Street where I turned north and drove until I hooked up with Interstate 70, which would take me on a straight shot to the "motor," as we cabbies refer to the taxi company. Getting onto an interstate was like stepping aboard a time machine. It had taken a half-hour to get to the haunted house on the old-fashioned two-lane blacktop, but by stepping onto the time machine I would get back to Denver in no time flat, which I did.

I timed it.

As I was driving along I started thinking about the novel, *The Time Machine*. It was a good thing H.G. Wells had already written that book because the odds were fair that I might have ended up writing a failed novel about a time machine. I was ten years old when I saw George Pal's film version of *The Time Machine*. It drove me insane with desire. At the age of ten there was nothing I craved more than to leave the town where I lived—Wichita, Kansas—and a time machine seemed like the ideal vehicle since I was too young to drive a car. I thought it would be great to hop into a time machine and travel thirty years into the future and see the wonders of the space age unfolding around me—the rocket ships, the moving sidewalks, the people wearing transparent helmets and carrying ray-guns. If I had actually accomplished such a feat I would have found myself in Wichita as it appeared last year when I went home for Christmas. The town looked exactly the way it did when I was ten. Nothing had changed, including my craving to get the hell out.

I pulled into the RMTC parking lot at 7:20 with ten minutes to spare on my singleton late fee. Out of the twenty-five bucks I had received from Shantel I had to give five bucks back to what I think of as The Black Hole. Any time money leaves my possession it goes into The Black Hole regardless of what I get in return—groceries, scotch, embarrassment—it's gone and I'll never see it again, so I purposely try not to think about it. However, since taxes are especially vexing I take a slightly different approach. For example, if I earn $10,000 in a year and pay $2,000 in taxes, I just pretend I earned $8,000 and didn't pay any taxes. This gives me the same heightened feeling of empowerment that I get after downing three shots of scotch. If every working American would embrace self-delusion on April 15th, I believe it would reduce the aggregate percentage of springtime hangovers.

I walked into the on-call room. Stew was seated in the cage reading a model railroading magazine. There were no other drivers present. The graveyard shift-change had taken place at seven, so I was spared the embarrassment of someone overhearing Stew say quietly, "You owe an additional five." I don't like people to know I have flaws. I'm not sure if this makes me human or not. Not the "flaws" part, but being embarrassed about it. It's possible that I might have been born with an innate sense of perfection, which would be ironic given the number of rejection slips I have acquired in the past twenty years.

As I dragged my incriminating billfold out of my back pocket I told him about the long run to the haunted house out toward Golden. But Stew had been a taxi driver when I was still a teenager. He wasn't impressed by my sob story. He handed me a receipt for the five, which I quickly crumpled into a ball and shoved into a pocket out of fear that a driver might walk into the room and see the receipt and "know" that I had flaws.

"See ya tomorrow," I said.

Stew nodded and went back to reading about tiny railroad tracks.

I walked out of the on-call room and headed for my '64 Chevy feeling like a rat trapped on a treadmill. By this I mean I was forced by the immutable laws of economics to work the next day—Thursday. Every fourth week of the month I have to work five days in a row in order to cover my rent. I refer to this phenomenon as "work week." I suppose I could label it "normal week" since normal people work five days a week. In fact if I had the time, the energy, and no reason to go on living, I could come up with all sorts of imaginative names for my monthly obligation, but I don't like to use my imagination for anything except getting paid to write novels. But since I have never gotten paid to write novels I don't want to risk wasting a word that could conceivably play a pivotal role in the acquisition of an acceptance slip—especially if that all-powerful word was inextricably tied to a plot. I spend a lot of time trying to psych out the minds of book editors in New York City. If *only* I knew what they *wanted*.

Fortunately I would not be starting any new novels that week. Ever since the day I had decided to become a novelist it had been literally impossible for me to write books when I was working a normal job. As a result, I did everything I could to avoid normal jobs in order to improve my chances of getting published. There seemed to be some kind of mysterious connection between manual labor and rejection slips, and I wanted to eliminate every conceivable risk.

Due to economic factors, I did once get a normal job, but it lasted only a year. I wrote monthly brochures for a company called Dyna-Plex. It took me one hour to write one brochure. The fact that I worked only twelve hours a year did nothing to invalidate the "normality" of the job because I still had to arrive at work at 8:00 a.m. and couldn't go home until 5:00 p.m. We were given an hour for lunch. I felt that anybody who needed an hour to eat anything at all was a candidate for some kind of goddamn therapy. I would have preferred that they cut down the lunch hour and let me go home at 4:03.

On the other hand, when I was in the army we were given an hour and a half to eat lunch. But army lunches were different from civilian lunches. First of all you had to stand in a slow-moving line outside a mess hall door. Then you had to sit down at a table and try to figure out what the hell was on your tray. The final step, of course, was to psych yourself up to eat it. The army had it timed perfectly.

On the way home from RMTC, I stopped off at a Burger King and bought a couple of hamburgers, but no soda. I rarely buy soft drinks at fast-food joints because I keep a handy supply of sodas at home. As a consequence, each time I order a burger and don't ask for a soda I get the impression that the cashier suspects I'm trying to pull a fast one. I worry that the manager and the cook might step out to the drive-up lane and ask me just what the heck was going on here. They might even suggest that I take my business elsewhere unless I start ordering normal meals. "Normal" in America is two hamburgers, a soda, and a sack of fries. The upshot is that whenever I order my meals at a Burger King, I feel like a goddamn communist.

CHAPTER 4

I arrived at my apartment at twenty minutes to eight. This completely threw off my schedule, since I am used to arriving home at a quarter after seven. Those twenty-five minutes play a pivotal role in my life because they give me fifteen minutes to eat and prepare myself to watch *Gilligan's Island,* which comes on at seven-thirty, broadcast out of a sister-station in Chicago. I prefer not to eat during *Gilligan* because I like to focus all my attention on the character known as "Mary Ann." Chewing diminishes my concentration by 17 percent, which is like missing 17 percent of Mary Ann, which in turn is like drinking watered-down scotch.

But this was "work week" and during work week I have to deal with a lot of inconveniences in my life. It took fourteen years of cab driving to adjust, but somehow I managed it. Denial plays an enormous role in my adjustments, so that night I just pretended I hadn't missed ten minutes of *Gilligan.* I switched on the TV and unwrapped my first burger, aware nevertheless that I had missed 30 percent of Mary Ann, combined with the 17 percent that I would miss by chewing while staring. I wasn't certain just what that added up to in terms of (30 (minutes) − (time+visual imagery)) so maybe I should have stayed awake in algebra class. At least then I'd know what I was missing. But my denial was rendered moot when the picture came on the tube.

I froze.

Bob Denver was a vampire.

It hadn't occurred to me that Chicago would be broadcasting one of my all-time favorite *Gilligan's*es. But it made perfect sense. It dovetailed neatly with the Halloween season. It was an episode where Gilligan gets bitten by a bat and thinks he has become one of the living dead. It's a real knee-slapper. I was enraged—I missed ten minutes.

I simultaneously did two things, which Albert Einstein supposedly proved impossible (re: The Theory of Simultaneity)—I lost my appetite and I switched off the TV.

Why the hell do I drive a taxi for a living? I asked myself as I tossed my sack of food onto my beer table and slumped down in my easy chair.

If I had worked a normal job I would have been home by six-thirty, which would have given me plenty of time to eat, bathe, put on a robe and slippers, and prepare myself for thirty blockbuster minutes of island hopping. I assumed that all normal men wore robes and slippers when they got home from work, although this was pure speculation on my part. Some of it derived from reading Conan Doyle. Sherlock Holmes dressed that way, and he struck me as normal, since he was the only private detective who lived in London during the late 1880s and therefore embodied The Norm. I don't want to mislead you, though. Most of my assumptions are not based on things that I have read, viewed on TV, or personally experienced. I make up a lot of them and then wait breathlessly to see if they coincide with reality. Surprisingly, they often do. For example, when I was in high school I began to suspect that having a job as an adult would amount to a living hell.

I sat in my easy chair feeling the pangs of hunger gnawing at my vitals, and thinking about the people who were responsible for the mess that was my life. I'm talking about the five kids that I had taken to the haunted house. If they had not climbed into my cab I would have gotten home at a decent hour. I would already be fed, relaxed, and gazing anxiously at *Gilligan's Island* hoping for a glimpse of Mary Ann.

But then I remembered that the kids had climbed into my cab because I had parked to gawk at the women dressed in Halloween costumes instead of driving back to the Brown Palace for another quick money run.

That made me start thinking about Wonder Woman again. When *Wonder Woman* came on TV starring Lynda Carter I never watched it. Call me a sexist but I had been programmed by life in these here United States to expect my superheroes to be men. Even if I had watched the TV show, I probably would have done it just to gawk at Lynda, so either way I would have come off as a sexist. Face it, men can't win in this world—except James Bond and Spider-Man. They always win, although usually by the skin of their teeth. But that's what gives their stories the edginess that is sought by all couch potatoes who crave excitement.

Ergo, I began to realize it was my own fault that I was sitting in my living room starving to death and mooning around about Mary Ann. But I finessed that self-confrontation by thinking about the smart-aleck kid who had been dressed as Dracula. I envisioned him taking the haunted house tour and sneering at the exhibits. But then I remembered him saying that the house was supposed to be haunted. I envisioned him taking the tour and lagging behind his friends, peering around curiously as he walked through the dim rooms, climbing up and down creaking staircases and glancing into dark alcoves wondering if perhaps he might sense the presence of an unearthly spirit. If I believed in ghosts that's what I would do—minus the lagging behind my friends part.

Then I started wondering if the kids would have any problem getting a taxi back to downtown Denver. Just because I had a seen a couple of taxis near the haunted house did not mean there would be other cabs headed out there at this time of night. Maybe the kids would not be able to flag one down, and would subsequently find themselves having to phone for a taxi. This made me uneasy. The house was located in an area where cab drivers might not be willing to go. I'll admit it. If I was pulling a graveyard shift I wouldn't want to travel fifteen miles into the wilderness to pick up a fare. It's true that cabbies cover the entire metro-area, but still, that's a long way to go at night when you are haunted by the one thing that cab drivers fear most: The Dreaded No-Show.

I even avoid taking calls at supermarkets in the daytime because I have been burned too many times by customers who disappear before I arrive. This is usually due to the fact that most cab drivers are like me. By this I mean they will stop for anyone who flags them down, and if I myself happen to drop someone off at a Safeway and a woman is standing outside with a bag of groceries and has phoned for a ride home, I will pick her up with no questions asked. This sometimes happens at the Cherry Creek Shopping Center. Okay. I'll admit it. I possess absolutely no ethics, but let's ignore that forever and concentrate on the subject at hand.

When I was a newbie I once jumped a bell at a truck-stop ten miles east of the city limits, way out on the lonesome prairie. When I arrived, the customer had vanished. That pretty much cured me of jumping long bells because I didn't earn any money for that hour. The fact that I frequently sit outside a downtown hotel for an hour reading a paperback without picking up a customer invalidates the essence of my gripe, but I'm not trying to be logical here, I'm just trying to make sense. Suppose no cab driver was willing to jump a bell on the far west side of Denver at that time of night. How would the kids get back to DCPA?

I know what you're thinking—don't I have anything better to do with my time than carry the weight of the entire world on my shoulders? Well—this depends on your definition of the word "do." I never do anything, so I certainly have time to save humanity from itself. But on that Wednesday night there had been a number of other relevant factors at work. I will list two of them. (#1) I was off duty and (#2) I was hungry.

I picked up the sack of burgers and began eating them one at a time. When I was in college I tried to eat two hamburgers at a time while hurrying to a literature class. I ended up missing the lit class. It's a dull story that involves the Heimlich Maneuver, so let's move on.

By the time I finished my supper, *Gilligan's Island* was over and there was no possibility of my ever seeing the vampire episode again unless I tuned in the Los Angeles station at 3:00 a.m., which was beyond the realm of possibility because I had to work on Thursday and I absolutely never stay up late on week nights unless I don't have to work the next day, in which case I stay up late on Monday, Wednesday, and Friday.

I began channel surfing.

I knew I would find a lot of horror movies since it was the Halloween season. The first movie I came across was *The Wackiest Ship in the Army* (1960). I saw that movie when I was ten. It infuriated me. The only funny thing about it was the title. At the very least I expected a cameo appearance by Francis the Talking Mule. I hate slick marketing. The next movie I surfed was *Boys' Night Out* (1962). Both Tony Randall and Howard Morris were in that one, a double threat. Howard Morris played Ernest T. Bass on *The Andy Griffith Show*. I'll follow Howard anywhere, even to New York City, but I wasn't in the mood that night to have my ribs tickled by sophisticated East Coast corporate humor. I wanted to be terrified. The next movie I surfed was *Pillow Talk* (1959) starring Doris Day. What the hell kind of Halloween programming was this? Where was *Frankenstein*? Where was *The Wolf Man*? Where was *The Blob*? I'm talking Steve McQueen, not Kevin Dillon—with all due respect to the strides that have been made in computer animation, when it comes to monster movies I prefer the quaint charm of old-fashioned amateurish special effects manufactured by desperate film crews working on shoestring budgets. If it's crude, you're talking my language. This applies to other aspects of my life but let's not get into that.

I was just about to give up when I surfed Channel 6, the PBS station in Denver. They were showing *Dracula* (1931). PBS always goes for the horror films that have stood the test of time and proven their artistic merit, as opposed to *The Attack of the Killer Tomatoes,* which ironically will stand the test of time due to VHS, DVD, TIVO, and teenagers.

By that time, though, I was too depressed to watch a horror movie. The sight of Doris Day took the wind out of my sails. I decided to stick with *Dracula* only long enough to watch Renfield laughing maniacally at the bottom of the ladder in the bowels of the sailing ship that had brought Count Dracula to England. After I turned off the TV, Renfield's laughter echoed in my mind. This was normal. I hear Renfield's laughter every time I make a decision. In this case my decision was to leave the foyer light on before I went to bed. If you are ever driving past my apartment building on Capitol Hill in the middle of the night and see a light shining through a third-story window, you can bet I've made another decision.

I went into my bedroom, kicked off my Keds, and collapsed onto my mattress. As I lay there I again started thinking about the costumed teenagers that I had dropped off at the haunted house, and worrying that they might not be able to get a taxi home. I then realized that I had forgotten one important factor: parents. If they couldn't get a taxi, they could always phone their parents and arrange a ride home. That's what either parents or teenagers are for, I forget the hierarchical pecking order of domestic exasperation.

This made me chuckle to myself. It was a breathy, burbling chuckle that I quickly stifled because I was starting to sound like Renfield, and nobody in his right mind would ever do anything Renfield did. In the Bram Stoker novel, Renfield's doctor diagnosed him as a zoöphagous maniac. If you don't know what "zoöphagous" means, you're best off not knowing.

I had always liked the name "Stoker." When I was in the army I tried to get my buddies to nickname me "Stoker." My hope was that barmaids would start saying things like "Hey Stoker, how's your love life?" There had always been somewhat of a disconnect between me and hope.

I started thinking about *The Blob* again. Believe it or not, the original working title of that movie was *The Glob that Girdled the Globe*. This is the kind of information you pick up after you have abandoned your search for the ultimate truth, which happened to me during a wet T-shirt contest at The Campus Lounge in Wichita twenty years ago. I was attending Kansas Agricultural University (KAU) at the time. I read a lot of existential books in those days in both my English and philosophy classes, and I slowly came to the conclusion that there was only one ultimate truth. I was so pleased at having narrowed The Truth down to a single digit that I decided to put off figuring out exactly what it was until after the T-shirt contest. But like everything else in my life I kept putting it off, and putting it off, and the next thing I knew I was a forty-five-year-old taxi driver in Denver, Colorado, drifting off to dreamland.

CHAPTER 5

I woke up Thursday morning feeling the same way I felt when I woke up the previous Tuesday morning. I always feel that way when I have to work on days that I want to work even less than on the days I have to work or risk not having money for the really important things in life. I divide the world into really important things and necessities. I won't list any of them here except cable TV and rent—the Scylla and Charybdis of my billfold.

I ate a quick breakfast of cheese and white bread then departed by the back door of my apartment, which I call my "crow's nest" although I've never said that audibly to any human being. I climbed down my fire escape to the dirt parking lot where my 1964 two-door two-toned Chevy Impala sat covered with October frost. The two tones were black and red. The doors were the red part. It's a long story. But lately I had been thinking about going to a junkyard and searching for black doors. I had recently seen an episode of the *Batman* TV series starring Adam West and I had forgotten how snazzy a totally black car looked. When Batman and Robin zoomed down the boulevards of Gotham City, the barmaids took notice.

Up until then I had never been bothered by driving a car that looked ridiculous. Don't ask me why—maybe it had to do with the "important/ necessity" dichotomy, but certain things in life don't bother me, whereas other things that make no sense *do* bother me, like people knowing that I have flaws. I don't care if they know my car has flaws, but I feel uncomfortable giving people a peek at my checkered soul. Thus, in order to avoid letting people know what kind of a person I really am I spend a great deal of time pretending to be something I'm not. This primarily has to do with increasing the tips I receive from fares. To sum it up briefly, I will say anything to, or do anything for, a taxi customer as long as it increases my tips, barring socially unacceptable behavior. But I'll let me be the judge of that.

Before I go any further, let me state here that if you ever take taxicabs anywhere, you would be best advised not to try to find out what kind of a person your driver really is. Just play the game. Be affable. Tip generously. Say, "Have a nice day," as you climb out of the cab. Then put the entire episode behind you and try to get on with your life.

Nuff said.

It may have something to do with the season of the year but I always feel especially comfortable pretending to be something I'm not when Halloween rolls around since everybody is wearing costumes. I myself like to pretend I'm a cab driver. This may explain why I didn't descend into a state of total despair as I drove my Chevy into the RMTC parking lot that Thursday morning. I felt comfortable. A lot of the fares I would be picking up would be wearing masks, therefore I knew that being a fake, a phony, and a fraud would be socially acceptable all day Thursday and all day Friday. On the following Monday it would become socially unacceptable again although I would still do it. Habit.

The days were getting colder so I had brought along my deep forest green Rocky jacket to wear during the short walks from my cab to the front doors of houses where the fares weren't nervously peeking through the curtains as they waited for their taxi to arrive. Some people seemingly are not afraid of making a cab driver climb out of his vehicle and walk all the way up the entire length of a sidewalk and knock on a door. I have never understood the courage of those people. Half the fun of being a cab driver is making people think I'm too important to get off my duff.

I gathered my plastic briefcase and toolbox and carried them toward the on-call room where I would be picking up my trip-sheet and key to Rocky Mountain Taxicab #123, the vehicle that had been assigned to me after Rocky Mountain Taxicab #127 had caught fire one day while I was driving along Interstate 70. RMT #127 was the first cab ever assigned to me. After it succumbed to an inferno near Vasquez Boulevard, the tires exploded. They made a series of sounds like this: blam blam blam blam!

The memory still brings a grin to my face.

I opened the door to the on-call room and started toward the cage, a small room that serves as a cashier's booth where my arch enemy Rollo sat eating a donut and reading a comic book.

I froze.

He was reading a copy of Classics Illustrated #124: *The War of the Worlds* by H.G. Wells.

It was the very same edition that I had first read as a child. During art class in the second grade our teacher handed out white sheets of paper and crayons and told us to draw a picture of anything we wanted as long as it came out of our very own creative imaginations. While the rest of the children were laboring over drawings of ponies I was rendering from memory the cover of *The War of the Worlds,* which depicted a giant three-legged robot blasting the hell out of everything in England. Even at the age of seven I was a fraud.

I hadn't seen a copy of that comic since I was a kid, and suddenly I wanted it bad.

Real bad.

I might as well admit that I collect comic books. I don't have a large collection. I am selective in my accumulation of cultural icons. Sentimentalism plays a significant role in my decisions, but I also take into consideration the physical condition of the comic book, the scarcity of the item, and the cost. Mostly the cost. I will admit that I have purchased comic books that didn't cost much. I own a mint-condition Classics Illustrated version of a thing called *Silas Marner* that I would be willing to part with for a song if you're interested. I bought it on St. Patrick's Day a few years back. That was the same day that I bought my ThighMaster. Same cable channel. Same 800 number.

I continued toward the cage adjusting my facial muscles so that Rollo would not know what I was thinking.

When he saw me coming he sat up straight on his chair, grasped one corner of the comic book by a thumb and forefinger, and wiggled it gently in my face. Then he smiled a supercilious smile that resembled Victor Buono's mandibles, set the comic out of sight below the counter, and picked up a blank trip-sheet. Rollo never wears a mask. He really is like that.

"Full shift," I said, then regretted it immediately. I never say "Full shift" when I sign out a taxi. I just hand over seventy bucks and take my key. But I was trying to cover up my irritation at his symbolic gesture of superiority, and there was no doubt in my mind that Rollo knew it. What I didn't understand was how Rollo knew I wanted the comic book so badly that I was willing to pretend I didn't. Could he read me like an X-ray? I thought only Big Al could do that.

I yawned and walked out of the room trembling with rage. As the door closed behind me I started thinking that if Rollo and I became friends he might be willing to give me the comic, or at least sell it to me. On the other hand, if we became friends he might start coming over to my apartment. That sobered me up fast. I forgot about my fixation with pulp magazines and climbed into #123 and got on with the job at hand, which was getting through Thursday without being crushed flat by the realization that I was working hard.

I had no intention of working hard that day, but it's just that driving five days in a row automatically qualified as working hard. I planned to sit outside hotels, transport people back and forth, collect my fifty dollars profit, and go home. "Working hard" is a term I normally use to describe taking calls off the radio, which I do as little as possible because it's too much like cab driving, and if I wanted to work hard I would not be driving a cab. I would be doing whatever it is that Americans do who don't drive cabs.

I stopped at a 7-11 store, gassed up 123, bought a cup of coffee and a package of Twinkies, and drove straight to the Brown Palace Hotel. There were three taxis already in line at the cabstand. I parked, pulled a paperback out of my briefcase, opened my Twinkies, took a sip of joe, and started reading. The day was starting out so normal that I should have known it was too good to be true.

A half-hour passed before I pulled up first in line at the stand. I put my paperback away and began staring at the front door of the Brown. I can't function on a normal level when I'm first in line at a cabstand. I can only sit and stare at the door and try to "will" a customer to come out of the hotel and climb into my cab and say, "DIA," meaning Denver International Airport.

During the next fifteen minutes three taxis pulled up at the curb in front of me to discharge passengers. It was a pleasant diversion. I watched the unloading of luggage from the trunks, which was overseen by William, a black man who had worked at the Brown since before I became a cab driver. He was pocketing tips left and right. I sometimes fantasize about becoming a doorman at a classy hotel. They do collect the tips. But they also have to stand up all day. I categorize standing up as "working hard." I categorize practically everything on the planet as "working hard" so it is unlikely that I will ever do anything except drive a cab for a living and write novels, but I don't want to get into that. Novelists never collect tips.

While I was eyeing the greenbacks being discreetly pocketed by William, my back door opened and a man climbed in and said, "DIA."

I glanced around at him and saw that he was a businessman holding a briefcase. He must have come out of the hotel while I was fantasizing. All sorts of unexpected things happen to me when I fantasize.

"Yes, sir," I said, starting the engine and pulling away from the curb. Businessmen with briefcases are my number one all-time favorite customers because they have no luggage, which means I don't have to get out of the cab when I arrive at the airport.

After we got to DIA he handed me sixty bucks and told me to keep the change. I filled out a receipt and gave it to him, then I headed back toward Denver. I didn't bother cruising past the taxi staging area where scores of cab drivers were waiting to pick up arrivals at the terminal. I intended to deadhead back to downtown Denver and park at the Brown again. I had already made more than one-third of the gross that I needed to net my fifty-dollar profit for the day so I was feeling extremely pleased with myself. I was lulled into a lightheaded sense of complacency and self-satisfaction. This is what easy money does to me. If I ever become a millionaire I will probably melt into a puddle of putrefaction.

"One-twenty-three!" the radio barked. "El-two!"

I was startled out of my complacency. The dispatcher was telling me to return to the motor to talk to Hogan. That's what "el-two" means. It stands for "L-2." I don't know what the "L" stands for. Licensed cabbie. Loafer. Lunkhead. Loser. Take your pick. All I knew was that I had to return to the motor immediately with no questions asked.

I grabbed the microphone off the dashboard and said, "Check."

I hung up the mike wondering what Hogan wanted to see me about. One thing I knew was that Hogan did everything within his power to avoid talking to me, so whatever it was, it made me uneasy. I always feel uneasy when anybody wants to talk to me. I do everything within my power to avoid interacting with the human race at all times, yet it never seems to work. If I was a millionaire though, I would make it work. I would pay off all the taxes I owed and go live as a hermit in a cabin. I would never communicate with anyone ever again except the technician who would be forced to climb to the top of Mount Everest to install my cable service.

I pulled into the RMTC parking lot and got out. When I walked into the on-call room Rollo was no longer reading the comic. He gave me a look that was devoid of expression. This made me more uneasy. It meant that Rollo had taken a hiatus from playing the pathetic "mind games" that consume his empty life.

"I got an el-two," I said.

Rollo nodded and said, "Go on up."

He knew I had been given an L-2. The man in the cage knows everything that goes on at the motor. I climbed the stairs to Hogan's office and knocked on the door.

"Come in," Hogan said.

This shattered my nerves. Hogan usually said "Yeah" in a muted voice that communicated disgust and indifference to the world outside his door. But when he talked like an affable human being I knew that two detectives from the Denver Police Department were waiting to question me about my involvement in a possible homicide. It was a learned thing.

CHAPTER 6

I pushed the door open and gazed around the office with wonder. Hogan was alone. I was overcome with elation.

"Thanks for coming in Murph," he said. "Why don't you have a chair."

My elation evaporated. Hogan usually makes me stand because our one-on-one conversations never last long enough for me to sit down. They usually amount to him reminding me to take my annual physical. At the risk of being redundant, that takes place once a year.

"We have a kind of strange situation here," he began, as I sat down on a chair in front of his desk.

"How so?" I said.

"I got a phone call this morning from a woman whose last name is Harris. She told me that her daughter and four of her friends took a taxi to one of those haunted house deals last night."

I froze.

"By any chance did you take some kids to a haunted house last night?" he said.

I swallowed hard, then said, "I picked up five kids at DCPA around six-thirty p.m. and took them to a haunted house on west Thirty-eighth Avenue near Golden."

Hogan pursed his lips and nodded.

"Is there a problem?" I said, even though I knew the question was rhetorical. The entire room reeked of problem.

Hogan frowned down at his desktop, then looked up at me.

"Let me fill you in on what's going on here, Murph. According to this woman's story, these kids were at a costume party at DCPA, but they left the party without telling their parents where they were going."

I felt the hairs on the back of my neck bristle.

"When the parents realized the kids had disappeared, they started looking around for them, but couldn't find them anywhere at DCPA. So they put out the word among the other adults at the party, then they went home and made some phone calls and so forth, but they were not able to track the kids down."

I felt my entire body starting to calcify. There were a lot of things I wanted to say but I let Hogan continue talking. I had learned long ago not to interrupt my managing supervisor when he was delivering the devastating news once again.

"Mrs. Harris and her husband called the police at one o'clock in the morning," Hogan said.

I clenched my teeth. Two words welled up in my brain. One word was "Duncan" and the other was "Argyle." I'll explain later.

"They reported the kids missing. Around four a.m. their daughter Shantel came home. The girl said they had gone to another party. She said she was sorry she had left DCPA without permission, and on and on, but she was vague about where they had been except to say that they had gone to a haunted house near Golden. You know teenagers."

Oh yeah. I do know teenagers. I used to be one.

"Did the other kids get home okay?"

"The parents checked with each other, and all the kids got home, but the kids were as vague as the Harris girl about where they had been and what they had been doing."

At this point in time my body had achieved almost 100 percent calcification. I was now certain that two detectives named Duncan and Argyle from the Denver Police Department were about to play a key role in my immediate future.

"Here's the thing though, Murph," Hogan continued. "One of the kids mentioned that they had taken a taxicab to the house out by Golden but he couldn't remember the name of the taxi service. So the Harrises started calling the cab companies trying to find out who had taken the teenagers to the house. I'll be straight about this. They were mad as hell. I called the managing supervisors at Yellow and Metro and the other companies and it looked like all the parents were playing detective. They wanted to find out who the cab driver was that had taken their … under-age kids to Golden last night."

Aaaah Jaysus.

I sat back on the chair and slumped down. Up to that point I had been sitting on the edge of my chair the way I sat on my easy chair at home when I watched horror movies. You wouldn't believe how awkward it is to sit on the soft edge of an overstuffed chair, but somehow I manage it.

Hogan picked up a trip-sheet that had been lying on top of his desk. I hadn't noticed it until then, but before he even spoke I was way ahead of him.

"I checked with the dispatcher. We didn't have a radio transcript of anyone calling for a cab, so I looked through all of the trip-sheets from last night and I came up with this." He held up my trip-sheet so I could see it.

I gave my handwriting a cursory glance.

But I didn't really see it.

Instead I saw a group of men standing in line at the unemployment office.

"That's why I called you in, Murph. It looked to me like you made a long trip from the cabstand at DCPA to Golden around the same time the kids disappeared."

I nodded. "Yes, I'm the one who took them there. But they …"

I stopped. I immediately began to feel like a stool-pigeon. I was going to tell him that the kids had said their parents had given them permission to go to the haunted house. The instinct to say this made me feel like I was trying to evade responsibility. All of my instincts make me feel this way.

"They what …?" Hogan said.

I sighed. I raised my hands with my palms held vertically as if I was holding a cardboard box, or lying about the size of a trout that got away.

"I asked the kids if they had permission to go to the haunted house. In fact, as I recall I broached the subject twice just to make certain. The girl assured me that they did have permission. I even tried to talk them into going to a haunted house down on south Broadway since it was in town, but they (*Dracula!*) insisted on going to the house out by Golden."

Hogan nodded and set the sheet down. "I want you to know that I did not give Mrs. Harris your name," he said. "But I did tell her that

I would have a talk with the driver who took the kids to the haunted house. I did my best to make it clear that our driver had not, to my knowledge, broken any specific regulation. But I got the impression that she was not interested in a strict interpretation of taxi regulations."

"That's understandable," I said in a voice that came out rather thin.

"I'm glad you see it that way, Murph," Hogan said. "It appears that the kids are okay, but the parents seem to think that the taxi driver should not have taken a group of underage children anywhere at that time of night without clearing it with an adult."

I nodded again. Nods were about all I had left in my arsenal of self-defense. I now saw with clarity that I had made a number of mistakes on Wednesday night, not the least of which was taking a teenager's word for it. Even though I had no intention of making excuses aloud to Hogan, I knew what those excuses would have consisted of, i.e., it was late at night, I wanted to get home, I knew I would be charged a late fee when I arrived at the motor, I was in a hurry, the kids assured me they had permission, blah blah blah, etc. etc. etc., but those excuses were as old as the concept of transporting human beings across the face of the earth. I'll bet Christopher Columbus had a treasure chest full of excuses in the hull of the *Santa Maria* "just in case."

"I told Mrs. Harris that I would talk to the driver, and I have talked to the driver," Hogan said. "In my opinion you did not break any rules or violate any procedures or protocols. As far as I am concerned this brings the situation to a close. Our meeting is over. You can go back on the road now."

I nodded, but the nod slowly transmogrified into the opposite of "yes." It would be "The No Nod," only I don't know if such a word exists in the English language. The closest I can come to it is "uh-uh," or the variation, "unh-unh" with the subtle "n" sound. Strangely, the word "uh" does not appear in the dictionary, which is ironic because it is the most commonly used and most annoying word in the English language if … uh … you know what I mean.

By the way, did you know that the word "no" is an adverb? On the other hand, the word "adverb" is a noun. I know what you're thinking: just cut the nylon line and buy a new fishing reel.

I ceased shaking my head sideways and said, "Are you going to tell the top brass or the insurance company or anybody else about this situation?" This was a learned thing too, although it was not a habit. I had never said it before although God knows why not.

Hogan sighed. "The case is closed, Murph, and I am going to do everything I can to see that it stays closed. The buck has stopped. It was the responsibility of the parents to watch out for their children, and not the responsibility of the Rocky Mountain Taxicab Company. I suspect that they're just trying to spread the blame around. They were doubtless afraid for their children and they're letting off steam. That is why cooler heads must prevail. The fact that the kids lied cannot be pinned on you. You did everything that was legally required of you."

I wished he hadn't thrown in the word "legally." People do lots of "legal" things that aren't necessarily ethical—but I won't say which people or how much they charge per trial.

I fought another unh-unh and forced it into a nod. I wanted to tell Hogan that I would understand if he called me in on another el-two and gave me more bad news—such as a group of angry parents filing a class-action lawsuit naming me as the defendant. But I didn't want to jinx the delicate balance of the situation. I once did that while sitting in a booth in a sports bar. I made the mistake of idly remarking that the Broncos might lose the playoff game that everybody was watching on TV. I was lucky to crawl out of that bar alive.

My meeting with Hogan was over. The only thing left to do was get up off the chair. I managed to do that with a modicum of difficulty, then I thanked Hogan for filling me in on the situation. He thanked me for coming off the road even though I had no choice, although technically I did, in the sense that I could have simply walked off the job and headed down to the employment agency. But I hate choices like that. I view them as a mockery of free will.

When I got outside I trudged over to #123 even though I wanted to trudge over to #64—my two-door Chevy. I felt morose. I get that way whenever I have a close encounter with a screw-up. The fact that it had not evolved into a full-blown catastrophe did nothing to alleviate the impact on my emotions. My emotions have never been properly linked with reality, which is the way I usually like it, but I felt bad after Hogan had politely dismissed me. I felt like a rank amateur. It seemed as if no matter how hard I tried or how many years of experience I had under my belt as a cab driver, a situation always arose that I could have handled better. I didn't know if this was because my years of experience had lulled me into a lightheaded sense of complacency or if I was simply—flawed.

You be the judge.

I climbed back into 123 and sat behind the steering wheel staring at the skyline of the Rocky Mountains in the distance. Somewhere at the base of those mountains was an old house that had been turned into a fantasy exhibit designed to tap into the wallets of people who liked to pretend on an annual basis. My pretense on the other hand was perpetual, which was ironic because I did not believe in ghosts and had no interest in the supernatural beyond B movies. At some point between graduating from high school and receiving my draft notice I had lost all interest in death. I would no more go to a haunted house, a Halloween party, or a DCPA costume ball than I would go to an afternoon lecture on paleontology at the Museum of Natural History in City Park. I didn't care about dinosaur skeletons anymore, and believe me, when I was ten years old nothing blew my mind like a thirty-foot tower of T.rex bones. But nowadays I wouldn't go anywhere for any reason if I could swing it. However "going" is just a part of life that everyone has to accept—or else. The cemeteries were full of people who had stopped going.

I decided to get going.

I had nine hours left of my cab shift, and due to my el-two with Hogan I would have to work hard for the rest of the day to make up for lost time and money. Not that I had really "lost" any money. I never possessed it to begin with. It always makes me laugh when I hear businessmen complain that they "lost" money due to, for instance, weather conditions that didn't cooperate. If it doesn't snow in Colorado until December, you hear owners of ski lodges complaining that they lost hundreds of thousands of dollars in ski-ticket sales, when in fact they lost nothing because they never had it to begin with. This is one thing that I do have in common with millionaires: grousing about projected profits that failed to materialize. Disappointed millionaires make my heart bleed.

CHAPTER 7

I turned on the Rocky radio as soon as I drove out of the lot. Whenever I work hard I have to make an attitude adjustment, which consists of accepting the things I cannot change, and trying hard not to think about it. One of the things I cannot change is the fact that I have to listen to the dispatcher and be ready at any moment to jump a bell. Being ready for anything is an excruciating experience for me, which is why I like to sit at hotels and allow luck to determine my fate. Self-determination leaves a bad taste in my mouth.

I began taking calls. They were my usual daytime trips to grocery stores or the Cherry Creek Mall, although I left the mall as soon as I dropped off my fares. I wasn't in the mood to steal fares from Yellow Cab drivers by prowling the parking lot looking for people with shopping bags. Taxi drivers are supposed to go to the official cabstand at the main entrance of the mall to wait for fares—but is it my fault that the shoppers don't always understand this?

I worked the downtown area making short runs to stores or to dentist and doctor offices. Most of the rides were less than five dollars, but when you run four of these an hour you can earn decent money. I picked up a fare in LoDo, a waitress who worked at a fern bar. She wanted to go to the Baker neighborhood on the west side of Broadway. She lived on the block where the Mary Chase House is located. It's a local landmark, the childhood home of Mary Chase, who wrote the Broadway hit, *Harvey*, which was made into a Jimmy Stewart movie. He played the main character, Elwood P. Dowd. After I dropped off the waitress I drove slowly past the Chase house wracked with envy. Imagine living on the same block where a famous playwright grew up. I'll be honest. I had driven past the house a few hundred times before. I was hoping some of the magic would rub off on my tires.

I drove back to Capitol Hill listening to the radio. I was garnering a steady flow of cash, which took the edge off the pain of having to stay on the ball, listen to the radio, and drive without a break—not counting quick stops at 7-11 for the cab driver's 3-J combo: john, joe, and junk food.

It didn't work out very well.

Sure, I was making more money than I did when I sat outside hotels, but I couldn't get my mind off the fact that I had been called on the rug over those kids that I had driven to the haunted house. I kept telling myself that Hogan was right, that I hadn't violated any regulations or protocols. But there are protocols and protocols. One of my personal protocols is to avoid doing anything that might annoy or anger people, and I had learned that the only way to do this was to master my job thoroughly and execute my duties with impeccable precision. Some people call it "professionalism." I call it "cowardice." If you get sloppy, events go haywire and the next thing you know total strangers are intruding on your life—like Mrs. Harris.

Due to the fact that I had not checked to make certain that those teenagers had permission to go to the haunted house, Mrs. Harris had come looking for me. And it wasn't just her. She stood proxy for all the parents who wanted to know the identity of the taxi driver who had picked up a bunch of kids at night and drove them into the dark wilderness where he took their money and abandoned them to their fate.

I realized what I ought to have done.

I ought to have waited at the haunted house for the tour to end, and then brought the kids back to DCPA—gratis.

This never would have occurred to me if I wasn't wracked with guilt.

I have already delineated my feeble excuses, i.e., I had picked up the kids close to my shift-change, I wanted to avoid a double late-fee, I was hungry, etc., but still, I could have parked and pulled out my paperback and read while I waited for the kids to come out of the house. So what if I hadn't had a beer in twenty-four hours? So what if I would have been forced to wait an extra sixty minutes before scarfing down two prefab hamburgers? So what if I was missing *Gilligan's Island*? I missed it anyway. I ended up turning off the TV and starving myself to death while brooding about my lousy life. Hell, I could just as easily have done that outside the haunted house. I could have taken the time to make certain that the kids got back to Denver safely. But no. Not me. Not Mister Center-of-the-Universe. I had to slake my craving for pleasure as quickly as possible, and to hell with humanity!

I was beating up on myself pretty badly when a radio fare came out of an apartment building and climbed into my backseat and asked me to drive him to the Arapahoe County Jail on the southeast side of the metro area. I'll admit it. I was shocked when he told me his destination. He seemed even more morose than me. He told me he had been ordered by the court to report for a thirty-day jail sentence on his own recognizance. Given the fact that I am human I wanted desperately to know what his crime had been, but I am sorry to report that I kept a leash on that inclination.

He didn't say much during the ride. He stared out the side window at the passing landscape that he would be saying goodbye to for the next thirty days. When we arrived at the jail he gave me twenty dollars and a tip. I was surprised by the tip. The guy looked about twenty-two years old, and American males don't learn about tipping until they reach twenty-five. That's been my experience anyway. But maybe young men who commit crimes are more sophisticated than college kids.

I sat in my cab and watched him trudge toward the jail. His shoulders had a perceptible droop. He opened a big glass door and stepped inside. The door slowly closed behind him.

Rather than drive away, I sat in the parking lot of the jail and filled out my trip-sheet. Maybe I took the time out to complete the legal requirements of driving a taxi because I was so close to a law-enforcement building, or maybe I was hoping that a reformed customer would come out and hop into my backseat. Or maybe—just maybe—I had lost all desire to go on working, eating, and breathing.

But—after completing the trip-sheet—I did all three.

I took a deep breath, started the engine, and popped my last Twinkie into my mouth. I kept my ear attuned to the radio. I rarely work the east side. I had given up on Aurora after a bad experience I'd had awhile back jumping a bell that was too far away and took too long to get there. The people ended up asking a neighbor to drive them to DIA—and then on my way back to Denver with an empty backseat, my taxi broke down. There is also a bank robbery, a corpse, and a suspected assault on an elderly lady related to this story but the point I'm trying to make is that I steer clear of Aurora whenever I can.

Just my luck, though. A call came over the radio for a trip to a strip-joint in Glendale. I jumped it. Two sinners in their early twenties hopped into my backseat and talked about women during the entire ride, then tipped me five bucks at the end of the trip. Maybe I had most young men figured wrong when it came to tips. Maybe most young men just didn't tip *me*.

I tried not to think about it.

Instead I thought about the fact that it was four in the afternoon and I had grossed $150.00, which was twenty bucks more than I needed to call it a day. I had earned my standard fifty-dollar profit and I could go home.

Or …

I could stay on the road for the next three hours and garner anywhere from $30.00 to $60.00 more in clear profit depending on the variables. This is one of the major problems of being a taxi driver. After you have earned back your lease payment and the cost of a tank of gas—which comes to a total of $80.00—it's like your billfold has broken free of the gravitational pull of the earth. After that, every dollar you earn floats right into your billfold, your brain floats out the cockpit door, and you become motivated to work harder, smarter, and faster, the three warning signs of insanity. You become obsessed by the idea that your potential profits are as unlimited as the far reaches of outer space. I label this "The Mine-All-Mine Syndrome."

But whoa, space-jockey. That's the time to hit the retro-rockets and return to earth.

Unlike outer space, a cab driver's universe is bounded by an invisible "wall," which I refer to as "seven p.m." When you start your shift you can legally drive for only twelve hours. So whether you are traveling thirty-five miles per hour or one hundred and eighty-six thousand miles per second down Colorado Boulevard, your journey ends at the twelve-hour mark. That is the inviolable enforcement mechanism that pertains to the laws of taxi physics.

I know a lot of drivers, both newbies and old pros, who labor con-stantly under the delusion that they can violate those laws. They are like people at a dog track who keep coming up with new betting systems. But I have found that it is impossible to win because no matter how fast I drive or how many customers I pick up, I still end up paying the same amount of taxes to Uncle Sam on April 15, which is another kind of "wall." The point I'm making is that there is no point in going on driving after I have met my minimum standard profits for the day: $50.00. For some drivers, such as Big Al, it's $100.00. I know drivers who work so hard that they actually rake in $150.00 per shift. Stars like that don't last long, but they do burn bright.

I decided to call it a day.

I was quitting work three hours early, which was tantamount to closing the door on an unguarded bank vault. I am sometimes mystified by my willpower. But on that day there were other aspects of my mental-being at work, such as my perpetual desire to do nothing. That trumps everything.

By "nothing" I mean watch TV. Some people have hobbies. Some people attend adult education courses. My landlord goes to a free school where he studies macramé. Big Al plays the dogs. People do things. I watch TV.

Okay, I'll admit that I occasionally do other things, like collect comic books. But I collect comics the way a sock collects lint, or the way dead leaves fall from trees. It just happens. I'm not big on volition.

I drove back to Rocky Cab and parked in the lot. I sat in my cab and took a few minutes to cross my eyes and dot my tees on the trip-sheet. After I completed the paperwork I looked up and admired the skyline of the Rocky Mountains in the distance. When the weather is right in Denver, the smog fades like a ghost and you can actually see the snow on the high peaks beyond the Front Range. The air is so pristine and crystal clear that you can view the exact same sight that the early pioneers viewed when they arrived in Colorado more than a hundred and fifty years ago. They must have been horrified. "How in the hell are we going to haul our wagons across that mess?" Their wives probably wept. The anguished children clung to their mothers' skirts. The men gazed westward with their jaws set firmly, and decided to give up. Thus was Denver founded.

I climbed out of my cab and walked toward the on-call room. When I got inside I saw Rollo sitting in the cage reading the sports page. I approached him holding out my key and trip-sheet. Rollo did a double-take because it was unusual for me to quit work so early. He closed the paper and made a move as if to reach under the counter but I shoved the trip-sheet and key toward him before he could complete his maneuver. I knew exactly what he was up to. He had intended to reach beneath the counter and pull out his copy of *The War of the Worlds* and place it in front of him, but there was no room now. My trip-sheet took up the empty space on the counter that would have been occupied by the comic book had he been warned ahead of time that I was coming. I had caught him off-guard. Even though there were no mirrors in the vicinity, I knew that I had the glint of victory in my eyes.

Rollo took the trip-sheet and placed it on a stack near his left elbow, then hung the key on a hook among dozens of other keys on the wall. He quickly reached under the counter—and pulled out a voucher.

A voucher is like a credit card receipt. Businessmen often use vouchers in lieu of cash payments. Rollo held it up and said, "Mr. Hogan passed this along to me. You forgot to date it. You need to write the date and then initial it for the records."

Stunned, I took the voucher and looked at it. I had received it from a businessman on Tuesday. He had gone to the Denver Tech Center down south. It was like a knife in my heart. I had failed to write the date in the little rectangle in the upper right-hand corner. I hadn't made a mistake like that in so long I couldn't remember. I felt like a newbie. A lunkhead. A loser. I quickly wracked my brain to fabricate an excuse, but there was no excuse for what I had done, there was only a reason, i.e., I had screwed up.

"Oh," I said.

It came out like a tiny burp.

I took the voucher from his fingertips and placed it on the counter and filled in the date, then initialed it under the piercing glint of Rollo's eyes. I could feel my cheeks burning crimson. Another flaw exposed. Since I had no excuse for my mistake I did the only thing I could do. I took a moment to frown like an important person and examine the entire voucher to make certain there were no other tees to cross. I even went so far as to purse my lips and nod. It is somewhat difficult to describe the subtle nuances that I incorporate in the never-ending battle of the intellects that Rollo and I engage in, but the purse and the nod are like feeble parries in a fencing duel—they were all I had left.

I smiled and raised my eyes and held out the voucher.

It was too late.

He was chewing on a donut and holding *The War of the Worlds* open in one hand.

He glanced at me and said, "Finished already?"

I parted my lips and started to say, "What do you mean, finished 'already'? How long did you expect it to take me to write down the date fer the luvva ...."

But I snapped my lips closed.

As I sometimes say, even losers know when to quit. It just takes them longer than winners.

I nodded, set the voucher on the counter, and slunk out of the room.

I crossed the parking lot and climbed into my Chevy. I sat staring at the mess in the distance. I was demoralized. I had never come so close in my life to outwitting Rollo on a physical level. Our duels were almost always verbal in nature. It was rare that they descended into the crude arena of physical action. By shoving my trip-sheet and key into his face I had thwarted his attempt to pull the comic book out from under the counter—but with the expertise of a Samurai warrior he had unsheathed a voucher and shoved it in my face—the voucher that I myself had failed to date!

I had been hoisted by my own petard.

The reason I have gone into such detail to describe the irreversible calamity that took place in the on-call room that afternoon was because it dovetailed with the L-2 that I had received from Hogan. Both incidents had resulted from a lapse of professionalism on my part, they had both taken place on the same afternoon, and their combination depressed the hell out of me. Was I losing my touch? Did I even have a touch to begin with? What was wrong with me?

I inserted my key in the ignition, twisted it in a clockwise motion, and started the engine. Just before I placed the gearshift into Drive, I sensed an ominous truth approaching like a wave about to crash over me. All the signs were present. There was no denying the inevitable. I would have to become humble.

The drive back to my apartment seemed to take forever. I no longer had the energy or the will to cook a hamburger that night so I stopped off at the Burger King. I ordered two hamburgers and a bag of fries. I also ordered a soda in order to avoid feeling like a communist. I didn't want anybody to suspect that I had sodas at home. I wanted to stop pretending that I was capable of outwitting the world. I wanted to fade into the woodwork, expunge the hubris that permeated my soul, and get on with the task of being humble forever.

Looking back on that strange week in October, I cannot help but feel that I really do need some kind of goddamn therapy.

CHAPTER 8

I arrived at my apartment building at 4:30. I parked in the choice V-spot in the dirt lot behind my building and climbed out with my stash of food and drink. I was unused to carrying a paper sack and a paper cup full of soda up the fire escape, which may not sound like much of a problem to a layman, but people who enter apartments by fire escapes know what I'm talking about.

It was awkward trying to brace my hand against the railing with my fists full, but somehow I managed to arrive at the top landing without doing one of the three potentially disastrous things that can happen in such a situation. I even managed to unlock my door and step inside with my meal intact. My spirits were somewhat buoyed by this paltry achievement. But then I felt foolish as I sipped my paper cup of soda knowing full well that I had eight cans of pop sitting idly in the fridge, like a profligate millionaire who didn't give a damn about the thirsty humanity.

It was 4:45 when I finally finished burping and tossed the sack into the trash. Before I tossed the sack though, I placed the cup inside it so I wouldn't see it while roaming around my apartment and accidentally be reminded of what a selfish bastard I was.

I turned on my cable and began surfing for *Gilligan's Island* even though I knew it wasn't scheduled at that time of day in Denver, Chicago, Los Angeles, or any other sister-city where bulk reruns fill dead airtime. But you never know—the programming directors of America are a whimsical bunch. I once turned on my TV at 11:30 Sunday morning and saw a *Gilligan* that wasn't listed in the *TV Guide*. I was still in my PJs and there stood Ginger and Mary Ann doing the Twist. I nearly broke my ankles pulling on my jeans, but at least I had the decency to get dressed with the sound off.

I finally shut down the cable box, sat back in my easy chair, and stared at the wall. I began thinking back over the events of the day. The call to Hogan by Mrs. Harris. My subsequent L-2. My trip to jail. My defeat by Rollo, or "Rollo's Victory" as it would come to be labeled in the partition of my brain where I store psychological tics. My trip to the Arapahoe County Jail did not technically belong in the tic box, but it acted as a kind of link to the guilt I felt about having fumbled the ball the previous evening by abandoning the kids at the haunted house instead of driving them back to DCPA. You perhaps might wonder why I was obsessing on that episode, since Hogan had stated categorically that the buck had stopped. He had called me in to have our talk, and he had exonerated me of any guilt or responsibility for having taken the kids to the house without permission from the parents. But the thing is, I had made similar blunders in the past, poor judgment calls that had blossomed into murders, kidnappings, robberies, assaults, and other misconceptions by the detectives who had grilled me in small rooms down at DPD. Never in the same small room though. Apparently they have quite a few small rooms available for use down at headquarters. They all look alike. Four walls, a table, chairs. That describes every apartment I lived in before moving to Denver.

I should add that there never actually were any real murders, kidnappings, or assaults, although there was one bank robbery. The robber died, but I didn't have anything to do with his death. Thank goodness he died in police custody, or I might have found myself living in a small room in Cañon City. I'm talking "Supermax."

It was 5:15 when I finally glanced at my wristwatch and decided there was only one thing that could take my mind off my troubles: write a novel. Sure, it was Thursday, and no cab driver in his right mind ever attempted to start a novel on a Thursday because the prospect of working on Friday—the busiest day of the week—rendered it virtually impossible to think about anything except the money he would earn the next day. The irony is that money is the only reason I write novels. But taxi money isn't like novel money. For one thing, the Rocky Mountain Taxicab Company does not pay $100,000 advances to first-time drivers. Conversely, New York publishers do not pay authors fifty dollars a day to write books, although I would gladly take a stab at it. Heck, I would work *five* days a week if I could get a deal like that. I don't know why publishers don't simply hire guys like me to write their novels instead of relying on the slush pile and fly-by-night literary agents to scout new books. I mean, look at the early days of Hollywood. They used to have stables of writers to crank out screenplays. Why doesn't Scribner have stables?

These are the kinds of thoughts I have when I'm trying to avoid going to my word processor and filling a blank page with words. Wallowing in umbrage wastes at least as much time as sharpening pencils. But I have found that the best way to waste time is to plan a novel. Add to this mixture the fact that I don't know how to plan a novel, and you're looking at a good possibility of never getting started on a book at all. The great thing about planning a novel though, is that you don't have to be seated in front of your computer. You can do it from the comfort of your easy chair.

I settled back in my easy chair and started contemplating potential premises for a novel. Contemplating premises is not as difficult as planning a full-blown storyline. For instance, I might come up with a premise about a man who goes to work wearing a green shirt, but when he arrives at work he's wearing a red shirt. Wow! How did that happen? That's where the "planning" part is supposed to kick in. I'm not so good at that—but again, not being good at something is an effective way to avoid accomplishing anything.

Given the fact that this was the Halloween season though, I decided to give a horror novel some thought. I cast about for a few original ideas. That didn't work, so I started thinking about horror movies that I had seen in the past. Maybe they would inspire me. The first horror movie I can remember seeing was called *The Day the World Ended*. I was six years old. The movie scared the hell out of me because it was so realistic. I saw it for the second time in my mid-twenties. To my horror I realized it was neither scary nor realistic. It was a Roger Corman film.

The next movie I thought about was the first horror movie I had ever seen in a theater at nighttime. I was ten years old. I went alone to see a six p.m. showing of *Jack The Ripper* (1960). It ended at eight. The movie was scary but not as scary as the walk home alone in the dark. There are a hell of a lot of trees in residential Wichita, and I don't suppose I need to tell you who was hiding behind every one of them.

But the thing that scared me most was the knowledge that Jack the

Ripper had been a real person. Blimey. But somehow I made it home alive. I spent the rest of the evening hanging around in the kitchen while my Maw did the dishes and mopped the floor.

As I sat in my easy chair I started thinking about the fact that Jack the Ripper had never been caught, or even identified. What could have become of Jack the Ripper? I began to extrapolate. Maybe he had emigrated England and immigrated to America determined to change his identity and erase all evidence of his past. Since he was British, it seemed plausible that he could have disguised himself by becoming a manservant, like Mr. French on the TV show *A Family Affair*. I pictured Sebastian Cabot sitting on his bed in his room gazing nostalgically at a black bag filled with medical instruments. He would pick up a chrome-plated scalpel honed to a razor's edge and gaze at his image in the reflection of the six-inch blade. The "craving" would come over him again. Meanwhile, Brian Keith would be sitting in the living room sipping a dry martini and relaxing after a hard day at the architect firm.

No doubt Jack would be forced to flee New York City after perpetrating another despicable and motiveless crime. He would probably leave a trail of bodies from Philadelphia to Cincinnati to Kansas City to Seattle to Los Angeles ... suddenly I realized I was describing my own travels around the country after I left Wichita.

A voice inside my head told me not to write that book.

With my luck, a murder had taken place in each one of those cities after I left. A smart homicide detective just might read my novel and erroneously connect the dots that would get me a life sentence in Supermax based on circumstantial evidence.

It was with a sigh of relief that I decided to drop the idea of writing a novel. I had to be up early Friday morning anyway to start raking in taxi money. Even though I would have preferred to rake in a one-hundred-thousand-dollar advance from Scribner, I didn't want to risk going to prison. I couldn't imagine anything worse than writing a bestselling novel and then find myself hanging around "The Yard" among a sea of convicts who knew I was filthy rich.

Nothing cheers me up quite like abandoning a novel, so I felt better as I walked around my apartment turning off the lights. The disasters of the day dwindled to their proper perspective, which I sometimes refer to as "meaningless." I still hadn't given up on the idea of being humble, but this was not unusual. The sensation was oddly similar to that of trying to give up cigarettes.

I started smoking in high school, the same year the Beatles released *Revolver*, although I don't think there was a connection, beyond the general concept of wanting to be thought of as "cool" by the varsity cheerleaders. I don't know what made me think that girls who could do back flips while holding spinning batons would think that destroying my lungs was cool, but I labored under a lot of erroneous assumptions during my teens, twenties, and early thirties. For instance, when I started driving a taxi at the age of thirty-one, I assumed it would be a brief gig until I sold my first novel for a million bucks. This assumption came from reading a book called *Youngblood Hawk* by Herman Wouk. The first novel I ever wrote in college was titled *Youngblood Stoker* but I don't want to talk about it. In fact, I have quite a few unpublished novels that I don't want to talk about. However if you want me to describe any of them in longwinded detail, I prefer Johnnie Walker over Cutty.

I went into my bedroom, kicked off my Keds, and collapsed into bed. As I lay in the darkness staring at the ceiling I started thinking about humility. I knew from past experience that becoming humble was easy. The hard part was sticking with it. Just like kicking cigarettes. It's easy to give up cigarettes for a couple of days. All smokers do that. They even go so far as to announce to their friends, "I've quit smoking!" But that's because they believe in the magic of language, i.e., if you say it, that makes it true. I'll be honest though. I have never once said to my friends, "I've become humble!" I knew intuitively that they would give me withering looks, and then offer me a light.

No—just saying it would not make it true. I would have to actually "do" something that would prove my humility to be a fact. This thought made me groan aloud, which is eerie when you're all alone in a dark room on the third floor of a mansion built by people who have been dead for a hundred years.

But the reason I groaned was because I had known all along that the only way to stop feeling guilty for having shown so little concern for the welfare of my teenage passengers on Wednesday night was to come clean and apologize to the parents.

I'm talking "in person."

I had no trouble envisioning the emotions that they had experienced when their children disappeared from the DCPA party and did not come home until nearly dawn. I knew that the parents had been frantic. I knew that nothing short of wringing the cab driver's neck would ameliorate their anger. I knew this because I had gotten involved in the personal lives of previous taxi fares, sometimes teenagers, and had witnessed first-hand the despair of parents who were worried about their kids. I also knew that I had violated one of the ironclad laws of cab driving, which mandated that a driver was responsible for the safety and welfare of his customers while they were in his vehicle. The fact that the kids were no longer under my legal dominion after they had gotten out of my taxi at the haunted house was irrelevant, because there is such a thing as "the spirit of the law." That has been my bête noire ever since the day I received my Herdic license from the City and County of Denver.

I knew I had violated the spirit of the law when I failed to consider how those underage kids were going to get home from the haunted house, aside from advising them to "hail" a cab after the tour was over. The memory of this lapse in judgment made me want to wring my own neck. And the memory of my lame excuses, which I have delineated for you, made my hands slowly creep toward my throat. Fortunately I fell asleep before they got there.

By the way, just so you know, "Herdic" is the legal name for a taxi license in Denver. Don't ask me why. Maybe the first cabbie in Denver was named Geoffrey Herdic. He might have even emigrated from … England.

CHAPTER 9

When I woke up Friday morning I was wracked with the kind of psychic pain known only to people who are brought to their knees and forced to admit the truth. On top of that, I knew that I would be forced to work hard that day because I was going to take time off to visit the home of Mrs. Harris and apologize to her for my lapse of judgment on Wednesday night.

I prayed that this would not take more than an hour out of my work day. The most unbearable part of this scenario was the fact that under normal circumstances, guilt doesn't bother me. In fact, when it comes to my response to the crimes that I normally get away with, "guilt" is a complete misnomer. The closest I can come to it linguistically is "indifference." The crimes that I normally get away with are referred to by the police as "petty"—or more correctly "petit" (from the Old French)—such as the aforementioned U-turns and parking in no-parking zones. But when it comes to the big issues like homicide and suchlike, neither the police nor me are quite that disingenuous.

As I trudged off to work I also prayed that my apology to Mrs. Harris would stand proxy to every one of the parents who had been fraught with anxiety on Wednesday night. My fervent hope that I could dodge those bullets made me feel a little better as I started my Chevy and drove out of the parking lot of my building. Dodging bullets, pulling fast ones, and getting away with anything in general lifts my spirits. It makes me feel like I won five bucks on a scratch ticket.

By the time I got to work I had the solid sensation in my gut that a guilty man feels after he has come clean. It was an unusual feeling but I didn't question it. I simply "went with the flow." I planned to visit Hogan and tell him what I intended to do, and ask if he would contact Mrs. Harris by phone and let her know that I wished to speak with her.

I would request permission to visit her house and get this thing settled. According to the how-to-write-novels books that I secretly read, this is referred to as a "satisfactory resolution." That would also be unusual for me.

In fact, this entire scenario was unusual. It had been a long time since I had followed through with a "plan." I admit that I do occasionally embrace plans, and I will admit that those plans almost always are linked directly to having made the mistake of getting involved in the personal life of a fare. But this particular "plan" was especially unusual because it did not come as a result of a frantic effort to fix a situation that I had metaphorically "broken." Take for instance the time I was suspected of kidnapping and murdering that eighteen-year-old actress. If I had left well enough alone she wouldn't be in college right now. But thanks to me, she has to do homework.

As I entered the on-call room I felt like a freed man walking out of a penitentiary. I took a deep breath of air and smelled eclairs. Rollo was at work in the cage. He always eats eclairs on Friday, and I knew why. It was because Friday was a "special" day for Rollo. Friday is a "special" day for all cab drivers because it's the busiest day of the week—and because the snack truck pulls up in front of the RMTC offices every Friday morning with a discount on eclairs—I'm talking "twofers."

I felt so damn good about the cleansing of my soul that I decided to put our "battle of the intellects" on hold. Rollo and I have been engaged in a mental duel for the past fifteen years. None of the other cab drivers are aware of this battle, though, because Rollo and I have an unspoken agreement to keep it strictly between ourselves. At least, to my knowledge Rollo has never spoken about it. I myself probably would speak about it if anybody showed any interest, since I am a sucker for attention, but all of the other cab drivers seem primarily interested in getting on with their lives and talking to me as little as possible. Objectively speaking, I would have to say that for the most part none of the other drivers have the slightest interest in my existence, which is the way I prefer it. But I suppose that if I ever get any goddamn therapy I might mention the protracted and enduring intellectual battle between myself and Rollo to the shrink.

Or maybe not.

I'll have to wing it.

"I need to run upstairs and talk to Hogan," I said.

Rollo began nodding and pointing at the ceiling. He was chewing on an eclair so I hardly expected him to speak. It's almost impossible to have a dialogue when your cheeks and esophagus are bloated with whipped cream and lemon-flavored frosting, though God knows I've always wanted to.

I nodded and started to move away from the cage, hoping that Rollo would appreciate the subtle nuance of this maneuver and realize that our battle was on hiatus. I liked to think of the relationship between he and I (or is it him and me? I have an English degree but when it comes to the nuances of personal pronouns I'm all thumbs) as that of two WWI flying aces who comport ourselves like gentlemen while dueling in the sky. Neither of us takes advantage of the other when, for instance, we have engine trouble or when one of us runs out of bullets. We disengage from combat, salute each other, and part ways to fight another day.

"He's waiting for you," Rollo said with a slight wheeze in his voice that might have come from lemon frosting stuck in his windpipe. He sounded like he was having engine trouble.

I nodded, then did something I had never done before, which was to tap my forehead in a small salute and walk away. I hoped he picked up on the significance of that subtle gesture.

Suddenly I stopped.

I turned back to the cage. "What do you mean … he's waiting for me?"

Rollo finished swallowing the remains of his eclair. He coughed and cleared his throat. "He told me to send you upstairs as soon as you got here."

A chill gripped my heart.

"Why?"

Rollo shrugged. He reached under the counter, pulled out his copy of *Worlds*, and began leafing through it.

Believe me, brother, I picked up on the subtle nuance of *that* gesture: conversation over.

But I couldn't let go of it.

"Is Hogan alone in his office … or are the police with him?"

Rollo raised his eyebrows querulously. I realized I had "shown my hand." I was furious with myself.

"He's alone as far as I know," Rollo said with a smile.

I nodded and hurried away.

Score two for Rollo the Flying Bastard of Dusseldorf. He had out-foxed me again. Or had I outfoxed myself? I do that frequently.

I trudged up the stairwell to Hogan's office and knocked on the door.

"Yeah," Hogan said in a muted voice.

I opened the door and stepped inside. I noted that he was alone. This ought to have come as a great relief to me, but it didn't.

"Thanks for coming in, Murph," Hogan said, brightening up.

I will go on record here and say that Hogan is the only human be-ing I have ever met who brightens up when I walk into a room. End of observation.

He frowned and tapped a finger on his desk. "Let me cut to the chase here and tell you what's going on."

I was petrified that he was going to offer me a chair, but he didn't.

"I got a phone call from Mrs. Harris, the mother of that girl you drove to the haunted house last Wednesday."

"Oh?"

"She called to ask if it might be possible for you to come by her house today. She wants to have a word with the driver who chauffeured the kids."

I froze.

"But the thing is," he quickly went on, "she didn't seem to be angry. I made it clear to her that I could not order you to go see her, but I said I would pass the word along and let you decide if you wanted to take time off from work to visit her."

"Can I sit down?" I said. My knees had gone weak. The weak Irish part anyway.

He nodded and pointed at "my" chair.

I sat down quickly and frowned. "Did she say what she wanted?"

"No she did not," Hogan said, "and I didn't ask. As far as I'm con-cerned, this is between you and her. I hope you understand where I'm coming from, but as I told you yesterday the buck has stopped and I intend to keep it that way. I don't want to see Rocky Cab entangled in what I view as a private matter between a customer and an independent contractor, meaning you."

I nodded. Hogan is an expert when it comes to dodging bullets. He's my hero.

"Listen, Murph, I really think you should go see her. This isn't Rocky Cab talking, this is just me. I've found that the quicker a situation like this can be resolved, the better off everybody will be in the long run."

I frowned slightly when I heard Hogan use the word "resolved." I wondered if he was an unpublished novelist.

But now I realized I was faced with an excruciating decision. I could just nod and act as if I was surprised by the idea of having a conversation with Mrs. Harris, or I could tell Hogan that I had already made the decision to request a meeting with her. But if I told him that, though, it might sound like a crock of bull. He might "eye" me with suspicion. It would be similar to a situation in which you inform somebody of an obscure fact and they say, "I knew that," when you knew damn well they couldn't possibly have known it and were just trying to cover up their sense of inferiority.

Been there.

"I agree with you," I said, trying to sound mature.

"I'm glad you see it my way, Murph." He picked up a Rocky Cab receipt that was lying on his desk and handed it to me. "I jotted down her phone number. She said you could call her any time and set up an appointment. She said she would be home all day."

I reached for the receipt feeling as if I was reaching for a scorpion, but I didn't let it show. I'm pretty good at hiding my feelings as long as there isn't any scotch around.

I took the card and looked at it, then nodded at Hogan.

Meeting over.

Everything that could have been said had already been said.

Not literally of course. I could have recited the contents of the *Encyclopedia Britannica* like a slick congressman pulling a sneaky filibuster, which was exactly what I felt like doing, since the last thing in the entire world that I wanted to do now was have a one-on-one dialogue with Mrs. Harris in spite of the fact that I had come to work fully intending to have a talk with her. I experienced the gut-wrenching feeling of dread that I always get when I am faced with the prospect of coming clean, looking into a mailbox, or meeting old friends.

As I trudged down the stairwell the thing that bothered me most was that my original "plan" had been rendered moot. Mrs. Harris had finessed me. I felt like an inventor who had been struggling for years to perfect a device that would make life better for all mankind, only to see it advertised on TV for $9.95.

I stepped up to the cage and handed seventy bucks to Rollo. As he retrieved my key and pulled out a blank trip-sheet, he kept moving *Worlds* around on the countertop with his fingertips as if it was getting in his way, but I kept a blank expression on my face and didn't look down at the scene where the main character is frantically guiding a horse-drawn wagon along a dirt road and suddenly comes face-to-face with a giant Martian robot ripping trees apart with its octopus-like metal tentacles.

Didn't even glance at it.

I knew that my indifference to Rollo's subtle fingertip-gestures would ruin his day.

We were back in our respective cockpits, dive-bombing each other over the fields of Flanders.

"Hogan phoned from upstairs just now and told me to credit you for an hour of down-time on today's shift," Rollo said.

"Huh?" I replied.

"I could apply the credit to your next shift, or I could just give you back six bucks on today's lease."

"Uh … I'll take the six bucks," I said.

Rollo handed me a fiver and a singleton.

I mumbled thanks and hurried out of the on-call room trying to get a fix on Rollo. He didn't seem to understand that the *battle royale* was back in play.

I wandered around the parking lot searching for Rocky Mountain Taxicab #123. At any given time there are at least twenty cabs in the parking lot. The lot is not paved, it's just dirt, so there are no white lines to act as parameters for the ranks of cars. The drivers park pretty much the way civilians park at a shopping mall when it snows, i.e., the rows of cars are like the long sweeping curves of a Jackson Pollock painting. I've heard rumors that the big-deal-Charley parking lot at Yellow Cab is paved with asphalt.

I don't want to talk about it.

I found 123 parked at a skewed angle that Jackson Pollock would have been proud of. God knows Peggy Guggenheim would have loved it. I climbed in and set my briefcase and toolbox on the shotgun seat, then looked at the Rocky receipt with the phone number of Mrs. Harris on it.

I wondered if there was a *Mister* Harris.

That's a knee-jerk reaction I experience whenever I get hold of a woman's phone number and it has no relevance here. I won't keep you in suspense though. There was.

I decided to get this chore done and get it out of the way. It was generous of Hogan to offer me sixty minutes worth of credit for the downtime it would take to visit Mrs. Harris. I again hoped it wouldn't take an hour to get my excruciating penance over with. If I could whittle the visit down to twenty minutes tops, I could get back on the road with forty minutes of free drive-time and thus rip off Hogan for the remaining four dollars out of the six that Rollo had given to me. As I stated earlier, I possess absolutely no ethics. That's the only thing that keeps me going.

CHAPTER 10

I drove to a 7-11 where I gassed up and bought some joe and a Twinkie, then went outside and drove my taxi from the pumps to the public telephones hiked on the wall outside the store. Before I got out of my cab I took a good long hit of coffee for a caffeine rush that would bolster my tepid determination. I wished the cup contained scotch, but according to my understanding, it is illegal to drink alcohol while driving a taxi.

I climbed out and walked up to a vacant phone, inserted two quarters, and dialed as quickly as my free will allowed. I knew that if I hesitated to act right away I would put off calling Mrs. Harris in the way that I put off doing my homework until Sunday nights when I was a kid. But there are no Sunday nights in the real world.

She picked up on the second ring.

I don't want to embarrass myself by transcribing our conversation verbatim. I will tell you only that I pretended to talk like the most grownup man in all of Denver. To my knowledge that title is held by an appellate judge.

I told Mrs. Harris that I was a driver for Rocky Cab, my last name was Murphy, and that Mr. Hogan had given me her phone number in reference to the situation involving her daughter. She said she was glad that I had called.

I was hoping she would let me get away with a phone confession, but instead she gave me her address and said I could drop by within the next half-hour. I began breathing heavily, but not until after she hung up her phone, thank God.

The reason I breathed that way was because the address she had given me was two blocks north of the Denver Country Club, which is just about the ritziest part of Denver proper. There are ritzier places in the overall metro area, but this was "old" ritzy—I'm talking the early pioneers of eighteen-hole golf.

My heart sank, and not just because I would be driving past a golf course. Hell, I drive past the Denver Country Club all the time. It's right across the street from the Cherry Creek Shopping Center so I've gotten used to the sight of men hitting little white balls with skinny sticks for reasons that must exist because so many men do it. But I had never picked up a fare in that part of Denver.

I decided to take University Boulevard south to 1st Avenue and then cut west to the street where Mrs. Harris lived. University Boulevard was probably so-named because it runs past Denver University farther to the south. I've often wondered who named that street. Was there a vote taken by the city council, or did some simpleminded tyrannical mayor insist on it?

I turned west at 1st Avenue. The Denver Country Club was to my left as I drove along but I tried not to look at the men standing in the fairways. I hate to see people play when I have to work. I hung a right onto the street where the Harris house was located.

The mansions in that part of town are indescribable, so I won't. But it was like stepping through a looking glass into a magical realm. The odor of wealth was in the air along with falling leaves. The leaves were golden, but the hue was due to the fact that it was late October and not because the mansions were inhabited by the sorts of people who could afford to play golf down the block. In the springtime the leaves probably looked like emeralds but don't get me started on the financial aspects of my long-range writing goals.

I crossed an intersection. I was driving very slowly. There was no traffic, but for some reason I thought cops might be watching me. I had the same feeling once when I drove through Beverly Hills in a rental car. But that was long ago and in another pocket of wealth. Ironically my "Beverly Hills Moment" was related to the daughter of a wealthy man who lived on east 8th Avenue and was not so far away from where I was driving at that moment. I don't want to go into detail about that, except to say that his daughter is the actress that goes to Denver University nowadays and I did not kidnap her, although I did have to do some fancy explaining to the cops.

I pulled up in front of a house that had a vast, broad lawn. The facade of the house reminded me of the White Cliffs of Dover. I don't know when the houses in that particular part of town were built. My guess would be 1890–1920. The architecture was eclectic, yet the designs blended well in spite of the types of materials used on the facades, whether white brick or red brick or painted plaster or wood or whatever the hell houses are made of. I failed shop in high school.

I climbed out of 123 and began walking toward the front door along a sidewalk that had been fashioned in an elongated "S," which unfortunately reminded me of the first page of *Ulysses* by James Joyce. This was ironic because James Joyce never made a dime off his novels—or a pound or a quid or a farthing or whatever Irish writers don't make.

As I approached the house, two psychological things began to happen to me, which I attributed to the fact that I was approaching a house in a wealthy neighborhood. One was that I began to feel as if I was growing tiny. The other was that the front of the house seemed to rock slightly as if I was peering through the lens of a camera affixed to a canoe. It was very quiet in the neighborhood but for the soft crisp patter of falling leaves settling on the ground. The narrow-trunked, white-barked trees in the front yard of the Harris house were sparse yet very tall. I couldn't see the upper branches but I didn't raise my head to eyeball them because I was afraid I would look like a rube from Hicksville gawking at skyscrapers, and because I was afraid I would see the ceiling of a soundstage on a Hollywood backlot. Both reactions were normal, primarily because I actually am a rube from Hicksville and I have spent my entire life feeling like a character performing in a movie directed by an unseen hand. I sometimes tell fares that driving a cab is like being an actor, except for the getting paid part—cab drivers do get paid.

"… Ding-dong …"

That is the actual sound the doorbell made within the house after I pressed the button. This indicated to me that the house was built in 1923, six years before Americans became self-conscious about corny noises.

I waited patiently for thirty seconds. Then I became wracked with indecision. Thirty seconds is the limit of my patience when I am ringing doorbells on Capitol Hill, the part of town where people like me come from. I'll admit it. I was intimidated by the idea of ringing the bell a second time to motivate the occupant of the house to quit horsing around and get a move on. I began to feel like F. Scott Fitzgerald. Not the novelist Fitzgerald, but the hick-from-Minnesota Fitzgerald who thought the rich were different from everybody else. I don't know why Ernest Hemingway disagreed with F. Scott, because on that morning I learned for a fact that the rich actually are different from everybody else—to wit: they take longer to answer doors, and you never hear their clodhoppers stomping the floor as they rush to answer the bell.

I decided to capitulate to my intimidation and simply wait it out. I didn't want the lady of the house to feel pity and perhaps even vicarious embarrassment for the uncouth peasant slouched on her front stoop.

Okay. I'll come clean. I'll lay all my cards on the table. Just before the front door opened I quickly reached up and patted down my ponytail.

The door opened with a slow and steady and even regal bearing— meaning it wasn't yanked—and a woman who appeared to be about my age peered out with a pleasant smile on her face. I don't know why I say "on her face." Where the hell else would it be? This gotrocks jazz was starting to rattle my gourd.

She gazed at me silently for a few seconds. People often do that. Mrs. Harris was a head shorter than me and her eyes were flecked with gold. She tilted her head at a slight angle and looked upward as if she was not only examining my baby-blues but was peering deeply into my soul. "Mr. Murphy?"

"Yes, ma'am. I'm with the Rocky Mountain Taxicab Company."

"I'm Shantel's mother," she said. "Please come in." She stood back and pulled the door open farther revealing a long hallway that reminded me of the green tunnel that led to the Wizard of Oz's throne room. It occurred to me that on the night I took the teenagers to the haunted house I had the tin-man and the scarecrow in my cab, and Shantel could easily have stood proxy for Dorothy, however two of the other main characters were missing. I thought about this as I walked down the hallway. Suddenly a little dog dashed from a side room and began snarling. That took care of Toto. All I had left to do in this scenario was cast the Cowardly Lion.

"Peanut!"

Mrs. Harris stooped and signaled with her hands, and the dog leapt into her arms.

I chuckled. "When I was a kid my family owned a Sheltie dog named Shelteen," I said. "I never knew her to obey an order, and when she leapt in my direction she was all teeth." This was standard canine-chat. I often used it when fares climbed into my cab with dogs, sometimes seeing-eye dogs. This may sound crazy, but whenever a seeing-eye dog is sitting in my backseat I feel like it knows what I'm thinking. You can image what talking parrots do to me.

Mrs. Harris smiled. "Don't worry, Peanut doesn't bite."

I let that one slide. Dog owners are cockeyed optimists.

Mrs. Harris led me into what I assumed was the living room. I don't really want to describe it except that it didn't look like anybody lived in it with the possible exception of Howard Hughes. Expensive carpet, drapes, furniture, vases, polished things—you can take it from there.

"Excuse me while I put Peanut out back," she said.

I nodded and tried not to visibly heave a sigh of relief. Small dogs. I don't know. I sat down on either a chair or a polished thing and waited for Mrs. Harris to return. When she did she had a smile/frown. You often see the smile/frown on people who are about to beseech forgiveness, although I once saw it on the face of a man who fired me. He was the foreman's assistant. I forget which hellish job that was, but the city was Philly.

"Thank you for coming over to see me," Mrs. Harris said. "After we have spoken, I would like to pay you for your time."

I nodded and didn't argue. I know what you're thinking: no ethics. Hogan had already—in essence—paid me six bucks to come here. I had long ago given up bickering about money, whether debit or credit. I hate money to begin with. If I wasn't for money I wouldn't have to work.

"Thank you ma'am," I said, bringing closure to that dull moment.

She sat down on a chair across from me and folded her hands on her lap. She was wearing a white pantsuit but let's move on. I hate clothes even worse than I hate money.

"Let me explain why I asked you to come over here," she said. "I want to apologize for any trouble that I might have caused between yourself and your employer. The other night after you drove Shantel and her friends to the haunted house, my husband and I made the mistake of trying to place the blame on you for the irresponsible behavior of our daughter."

I sat as still as humanly possible and tried to keep a pleasant look on my face, which is difficult to do without a rearview mirror for reference. Once again I had found myself in the position of being forced to act like an adult. This is one of the many reasons why I hate talking to people. I wouldn't do it at all if they didn't pay me.

"The parents of the other children got it into their heads that you were the irresponsible person in this situation and that you should not have taken a group of sixteen-year-old kids to such a distant location at night without checking with the parents first."

It was as if she had reached back twenty-four hours and taken the words right out of my mouth. I didn't know whether to moan with horror or bust out laughing, my standard response to everything.

"But I had a long talk with Shantel," Mrs. Harris continued, "and she confessed that she had lied to you. Apparently she had given you the impression that she and her friends did in fact have permission to take a taxi ride."

It took quite a bit of my willpower not to nod in agreement. The reason I didn't do it was twofold, i.e., if I had nodded I would have felt like I was squealing on Shantel—but by not nodding I felt like I was lying to Mrs. Harris. I was ambivalent about this, but as a taxi driver I had learned to deal with ambivalence by ignoring it.

"I don't know how all of us could have come to the conclusion that you were to blame for the actions of our children," Mrs. Harris said, clasping her hands tighter and shaking her head. "We started phoning around to the cab companies trying to find out who had taken them to the haunted house. The husbands wanted to see you fired, and I suppose we wives did to."

My lips practically got a hernia as I tried to keep from smiling. Mrs. Harris had no idea how many times I had been fired from Rocky Cab, although technically they were merely "suspensions." Sort of like getting 86'd from Sweeney's Tavern.

"We finally tracked the driver down to the Rocky Mountain Taxicab Company," Mrs. Harris said, nodding toward me like a nun with a rubber-tipped blackboard pointer. "I spoke with Mr. Hogan and he said he would have a talk with you. I will admit that I was feeling vindictive, but after Shantel told me the truth about what had taken place on Wednesday night, I realized I had faulted the wrong person and I was afraid I might have gotten you into trouble with your employer. So if I have caused any friction between yourself and the taxi company, I want to apologize and ask your forgiveness."

I was completely out of my element now. Forgiveness is a priest's game.

"Oh Margaret … I'm home!"

Mrs. Harris glanced toward the hallway. I heard a door close.

"That's my husband," she said, rising from the chair. "We're in here," she said, raising her voice one degree on the decibel scale. I could tell that this was not a "shouting" house. Mrs. Harris looked down at me and smiled. "My first name isn't really Margaret. But Jerry thinks it's funny to say that when he enters the house."

I thought it was pretty funny myself because the man had perfected the soft orotund vocal tone of Robert Young. I was immediately wracked with envy. I can't imitate Jane Wyatt's husband worth beans, although the barflies down at Sweeney's tell me I do a pretty good Bullwinkle.

Mr. Harris strode into the living room grinning big. He had the healthy, wholesome, pleased expression that you often see on the faces of people who enjoy life. He was wearing a golfing outfit—cap, sweater, plus-fours, the whole shebang. I felt like Superman in the presence of kryptonite.

"Jerry, this is Mr. Murphy, the taxi driver we spoke about."

"Oh hey, I thought I saw a cab parked in front," he said, holding out his right hand. "I was hoping I would get back before you arrived. I just finished nine holes down at the club."

I smiled and shook hands with him. Mr. Harris reminded me of the rich man who lived on 8th Avenue so I immediately felt comfortable in his presence. I knew that even wealthy people had problems that could not be solved with money, which is the only thing that makes the rich different from me.

After we shook hands, he frowned and said, "Listen, Mr. Murphy, we're really sorry about any problems that might have arisen between yourself and the taxi company due to our response to the events that took place on Wednesday night." He glanced at his wife. "I suppose Beth has already explained the situation to you."

"Yes sir," I said, "your wife did explain it, and I just want you to know that there is no problem between myself and the taxi company."

I said this knowing full well that I was blowing a great opportunity. Any time people apologize to me, I milk it.

"We panicked and started calling taxi companies trying to find out who had driven Shantel and her friends to that haunted house. We got off on the wrong track there. We should have given ourselves time to cool down and look at things from the proper perspective. In fact, that did happen, but by then we had already spoken with your managing supervisor. So again, I just want to say both my wife and I are very sorry."

I took a deep breath, cleared my throat, and said, "When Mr. Hogan told me what was going on, I realized I should not have taken those kids there without personally checking with their parents. So I would like to apologize to the both of you and to all of the parents whose children I took to the haunted house. It was a lapse in judgment on my part. I do feel that I am responsible for any anxiety that you experienced, so I just wanted to say I'm sorry, too."

"Not your fault," Mr. Harris said. By this time he was standing with his arms folded, though not a regular fold but a half-fold where his right hand was cupping his left arm which was hanging downward. John Wayne stood that way at the end of *The Searchers*, although he was just acting. I doubt if he was sorry.

"Shantel told us that she lied to you about getting permission from us, and we realized you could not be blamed."

I had the urge to disagree, but I could see that Mr. Harris wasn't so much interested in parsing the truth as receiving absolution. Our conversation was like an absolution tennis match.

I nodded in acquiescence.

"Well, at least everything worked out okay," he said. "The kids got home all right. Can't ask for more than that. I wish I could stay and talk a little longer but I've got to get to the office. Thank you for coming by Mr. Murphy. I want to pay you for your time."

I almost went ahead and said he didn't have to pay me, but I put a leash on it. Trying to stop people from giving me money was like battling dandelions.

Mr. Harris glanced at his wife. "Could you take care of that, honey? I need to grab a quick shower. I'm running late."

We shook hands one more time, then Mr. Harris left the room. I couldn't believe he had played a round before going to work. If I was rich, you wouldn't catch me doing either of those things. Whatever I did do, it would lie somewhere in the shadowlands between work and play.

"Thank you so much for coming by," Mrs. Harris said.

She picked up an envelope from a well-varnished antique table. "I hope this compensates you for your trouble."

Trouble?

I put a leash on it.

"Thank you," I said. "I'm glad we got everything cleared up."

"I am too," she said.

She escorted me toward the front door. As we walked down the green hallway I started thinking about the Cowardly Lion's exit from the Wizard's throne room. He ran full-tilt down the hallway and dove head-first through a window. When I was a child I thought his leap was an awfully dangerous move, even for a lion. How could he possibly have known what was on the other side? What if he crushed a Munchkin? Four years old is a terrible age to develop a psychological tic.

CHAPTER 11

I strolled along the S-shaped sidewalk feeling once again like a man freed from prison. I've never actually been in prison, but I have walked away from police stations—the sensations are probably indistinguishable. I also graduated from high school, and I was discharged from the army. They handed me official certificates for both of those deals. You may have experienced that yourself. I graduated from college, too, but my emotional response wasn't the same. I felt like I was leaving Studio 54.

I climbed into my taxi and took a moment to peek into the envelope. Jackson. I still had forty minutes left to run bells before my real drive-time began, so I felt like I was "in the chips." On a normal day this meant I would come out twenty bucks ahead for the hour, but being "in the chips" had its standard effect on me. I became lethargic. Instead of turning on the Rocky radio and grabbing calls left and right, I drove to a kwickie-mart on Speer Boulevard and bought a cup of joe and another Twinkie to celebrate the cleansing of my soul.

As I sat in front of the mart sipping and chewing, I contemplated the fact that Mr. and Mrs. Harris were two of the nicest people I had ever met, and I had met a lot of nice people in my time. I started wondering about Shantel. I wondered why she had felt compelled to lie to me on Wednesday night. After all, she came from a nice family. In theory I did too, so I wrote her duplicity off as standard teenage antics. Half the fun of being young is rebelling against authority, especially when the rebellion is funded by a weekly allowance.

But I intentionally had not asked about Shantel or her whereabouts that morning. I assumed she was in school, the place where society warehouses its mutineers. Nor did I inquire as to the consequences of her actions, such as being deprived of TV for a week. Thank God for television.

I have no idea how parents punished their children before electricity was invented.

The point is, I had consciously and deliberately tried to avoid bringing up any subject that might have interfered with my absolution. Whenever I knelt in the confessional at Blessed Virgin Catholic Church in Wichita, I never shot the breeze with Monsignor O'Leary. Get in, get out, and get my three Hail Marys said, that was my motto. It stood me in good stead for nine out of twelve years.

As I sat there chewing my cud with the clock ticking away, I started wondering where Shantel and her friends went after they left the haunted house. Hogan had said something about the kids having gone to another party. Mr. and Mrs. Harris had not mentioned it, and that was understandable. None of my business.

I sat there chewing and thinking, and after a while the Twinkie didn't taste so good. I had been kidding myself all along and I knew it. The kids hadn't gotten home until four in the morning. Where could they have gone? Did they meet someone at the haunted house, other kids maybe who told them about a party in another part of town?

Jaysus.

Four o'clock in the morning.

I spat the last remnants of the Twinkie into a napkin and climbed out of my cab. I tossed the cup and the napkin into a trash barrel and got back into 123. By then my sense of guilt had settled over me like a London fog. My lapse in judgment could have put those kids in harm's way. I knew that in spite of the absolution I had received from the Harrises, I was as guilty as ever. I had never met a person capable of truly absolving me of feeling guilty. The passage of time combined with intense grilling by detectives sometimes helped, but in the end I always had to face the fact that I had screwed it up, whatever "it" was.

I hate it when I am forced to admit to myself that I am not good at everything. Why can't human beings be born perfect? Our hearts and lungs and digestive systems work perfectly when we are born. Why doesn't that apply to our brains?

I wiped my lips with the back of my hand and squinted into the rearview mirror, then started the engine. I knew that the only "cure" for my sense of guilt would be to embrace acute depression. Whenever a heroin addict goes in for treatment, the doctors substitute methadone for heroin, and depression is as close to methadone as I can get without a trip to Sweeney's.

I looked at my wristwatch and noted that I had blown the free time that I had been counting on to keep me "in the chips" for the rest of the day. If I went to a hotel and waited in line, the sawbuck would be further eaten away, like the face of the dead Morlock in *The Time Machine* after Rod Taylor gave him a haymaker to the jaw. Cabot appears as a character in *The Time Machine*. He plays a cynic. Ironically Jack the Ripper is a character in *Time After Time*, where Malcolm McDowell plays H.G. Wells. It makes me dizzy to think how derivative screenwriting can truly get.

I started jumping bells. It was Friday and there were plenty. Normally jumping bells depresses me because it entails working hard, but since I was already depressed it had the double-negative effect of canceling out my blues, thus allowing me to perform my duties "on an even keel." I took one call after another and pocketed my take without bothering to add it up after each fare climbed out, which is a normal psychological tic when you have a job that involves cash transactions. Unlike Kenny Rogers' gambler, taxi drivers have a tendency to count their money before the game is done due to the fact that cab driving does not entail betting, bluffing, or tipping men in black vests. You have to stay on top of things. The Public Utilities Commission long ago set into place a rigid system of regulations that virtually forces cab drivers to live from hand-to-mouth, thank God.

My plan was simply to drive until the end of my shift, sign out, go home, stash my cash, turn on my TV, eat, surf, laugh, and crash. I would count my money on Saturday.

That was my "plan."

But then, at ten minutes to six p.m., I got a personal.

To sum it up briefly, a "personal" is a call from a taxi customer who knows my name. As you might or might not surmise, I get very few personals over the radio since I consciously and deliberately go out of my way to avoid letting anybody on earth know that I am alive, much less that I live in Denver.

I picked up the mike and answered the call. The dispatcher told me that a fare named Nagle had requested my services at an address on east

5th Avenue. The customer was going to Larimer Square. I wracked my brain but couldn't recall anybody I might have chauffeured named Nagle.

"Check," I said. This would be my last call of the evening. I suspected I had earned almost seventy dollars for the day. Even without consciously counting the money I still had a "feel" for how much I possessed, in the way that skag addicts are said to know intuitively how much horse is in their hidden stash down to the last tenth of an ounce. I read that in a psychology journal or a suspense novel, I forget which.

I worked my way over to 6th Avenue and crossed Colorado Boulevard. I entered the part of Denver that is midway between filthy rich and regular rich. During the past fifteen years I had dropped off lots of people in that part of town who had come from the airport—either Stapleton or DIA. I miss Stapleton. Going to Stapleton was like passing through the drive-up lane at a fast-food joint. Going to DIA is like a trip to Aspen with no hope of a return fare. DIA took all the fun out of living hand-to-mouth.

It was dark by then. Colorado had gone off Daylight Savings Time. In the summertime the sun is fairly high at six o'clock at night. I don't know why Colorado doesn't stay on DST all year long. It makes me uneasy when the government starts playing God with store hours. But then the position of the earth's axis relative to the sun has never affected my tax returns, so why should I care?

I pulled up in front of the address. I didn't recognize the house. Even though I rarely remember the number part of addresses, I can usually remember a house where I had dropped off a fare. I don't know if this ability is a cabbie thing or just a human thing. Leave it to any brain to remember everything that is absolutely meaningless except algebra theorems.

The yard had a high brick wall around it and a wrought-iron gate. I knew I would have to go to the front door in person. I had learned during my years as a cabbie that the rich don't peek out windows. They wait. I never honk my horn for a fare but especially not a rich fare. Tips are inextricably linked to good service and courtesy, and the rich do know how to tip. Witness my Jackson.

I walked up to the gate and pulled it open. As I did so the porch light came on. It was dim and yellow, perhaps sixty watts. The distance from the gate to the porch was approximately thirty feet. This house was not at all like the Harris house. It was a classy red-brick job but not a mansion. There were similar houses close by. The yards weren't as big as the Harris estate. The trees were not so tall. The branches of the trees hung low and thick. Half the leaves were still hanging on, and the rest were crunching under my feet. As I drew closer to the porch I realized the front door was open. Standing motionless in the doorway was a solitary figure. A hallway bulb backlit the figure, which made it difficult to discern the person's features. By the time I was fifteen feet away I had come to a complete halt.

"Rocky Cab," I said.

The figure did not move.

"Mr. Nagle?" I said.

Still he did not move.

I raised my voice. "Did you call a taxi?"

The figure raised his right hand, and the hallway light went out.

"Goot evening, Mr. Murphy," he said.

Goot?

The screen door opened and the figure stepped onto the porch. It was Dracula.

CHAPTER 12

By "Dracula" I mean the kid that I had driven to the haunted house on Wednesday night. I recognized the makeup job and the cape that hid his entire body. He was wrapped like a black cigar. The voice was that of Bela Lugosi.

"Is your father home?" I said.

He didn't reply.

He slowly stepped down off the porch and approached me. I countered his move by walking past him and climbing onto the porch. I quickly found the doorbell and rang it.

"What are you doing?" the kid said in a voice no longer like Bela's. He sounded like a young Dean Stockwell.

"Your father called the Rocky Mountain Taxicab Company," I said, knowing full well that I was in for another parental meeting. I felt I had been "taken in" by Mr. Nagle. He had pulled a fast one on me. He had called for a taxi and requested a personal just so he could lure me to his house for a well-deserved horsewhipping. Despite the fact that I was chagrined by the ruse, I was impressed. I just might have a few things in common with the talented Mr. Nagle.

"That's not likely," the kid said.

"What's not likely?" I said, peering through the window on the front door and waiting expectantly for the hall light to come back on.

"It is unlikely that my father called for a taxi."

"Why?"

"Because my father died ten years ago."

I froze.

I had not been in a situation this awkward since nine a.m.

I turned around and faced the kid who was standing on the sidewalk glaring at me. Falling leaves fluttered past his shoulders and settled with a scuffing sound at his feet.

I cleared my throat and said, "I'm sorry to hear that. Are you the person who called for a taxi?"

"Yes," he said.

"Well … I'm also sorry to have to tell you that I am not going to take you anywhere."

"You have to," he said. "You work for the government."

"What?"

"You work for the Public Utilities Commission. They regulate taxis, so you have to obey their rules. The rules say you have to drive people where they want to go."

My heart suddenly went out to this kid. I realized in a flash that he had no grasp of reality. He reminded me of a certain young man I once knew a long time ago, a wet-behind-the-ears, naive, deluded boy who didn't know his left elbow from his right foot. His name was Wardholtzer. He was in my basic training platoon.

I stepped down from the porch and walked up to the kid. He was about five-foot-seven. I tried to recall if this was a normal height for a high school student but I couldn't remember. I tried to forget as much about high school as I could after I graduated, and the average height of the aggregate student body was one aspect of my blackout. I myself topped out at six feet during my sophomore year. I am tall and fast on my feet but it didn't motivate me to go out for basketball. And I didn't have a gut in those days. That's "gut" and not "guts." I didn't have any of those either, and believe me, it takes guts to tell a gym coach that you think intramural sports is for cretins.

"If I recall from Wednesday night, your name is Lester, is that correct?" I said in as courteous a tone of voice as I could muster.

"That is correct, Mr. Murphy."

Have I ever mentioned the fact that I hate being called Mister Murphy? That's because the noun "Mister" implies that I am a mature adult, and I'll be the judge of that.

"Well, Lester Nagle, I'm afraid you're wrong. A cab driver doesn't have to take anybody anywhere if he doesn't want to. PUC regulations do not cover that aspect of cab driving. But that's not relevant here. The reason I am not going to take you anywhere in my taxi is because of the problems you and your friends caused everybody's parents on Wednesday night. You not only lied to me about having permission to go to the haunted house, you didn't get home until four o'clock in the morning."

Even though Lester was wearing fright makeup, a look of horror came over his face.

"How did you know about that?" he said.

"Because I almost got into trouble for taking you kids to the haunted house. I had a talk with Shantel's parents this morning and they told me that the parents of all the kids wanted me fired from my job. They even called the police."

A blank look came over his pasty white face. It was a look of incomprehension. I had seen it many times on my own pasty face, either in mirrors or in candid photographs taken by Wardholtzer at the judo range. He owned a Polaroid.

"Did your mother inform you that she talked to the other parents about that situation?" I said.

He didn't reply.

His silence spoke volumes. Teenagers are not very enigmatic to begin with, and even though I am lousy at math I have never had much trouble putting two and two together.

"Is your mother home?" I said.

He nodded.

"Well listen, Lester, unless I talk to your mother, I'm not going to take you anywhere tonight. I need her permission to drive you wherever you're going." I paused a moment, then said, "Where are you going anyway?"

"To The Flicker on Larimer Square," he said. "They're showing some Halloween movies."

The Flicker.

I knew The Flicker.

I knew it well.

It was a small theater located at 15th and Larimer. When it was first built it was referred to as a "mini-art" theater because it had a small screen. Today it is referred to as "normal" since most theater screens in America nowadays are an insult to the memory of Cecil B. DeMille. But there was something else about The Flicker that gave me pause. It had to do with kidnapping, murder, robbery, and other misconceptions that set the DPD bloodhounds on my trail. But I don't want to get into that, save to say there was no kidnapping or murder or robbery, although there were two bloodhounds. I call them "Duncan and Argyle" but let's move on.

"Why don't you go ask your mother to come to the door," I said. "If she okays it, I'll take you there."

He frowned. This was amusing because I had never seen Bela Lugosi frown, even when he was cornered by Van Helsing.

"Do I have to?" he said.

"No," I said. "You don't have to. You can stay home if you want, and I'll drive away. It's up to you."

Lester glanced at the front door, then did a kind of sideways rock with his cape-wrapped shoulders as if he was debating whether or not to give in. I sympathized with him. It's difficult to think when your arms are hamstrung by a strait-jacket. Don't ask me why I know this. I just do.

"Wait a sec," he said.

He stepped back up to the porch and went inside the house. I gazed at the door for a bit, then turned around and looked across the yard toward the street. I could see leaves falling farther down the block in the light cast from a high pole. The scene reminded me of a street pole as viewed from my bedroom window up in my crow's nest. In the winter, heavy snowflakes flutter around the light bulb like moths. In the summer, moths flutter around the light bulb like heavy snowflakes. The two images are virtually indistinguishable. If I wasn't too cheap to buy a Polaroid I could provide photographic evidence of how poetic my life gets when I'm sprawled on my mattress plastered to the gills.

I heard the screen door open.

I turned around and saw Lester coming back out the door. Behind him was a woman wearing a robe. She had a look on her face that I can only describe as "dazed and confused."

"Yes, what is it?" she said, holding her robe tightly at the neck with one hand and touching the closed screen door with the other.

"Mrs. Nagle?" I said.

"Yes," she said, nodding.

"I'm with the Rocky Mountain Taxicab Company. Your son Lester called for a cab. But because he's underage I need your permission to drive him down to The Flicker on Larimer Square."

She continued nodding. She looked like she had just woken up. "Yes, that's fine, he has my permission," she said.

There was a moment of awkward silence as I waited for her to say more. But she didn't.

I did though.

I wanted to ask if Mrs. Harris or any of the other parents had contacted her about the events of Wednesday night. I glanced at Lester. He was dressed like the living dead and he looked the part. He was gazing vaguely at a spot on the frame of the doorway.

I started nodding. "All right, I just needed to check. Sometimes … sometimes it's hard to judge the age of my fares … especially when they're wearing costumes."

Mrs. Nagle was still nodding. She had an inquisitive look on her face that I interpreted as either "Why are you telling me these things?" or "Why isn't this conversation over?"

"I guess we can go now," I said to Lester, and before the words were out of my mouth I heard the front door close.

I stepped down off the porch and walked toward my cab feeling very odd. Mrs. Nagle didn't seem particularly interested in the fact that her teenage son was going out on a Friday night alone … and it seemed to me that she might not have known he had intended to do this in the first place.

I heard Lester's feet crunching the leaves behind me as I approached the cab. They stopped. I looked back and saw him pulling the gate closed. As he did this, the porch light went out. This made me feel even odder. Why wouldn't his mother leave the light on? I pondered the light as I opened the driver's door. I didn't see any lights on in any windows of the house. I waited while Lester climbed in.

I felt so odd that I decided there was only one thing to do: act like a professional taxi driver and treat Dracula as an ordinary fare.

"The Flicker?" I said, as I climbed in, started the engine, and dropped the flag.

"Yes," he said quietly.

I pulled away from the house and headed for 8th Avenue. Due to the fact that it would take more than ten minutes to work my way over to 15th and Larimer I decided to strike up a conversation. Silence can be unnerving in a taxi, and the events of the past few minutes had given the ride an edge—as in "razor's."

"What movie are you going to see?" I said.

"*Night of the Living Dead*," he replied.

But of course. They show that every Halloween at The Flicker. I had been to some of the showings going as far back as my college days at UCD. People always arrived wearing Halloween costumes. They showed *The Great Gatsby* at The Flicker one time and people showed up dressed like Mia Farrow.

"That's a good one," I said. "I've seen it a couple times."

"Me too," he said.

A silence ensued. Lester was not acting the way he had acted on Wednesday night. Nor was he acting like Bela Lugosi. He was acting like a teenager who was embarrassed because his mother had to give him permission to go to a movie. Maw never gave me permission to go to movies. I just went. That's how I happened to catch the six p.m. showing of *Jack the Ripper* when I was ten. Maw had been under the impression that I was "going out to play" with my friends. Little did she realize that—at the age of ten—I had no friends.

The word "goot" welled up in my mind. Lester had been play-acting when he had first appeared in the doorway, talking like Bela, having some fun, but the surprise appearance of his mother must have dampened his enthusiasm. I felt badly about raining on his parade. But I didn't have any choice. I wasn't about to go through another "Hogan Moment" involving one of the kids who had lied to me on Wednesday.

I glanced at my mirror. Lester was gazing out his side window. I had the feeling I had ruined his fun. I felt badly. I remembered what it was like when I used to have fun. Those were the days.

"Listen, Lester, I'm sorry if it sounded like I was getting on your case back there. It's just that when you drive a taxi for a living, you run into unusual situations every once in a while and you have to be careful. I've been in situations where the police got involved, so I wanted to make sure something like that didn't happen again."

"Why did the police get involved?" he said. "What did you do?"

"I didn't do anything," I said quickly. "But I was a part of some investigations that … that …"

I became fumblemouthed, if there is such a word. I didn't want to tell this teenager about the murders and kidnappings and robberies and—I can't even remember half of the crimes I never committed, but there was no reason to tell Lester about the "funny business" that took place on Lookout Mountain, or the dope-smoking teenage girls who disappeared, or … well … you get the picture.

What I mean is, I've had fares in my taxi that the police took an interest in, but that happens to all cab drivers, I guess.

I glanced back at him and said, "Sometimes my fares jump out of my taxi at stoplights and run away without paying."

I saw him smile. "Do the police arrest them?" he said.

"No. I always let them go. It's too much trouble to chase people like that, although I did call the police a couple of times when I first started driving."

"Did the police catch the guys?"

"Yeah. But the guys were drunk so they were easy to catch."

I had never said that sentence before in my life. I decided to file it away in the "gentle reminder" drawer in my brain. I placed it next to the reminder not to get involved in the personal lives of my fares.

"Can I ask you something?" I said.

"Yes."

"Why did you call Rocky Cab and ask for me to come and pick you up?"

A long silence ensued. I glanced back to see what Lester was doing. Maybe he was getting ready to bolt. As I turned my head I saw him peering out the right-side window. He quickly glanced at me. The "vibes" had become thick again.

"Was it just because you know my name?" I said.

"Sort of," he replied.

"So you just wanted to give me your money rather than give it to a strange cab driver?"

I heard Lester inhale and exhale with what I interpreted to be resignation. When you drive a cab for a living you become acutely sensitive to sighs, vibes, and the general nuances of body language. This is related both to tips and survival.

"Shantel told me I should call you," he finally said.

"You mean the girl who was dressed like a princess the other night?"

"Yes."

"Why would she do that?"

"Because she knows I'm going to the movie and she wanted me to tell you that she was sorry she got you in trouble."

I nodded as if I understood. I have no idea whether or not I understood but I "went with the flow."

"How come she wanted you to make the apology for her?" I said. "Was she too embarrassed to apologize to me in person?"

"No," he said. "She was supposed to go with me to the movie tonight, only her parents grounded her. She was going to call the cab company and ask them to send you over to her house and then come and pick me up. She wanted to tell you that she was sorry about everything."

"When did her parents ground her?" I said.

"About an hour ago."

I nodded, but that was just a ruse. In reality, I was thinking about the fact that Lester's mother had not grounded *him*. I was also thinking about the possibility that his mother did not know that he had wandered in at four in the morning after visiting the Halloween house on Wednesday night.

"You can tell Shantel that it's all right," I said. "I didn't get into any trouble."

"Okay."

"Are you taking a taxi home after the show?"

"Yes."

"If I was working I'd pick you up myself," I said, "but I'm heading home after I drop you off."

"I'm going to call a taxi from the theater," he said.

"If you want, I could set up a time-call for you," I said.

"What do you mean?"

"I can tell the dispatcher to have a cab waiting for you when the movie gets out. That would be about nine o'clock, right?"

"I didn't know you could do that," he said.

I nodded and simultaneously made a mental list of all the astounding things that teenagers have no idea you can arrange to have done in this world, especially if you are rich. "Heck, you can phone a taxi company a week in advance and arrange to set up a time-call."

"Really?"

"Yeah."

His response to this enlightenment depressed me. I had the feeling I was teaching him something that they don't teach in high school. Wouldn't it be nice if they actually taught useful skills in high school? I will admit that girls learn useful skills in Home Ec, but when was the last time you climbed a twenty-foot rope?

"Do you want me to set up a time-call for you tonight?" I said.

A silence emanated from the backseat. It had the quality of "uncertain" silence. I sensed that the kid was leery of trying something new and complicated. But what kid doesn't do this? To my knowledge I have never cooked an omelet.

"I'm not sure what time the movie will get out," he said, verbally backing away from my offer.

I let it go. I myself have always been leery of unsolicited offers of help. High school counselors sometimes did that, usually in reference to applying myself to my studies. But I managed to dodge those bullets. Hell, if I had listened to those clowns I wouldn't be where I am today.

CHAPTER 13

I pulled up to the curb in front of The Flicker. Scores of kids wearing Halloween costumes were lined up to get into the movie. I won't describe the costumes. You've seen kids before. I shut off the meter and reached into my plastic briefcase. I pulled out a 2x3 card, a Rocky Cab receipt. The fare came to just over seven dollars. Lester handed me a ten-dollar bill and stunned me by saying, "Keep the change." I won't bother to explain why that stunned me.

"The phone number for Rocky Cab is printed here," I said. I took out my pen and wrote my full name under the number, except for my middle name, which is "Aloysius." I left that out because it's just down the road from "Argyle."

"When you call the company, tell them Murph sent you." But I said this for effect only. My name means nothing at Rocky.

"Thanks," he said.

He hustled himself onto the sidewalk. I watched him walk toward the rear of the crowd. I was curious to see if anyone would recognize him, wave to him, and maybe offer to let him cut in line. I've heard of things like that happening but I've never experienced it myself.

Neither did Dracula. He took his place at the end of the line behind Yoda.

While watching all this I suddenly realized that by remaining parked at the curb I was taking a terrible risk. Someone might climb into my backseat and ask for a ride to a distant location that would overextend my shift and cause me to end up paying a late fee.

I looked back to check the traffic, then sped away from the curb. I glanced at my rearview mirror and saw more people arriving for *Night of the Living Dead*. It made me wistful. It not only reminded me of my college days, it reminded me of the actress that I supposedly "murdered" awhile back. I assure you that I did not murder her, but it's a long story and I don't want to go into the details of how the police finally concluded that I did not kill her or any of the other victims that the police have questioned me about for reasons that made sense at the time but were proven wrong because there were no dead bodies and … actually there were two dead bodies that I can think of, but I assure you that I did not have anything to do with their deaths except in what might be viewed as a peripheral connection which … well … perhaps I've said too much.

I drove back toward the motor feeling generally good about myself. I felt that I had handled things well that day. I was glad Shantel had wanted to apologize to me, and that her parents had contacted me to clear things up, and that Lester Nagle had broken through the "fourth wall" of his Dracula schtick to set things right.

Yes, as I drove back to the Rocky Mountain Taxicab Company on that Friday evening one day before Halloween I can honestly say that I experienced what some people refer to as a "clear conscience." It was an unusual feeling, and not necessarily one that I would recommend to other people for the simple reason that the journey to a clear conscience can be bumpy.

All things considered, I prefer guilt. For one thing, having a clear conscience is like buying a new car. You live in fear of the day that a scratch will appear on a fender. I feel that in the long run, guilt is psychologically cheaper yet just as effective as absolution if you give it enough time, though I will concede that not everybody can handle guilt. Like mescal, it's an acquired taste.

I arrived at the motor with five minutes to spare. I would not be paying a late fee. This made me feel competent. It was an illusion of course, like everything that makes me feel competent. I don't know why people get down on the concept of illusions, as in the famous phrase, "Happiness is just an illusion." Pain is just an illusion generated by the brain in conjunction with the central nervous system, yet it is as real as reality gets. On the other hand, paying taxes is not an illusion—let's see a home-grown cynic field that one.

I climbed out of 123 and said goodbye to it. We wouldn't be seeing each other again until Monday. I walked toward the on-call room trying to determine whether we would see each other in two days or three days, given the fact that this was a Friday. I realized that I could almost say it would be four days if I said to myself, "Friday, Saturday, Sunday, Monday," which I did.

I was looking at the ground as I said this so I didn't see Jacobsen until I got close to the on-call room. He was standing outside the door smoking a cigarette. Jacobsen was an old pro who had been driving a taxi six years longer than myself.

"What the hell are you mumbling about, Murph?" he said.

I froze.

There is nothing in the world that I fear more than letting people know I mumble things.

"I was cursing," I said. "A runner cheated me out of eight bucks."

"I hear you, man," Jacobsen said, flicking ash to the ground.

I felt guilty about having lied to Jacobsen. But that was okay. I handle guilt much better than I handle embarrassment.

I started to open the door but Jacobsen put a hand on my shoulder. "Before you go inside, I want to tell you something."

If it had been anyone but Jacobsen who had physically and verbally stopped me in my tracks I would have been livid. I never want anybody to tell me anything. But during the past fifteen years we had spoken perhaps a dozen times and I had learned that Jacobsen wasn't the kind of man who talked when he had nothing worth saying. That's one thing I do not have in common with him.

"Brace yourself for what you are about to see," he said.

"What am I about see?"

"I can't describe it," he said. "Just prepare yourself mentally in a way that you have never prepared yourself for anything in your entire life."

When an old pro says something like that, I know it's time to resign and get a real job. But it was six forty-five on a Friday night and I have never wanted a real job.

"How about a hint," I said.

He tossed his cigarette to the dirt, stepped on it with his toe, and ground out the ash like he was grinding out all hope in the universe.

"I can say only this," Jacobsen said. "Hapworth's wife made him do it."

Then he was gone.

I listened to the crunch of Jacobsen's boots as he disappeared into the darkness. Jacobsen wears cowboy boots. I've never asked why. Hapworth, on the other hand, is the name of the owner of the Rocky Mountain Taxicab Company. His wife comes around every so often. She likes to "meddle." I hope I don't have to explain that to you, save to say that her husband is rich, which means she is too. I suspect she is also bored.

I opened the door to the on-call room. I didn't bother to brace myself—I gave up doing that after receiving my draft notice. That was the day I learned that bracing yourself for the worst is the most irrelevant act a human being can perform. I suspected that Jacobsen knew this too, but had felt morally obligated to go through the ritual of saying it. After all, rituals are a universal aspect of the human experience. The mythologist Joseph Campbell wrote twelve thousand books on the subject.

I stepped into the on-call room and quickly scanned it with my army-trained eyes. I did not see anything out of the ordinary. I continued to peer around surreptitiously as I walked up to the cage. Then I looked at Bozo the Clown sitting inside the cage where Rollo normally sat.

The fright wig. The bulbous nose. The twisted red lips. I could not see any of those features because Rollo was wearing a full-head mask.

He was also wearing a tent-like costume that covered the rest of his body. It had blue polka dots. It reminded me of the costume that Clarabell the Clown used to wear on *The Howdy-Doody Show* in the 1950s. Clarabell was played by Bob Keeshan who went on to become Captain Kangaroo. Clarabell couldn't talk, so he had horns on his belt that he honked in response to anything Buffalo Bob said. When I was a kid I couldn't decide which would be worse, knowing someone who couldn't talk, or knowing someone who honked big horns at you. The jury is still out.

I handed my key and trip-sheet to Rollo. He reached out with a hand encased in a white glove. We're talking full-frontal ensemble. There was no doubt in my mind that his shoes were two feet long.

I glanced at Rollo's eyes. They bore the look of a terrified animal.

Rather than say the sorts of things that a lesser man might have said, I simply shook my head with sympathy. "I don't know which I hate worse, holidays or rich women." I had to reach deep down inside my soul to utter that blasphemy. In truth, I have nothing against rich women. I wish I knew some. And as far as holidays go, my life is an endless series of firecrackers and valentines.

"She thought it would be festive," Rollo said with a note of despair.

I replied by making a sound like this: "Tsk."

Then I walked out of the on-call room.

As I drove toward my crow's nest that Friday night I started thinking about the concept of humiliation. I was reminded of a Halloween that took place when I was in my late twenties. It was the first and last time in my life that I made an attempt to change the world.

I was living in a low-rent neighborhood in Cleveland. The small house that I rented has since gone under the plow. The landlord told me that the place was scheduled to be razed within a year to make way for an addition to an interstate highway. The government called it "eminent domain." I called it "justifiable homicide." You wouldn't believe the rat hole my house was. Anyway I decided on that particular Halloween not to hand out candy to children. Instead I would hand out paperback books.

I went to a Salvation Army store and picked up as many books as I could find that cost a dime. I bought things like *Treasure Island, Henry Huggins, Charlotte's Web, Tom Sawyer*. I also found *The Wonderful Flight to the Mushroom Planet* by Eleanor Cameron but I kept that for myself. I first read *Mushroom* when I was ten, and I am still convinced that Tyco Bass permanently altered the fundamental structure of my brain, although I have no neurological proof—yet.

When the kiddies began knocking on my door on Halloween night I surprised them by placing paperbacks into their candy sacks. Due to the fact that they were wearing masks I could not see the delighted expressions on their faces.

I still had a few books left in my bowl when I heard a loud knock on my door. I opened it and saw two uniformed policemen. I looked beyond them to the sidewalk where a group of adults had gathered. By "group" I mean two dozen. They were accompanied by kids who had knocked on my door earlier. I recognized the costumes.

"Are you the gentleman who has been handing out books to the little ones?" a cop said. He had red hair. I glanced at his nameplate. It said "O'Rooney" although that never became relevant.

"Yes, sir," I said.

"We've been getting complaints down at the station house."

His partner was holding a transparent plastic bag containing books that I had given out. I looked back and forth at the cops, then I looked at what I now discerned was a "surly" group of parents.

"I decided to hand out books tonight instead of candy," I said.

"That's not how it's done, laddie," O'Rooney said. "On Halloween you give sweets to the tots. The only acceptable substitutes are candy-apples and popcorn balls."

One of the parents barked, "What's the big idea of giving my kid a book!"

This was followed by a round-robin of yeahs like you hear in movies about lynch mobs.

O'Rooney turned around and held up a hand. "All right now folks, simmer down, I've got everything under control."

He turned back and gave me the fish-eye. "What possessed you to hand out books to the children?"

I cleared my throat, "I wanted to change the world."

"This is Cleveland," he said. "We don't do that here."

I nodded.

His partner handed the bag of books to me and said in a level tone of voice, "Sir, in the future I would advise you to stick with the traditional penny candy."

O'Rooney leaned closer and spoke softly. "If I were you, laddie, I wouldn't be opening the door again tonight."

"Yes, sir," I said clutching the bag to my breast.

The cops turned and stepped down off the porch. "All right now folks, you can go on back to your homes, everything has been straightened out."

"What about candy!" someone shouted, but I quickly closed the door.

I didn't open it again for the rest of the night, and not only because Officer O'Rooney had advised me not to open it but because I kept hearing thumps on the front wall of my house. The next morning I peeked out the window and saw books scattered all over the front porch. By six o'clock that evening I was on a bus headed for Seattle.

CHAPTER 14

I woke up Saturday morning feeling content. Halloween was the best holiday in America next to Christmas because it was another "Day Of Free Things." Even though I had given up trick-or-treating during my late teens I still liked it when Halloween rolls around. It "felt" good. It made me want to watch movies about wolfmen, ghosts, and man-made monsters, the sorts of movies I watch every weekend. My plan for that day was to make a run down to an independent video store on south Broadway called Gandalf's and peruse the "recommended" shelf, a wall of tapes in a far corner where the sorts of people who earned the minimum wage were given an opportunity to publicly expose the range and depth of their taste in the art of the cinema. That's where I first encountered *Evil Dead 2*. The clerk who recommended it was named "Trixi." I gave her four thumbs-up.

Before rolling out of bed, I parted the curtain above my pillow to check out the weather. The sky was cloudy. This depressed me. On the one hand the mood was proper for Halloween, but on the other hand I was afraid it might rain or even snow and thus wreck trick-or-treat for the kids. This is the only flaw I associate with Halloween. The weather doesn't always cooperate. When I was nine years old it snowed in Wichita on Halloween and destroyed my life. I should add that I was living in Wichita at the time. If I had been living in Orlando it probably wouldn't have meant anything to me. I know what you're thinking: Mister Center-of-the-Universe couldn't care less about suffering humanity.

Eight inches of snow had fallen in Wichita that day and the sidewalks were virtually impassable. But Maw did allow my older brother Gavin and myself to make a circuit of the block even though it was "not a fit night out for man nor beast." Apparently mothers have no idea just how powerful the lure of free anything can be to a boy. Like the greed-head sourdoughs who ran off to the Klondike, Gavin and I were determined to dig a few nuggets out of the permafrost. As soon as we got home though, Maw made us share the mother lode with our sisters.

I don't want to talk about that any further.

In spite of the fact that I was both depressed and contented, I rolled out of bed. It was 10:00 a.m. and I had two whole days of free time ahead of me to do nothing. It's true that I could have started writing a novel but I never compose novels on holidays. I'm afraid I might start a book that could turn into a bestseller but then get interrupted by an invitation to a party. Think of how awful it would be to come that close to earning a million dollars only to be lured away by free beer. It simply was not worth the risk.

Then the phone rang.

I glanced at the digital clock on my radio. It was 10:01. I quickly deduced that the phone call was from someone who knew exactly what time I awoke on my day off. This did not bode well.

Rather than go into the living room to listen to the voice on my Audio-Master Deluxe answering machine, I stood hidden next to my bedroom door and kept my ears cocked.

"Murph, this is Stew down at Rocky. If you're there could you please pick up?"

I wanted badly to slump against the wall and rub my face—standard operating procedure when I get a call from someone I know. But I didn't want to keep Stew waiting. When you hack for a living you don't want to annoy anybody above the rank of "taxi driver." I'm talking office politics.

"Hello Stew," I said into the receiver.

"Sorry to call you on a Saturday, Murph."

I nodded, then quickly added, "No problem." That's one of the many things I hate about the telephone. You can't use body language to communicate your lies.

"Here's the deal, Murph," Stew said. "We got a call this morning from a woman who asked if you could drive over to her house. I told her you weren't on duty today, so she asked if I could call and let you know that she wanted to talk to you."

A chill crept down my spine. This happens whenever weird things occur in my life—like when women want to talk to me.

"But I told her that it was against company policy to do what she was asking," Stew continued. "She then told me it was a kind of emergency, so I told her I would talk to the managing supervisor and see what we could do. I said I would try to get back to her within a half-hour."

I slumped against the wall but I won't put you through the rest of it.

"Who was this woman?" I said.

"Her name is Shantel Harris."

I froze. I was in the middle of rubbing my face. "Did she tell you the nature of the emergency?"

"No she did not."

I closed my eyes and tried to think, which is virtually impossible on Saturdays. "You say you talked to Hogan about this?"

"Yeah. He seemed to know who this Harris woman was, and he told me to call you at one minute after ten to let you know what's going on."

I nodded but didn't say anything. I was still trying to think. I was thinking about my conversation with Hogan on Thursday and how he had said the buck had stopped. I wanted to make sure it stayed stopped. I didn't want Rocky Cab involved in this situation in any manner. That was the least I could do for Hogan. "Listen Stew, I do know this woman. Here's what I would like you to do. Call her back and give her my phone number and tell her to call me. I'll be waiting."

We rang off.

I set the receiver on the cradle thinking about the fact that I had not spoken that many words on a Saturday morning since … well … I couldn't remember the last time but I had to assume it was the last time I got involved in the personal life of a fare—meaning the last time my life went to hell in a hatbox.

As often as that happens, you might think I would remember my most recent verbal-Saturday, but I have always made a conscious and deliberate effort to forget everything that can conceivably be contained within the parameters of what I label my "past." I have no idea what my success rate is. I'm not sure I even have a success rate.

I stood for a moment wondering whether to start breakfast or to extrapolate on the many possibilities that Shantel Harris might define as an "emergency." Starting breakfast would consist of putting eggs into a pan of water, whereas extrapolation would consist of putting thoughts into my head. I felt incapable of doing either. I was barely capable of falling onto my mattress, but it didn't matter because the phone rang.

I decided not to put off the inevitable, which was a first for me. I knew who was calling. I felt psychic.

"Hello?"

"Mr. Murphy, this is Shantel Harris."

"Yes, Miss Harris," I said—I'm not into the "Ms." construct when it comes to teenage girls. "My boss down at Rocky Cab told me you wanted to talk to me."

"I'm sorry to call you at home Mr. Murphy, but there's something important that I need to talk to you about."

"It's quite all right," I said, then quickly continued. "I came over to your house on Friday morning and talked to your mother and father. Did they tell you about my visit?"

"Yes they did. They told me they wanted to apologize to you about the things that happened because of Wednesday night. I wanted to apologize, too."

The girl obviously was well-bred. She probably wrote thank-you notes for birthday gifts. Well-bred people are way out of my league.

"The reason I called you today is sort of connected with that," she said.

"How so?"

"The thing is, Mr. Murphy, last night I was supposed to go to a movie with Lester Nagle. He was the boy dressed like Dracula on Wednesday night."

"That's right. I picked him up at his house. He said that both of you originally were supposed to go to the movie but that you had been grounded."

There was a pause. I assumed she was experiencing a brief moment of embarrassment. That's one of my own ten top reasons for pausing over a phone—and believe me you don't want to hear the other nine.

"You see … the thing is, Mr. Murphy … Lester didn't come home from the movie last night."

My first instinct was to tell her to call the police. I even knew which police: Duncan and Argyle. But no sooner did those two names pop into my head than a third name popped into my head: Murph.

That's a name I did not want associated with Duncan and Argyle. Without going into too much detail, every time anybody in the entire metropolitan area disappeared I had the sudden urge to leave town. The only thing that stopped me was the police acronym "APB."

"May I ask you why you're telling me this?" I said as politely as possible.

"Because I don't want Lester to get in trouble with the police."

This girl was one step ahead of me. How could that be? She was only sixteen.

"If he's missing, maybe you really ought to call the police," I said.

"I don't actually think he's missing," she said. "I think I know where he is. That's why I called the taxi company. I wanted you to accompany me to the place where he might be."

"Where is that?" I said.

There was another pause. It held a vague resemblance to the seventh reason why I often pause.

"Could you meet me at the Cherry Creek Shopping Center?" Shantel said. "I have a couple of things to tell you and I told my mother that I was going shopping this morning and if she comes home and I'm not gone she might wonder why I'm still here."

If it wasn't for the fact that I have younger sisters, I might not have been able to follow the thread of logic in that sentence. Ergo, I tried to stay one step ahead of her. "I thought Lester said you were grounded," I said.

"I am grounded," she said. "But that's fun-grounded, not shopping-grounded."

I took a deep breath and said, "I don't know about this. It sounds like you ought to tell your parents and let them handle it."

"I can't do that," she said.

"Why not?"

There was a long pause. I do not suppose I need to explain to you that it held an exact resemblance to Pause #1 on my list.

"It's because I didn't tell them the whole truth about what happened last Wednesday night," she said.

"What happened on Wednesday night?" I said.

"That's what I want to tell you about. Can you meet me at the mall?"

"Listen," I said, "why are you so concerned about Lester? What I mean is … did his mother tell you that he didn't come home last night?"

"She doesn't know."

"How do you know that?" I said.

"Because he told her that after the movie got out he was going to spend the night at Herbert's house."

"Who's Herbert?"

"He was the boy dressed like the tin-man last Wednesday. He called me this morning and said Lester never showed up."

My sisters were no help to me now, but that was not unusual. I was starting to feel like a performer trying to keep track of plates spinning on top of skinny sticks on *The Ed Sullivan Show.* If you don't know what I'm referring to, it would take too long to explain.

"I understand why you wouldn't want to get Lester in trouble with the police, but I don't understand why you're asking me to help you," I said.

She paused only briefly … it was more of a verbal ellipsis. "It's because you're the last person I know who saw Lester," alive.

She didn't say alive. My mind said that. I don't know why I'm always the last person to see someone alive. Can't anybody else in this cow town see someone alive?

"I thought maybe Lester might have mentioned to you what we did on Wednesday night," Shantel continued.

I took a deep breath—to this day I'm not sure I ever let it out.

"He didn't tell me anything about Wednesday night," I said.

"Can we …" Shantel said, then she choked a bit. I sensed that she was trying to keep from crying. I glanced at my wrist where I usually park my watch. I noted that the tanned flesh was stark white where the wristband normally resided. This was because I often drove with my left elbow resting on the window frame where it got a lot of sunlight. It made me feel jaunty.

"All right, Shantel, I'll meet you at the mall," I said. "But I want to meet you in a public area. Do you know the part of the mall where the snack bars are located?"

"In the downstairs?"

"Yes."

The snack area of Cherry Creek is mind-boggling. It's like a cul-de-sac packed shoulder-to-shoulder with little concession stands that sell everything that can be humanly cooked, roasted, broiled, or baked: giant pretzels, frosted German hot-cross buns, chili dogs, spareribs, deep-fried chicken. It's a cardiologist's dream come true.

"I'll meet you there," I said. "Are you going to need a ride—I mean, is that why you called for a taxi?"

"No, I have my own car," she said. "I called for a taxi this morning so I could talk to you while you were driving."

Without reference to the white stripe on my left wrist I said, "Why don't we meet at eleven o'clock."

"I'll be there. Thank you for doing this for me, Mr. Murphy."

"You're welcome," I said. I hate lying to teenagers. I pride myself on my honesty when it comes to the untutored of the earth. But I felt compelled to tell her she was welcome. I was playing what is known in most circles as "The Game."

I went back to my room and collapsed face-down onto my mattress just to prove to myself that it could be done. I closed my eyes and mumbled the Taxi Driver's Prayer—to wit: "It doesn't matter, it doesn't matter, it doesn't matter ..." There is no "Amen" to the taxi driver's prayer. It just withers to nothing.

CHAPTER 15

After I finished praying, I got up and put myself into a state of mind that I call "robo-brain." It's similar to the state of mind that I embrace when I am obligated to do anything. You name it—I'm on robo-brain.

I got dressed but didn't have breakfast. I decided that since I was going to a snack bar I might as well start the day off with a couple of those frosted German hot-cross buns. By "frosted" I mean "industrial-strength." I'm not schooled in the history of German pharmaceuticals but it wouldn't surprise me if the icing on those rolls was the inspiration for amphetamines.

I peeked past a kitchen curtain to see what the weather on the west side of my building was like, and to see if my Chevy had been stolen. It gets stolen at both inconvenient moments and convenient moments. This would have been an inconvenient moment because I would have been forced to call a taxi and I hate calling taxis, but I don't want to explain that. I will only say that my Chevy was resting in the parking lot like a faithful mutt.

I suited up, left my crow's nest and went down the fire escape. I drove to University Boulevard in partial-robo mode, meaning I paid attention to my driving like I always do but I didn't think about where I was going. I just went there.

It was both Saturday and Halloween so the parking lot was crowded. I decided not to play the parking game that most civilians play, meaning I did not drive up and down the rows and through the parking garage looking for an empty space. I found a slot way the hell out in the asphalt boonies and hiked my way to the mall. This involved two minutes of walking, which was unusual for me but helped to wake me up. The hot-cross buns would take care of the rest.

The mall was crowded. You've seen crowded malls. Let's move on. I took a supersonic see-through elevator down one floor to the bottom level in order to compensate for my two-minute walk. I have never liked stairs anyway—neither up nor down. I prefer level ground. Maybe there's a bit of pioneer blood in my veins.

I hiked along the vast shopping corridor until I came to the snack cul-de-sac where I stopped dead in my tracks. The entire area had been decorated for Halloween—I'm talking orange and black streamers, cardboard cutouts of skeletons, witches, and black cats dangling from the ceiling. And to top it off, the clerks were wearing costumes. I would have lost my appetite if it hadn't been for the overwhelming aroma of freshly baked amphetamines.

I looked around for Shantel, didn't see her, then went up to the German concession to order a roll. The clerk was dressed like a peasant. Her cheeks were decorated with two big circles of pink rouge, her hair consisted of a bright yellow wig, and when she smiled I saw that two of her teeth had been blackened out with wax. I nearly vomited. Fortunately my stomach was empty, but I knew the cure for that.

I bought a bun and a soda and found an empty seat at a vacant table in the middle of the cul-de-sac. Little kids were running around screaming but I won't mention it again. I sipped at my morning soda, took the first bite out of the bun, and braced myself for a trip to pre-war Berlin.

The sugar rush came on quickly. I was tapping my right toe and humming a tune from *Cabaret* when I saw Shantel coming through the crowd toward me.

She was wearing a gray sweatshirt, faded blue jeans, and tennis shoes. She looked like 90 percent of the female cab drivers who work for Rocky, although one of our female drivers dresses like June Cleaver. I'm talking a fancy skirt and a coiffed hairdo. I figure her tasteful get-up as a tip magnet, and a pretty good one at that, but I don't know for sure—like all of the males at Rocky, I'm scared to talk to her. She's too beautiful. Driving a cab is like being in high school.

"Hello Mr. Murphy," Shantel said, as she approached the table. "Thank you for meeting me here."

"Hello Shantel," I said, standing up in accordance with Emily Post. "Can I buy you something to eat?"

"No thanks, I'm not hungry," she said, as she sat down on a plastic chair opposite me. She was carrying a small brown purse strapped over one shoulder. After she got settled she lay the purse on the table. I set aside part of my brain to keep tabs on the purse in order to make sure she departed with it. As I hinted at earlier, a lost purse once brought me to within a hair's-breadth of a kidnap/murder charge. But it ended happily, like all of my brushes with John Law. By "all" I mean "major criminal investigations."

Shantel clasped her hands and rested them on the table, then looked at me with mournful eyes. "I'm sorry to interrupt you on your day off, but this is really important to me."

"That's okay," I said. "I wasn't doing anything anyway." Normally I wouldn't say that to any human being on earth. When people get the idea that I don't do things they tend to think up things for me to do. But I wanted to put Shantel at ease. I took a sip of soda, set the cup down, and smiled.

She smiled back but didn't say anything. I figured that she was going to have trouble cutting to the chase. I groaned inwardly for two reasons: #1, I knew I would have to act mature by #2, treating Shantel as if she was a passenger in my taxi. By this I mean I would have to coax her into talking. Cab drivers are good at getting people to talk about their personal lives. A few well-chosen questions can motivate a fare to talk virtually non-stop for an entire ride, and believe me, the monologue is preferable to the dialogue.

To my surprise though I didn't have that problem with Shantel. She cut right to the chase.

"The thing is, Mr. Murphy, last Wednesday when we were at the haunted house, we met a group of people who invited us to a party. I didn't really want to go but Lester talked me into it. The other boys wanted to go too, and since the party was at a house here in town Lester said we wouldn't have to take a taxicab back to Denver after all."

"Who were these people?"

"One of them was named Rodney. The haunted house is where he lives."

"How old is he?"

"Pretty old. He's like thirty. He said he held the haunted house party at his place last year too."

"Who were the other people?"

"Just kids like us. Some boys and girls. Lester was the one who met them. They were behind us while we were walking through the house. Everybody was screaming and laughing at the ghosts and stuff that they had there, and we just kind of all mingled together and became one group. But it was Lester who started talking to Rodney. Rodney was walking around in a vampire suit like Lester. He told Lester about a party that was going to be held here in Denver after the haunted house thing ended. He started talking about the kinds of stuff that interest Lester. He told us that the other kids had come in two cars and they would drive us back to Denver and take us to the party if we wanted to go."

"What kind of stuff interests Lester?" I said.

"Supernatural stuff like ghosts and Ouija boards, and even flying saucers. Rodney said he was a palm reader. He tells people's fortunes with Tarot cards and crystal balls."

"Is that what he does for a living?"

"I don't know how he makes a living but he told us that he does these palm readings and charges people for it. There was a sign in his front yard that said people could make appointments."

This put me in mind of signs that I had seen posted around Denver that had to do with fortune telling. You see them here and there, discreet signage in front yards that offer psychic readings. But until this conversation I had never thought much about them. It made me wonder if it was illegal to seriously claim to be able to tell people's fortunes. I hoped not. America had enough unenforced laws on the books without creating a new class of criminals who would bring the curse of the banshee down on the taxpayers.

"Lester said he wanted to go to the party, and that it would be better than trying to get a taxicab. So we all rode with Rodney and his friends."

"Why did you guys stay so late?" I said.

Shantel pursed her lips and looked down at the table, then looked up. "That's the part I didn't tell my parents about. Rodney told Lester that after the party was over they were going to hold a seance. The party actually ended around two o'clock. Rodney had a video camera that he was using to take movies of the party. He showed us a video about a seance."

"Did ghosts appear in it?"

"No, but there were these people sitting around a table in his house out by Golden, and Rodney was sitting with his eyes closed and answering questions that people were asking. He was supposed to be talking in the voice of the spirits." She paused a moment and thought about it, then said, "It was like watching an instructional tape in school."

"You mean it looked staged?"

"Sort of. I mean it didn't look like a real seance, if you know what I mean. It was like how a seance was supposed to look. After the tape ended he said he was going to hold a seance upstairs."

Promo tape.

That's what Rodney was showing them, I was sure of it.

In the olden days, snake-oil salesmen used dancing girls and banjo players to lure a crowd. Now it was VHS tape. Same con, different era. Even Shakespeare must have hyped Yorick's skull.

"A lot of people had left by then, but Lester told us he wanted to stay for the seance. I didn't really want to, but Lester thought it would be fun. So we all stayed."

She frowned and shrugged her shoulders. "I wish I had just called a taxi and gone home."

"Why? Did something weird happen?"

"I didn't take part in the seance, but Lester did. The rest of my friends just hung around downstairs and watched part of a video."

"What video?"

"It was a movie called *Plan Nine From Outer Space*. It was pretty awful."

I was ambivalent about her critique, but I let it pass.

"The seance lasted an hour," she continued. "It was like three o'clock when we finally left. Rodney drove all of us home. Lester and I were the last two people he dropped off. Rodney let me out at my house, then he took Lester home."

On the surface I was calmly chewing on a hot-cross bun and sipping my soda, but deep down inside I was experiencing a state of apoplexy. Paul Lynde sang it best in *Bye Bye Birdie*: "… What's the matter with kids today? …"

I set the cup on the tabletop. "So basically you didn't want your parents to know that Lester had attended a seance," I stated.

She nodded.

I could have given her a lecture on the dangers of meeting strange people and going to strange houses—which pretty much described what I did for a living—but I had the feeling this girl had been giving herself that lecture for the past two days.

"Where is Lester right now?" I said.

"I think he went back to visit that guy Rodney."

"Why do you think that?"

This was where she temporarily clammed up. I had the feeling she was about to start wringing her hands. Her eyes became rimmed with tears.

"Did you have breakfast this morning?" I said.

She reached up quickly and wiped an eye, then shook her head no.

"I'm going to buy you a hot-cross bun and a soda," I said. "You don't have to eat it, but I feel impolite eating in front of someone else."

This wasn't true. I'll eat in front of anybody at any time in any place, barring the obvious places where you wouldn't want to put food into your mouth, like an army mess hall.

I didn't wait for a reply from Shantel. I stood up and walked over to the counter and ordered two sodas and a bun—then went ahead and ordered my second German power-booster for the day. The real reason I did this, though, was to give Shantel time enough to work herself up into telling me the rest of the bad news. I wasn't kidding myself. The Cherry Creek snack emporium reeked of bad news. I could barely smell the chili dogs.

It worked.

By the time I got back to the table Shantel was sitting very erect. Her eyes were as dry as the bones of the cardboard skeleton dangling above our table.

"Thank you," she said, after I placed the confection in front of her.

I sat down and set my frosted bun in front of me and pretended to ignore it.

"Why do you think Lester went to see Rodney?" I said.

Shantel took a deep breath and sighed. "I got home on Wednesday night about four o'clock. All the lights were on in my house and my parents were still awake. They were really upset. They told me they called the police. I got a lecture. Then they sent me to bed."

I nodded. I wanted to say she didn't have to paint me a picture. I know all about upset parents. I had two.

"About half an hour after I went to bed I got a call on my cell phone," she said. "Lester hadn't said anything to me after he and the other kids came downstairs from the seance. He usually makes jokes and things, but he was real quiet on the ride home." She paused, then looked me in the eye. "He called to tell me that during the seance he contacted his dead father."

CHAPTER 16

I casually reached out, picked up the hot-cross bun, and took a bite of the frosting, avoiding the bun entirely. This was analogous to "eating the worm." If you don't know anything about mescal, I advise you to keep it that way.

I washed it down with a sip of soda and waited for Shantel to go on, but the look on her face told me she had said everything she wanted to say. I tried to look as if I wanted her to tell me more but I wasn't able to pull it off because that's one aspect of body language I never mastered. I never want anybody to tell me anything.

I finally capitulated and went for the last resort: talking.

"You do realize, don't you Shantel, that seances are a fraud? It's impossible to communicate with the dead."

She replied with the resigned nod of a person who is acknowledging the truth of something that has never been scientifically disproven. Disproving negatives is not within the purview of the bright boys who have degrees from institutes of technology. M.I.T. comes to mind.

"I know," she said, "but ever since I've known Lester he has always talked about E.S.P. and stuff like that."

"How long have you known him?"

"All my life. We grew up together. He's my cousin."

A wave of foolishness passed through me. The whole time we had been talking I had been fighting the urge to ask why she cared what this friend of hers did. Not caring a whit about what friends did was a method of dealing with difficult relationships that I began practicing in kindergarten.

"Lester's mother is my father's sister," Shantel continued. "My uncle's name was Herbert. He died when Lester was six years old. Lester used to have dreams that his father was alive and still at home. He once told me he believed his father's spirit came into his dreams to talk to him."

I understood. My father died nine years ago and I have had numerous dreams where I am back in the house where I grew up in Wichita, and there's my father walking around in the living room as alive as Joe Hill. In those dreams I never speak to him, I just look at him querulously. I want to ask what he is doing there, given the fact that he died nine years ago. But I never felt that my father had returned from "the other side" to tell me anything. He rarely told me anything when he was on "this side" except when he handed me a quarter every Saturday and told me not to spend it all in one place. I have often wondered about the origin of that expression. Was there a time in America when spending all your money in one place was a perilous financial strategy? I don't know which is more baffling—dreams, fathers, or Keynesian economics.

"Did Lester tell you he actually heard his father talk during the seance?" I said.

"No, but he said Rodney detected his father's presence in the room and was able to answer some of the questions Lester asked."

All of the sudden the sugar-rush that I had been experiencing faded like an ebb tide. It was replaced by a simmering amalgam of revulsion and anger. I wondered if this was something I should take to the police. I knew there were a Homicide Division, a Bureau of Missing Persons, and a Robbery Division at Denver police headquarters, but I didn't know if there was a Bunko Squad. And frankly I never had any desire to find out. To date the police hadn't nailed me for homicide, kidnapping, or robbery, however "fraud" might just turn out to be the bullet in the game of Russian Roulette that I play with John Law.

"Listen Shantel, I have to be honest with you, this Rodney guy was conning Lester. I don't know why he would do it, unless Rodney just gets his kicks playing a medium."

"That's what I thought, too," she said, with a note of anguish in her voice. "But Lester believed him. He told me he was going to attend another seance. He also told me that Rodney said he would be able to communicate with his father using a Ouija board."

Rather than close my eyes and rub my forehead with disgust, I nodded. "Are you saying that last night Lester went back to the same party house?"

"Yes."

"Did he take a taxi there?"

"No. The plan was to meet with Rodney at The Flicker last night. We were going to go to the movie together, and then go back to that house."

"You were planning to go *with* him?"

She sighed, she shrugged, she looked at the tabletop and nodded. "He's my cousin. It seems like I've spent half my life watching out for him. I didn't want him to go there alone."

Half her life. She was sixteen. If I remembered my algebra correctly, that divided up to eight years of watching out for her cousin.

I opened and closed my lips three times. I kept starting to say the obvious things that a "mature" person would say, such as, "You were lucky your parents grounded you last night," but instead I said the kinds of things I often say.

"Where is this house?"

"It's on the north side of town."

"North Denver?"

"No. It's east of Interstate twenty-five. It's in a funny part of Denver. It's real old. I can't remember its name."

"East of I-twenty-five?" I said, attempting to sketch a mental map of my taxi AO.

"Yes," she said. "We had to drive under Interstate seventy to get up there."

"East of I-twenty-five and north of I-seventy?"

"Yes."

"Globeville?" I said.

"That's it," she said. "His house is in Globeville."

Oh brother.

Globeville.

But that wasn't the best part.

"The house is this old mansion that's built right next to a cemetery."

"Riverside Cemetery?"

"That's right!" she chirped, as if I had correctly answered a question on *Wheel of Fortune.*

If you've never been to Denver, let me tell you something about Riverside Cemetery. It's the oldest boneyard in Denver. It's where they buried the first quitters who wouldn't cross the Rockies. Globeville itself is a peculiar part of Denver. I think of it as "The Town That Time Forgot."

The last time I was in Globeville it looked the same as I imagined it must have looked in 1910, and the reason for this is the interstates. Interstate 25 was built in the 1950s, and I-70 came along later, and those highways—in effect—cut Globeville off from the rest of Denver insofar as there hasn't been any growth or change due to its awkward accessibility. Globeville is like a little slice of pie that has been left on the shelf for the past century. The houses are generally small and quaint. The streets are quiet, the type of streets where you might expect to find Gig Young wandering around wondering how he got back to the 1930s when he just left his 1960 sports car to be serviced in a gas station down the road.

During the past fifteen years I had dropped off exactly one fare in Globeville. Prior to that I didn't even know the place existed. It was never mentioned in the Denver history class I took at UCD, unless I fell asleep that day which was not beyond the realm of possibility. After I dropped off the fare I drove around marveling at how strangely well preserved the district looked. To be honest, it gave me the creeps. Everything about it felt "old." As I cruised around that museum of Denver's architectural past I found myself driving by a landscape that looked like something out of a Universal horror film: Riverside Cemetery.

The guy who named the place had probably arrived on a Conestoga wagon. The South Platte River runs along its northwest border. Every once in a while a local paper will print a filler about Riverside. I'm talking slow-news days. It was the kind of cemetery where the tombstones looked the way tombstones are supposed to look. But there are also statues of angels and animals and people, and even one monument shaped like a log cabin. But best of all there are crypts. I'm talking vine-covered doorways set into cliff-like earthen walls. The cemetery is not well kept up. I saw fallen tombstones scattered near one end of the cemetery, the precise locations of the graves doubtless lost forever. It made me wistful.

"I want to go there," she said.

I suddenly looked up. I had been staring at my hot-cross bun. The sugar rush had crept back into my brain like a ground fog and I had momentarily forgotten that I was sitting in an ultra-modern snack bar surrounded by skeletons.

"That's the reason I called the taxi company this morning," Shantel said. "I was hoping you would drive me to the mansion and find out if Lester had gone back there."

My heart sank. This was normal. Any time anybody asks me to do anything my heart sinks—unless I'm driving my taxi, in which case my heart soars like an eagle because I know I'll be picking up fast money.

"I'll pay you to take me there," she said.

This played havoc with my heart. Which is to say, I wasn't working, yet I was being asked to do something for pay. I could not for the life of me remember a time when anybody offered to pay me for not working. That's probably never happened to you either.

"Listen Shantel, don't you think it would be best to tell your parents about this … or at least tell Lester's mother?"

"All I want you to do is drive over with me and see if he's there," she said quickly.

"But …"

"I don't want my parents to find out about any of this if I can help it. They're mad at me for lying to them and if they find out Lester called and told me he was going back there they'll find out *everything*."

"What do you mean by 'everything'?" I said. "What else don't they know?"

She looked at me with a beseeching expression. "When I got home Wednesday night I told them that we went to a party at a friend of Conrad's house."

I paused a moment to translate this from "teenager" into "English."

"So your mother and father think you went somewhere else on Wednesday night instead of that mansion," I said.

She nodded.

It finally got through to me, i.e, Shantel was either a chronic liar or a normal adolescent. She had lied to me when I picked her up at DCPA, and she had lied to her parents about where she spent Wednesday night. I recognized the construct, which is commonly referred to as "a tangled web." I've woven my share.

Shantel started to weep. "I'm worried about Lester," she said. "That guy Rodney gave me the creeps."

Creeps.

She was talking my language.

I took a deep breath and sighed. I thought of all the other times that I had gotten involved in the personal lives of my fares. It almost turned my hair white.

"I'll tell you what," I said. "I'll drive up to the house by myself and knock on the door. I don't want you to come with me. I just need to know where the house is. Do you know the address?"

She shook her head no. "There aren't any other houses like it nearby. It's a two-story mansion that has funny roofs with little fences on top of them. You know … little flat roofs."

"You mean like on the house where the Addams family lives?"

"Yes, like that!"

Score two on *Wheel of Fortune*.

"Those are called mansard roofs," I said. I didn't really need to say that but I suffer from a psychological tic that prompts me to explain things to people whether they want explanations or not. It dates back to grade school where I never knew the answers to the questions the nuns asked. I'll be honest. I have a deeply rooted need to advance from D+ to C- in the report card of my life.

Shantel opened her purse and pulled out some folded money but I held up a palm the way people do to halt speeding trains. "You don't need to pay me right now, Shantel," I said in a voice that came to within a hair's-breadth of sounding stern. "In fact I don't want any money at all. I'm doing this as a favor. I'm going to run up to the house and see if Lester is there, and if he isn't there I'll call and tell you. I have your home phone written on a taxi receipt that my boss gave to me."

"I would rather you called my cell phone," she said.

"Okay. You'll have to give me that number. But let me just say that if he really is missing, the police might have to be called."

This was shaping up to be the worst Halloween since Cleveland.

Shantel shoved the money back into her purse and snapped it closed. "Thank you for doing this for me, Mr. Murphy," she said in a little-girl voice. Made sense. She was a little girl.

I might add that it grated on my nerves to be called "Mr. Murphy." I get enough of that from prosecuting attorneys. But I let it slide. If Shantel chose to go through life thinking I was a grownup, who was I to shatter her illusion? She would have enough psychological baggage to deal with after she discovered the intrinsic value of a high school diploma.

CHAPTER 17

Shantel gave me her cell phone number, then got up and walked away. I sat at the snack bar staring at the remains of my frosted German treat. I was going over in my mind the fix that I had gotten myself into. You heard me right: "myself." I usually blame other people for getting me into fixes. I had a 51 percent success rate, but this wasn't my day.

I recalled the events of Wednesday night when I had taken those kids to the haunted house. I had been thinking about nothing more than getting back to the motor on time to avoid a second late fee, which would have cost me five dollars on top of the first five-dollar late fee. Given the fact that I have absolutely no interest in money barring one million dollars, I don't know why I let late fees bug me. Nobody at the Rocky Mountain Taxicab Company cares what time I bring my cab in. There are plenty of wrecks that can be assigned to the newbies if #123 isn't there. The first cab I ever drove was #127, which accidentally burned to a crisp out near the I-70 viaduct, and nobody at RMTC batted an eyelash. They just handed me the keys to #123 and let me get on with my fabulous career.

After a few moments I realized I had unconsciously eaten the remains of the German bun. The sugar rush was back. I looked up at the snack stand where they sold the buns. I debated whether to buy one more, just in case. It was like looking at a clock near midnight and wondering if I ought to run to the liquor store and pick up a pint for the wee hours. Or sitting in a bar at last-call and wondering if I ought to cadge one more drink before cadging a ride home from someone whose name I had just learned.

I looked at all the concession stands in the snack area—the chili dog stand, the pizza shack, the cookie palace—and I wondered why they were referred to as "concession" stands. What were they conceding?

I thought about scouting a bookstore and finding a dictionary to look up the definition of the word "concession." Suddenly a voice deep inside me said I was stalling for time. I recognized the voice. I hear it twelve to sixteen times a day, depending on how late I sleep.

I canned the idea of scouting the massive mall in search of a bookstore. Needle in a haystack. I would have better luck finding a tattoo parlor. I shook myself out. I had a job to do, a job I did not want to do, which describes every job I ever did. The operative word there is "want." I never want to do anything, but cab driving is the only labor I've ever been compelled to do that did not …

The voice spoke again.

I stood up from the table and debated whether to police up the cups and napkins and toss them into a trash barrel. Would that qualify as stalling for time? I stared at the clutter on the tabletop until a screaming skeleton broke my trance. The sugar rush was in full force. The skeleton was six years old and being chased by a robot. Their mother was chasing both of them. I realized I had to get out of there. It reminded me of last Christmas.

I started to leave the snack bar when I noticed a small concession that sold espresso. I decided to buy a latte as a co-eye-opener. The noon hour hadn't arrived yet so it seemed right to have a cup of morning coffee before heading out to Globeville. I often do things that seem right.

After I carried my latte outside I had trouble remembering where I had parked my taxicab. But the brisk, fresh, autumn air cleared my head to the point where I remembered I had driven my Chevy to the mall.

From that point on it was smooth searching.

After I got seated behind the steering wheel I leaned over and opened the glove compartment and pulled out a plastic cup-holding device that I had picked up in Hollywood awhile back. Souvenir of Venice Beach. I attached it to my windowsill and placed the latte in it, then backed my car out of the slot and headed for an exit. Out of habit I kept my eyes peeled for women carrying shopping bags. Maybe one of them would agree to let me drive her to her house at a dollar-fifty per mile. They sometimes let me do that when my vehicle was green with a checkerboard pattern bordering the roof, but the few women I slowed down next to that morning looked at my black and red car with a jaundiced eye, proving once and for all that I do not resemble Adam West.

I couldn't remember the precise location of the boneyard, so I drove over to Downing Street and up to 38th and from there to Washington Street, which took me to Globeville. I ought to have brought my map of Denver. That was only one of the many mistakes I made that week, but I hadn't known I would be going to Riverside Cemetery. I will admit that drinking a three-shot latte after eating two German time-bombs was also a mistake, but at least it wasn't illegal.

When I entered Globeville proper I was so hopped up with artificial energy that I felt like honking my horn at every woman I passed. Fortunately my horn was broken and there weren't any women on the street anyway. There were no men or children or teenagers either. There was no foot or vehicular traffic at all. Globeville was like a deserted town. It reminded me of five different episodes of *The Twilight Zone*. I have often wondered what made Rod Serling so melancholy.

I knew that Riverside Cemetery was northeast of Globeville where the houses and commercial buildings thinned out. Calling on the remnants of my sense of direction I worked my way along a few back roads until I came to the South Platte River. I was almost there. It was just a matter of following the river until I came to the place of the dead. The cemetery came into view, and it looked just as seedy and poorly preserved as it had appeared on the day I had dropped off that fare a few years back. I loved it. The thought of a pack of do-gooders deciding to collect contributions to spruce up the boneyard sent a chill down my spine. Why can't people leave interesting things alone?

I made my way down to Brighton Boulevard and headed for the entrance gate. Driving my car into Riverside Cemetery was like driving onto the back lot of Universal Studios where the *Psycho* house stood. I'll admit it. I once took the Universal tour. I played the tourist game. I snapped a picture of the house where Tony Perkins had to live with his conscience. I also snapped a picture of the mechanical *Jaws* shark, except another tourist got in the way so the picture came out crappy. I was mad as hell because I knew I would never be in Los Angeles again. Turns out I was wrong about that. I later went back to L.A. in search of the actress I was suspected of murdering. That was the week I bought my snazzy cup holder.

I could tell by the strange buzzing noises in my head that I was "peaking" in terms of sugar and caffeine. I knew that I was as motivated as I would ever be to visit the house where Lester had attended a seance on Wednesday night—or "Thursday morning" as it is sometimes referred to. Even though Shantel had made it clear that the property was near the border of the cemetery I chose to enter the cemetery proper so that I would appear to be a tourist or whatever they call people who visit graveyards where nobody they know is buried. In this way I could scout the border of the cemetery from "within the box" if that's proper business terminology.

I drove along a bumpy dirt road between the funeral plots with my head turned toward the tombstones, but in fact my eyes were secretly looking at the landscape beyond the border. I did this in case somebody was watching me, and also because I was so high from the legal chemicals I had eaten that I had succumbed to a feeling that I call "The Fear."

This is a feeling that comes over me whenever I do anything to excess, and believe me, I rarely do anything to excess. But when I do, it scares me. Excess is just a stone's throw away from ambition, and I steer clear of that booby-trap. I'll admit that imbibing two frosted buns and an espresso isn't the same thing as that New Year's Eve in that city whose name I forget, but both events reminded me of a disaster called "Crazy Days" that took place in Wichita when I was a college student. But I'm getting off the track here.

As I made a clockwise circuit of the cemetery grounds I saw a likely structure in the distance, a two-story house with mansard roofs. I could not help but feel that I had pinpointed my target destination because there was not another house like it near the entire circumference of Riverside Cemetery. Deductive logic had always been my ace-in-the-hole.

The rear of the house faced the cemetery, if that's proper architectural English, but rather than drive directly past the house I made a turn down a small lane between some plots and got a fix on the location of the house before heading back out the main gate and working my way around to the far side via Brighton Boulevard, which runs at a northeasterly angle on the map. There is a small town located twenty miles farther northeast of Denver called Brighton, ergo I assume the "boulevard" was originally a dirt two-track created during the nineteenth century by a farmer who made a lot of trips to Denver on his buckboard to sell crops. I don't know if the farmer was a genius, but I'll bet he was lonely.

CHAPTER 18

The mansion was set on a large plot of ground that was indistinguish-able from the surrounding fields and weedy earth of the cemetery. I approached a long dirt drive that led up to the house. The drive consisted of a U-shape at the front of the house, and I quickly deduced that it must have been formed by circling carriages back when the house was built, given that carriages rarely go in reverse. This made me wonder if a study had ever been made about the effects of internal-combustion engines on landscape architecture with respect to cement driveways. I bet the sale of basketball hoops skyrocketed after the driveway was invented.

I pulled up in front of the house wishing I was in RMT #123. I always feel safe when I approach a strange house in my taxi because taxis have a kind of dispensation that allows them to go anywhere, thus camouflaging the true nature of a non-official visit. Believe me, I've made more non-official visits during the past fifteen years than I care to think about.

I slowly climbed out of my two-tone heap, giving the occupant of the house plenty of time to notice my presence and come to the foyer before I went through the onerous process of knocking on the door. In fact, the occupant could have done a lot of things during the time it took me to yawn and stretch and amble my way to the front porch, i.e., call the cops, grab a shotgun, sic the dawgs. But nothing like that happened.

I kept my eye on the window on the front door as I slowly trudged up the steps. I saw the dark reflection of my rising body. The sugar rush had diminished by 30 percent by now so I felt only lightheaded as I stepped onto the porch and approached the door with my knuckles raised for a knock. Instinct told me that this place didn't have a doorbell.

Just before I knocked I noticed a circular metal device attached to the jamb indicative of a doorbell. Rather than scold my instinct I simply decided that this house sported the first doorbell installed west of the

Mississippi. When you've driven a taxi as long as I have, you learn to expose, condemn, and absolve yourself of miscalculations in the time it takes to ring a doorbell.

I pressed the button but didn't hear a "… Ding-dong …"

This irritated me because I had to debate whether to try it again and press a little harder, but at the same time I was afraid the bell had rung in a distant room and if I pressed it again the occupants would think a pushy salesman was at the door and would answer the bell with an "attitude."

I decided to wait.

I glanced at my wristwatch and counted off thirty seconds. This time I pressed the button hard but I still did not hear a bell inside the house. I stopped worrying about seeming pushy and rapped the door with my knuckles.

I took a step back and waited, and it was only while I was gazing vacantly at the glass that I realized I could see through it and into the house. The window had no curtains. I stepped a little closer to the door and peered through the glass while trying not to appear to be doing so. I never try to appear to be doing anything, but it didn't matter in this case because I could see all the way into a big room beyond the foyer. It might have been a living room but empirical evidence told me nothing because there was no empirical evidence to be seen. The room was devoid of furniture.

Two large windows fronted the house on either side of the door. I walked over to one and peered through it, then walked to the other window and peered through it. There was no furniture inside the rooms that I could see.

I went back to the doorbell and pressed it a half-dozen times, then rapped on the window.

No reply.

I stepped down off the porch and looked up at the second story of the house and noted that none of the windows had curtains. I tried to recall what Shantel had told me about this place. Someone had thrown a party on Wednesday night. Had Shantel mentioned furniture to me? All of the sudden I felt like I was back in high school where the chemistry nun had tried to teach us "the scientific method." It was the same class where I once got splashed in the face with a beaker of ammonia but that's neither here nor there.

We students were told to look at a burning candle and describe exactly what we saw. If we said, "melting wax," the nun told us we were wrong. We were allowed only to say "liquid" because our eyes did not know whether it was wax or water. We were admonished to describe only what our eyes perceived, and not conjecture as to the nature of the substances on the lab table. As infuriating as her admonitions were, I nevertheless was fascinated by the idea of describing things solely as they appeared, and leaving my assumptions and conjectures at the door. It opened up a whole new world to me. It contradicted everything I had been taught up to the age of fifteen, which was to accept as ironclad truth anything the teachers said to us—especially the history teachers. Hippies called this "questioning authority." I called it "childhood's end."

When Shantel had described the party to me I envisioned a furnished house decorated for a Halloween party. But she had not described the house in detail. She had said only that there had been a party, and that a seance had been held in an upstairs room. My brain had supplied the furniture and festive decorations.

Okay. I'll admit it. My brain added a washtub filled with water and apples for a bobbing contest.

Or perhaps I should say, "Filled with a transparent liquid and globular red things for reasons that are not apparent."

I now felt duped by the very brain that was currently coming down from a sugar rush. I really ought to have eaten eggs for breakfast.

I began making an external circuit of the house. I pretended the house was a candle minus the teardrop-shaped bright semi-transparent flickering "thing" on top. By "thing" I mean "flame." Believe me, brother, it's hard to describe physical objects as they appear to the eye. I failed chemistry by the way.

The foundation of the house was made of the same cemented rectangular stones that you often see in Thurber cartoons. They were stacked four high. From there on up the walls were made of wood. I came to a cellar window and tried to peer through but the interior was too dark to see anything. I passed a cellar door at the side of the house. It was sealed by a rusted padlock. I went on around to the rear. The backyard had a nice view of the cemetery. I went toward the back door, which was accessed by four wooden steps. I climbed the steps and tried the doorknob.

It worked.

The door swung inward revealing a kitchen. In spite of the scientific method, I assumed it was a kitchen because I could see an old-fashioned stove and an icebox. Made sense. This was an old-fashioned candle.

"Anybody home?" I yelled, then tried not to be bothered by the echo that traveled through the house and up to the second floor.

I turned and looked at the cemetery. I didn't see any tourists. Call me a coward but I have a knee-jerk reaction against being seen breaking-and-entering, the one crime for which, to date, I have never been busted.

I sometimes have dreams that I drive my taxi into suburban houses. I don't mean crash into them, I simply drive through the houses as if I was on a bicycle, except I'm steering a one-ton vehicle. Strangely, I never sideswipe the walls in the narrow hallways. The dreams make me feel guilty. When I wake up I wonder why I drive exclusively through suburban houses. What the hell does my subconscious care about the suburbs? If I ever get any goddamn therapy I probably won't mention these dreams, but if I do, they will be at the bottom of the list. It's a fairly long list. Let's move on.

I decided nobody could see what I was doing so I stepped into the kitchen.

"Anybody home?" I hollered again.

I passed on through and stepped into what I assumed was a dining room. But was it really an "assumption"? After all, kitchens and dining rooms do go hand-in-hand. Perhaps it was not an assumption but a deduction. Was I splitting hairs? I can only say that Sherlock Holmes probably would have agreed that it was a dining room and he was the master of ratiocination. Or was that Poe?

"Anybody home!"

I hollered this frequently. I won't mention it again.

I listened to the silence.

I peered at the floor. No dust. This indicated to me that the floor may have been swept and mopped. I once mopped floors in a medical clinic in San Francisco so I recognized the end result. I even mopped army barracks. Also a college dorm during one particularly productive hyper finals' week but let's not get into that.

I might as well admit that I began to doubt Shantel's word when I saw that the house was vacant, however as I roamed through the living room I could see that something had taken place here recently. No dust, no footprints, but no trash either. Whoever had been here had apparently cleaned the place up before vacating.

One last time, I promise.

"Anybody home!"

I headed for the stairwell, which was down a long hallway off the living room. I stood at the bottom of the stairs looking up at a dimness that was more pronounced than that of the ground floor. It was the kind of dimness you see in poorly lighted movies. I hate movies shot with low-light lenses under natural illumination. Half the time you can't see a goddamn thing, especially if you're watching a thriller in the daytime with the window shades up. Give me a couple of studio spots, or at least day-for-night ya bastards!

That's what I was thinking as I stood at the bottom of the stairs looking up at the second floor.

I waited awhile. I often do that when crippled by indecision. I finally began ascending the staircase, which was solidly built. No creaks. The crackerboxes they build in the suburbs creak even when they don't have stairs.

My head came level with the second floor and I stopped and looked around. The hallway was like a balcony. I could see a number of doors between the balusters. "Balusters" are wooden posts that hold up handrails. Kids sometimes get their heads stuck between balusters, mostly in funny movies. The doors on the second floor were closed. I assumed there were bedrooms, bathrooms, storage rooms, and possibly even sitting rooms beyond the doors. I was trying to strike a balance between the scientific method and guesswork. Why, I don't know. I went on up the stairs and stood in the dim hallway that led to the rooms. I listened again. I heard nothing.

"Lester?"

I approached a door and tried the knob. The door opened into a small room. It may have been a kid's bedroom except I had heard that people in the nineteenth century were shorter than the people of today—or maybe it was just the fools who went west. But I do know one thing: I had seen actual nineteenth-century beds in person and they weren't built for six-footers. I saw the beds in tourist traps. You may have experienced this yourself. I don't know about you but I love tourist traps. The cheesier the better. The underlying theme of all tourist traps is "Take a gander at this!" It reminds me of writing.

I moved on down the hall and tried the other doors, and they all opened into small rooms. I started to get bored. Then I came to a door at the darkest end of the hall. It was at this point that I experienced two physical sensations: I smelled a strange odor and I felt the air grow colder. It may be that the strange odor gave me goosebumps, which in turn fooled my skin into thinking it was cold.

I stood before the door and listened, then said, "Lester?"

No reply.

I reached down and turned the doorknob. It opened into a room that was much larger than the other rooms and had a curtain on the far window, which effectively blocked out the sunlight and made it difficult to see the details of the room, aside from the fact that the room was empty. I noticed that each of the four walls leaned inward starting at a point approximately five feet above the floor. I looked up and saw that the squared ceiling was smaller in breadth than the floor. I deduced that I was looking at the underside of a mansard roof. I had seen a number of mansard roofs from the outside of the house but I had no idea which one this might be. My sense of direction was too fragmented from wandering around inside the house. But I knew the answer to that conundrum. I walked across the room to open the curtain. If I could see the Rocky Mountains I could get a geographic fix.

The toe of my tennis shoe struck something that flew across the floor and hit the baseboard with a metallic clang. The kick and the clang happened almost simultaneously and echoed off the walls. I spun around and stared at the open doorway. I could feel my brain starting to think up things so I edged over to the window and yanked the curtain rod away from its support screws. I held the curtain-draped rod like a baseball bat. It weighed only a few ounces but felt good in my fists.

Light flooded the room.

I looked at the floor to see what I had kicked. That's when I saw the pentagram.

CHAPTER 19

A black circle five feet in diameter had been painted on the wooden floor. Contained within the circle was a five-pointed star, the points touching the circumference of the circle. Planted erect at four of the five points were what appeared to my eyes to be metal candleholders. I say this because each holder contained what appeared to be the melted remains of a candle. Each candle was black. The melted part was gray. The gray was solid and not liquid, and that's as far as I am willing to go in terms of the scientific method. It is virtually impossible to talk like a scientist for an extended period of time. Sooner or later the English language demands assumptions, conjectures, and plain old common sense. In this case common sense told me I was looking at something supernatural. I say this because 17 percent of all the movies I had ever seen were produced by Hammer Films, and of these, 58 percent starred Christopher Lee.

I realized I had kicked one of the candleholders when I crossed the room. It was lying on its side beneath the window.

I stepped to the center of the room and looked down at the pentagram. I knew virtually nothing about the symbolic significance of the pentagram beyond the fact that it was somehow associated with devil worship. I realized with horror that I should have paid closer attention to the plots of Christopher Lee movies. To be perfectly honest, I find the plots of most grade-B movies so boring that I just sip my beer, puff my cigar, and wait for the monster to appear.

I got down on one knee the way people do when they genuflect. I touched the painted line of the circumference. I didn't do this for any reason other than the fact that I like to touch things. I had been admonished many times in my childhood for doing this but I'd never really outgrown it. Even army sergeants used to get on my case for touching things I wasn't supposed to touch. Remind me to tell you about my first day at the hand-grenade range in basic.

I couldn't feel the paint, in the sense that it wasn't very thick. The line was perhaps two inches wide and appeared to my eye to be a perfect circle. Oddly enough, I got straight A's in geometry class in high school. I'm not even going to try to account for that, beyond the fact that geometry doesn't involve numbers until you get into "Geometry II," where algebra is related to calculations that no high school graduate has ever used for anything in his entire life, except perhaps people who teach Geometry II.

The strange odor that I had smelled in the hallway was stronger at floor level, and I realized I was smelling the spent candles. I leaned close to a column of wax and took a deep sniff. It brought back the goosebumps I had felt in the hallway, but I wrote that off as Pavlovian conditioning. It doesn't take much to scar me for life.

I stood up and peered at the pentagram wondering how it might have been connected with the seance that Lester attended. I had seen plenty of seances in movies and they didn't involve pentagrams. They took place at large round tables surrounded by ordinary-looking people whose facial expressions communicated wistful hope.

But maybe the seance wasn't connected at all. Maybe it had taken place in a different room. Maybe this was "The Pentagram Room." As good a name as any, and I couldn't think of a better one.

I didn't know what to make of it. But I did know I ought to replace the candle I had kicked from its position—just in case. I walked back to the window and bent down to pick it up. As I did so I glanced out the window and noted the Rocky Mountains in the distance. Due to the fact that I was twenty feet above ground level I had a slightly different perspective on the snow-capped mess in the distance than I normally do. I felt as if I was standing on the steps of the state capitol building looking at the Rockies. The capitol building had been built on a rise known as "Capitol Hill," but don't get me started on people who name things. There's a small metal plaque affixed to one of the steps that says, "Elevation 5,280 Feet Above Sea Level." When you stand on that step you know you are exactly one mile above the people in San Diego. If you are the type of person who gets a thrill out of being that high, then you are not unlike me. However I do not recommend standing on the step for an extended period of time while under the influence of any sort of prescription or non-prescription drug, partly because the notion of being one mile "up" is a mind-bender, but mostly because the capitol security police will chase you off. They just want you to look at the plaque, not "experience" it.

I knew now that I was standing beneath a mansard roof on the west side of the house. I also knew that I had wrecked the curtain rod beyond repair. This made me uneasy. Why would someone leave a curtain hanging in this particular room but not in the others?

I leaned the rod against the wall and started to walk toward the door. But then I stopped. I went back and picked up the rod with its curtains, which were made of a wispy white material like that of a handkerchief. I arranged it on the floor in such a way that it looked like the wind might have blown it down. The fact that the window was closed and no air could get in was not a significant factor to me because I figured if anyone came in here and saw the curtains on the floor they would think something had made it fall, possibly the wind. They would subsequently frown with bafflement because the window was closed. At that point they would begin to speculate further as to how the curtain might have fallen, never once considering the possibility that it had been ripped from its moorings by a taxi driver scared out of his gourd.

Why would anybody think that?'

With luck, some of the devil worshippers had taken high school chemistry. I was banking on the scientific method to divert them from the truth.

I walked out of the room and went back toward the stairwell. I stopped at the top of the stairs and started thinking about the scene in *Psycho* where a slashed and bleeding Martin Balsam staggered backward all the way down a stairwell in one of the most peculiar rear-screen projection shots ever filmed.

That was not a good thing to think about.

Okay. I'll admit it. I turned my body 90 degrees so that I could look both up and down as I descended the steps. I held onto the handrail with both hands in order to avoid a misstep and find myself racing Martin to the floor.

When I got to the bottom I walked quickly to the kitchen, passed through, and stepped outside. I shut the door firmly behind me and went down the wooden steps to the ground. I almost looked back at the kitchen window, then decided I didn't want to do that. For some reason I felt nauseated. The odor of the spent candles was still in my nostrils. So was the odor of German buns. I walked quickly around the house and looked up at the mansard roof closest to the Rockies. There was no curtain on the window, thank God.

I walked back around to the front of the house thinking about the cellar door that I had passed. Should I try to open it? Should I descend into the basement of the mansion and peer around to see if anyone might be hiding behind the furnace? But deductive logic told me that the basement would be pitch black—and I did not have a flashlight. I used to carry a flashlight in the trunk of my Chevy, which had a small toolbox, but every time my Chevy got stolen the thieves always took the toolbox. I finally gave up buying new toolboxes. The trunk lid was held fast by a small loop of twine. The lock had stopped functioning properly years ago after I backed into something or other. It was raining that night and I may have backed into a telephone pole. I checked the next day and the pole was still there, but the point I'm making is that I did not have a flashlight and therefore I had no reason to go down into the cellar. There were a couple of other reasons but I decided to go with Reason #1.

Without looking at any of the other windows, I walked back to my car, climbed in, started the engine, and put the shift into Low. Only then did I look at the empty windows staring back at me like big black eyes. Being inside a car that can go ninety miles an hour made me feel brave.

The house looked the same as it had when I first drove up, but I knew it wasn't the same. I knew that a curtain was missing from one of the windows.

Suddenly I realized that my fingerprints might be on the curtain rod.

My heart skipped a beat.

Then I dismissed the thought. I figured that the kinds of people who worshipped devils probably didn't phone the cops a lot.

This made me feel good inside.

It's odd how self-delusion can heal a troubled mind. But it wasn't surprising. I sometimes think of myself as the Hippocrates of disingenuous logic. Whenever a despondent taxi fare asks me for advice concerning a personal problem, I have found that saying what he wants to hear is a far more effective remedy than telling him the truth. I've been doing that for fifteen years, and so far I've had no complaints.

CHAPTER 20

I put Globeville at my back and drove south toward Denver proper. I debated whether to phone Shantel or drive to her house. I dislike talking to people on the phone almost as much as I dislike talking to people at all, so I was torn. I have no problem talking to people when I drive a taxi because, like psychiatrists, I get paid when the conversation is over. But unlike telemarketers I never get paid to talk to people over the phone. I once dreamed I went door-to-door selling chicken eggs for fifty cents apiece. I don't know why I bring that up except to say that it seemed like a pretty good job, like most of my unrealistic dreams.

I finally decided to pull over to a phone booth and call Shantel. She was worried about Lester and I figured she would want to hear from me as soon as possible. I headed for a 7-11 store on Broadway and parked in the lot. They didn't have any "booths" at the 7-11 but there were telephones attached to the outside wall. You hardly ever see a phone booth anymore, except on *Doctor Who*. But that's a British phone booth. I wondered if Alexander Graham Bell made any quid when England was wired for sound.

"Hello?"

"Shantel, this is Mr. Murphy. I called to tell you that I just left that house in Globeville and I didn't find Lester."

"I know," she said.

"How do you know that?"

"Because Lester called me fifteen minutes after I got home from the mall."

I was nonplussed by her statement. This is one of the reasons I hate the general concept of talking—it almost always involves people.

"Did he say where he went last night?" I said.

She paused a moment, then said, "He told me he was just out all night with some friends." She paused again, then said, "Listen Mr. Murphy, I'm sorry if I put you to any trouble but everything's okay now, so …"

She went silent. I sensed she wanted to end the conversation. I often get that feeling when I talk to women so I'm familiar with the end result. But I wasn't satisfied.

"Did Lester say who the friends were?" I said.

"He just … he said he stayed overnight with some friends and then … you know … came home."

I deduced from the nature of her syntax that she was covering something up, but I didn't feel I was within my rights to grill her. However I did feel I was within my rights to take the conversation in another direction.

"I want to ask you something about that house, Shantel."

"What?"

"I looked through the windows and saw that there was no furniture. Was there any furniture in the house when you went to the party?"

Her pause lasted for an extended period of time. Then she said, "No."

Strangely, her no sounded like a lie, when I was certain it was true. I was having difficulty with this conversation. I had to remind myself that I was talking to a teenager. I did not have a great deal of experience holding conversations with teenagers even though I used to be one. The truth is, I hardly ever talked to other teenagers when I was in high school. I was the least popular kid in my class, thank God.

I suddenly realized that I was going about this all wrong. I had learned over the years that when you ask people questions you are basically giving them control over the direction a conversation takes. My Maw used to make this mistake with me in connection with missing cookies. Ergo, I was letting Shantel control the conversation. I had been doing it out of politeness, but I decided to back off and try a new tack. "New Tack" is a nautical phrase coined by desperate seamen.

"In fact I went inside the house, Shantel, but I didn't see any evidence that there had been a Halloween party. I don't think anybody lives there."

I quit talking and let that piñata dangle over her head.

"I don't really know who lives there, Mr. Murphy," she finally said. "I just know that we were at a party there on Wednesday night. I have to hang up now. My parents just came home."

And with that she rang off.

I stood holding the receiver and wondering why it was necessary for our conversation to end just because her parents came home. Teenage logic, I supposed.

I hung up and went back to my Chevy, sat down behind the steering wheel, and stared at the front door of the 7-11 for a while. Four of Shantel's words kept ringing in my ears, i.e., … "everything is okay now." My senses go on red-alert whenever I hear those words, especially if they come from my mouth.

On the one hand I felt like Shantel owed me a little further explanation. On the other hand, I once made a vow never to get involved in the personal lives of my fares. When placed side-by-side the two concepts generated static, like the horizontal electricity jumping between metal poles in a laboratory where an optimistic nineteenth-century scientist is trying to do with cadavers what he thinks he does with dead frogs, i.e., make them move. Sure, dead frogs twitch when you touch them with an electric wire, but the invention of the electric chair pretty much squelched the extended logic of that theory.

My vow won the day. I decided that I would take Shantel's word and ease my way out of the life of everybody who lived in the vicinity of the Denver Country Club. Lester was obviously one of our nation's troubled youths, and Shantel was his mother hen.

I drove out of the 7-11 lot and headed toward Capitol Hill. Not surprisingly, I had trouble letting go of the idea that I was no longer involved in a mess. I wasn't used to that. I wondered if I should drive over to Shantel's house and talk to her in person. But if I did that, her mother might find out what was going on, and Shantel had asked me to keep it under my hat—so to speak. She didn't actually say "Keep it under your hat," even though that's what she meant. I often misquote people in order to cut down on the wordiness of my explanations. I wonder what genius thought up the word "wordiness." It sounded like something a newspaper editor would have coined in the 1920s to show all the cub reporters how hep he was to purple poppycock, the type of guy who would put his feet up on his desk and puff on a cigar and spin yarns about "the good old days" when hard-drinking two-fisted reporters like Gene Fowler sniffed out real dope on corrupt politicians bought off by racketeers.

Anyway, Shantel asked me not to let her mother know, so I abandoned that idea.

It must have been a rapid drop in my blood sugar because suddenly I wanted nothing more than to go home, collapse into bed, and embrace the oblivion of death's counterfeit. That's Halloween talk for "sleep." I think it was coined by William Shakespeare but I was only half-awake in English class that day. Believe it or not, I did not fail any of my English classes in college. College is a snap. I highly recommend college to anybody who failed high school.

I drove down Broadway trying to ignore the fact that I had "done" something on my day off. I tried not to think about the fact that I had missed two episodes of *Gilligan's Island*, one broadcast out of Chicago and one out of L.A. I had willingly tried to help Shantel, but now that "everything is okay" I wanted to get my life back to normal. Sleeping on a Saturday afternoon is not normal for me, but I was tired. Normal involves drinking a few beers and surfing the cable in search of *Bowery Boys* movies. Huntz Hall kills me although he's no Bob Denver. When I was in fifth grade I knew a kid who looked just like Leo Gorcey. I once jokingly asked him for his autograph, and he threatened to pound me. At the age of ten my sense of humor was lost on my contemporaries, but that was before I learned how to do "set-ups." I was too young to appreciate the crucial significance of the straight line. Hell, that's 90 percent of the joke. Face it, there is nothing inherently funny about saying, "Can I have your autograph?" unless you're talking to a rubber chicken.

I glanced at my wristwatch. 1:00. Another Saturday shot to hell. The entire episode involving Shantel had eaten up only three hours out of twenty-four but I treasure the hours that I have nothing to do. Even the most molecular intrusion on my time is excruciating, especially when it forces me to sleep another few hours away. Is there anything in this world more infuriating than being forced against your will to sleep during the daytime? In the army they actually made us sleep during the *nighttime*, for crying out loud. What American male under the age of twenty-one sleeps at night? Fortunately I was able to take advantage of the GI Bill after I was discharged and go to college where I was able to get my sleeping schedule back on track. It's true that I attended classes in the daytime, but to me that was just night school.

I felt drained of energy as I drove home from Globeville, which made me feel guilty. As a professional taxi driver I am sensitive to the rules of safe driving. To be more specific, sensitive to violating the rules that can cost me my cab license, and falling asleep at the wheel is one of them. I know this may sound like petty nitpicking, but there had been a handful of times during the past fifteen years when I turned around on my way to Rocky Cab at dawn and went back home because I knew I was too tired to drive. This involved a sensation of impending drowsiness, like dark clouds gathering over a horizon, which makes everything feel slightly off-kilter. I first became aware of the symptoms when I was in college, i.e., if I was walking to class and felt my brain starting to shift into the drowse mode, I knew I could grab some Z's during a required American history class. Why they teach American history in college is beyond me. Any high schooler who didn't have the Teapot Dome Scandal shoved down his throat ought to sue the Department of Education.

I pulled into the dirt lot behind my building. After I parked in the choice V-spot I sat there for a while staring at the place where fence-meets-fence. It was directly perpendicular to my hood ornament, which looks like a naked chrome lady. My eyes were drawn to a sparkle of sunlight on one of her wings. I gazed at it until I caught myself doing that and quickly looked away, not because someone might have seen me staring at a naked lady but because I was afraid of burning a hole in my retina. When I was a kid I heard about other kids who looked directly at the sun during an eclipse and went blind. I never understood why looking at the sun during an eclipse was considered more dangerous than looking at it, say, at high noon. I mean, during an eclipse the sun is blocked out by the moon. I still don't understand it, although I am willing to concede that the adults may have been giving us kids a lot of hooey in order to keep us from doing permanent damage to our eyeballs. It must be a real trial to ride herd on little savages.

I blinked my eyes a few times, hoping I hadn't set into motion a chain-reaction of retina implosion. How would I earn a living if I was blind? My ultimate goal in life is to earn a living as a novelist, and I sure as hell ain't no touch-typist.

I climbed out of my Chevy and trudged up the fire escape feeling as if I didn't have the strength to make it to the top step. I couldn't believe it. I had never felt such lethargy in my life.

And then it happened.

My right foot slipped and I started to fall backward. I grabbed for the handrail and held on. At that point adrenaline kicked in and awakened the sleeping giant of my nervous system. Whereas prior to that moment my brain had felt like a fogbank, it now felt like a pointillist painting. I could see my white knuckles gripping the handrail. I looked down and saw my right tennis shoe shuffling for safe footing on the black grille of the step. I could see the ground two stories below wavering back and forth as my body swayed on the pivot of my grip. I could see rocks scattered in the parking lot. I could see ants carrying bits of food between the rocks. My retinas had become Hubble Telescopes as I clung to the handrail with my heart pounding and my ears ringing from adrenaline, although I have to give some credit to my contact lenses. I bought them at a place called SightCity!!!. Apparently I got a much better deal than I bargained for. I had been climbing up and down the fire escape for years and had never noticed any goddamn ants.

I ascended the remaining steps to the top landing gripping the railing with both hands. I was in a mild state of shock. The only time I could recall ascending the steps using both hands was at the tail-end of a St. Patrick's Day party a few years back after my friends had dropped me off. That was the same night I ordered a ThighMaster through an 800 number. Let's move on.

When I got inside my apartment I felt physically ill. I didn't know if it was the adrenaline, my low blood sugar, or the brush with death. I locked the door behind me, headed into my bedroom, and collapsed face-down onto my mattress. I didn't even bother to kick off my Keds. My descent into sleep was like falling into a wishing well—my brain let go of the bucket and plunged into a pool of blackness.

The last thing I remembered thinking was, "I wish I could do this every night."

I suffer from terrible insomnia.

CHAPTER 21

My ascent to consciousness was a slow and laborious process. I dreamed I was trying to crawl out of a cellar window but the tight window frame was crushing my chest. I've had this dream before. I blame the birth process, although I don't have any proof—yet. I slowly opened my eyes and gazed across a vast plane of white. I didn't have any idea where I was. Things were back to normal.

I raised my head, which felt like it contained an anvil. I don't mean it hurt, it just felt heavy. The plane of white turned out to be my pillow. I twisted my neck and looked at the clock.

6:00.

But was it six a.m. or six p.m.?

Why this question occurred to me is mystifying because time means nothing to me on weekends. I began to wonder if it was possible to set my clock so that it would show twenty-four hours instead of twelve, i.e., if it was six p.m. it would say 1800. This would cause me to think less, and I am always up for that. My friend Big Al tells me I think too much. Big Al is the exact opposite of a nun. In arithmetic class the nuns continually admonished me to think harder, but all I could think about was how bored I was. To this day I have no idea what a subtrahend is.

I raised my right hand, which also seemed excessively heavy. I parted the curtains above my bed. It was dark outside. This told me nothing. It was dark at both six and six at this time of year, so I didn't know if it was morning or night.

I lowered my arm and closed my eyes and did some arithmetic. I know what you're thinking. Arithmetic? I was too. But I knew I had fallen asleep around one in the afternoon, so I had slept either five hours or seventeen hours. Again, the numbers told me nothing. I finally took a few deep breaths and sat up straight. I rarely sit up straight in bed. I usually do the conventional sideways momentum-roll with foot-drop and torso-hoist, but I needed the exercise.

I heard dark laughter.

I turned around and parted the curtains and looked out at the neighborhood. There were lights on in half of the apartment windows across the street. I peered down at the sidewalk and saw ghosts. Witches too. And a Spider-Man. Trick-or-treaters. Ergo, I knew it was six at night and I had slept only five hours. This knowledge came as neither a surprise nor a relief to me. It simply communicated a useless fact, like most arithmetic. I say this because it was Saturday night, that time of the week when I am most useless.

The neighborhood was crawling with kids out doing trick-or-treat. "Trick-or-treating" as some people say. Other people say, "Tricks-and-treats." Perhaps you find that as uninteresting as I do, but uninteresting things comprise approximately 8 percent of all the thoughts that pass through my mind—although I will admit that my definition of "uninteresting" might be more narrowly defined than yours.

I watched the kids for a while feeling envious. They were getting free stuff. Those were the days. When I was ten years old I came up with what I thought was a great idea for a Halloween costume. It included a go-kart. I wanted to dress like a spaceman, rig up a go-kart to look like a rocket ship, and drive from door to door. My brother Gavin told me I was an idiot. I'll let you be the judge.

I finally hoisted myself off the bed.

I was pleased to find that I was already dressed. This saved me the forty-three seconds it would have taken to put on my jeans and tie my tennis shoes. I wondered how I might fill up the forty-three free seconds that had been given to me by the Hand of Fate. I wasted most of it wondering what was on TV, then blew the rest trying to decide whether to cook a hamburger or heat up a can of spaghetti. By the time I left the bedroom the second-hand had run out. You just can't win in this world.

I staggered over to the kitchen shaking the grogginess from my brain and knowing that, in a sense, I had blown the possibility of getting to sleep before three a.m.—again, a useless number. Worrying about the clock was a holdover from the days when I had a real job. By "real" I mean Dyna-Plex, the place where I actually had to be at work by 8 a.m.

That was the year I earned twenty-thousand dollars. If you're wondering what I spent it on, the answer is: haircuts. I banked the rest of it. That's how I've managed to survive driving a taxi part-time for the past fifteen years. I'm the type of person whom the Nobel Prize–winning economist Milton Friedman used to refer to as a "tightwad." I won't tell you how much money I have in the bank, but if the next fifteen years are anything like the last fifteen years, I'm sittin' pretty.

I decided to cook a hamburger since the effort didn't involve opening a can. Plus, I decided to avoid sugar drinks, such as the sodas stashed in my fridge. Caffeine was also out. No coffee, no colas, no stimulants of any kind. I would stick with beer, the wet blanket of refreshing beverages.

After I put the beef patty on to brown over a low flame I went back into the living room to pick up my TV remote. It was resting on my beer table next to my AudioMaster-Deluxe answering machine.

It was then that I noticed a blinking red number "1."

Somebody had called me.

My heart sank.

The only way to find out who had called me was listen to the message. Then a thought occurred to me. An acquaintance named Harold had once showed me how to operate a function referred to as "Caller I.D."

If I pressed Caller I.D. I could see the number of the person who had phoned, and thus get an inkling as to what new hell I was in for. Dorothy Parker coined the phrase "new hell"—as in, "What new hell is this?" In some ways Dorothy Parker is funnier than Bob Denver. She once wrote a whimsical poem about suicide.

I peered at the thousands of buttons on my AudioMaster trying to remember which button Harold had pushed. But I couldn't remember. I grew afraid. What if I accidentally erased the message—or worse, saved it permanently?

Rather than make a decision, I hurried back to the kitchen. I had a hamburger on the stove, and carbon waits for no man.

I flipped the burger, then turned off the flame. I went back into the living room. I had a brand-new excruciating decision to make. Should I call Harold? He worked as a bartender at Sweeney's Tavern and I had done everything within my power to avoid talking to him ever since I first met him, which was difficult because I went to Sweeney's a lot.

Then it hit me. Star 69—not to be confused with *Star 80,* which is a movie. I had never dialed *69 before because I had never wanted to know who called me. My heart soared like an eagle. I wouldn't have to talk to Harold. I picked up the receiver and very carefully punched * before punching 6 and 9. I made certain that I didn't punch #. I was afraid I might connect with another plane of existence where the long-distance rates had kicked in.

"We are sorry but that number cannot be checked."

I slumped against the wall.

You can't win in this world. I decided to capitulate. I didn't want to talk to Harold so I had only one choice left. I would have to do what a normal person would do: listen to the recorded message. I hate acting normal because it makes me feel so common.

I hung up the receiver and punched the play button.

How did the word "play" ever get associated with home invasion?

I listened.

And listened.

And heard nothing.

By "nothing" I mean the electric silence that accompanies recordings during which no one is speaking. It was similar to the silence I hear when asking women for dates.

I recalled a phrase: "white noise." An engineer who worked in a recording studio had told me about it. White noise is the phenomenon that results when a microphone is set up in an empty room to record silence, a nutty but intellectually satisfying concept—to my intellect anyway. The dead silence of blank recording tape is audibly different from the dead silence of nothing recorded in an empty room. I would advise against taking prescription drugs while mulling over this concept.

It seemed to me that I was listening to white noise over the phone. I reached down and turned the volume up to ten.

That's when I heard the chanting.

It was dim and distant. I had to bow down to the speaker holes on the side of my AudioMaster to hear it better. A kind of rhythmic droning. It put me in mind of Gregorian chants except it wasn't as melodic. Believe me, I know my Gregorian chants. I was a little kid prior to Vatican II when the Mass was changed over to English. I got in just under the wire.

I learned more Latin from Monsignor O'Malley's show-stopping alto solos than I picked up in Sister Bertram's frosh Latin class.

My brother Gavin made it all the way through *Civis Romanus* with an A+ but I don't want to talk about that.

I couldn't make out any of the words so I won't go on record as saying the chanting was Latin. It could easily have been Old English. I once took a college course where we were forced to study Old English. It was like being back in Latin class. It had declensions and everything. I still remember the first line of The Lord's Prayer that we were required to memorize: "Faeder ure ou oe eart on heofonum." Strangely, I have found myself unconsciously mumbling that line during stressful situations, such as childbirth. I have delivered three babies in the auld taxi during the past fifteen years. Maybe there's a bit of the Bard in me.

As I leaned in to listen, I squinted. I turned my head so my right ear was aimed at the speaker. I parted my jaw approximately one inch. I did all the things that normal people do to discern words. It didn't help.

More evidence that normality is useless? You be the judge.

The recording lasted approximately one minute, but during the last ten seconds I heard a single voice, the words of a man that were slightly louder than the chanting but still undiscernible—except for the very last word he spoke, which sounded like "Murphy."

I stood erect and groaned. My lower back wasn't used to being bent. I really ought to renew my membership in the health club where I paid a $250 annual fee. Maybe they would take pity on me and give me credit for the remaining $240.00.

I went to the kitchen thinking about the call. I turned the flame back on and finished cooking the burger. When it was done I placed it between two slices of bread and ate it without lettuce, onions, mustard, or catsup. The infusion of naked protein seemed to help clear my mind. This made me uneasy because I now knew what I had to do. I had to call Harold. I had to find out from him how to trace the phone call from the choir invisible.

I dialed Sweeney's Tavern.

"Hello?"

"Harold?"

"Speaking."

"This is Murph."

"Top of the morning to ye, Murph me boy."

It was six-thirty at night but let's move on. I'm not going to waste your time or mine trying to explain Harold.

"I forgot how to use Caller I.D. on my AudioMaster-Deluxe," I said.

He chuckled. I let it pass. The lives of techno-nerds are so empty and meaningless that you have to accommodate their egos once in awhile. "Feed the hungry bee," as Ken Kesey used to say.

"Do you see the words 'Caller I.D.' on the upper right-hand corner near the little plastic window?" Harold said.

"Yes."

"Press the button on the right side of the window."

"Thank you, Harold. I have to hang up now."

"Did you press it?"

"Not yet but I will."

"Why don't you press it now and see what happens?"

"I have a hamburger burning on the stove."

"Oh ... okay. But one last thing, Murph."

"What's that, Harold?"

"Happy Halloween."

"Happy holidays to you, too."

He hung up.

So did I, with a sense of relief. Then it occurred to me that he now had my phone number, compliments of Caller I.D.

I started to feel nauseated. Then I remembered that the telephone at Sweeney's was a pay phone hanging on the wall next to the men's room— I'm talking a good old-fashioned rotary dial. Suddenly everything was copacetic. It's odd how obsolete technology can heal a troubled mind.

I pressed the Caller I.D. button.

Nothing happened.

I pressed it again.

Nothing.

The first time in my life that I had ever pressed Caller I.D. I got the phone number of the YMCA, so I knew the damned thing worked. But maybe it was already worn out from use—"planned obsolescence," as the Big Boys call it. Except both Harold and the man who had given me the machine told me it was state-of-the-art. The man who gave it to me was a millionaire. Still is, I imagine. I once inadvertently filled his daughter's mind with delusions of grandeur. That was during "The Week of the Cup Holder." But he forgave me after I shattered his daughter's illusions. He sent his chauffeur over with the AudioMaster-Deluxe as a gift. He said it would make my life more manageable.

You be the judge.

I played the tape again.

The AudioMaster may have been state-of-the-art but the sound was as bad as it is on all little machines. Then I got an idea. I removed the tape and put it in the cassette player on my stereo. I could adjust the bass, treble, and all the other switches whose functions I did not understand. What does 400Hz mean?

I could now blow the roof off my apartment if I so chose, but I chose not to. I save that for the Beatles. I turned the sound up loud though, and messed around with the acoustic controls. I was able to hear the words more clearly, but it was like watching a Roger Corman movie on IMAX—i.e., it was still a Roger Corman movie. However, the word "Murphy" was preceded by two words that I was barely able to make out. They sounded like this: "staaay awaaay." The words had a slow, dragged-out tone as if the recording was a 45 R.P.M. platter being played on 33. The slow rhythm reminded me of the bass guitar on the Beatles' version of "You've Really Got A Hold On Me." I didn't even know there was a bass guitar in the background of that song until I bought my stereo from SoundCity!!!. My previous hi-fi was state-of-the-art 1959.

I removed the tape and set it on my stereo, then went to my bedroom and opened a dresser drawer and reached into a small cardboard box resting next to my overdue library book. The box contained 50 blank cassette tapes. The salesman at SoundCity!!! talked me into buying it.

I returned to the living room and placed the blank cassette into my AudioMaster. I wanted to keep the strange message. I have a box full of tapes containing strange messages, if you consider telemarketing pitches to be strange. I do. I like to listen to those tapes when there is nothing good on TV. It's amusing to hear desperate people trying to talk me into giving them money. But I had learned my lesson long ago during what I call "The Night of the ThighMaster." When I woke up the morning after

St. Patrick's Day and realized what I had done, I knew I had an important life choice to make: either give up drinking or give up listening to sales pitches.

I went back to my stereo and looked at the cassette tape with the peculiar chanting. I wasn't certain that the words really did say "stay away" because they were muffled, but it was the word "Murphy" that finally tipped the scales in favor of doing what I didn't want to do. I pulled out my billfold and looked at Shantel's cell phone number. I mulled this over for a while, then pulled out the receipt that Hogan had given to me and looked at the number of the Harris's land-line.

I decided it would be best to talk to Lester Nagle's uncle rather than talk to a teenage girl on her personal phone—that didn't feel right. Nothing about this situation felt right. I felt that if I talked to Mr. Harris I would be, in a sense, "squealing" on Lester but I wanted to make certain that "everything is okay."

Suppose Shantel had told her parents that she had met me at the mall, and that I had gone out to the Riverside house and had talked to her afterward. If something "peculiar" was going on with his nephew I could not help but feel that Mr. Harris would cast a jaundiced eye on what I projected would be a desperate attempt at some future date to explain to him that I had been running around behind his back trying to help both his daughter and his nephew.

I sat down in my easy chair and looked at the telephone. I took a deep breath and sighed. I tried to remember how I had gotten myself into this situation. I felt like a chess master mentally replaying a game while Bobby Fischer waved at his fans as they cheered another of his spectacular and—need I say?—predictable victories.

I thought about the Wednesday night trip, and my Thursday L-2, and my Harris visit on Friday, and my Saturday morning meeting with Shantel, but it all came down to the one crucial move that had tipped the balance in favor of Bobby Fisher: I had gotten involved in the personal life of a fare.

My friend Big Al had trained me to drive a taxi fifteen years ago, and at the end of the training day he had warned me to never get involved in the personal life of a fare. I wrote that down in a little notebook that I had carried throughout the day. It was the very last piece of advice he gave me.

That day, I mean. He has been giving me advice on a continual basis for the past fifteen years. There is a peculiar sameness to the advice he gives me, i.e., "Never get involved in the personal life of a fare, Tenderfoot."

He had called me "Tenderfoot" on my first day of training and he has never stopped calling me that, although he sometimes goes with a variation: "Greenhorn." I would ask him to stop calling me those obnoxious names except I'm afraid he would say, "Why?"

I dialed the Harris land-line and listened to it ring for a minute. I deduced that no one was home. I placed the receiver back on the cradle.

I looked at the digital clock on my cable box. It was ten minutes to seven. I groaned as I got out of my chair. I went to my closet and pulled out my deep forest green Rocky jacket and my taxi cap. If I was going to Lester Nagle's house I wanted to arrive in full dress uniform. I have always suspected that I possess a somewhat bland face that nobody remembers, with the possible exception of the police, and I wanted Mrs. Nagle to recognize me when she opened the door.

It hadn't taken but a moment to formulate my "plan." I would go to the house and talk to Mrs. Nagle and find out if Lester was okay. Upon being reassured that he was fine, I would then come home, write a million-dollar bestseller, and move to a cabin in a remote spot of the globe inaccessible to all mankind except for the Sherpa who would deliver my beer and *TV Guide* once a week.

But first things first.

CHAPTER 22

I guided my Chevy east along 14th Avenue, then cut down to 5th. I cruised the street until I came to the Nagle address. As soon as I parked and got out of my Chevy I looked at the windows of the house expecting to see every one of them dark. But I was wrong. A single window on the second floor was lit. I noted that the porch light was not on.

I zipped my Rocky jacket up to the neck and tugged the bill of my cap down a bit on my forehead to further counteract my blandness. I pushed the front gate open. Stepping out of character for a moment I did not slip quietly and surreptitiously along the leaf-strewn sidewalk. I made noise. Normally I try to keep my presence unknown. Without going into specifics, I have been in quite a few situations like this.

I kicked at the leaves like an uncouth peasant as I approached the porch. If anybody was watching my arrival I wanted them to think I was normal. If you have ever ridden in taxis you would probably be surprised at the number of abnormal people you have given money to.

I climbed the porch steps with a heavy tread, and did the same thing as I crossed the wooden porch. I pressed the doorbell. I heard chimes inside. I calculated the house was built between 1934–39.

I stood approximately three feet back from the door so the occupants would have a good look at me after the porch light came on. I waited almost a minute but nothing happened. I wanted desperately to step off the porch and look up to see if the second-story window was still lit. The reason this occurred to me was that I myself usually turn off all the lights in my apartment when I become aware that someone is climbing toward my back door, with the exception of the pizza Sherpa.

But I stayed on the porch. I rang the hell again. Did I say "hell"? I meant "bell."

I began to feel anxious. Already I was concocting a new plan, which consisted of either calling Shantel on her cell phone or driving over to the Harris house and laying a new set of cards on the table.

I heard the click of the doorknob.

I froze.

The door opened an inch. I saw the dark silhouette of a head.

"Rocky Mountain Taxicab Company!" I said brightly.

A soft voice muttered, "Just a moment."

The door closed.

The porch light flashed on, startling me as if a moth had flown into my face.

The door opened three inches and I saw Mrs. Nagle peering out at me.

"Who are you?" she said. She spoke very slowly and softly. I wondered if she had been drinking.

"I'm with the Rocky Mountain Taxicab Company, ma'am," I said. "I drove your son Lester to The Flicker last night."

I don't know if that qualified as a non-sequitur but I had found that if I said something that had no real point to it people often responded as if I had said something meaningful. Inflection has a lot to do with this. If you're a politician, you probably know what I mean.

She opened the door a few more inches and looked beyond me, then said, "I thought you might be a trick-or-treater. I do not give out candy on Halloween."

That made two of us, especially after Cleveland.

I reached up and pinched the bill of my cap. It had the word "Rocky" stitched in yellow thread above the bill. You wouldn't believe the debate that nearly tore Rocky Cab in two the previous summer when Hogan told us that Mrs. Hapworth wanted to embroider the logo utilizing the color of our main competitor. It wasn't the yellow thread that vexed me though, it had more to do with the Italian Stallion, but let's not get into that.

"The reason I came by, ma'am, is that Lester told me he was going to take a taxi home from the movie last night and I just wanted to make sure he got home okay. I was off duty by then so I wasn't able to give him a ride."

The reasoning here was tenuous, but I was walking the razor's edge. I wanted her to think that I was concerned about her son's welfare. The fact that I actually was concerned about his welfare was irrelevant. This was one of those situations where the truth gets so confusing I preferred to lie. I mean technically I was lying even though everything I said was true.

"Lester's not home," she said.

This threw me for a loop. I had achieved my goal before rifling my grab-bag of deceptive truths.

"Do you know where he is?" I said.

I metaphorically held my breath. I knew I was crossing the bounds of propriety, meaning I was asking something that was none of my business. But as I stated earlier, I have absolutely no ethics.

"Lester is out with his friends," she said.

"Oh!" I chirped. "You mean his cousin, Shantel?"

She frowned slightly. Then shook her head no. "His other friends."

The night was quiet. There was no wind. Any leaves dropping from the trees behind me were dropping of their own volition. By this I mean they had given up. Dead leaves give me mixed feelings—I mean, why hang on when you know it's all over? On the other hand, there's something admirable about clinging to futile hope. Been both places.

I finally gave up.

"Mrs. Nagle, last Wednesday night I drove Shantel and Lester and three of their friends to a party out near Golden on west 38th Avenue. It was one of those commercial haunted house affairs. They didn't get home until four o'clock in the morning. Shantel's parents told me that they called the police when Shantel wasn't home by one a.m."

She peered at me as I recited this litany of squealing, but she didn't say anything.

I continued: "Were you aware that Lester got home at four in the morning? That would have been Thursday morning just before dawn."

She slowly shook her head no and said, "Lester comes and goes. He has his friends."

She reached up and took hold of the collar of her robe and gently clutched it at the neck. Until this moment I had not noticed what she was wearing. I suddenly pictured her living out her days and nights wearing a robe and puttering around the house like Cloris Leachman in *The Last Picture Show*, or Joanne Woodward in *The Effect of Gamma Rays on Man-in-the-Moon Marigolds*, which was ironic because I sometimes hear Joanne Woodward's voice inside my head—not the Joanne of *Gamma* but the Joanne of *The Three Faces of Eve,* but let's not get into that.

I wanted badly to tell her about the meeting with Shantel at the mall, but I did not want to bring the girl into this. Consequently I said, "I just wanted to check up on Lester. When I talked to your brother he seemed pretty concerned about the kids on Wednesday night, so I wanted to make sure Lester got home from the movie all right."

She raised her chin and peered at me. "I have no brother," she said.

Then she gently and quietly pressed the door shut.

The porch light went out.

I stared at the window expecting a light to come on inside the house, but it remained dark. I had the feeling Mrs. Nagle was watching me through the glass so I turned and went down the steps and tried to maintain the posture of a normal person as I moved past the gate. I pulled it shut behind me, then stepped around my Chevy and got into the driver's seat and started the engine. I drove to the corner and parked at the curb and sat staring at the quitters along the tree-lined street who were fluttering to the asphalt.

I tried to sort through the conversations, confessions, and absolutions that I had taken part in during the past three days, looking for the person who had told me that Mrs. Nagle was the sister of Mr. Harris. I kept thinking it was Shantel but now I wasn't sure.

There hadn't seemed to be anybody home at the Harris house when I had called earlier, but maybe they were home by now. I decided to call again. I chose to scout a 7-11 store rather than a corner phone booth because the presence of a 7-11 acts as a kind of psychic balm on my soul when I am troubled. The 7-11 stores have a lot in common with self-delusion. But that's just my take. I'm sure there are people who would prefer to meditate on their troubles in a grotto, but I don't think Denver has any grottoes.

I was forced to drive all the way north to Colfax Avenue to find a 7-11. If you happen to live in Denver, what I am about to say may come as a surprise to you, but Colfax has the same effect on me as 7-11 stores do. I feel good whenever I drive along Colfax. Conversely, I never feel good when I am forced to take the Colfax Avenue bus, #15. If this makes no sense to you, we could start a club.

I pulled into a 7-11 parking lot. They didn't have any booths at the 7-11 but there were telephones attached to the outside wall. I could see from my car that one of the phones was out of order. It didn't have a receiver. I was fairly certain that the other phone worked because a dude was talking into the receiver. He had long hair. He looked the way I looked when I lived in Cleveland: unemployed. The resemblance was uncanny.

I checked out the landscape before exiting my Chevy. I made sure all my doors were locked. I did this out of taxi habit. Dudes tended to climb into the backseats of parked taxis on Colfax even when the drivers weren't present. They often had no money. A learned thing.

I stood by the hood of my Chevy and discreetly watched my doppelganger, making it obvious that I wanted to use the phone by picking through a pocketful of change and glancing at him now and then. He was speaking quietly and—I might say—surreptitiously. Perhaps he was talking to a pharmacist, but I tried to avoid speculating, which is hard to do when you look like I once did. I had long ago shaved off the beard that I sported in college because long-haired dudes sometimes mistook me for a pharmacist.

He hung up the phone and looked at me with wide eyes as I approached to make my call. "You're not gonna be long are you, man?" he said anxiously.

"No sweat, dude," I said, falling into hippie lingo.

I dropped my quarters and dialed the Harris number. I had it memorized by now. If I had gotten involved in the personal lives of strangers when I was in grade school I might have passed arithmetic.

I listened to the phone ring. As I did so I glanced at the dude. He was standing a few feet away and doing a bad job of not appearing anxious. He was standing sideways to me but he kept glancing over at the phone. Perhaps he had recently had a wisdom tooth pulled and needed to fill a prescription for pain pills. That happened to me once in Kansas City. I could sympathize with the dude. I don't know what sort of pain pills the dentist in KC prescribed for me, I only know that I walked out of the pharmacy with a small white paper sack containing an orange plastic bottle and I woke up three days later in Reno flat broke.

I hung up the phone. "All yours, dude," I said.

He was dialing before I got back to my car, a distance of approximately nine feet.

There didn't seem to be anyone home at the Harris household. I got settled behind the steering wheel and tried to think. That didn't work so I climbed back out and went into the 7-11 to buy a cup of coffee. My vow to avoid stimulants had gone where most of my vows go. I climbed back into my Chevy and sat sipping for a few minutes, knowing full well what was going to happen.

It did.

The caffeine woke up the part of my brain that I sometimes utilize to make crucial decisions. I hate that part of my brain. It has the same effect on me that money has on normal people: it gives me ambition.

I finished the coffee quickly. It was a "small" cup. I had bought a small in the hopes that it would affect only a few of my brain cells but it didn't work, in the same way that you can't get rid of love-handles by spot-reducing. The caffeine acted as a light switch on all the cells. I crumpled the cup and tossed it into my backseat. I never do the crumple-and-toss when I drive a cab, for obvious reasons. But when I'm off-duty I comport myself like a bachelor. In Kansas City my wastebasket was hidden under pizza boxes.

I started my car and drove onto Colfax. I headed over to University Boulevard, then drove south to Speer Boulevard and cut west.

I drove past the Denver Country Club and turned onto the street where the Harris family lived. As I approached the house I could see that it was dark. I won't kid you though. I knew it would be dark. But I had driven to the house for the same reason that I glance at the houses of wealthy playwrights. One never knows, does one? Horace Tabor became a silver baron by accidentally parking his tent on the right mountain.

I slowed but did not stop in front of the house. When you drive a rolling junk heap and look like me, you don't park in front of rich people's houses. This was not a learned thing. It was intuitive.

Since this was Saturday night I figured the Harris family was probably out for the evening. Maybe Shantel had gone with her parents to a play. I wondered if *Harvey* was being revived at the Denver Center for the Performing Arts.

I drove out of the neighborhood and made my way over to the Cherry Creek Shopping Center. I pulled into the asphalt lot near the corner of 1st Avenue and University. I parked and shut off the engine. I took out the slip of paper with Shantel's number and gazed at it even though I had it memorized. I thought about calling her again. Who says doing the same thing over and over again while expecting a different result is a sign of insanity? Maybe it's a sign of desperation. Even sane people get desperate. Look at Horace Tabor.

A disturbing thought occurred to me. What if I called her and the cell phone rang in the middle of *Harvey*? Think how annoyed the Mary Chase fans would be.

I didn't know what to do.

Then I saw a Starbucks.

It was across the street. The small 7-11 joe had already done its work and had clocked out. I was becoming indecisive again, which is how I usually like it.

Let's cut to the chase.

Eight minutes later I was sipping a triple espresso. I had capitulated again. I felt the same way I once felt after giving up smoking during my twenties, only to find myself cracking a cellophane pack in a bar and flicking my Zippo. I felt like a loser as I lit the very first cigarette I had smoked since giving them up two days earlier. I bought the Zippo in the army. Everybody I knew in the army owned a Zippo. I guess the army is a kind of "Zippo" thing.

I estimated that I had digested one shot of espresso when the decision came to me. I would call Shantel's cell phone and to hell with Mary Chase. If Lester was involved with the devil I intended to do whatever I could to keep him from harm's way. I told myself that if I had hung around in Golden on Wednesday night and drove the kids back to DCPA instead of racing to the motor worried about a five-dollar late fee, none of this would be happening.

I climbed out of my Chevy and walked up to a phone booth planted on a corner of the Starbucks' parking lot. It wasn't actually a booth, it was just an aluminum poll with a phone bolted to it, but I'm from the old school of describing things inaccurately. My father was the same way. Me ol' Dad always referred to World War II as "the last war" even though

America had been involved in subsequent wars. You may have experienced this yourself, especially if you have an ol' dad.

I dialed the cell phone number. Doing this made me cringe. What if the play had reached the knee-slapping scene where Jesse White looked in the encyclopedia and read aloud the definition of the word "pookah" and my call stepped on the punch line? I would never forgive myself.

"We're sorry, but the number you have dialed has been disconnected."

I hung up the receiver and stared at the phone for a while trying to remember the last time this magical invention of Alexander Graham Bell had ever done me one damm bit of good. I couldn't even remember the last time I ordered a pizza.

My shoulders drooped.

But isn't this how it always is? You worry yourself sick thinking you're going to wreck the world, and then bupkus. It reminded me of a time when I queried two literary agents simultaneously in violation of the strict rules of submission and then worried that they would both want to see my manuscript at the same time. Instead, they sent me simultaneous rejection slips.

Shantel's phone was disconnected. And the Harris house was dark. It occurred to me that perhaps no one was at home permanently. Maybe they had packed up and left town in a hurry. It's been known to happen. I've done it a dozen times, but that's just me. Mr. Heartbreaker.

I went back to my car and got behind the steering wheel. So far I was batting zero, which was like batting a thousand for me. I tried to sort things out.

The only thing I knew about Rodney was the information Shantel had given to me. Rodney was really old … about thirty she said. Rodney had a Ouija board. Rodney took the kids to a Halloween party at the house near Riverside Cemetery where he held a seance during which Lester supposedly contacted his dead father.

I again wondered why Shantel's phone was disconnected.

I took a deep breath and sighed. I placed my latte in my cup holder then started the engine. I drove away from the mall and headed north on University Boulevard. I didn't know if every part of my brain knew where I was going, but the part of my brain that processes information did. But

I tried to keep it under wraps. I didn't want the part of my brain that is prone to panic getting wind of my destination.

When I arrived at Colfax I pulled into the 7-11 parking lot. The dude was gone. I went inside and purchased a flashlight. I know, I know, I could have picked up a cheaper one at a supermarket, but I wanted to buy one fast and the price you pay for goods at convenience stores is compensated by the fact that they are open twenty-four hours a day. I live for convenience, and there is more to life than stumbling around in the dark just to save money.

You may have relatives who do this.

The flashlight came without batteries so I paid that price, too. I took a moment to load the batteries into the flashlight. I felt like I was loading an antique pistol with monster bullets. I flicked it on and off. Then I backed out of the lot and headed west on Colfax until I came to Lincoln. I turned north and drove to Broadway. I eventually came to the viaduct that passed over the railroad tracks. The viaduct dropped down into the Platte River Valley and cut right at a 45-degree angle where it became Brighton Boulevard.

From there I drove straight to Globeville.

CHAPTER 23

The cemetery was dark.

I followed a back road that took me to the house I had searched at high noon. I turned into the long dirt drive and slowed to a crawl. I thought I saw a light go out in a window on the ground floor, but it may have been a brief reflection from my headlights striking the glass as I turned into the drive. I hit the brakes and gazed at the house. It looked the same as it had when I had been there at noon, minus the sunlight reflecting off the walls.

Rather than park in front, I drove slowly off to the right. The earth was as dry and hard as the driveway, there was no grass, and no obstacles to prevent me from driving around the house. It was bumpy though. My car swayed like a canoe. I slowed as I drove past the cellar door at the side of the house. I shined my flashlight at the rusted lock, then moved on. I rolled around to the rear of the house. I braked and looked across the acres of cemetery. There are a lot of trees at Riverside Cemetery. Jack the Ripper would have found plenty of places to hide … and seek.

I shut off the engine and opened the car door. I listened. I was listening for chanting. It was the only thing I could think of to listen for. I heard nothing. I looked at the back door of the house, then measured the distance from the door to my car. I estimated thirty feet. I climbed out with the flashlight in my hand. I left the car door open.

I walked to the bottom step of the porch and stood listening. I heard nothing.

I climbed the steps and tried the door. It opened. I stood in the open doorway listening, but still heard nothing.

I shined the flashlight around the kitchen. It looked the same. I walked through the kitchen and stood at the entrance to the dining room. I shined the light around. Everything looked the same as it had at high noon.

You might be wondering why I entered a dark house built next to a cemetery, but the answer is simple, if not inexplicable. I don't believe in ghosts. If Lester Nagle was in this house, I would find out, if for no other reason than it was my fault. A lot of people in this world get their courage from a bottle, and I will admit that I have done that a few times myself. But I have learned that when it comes to bolstering courage, scotch whiskey can't hold a candle to Catholic guilt.

"Lester Nagle!" I shouted.

I waited for a reply. It didn't come. I shined the flashlight on the floor to see if there were any recent footprints.

Nothing.

I walked into the living room and looked around. I peered down the hallway that led to the stairwell. I swept the hallway floor with the circle of light. No footprints.

Then I heard a sound.

A soft, odd, *whump*.

I froze.

I listened for a moment, then shined my flashlight down the hallway. "Lester!"

I waited and listened.

The sound did not come again.

I began following the beam of light toward the stairwell.

I stopped at the bottom of the stairs and shined my light up to the second floor. I ran the beam back and forth along the balusters. I held the circle of light against the door of the room where I had seen the pentagram, and as I did so I thought I saw a faint flickering light at the opposite end of the hallway. I swung the beam in that direction but could see nothing. I then did something that I never dreamed I would do in my lifetime. I turned off the flashlight while standing inside a dark house next to a cemetery.

But I had to do it.

I had to see if another light was competing with my flashlight.

It was.

I saw a faint glimmering coming from beneath a door on the second floor. It wasn't The Pentagram Room though. It was the room at the opposite end of the hall.

"Lester!"

I started up the stairs.

I walked softly, listening hard, but I did not hear any chanting. I heard nothing at all. I arrived at the top of the stairs. I moved down the hall toward the light flooding from beneath the door. "Lester, this is Mr. Murphy the cab driver! I've come to take you home! Are you here?"

Nothing.

I debated whether the time had come to go back downstairs, drive to a phone booth, and call the police. I had to balance the time it would take a black-and-white to arrive against the time it would take to open the door. It was a no-brainer, like everything else going on in the house that night.

I reached down and took hold of the doorknob. I turned off my flashlight and shouted, "The police are on their way!"

I shoved the door open and stepped back.

The room was empty but for a flood of bright, flickering, yellow light.

Where was it coming from?

"Lester!"

I glanced behind me, then walked into the room and looked around. I realized the light was coming through a window on the far side of the room. I walked across the floor and peered into the night.

My Chevy was on fire.

CHAPTER 24

The lessons of my grade school days rushed back to me: "During a fire drill walk rapidly but do not run to the nearest exit." This thought passed through my mind as I sprinted out the door and practically fell down the stairs. I did keep one hand on the railing, the slick varnished bannister damn near putting blisters on my palm as I descended. I scrambled along the hallway with the ghost of Sister Bertram snarling at me for violating "*The Rules!!!*" I saw the glow of the fire flickering on the dining room walls.

I ran through the kitchen and stopped at the back door.

My Chevy was engulfed.

Had it not been for the fact that there was not one item of value inside the car including the engine and transmission, my heart would have sunk. Instead, my heart sank because I did not have a ride home. This thought preceded my next thought: how did this happen?

I hurried down the steps and circled the bonfire.

I backed away from my car and glanced around the terrain but the light of the fire made everything beyond the yard pitch black.

That's when I heard the chanting.

It was dim and distant. I couldn't tell where it was coming from. I slowly turned 360 degrees and tried to get a fix on the source of the sound, but it had the odd quality of coming from every direction and no direction.

I began backing away from my burning car. I was at least a half-mile from Brighton Boulevard in terms of following the road, but I was no farther than the diameter of the cemetery from the boulevard—four blocks "as the crow flies."

I continued to back away from the fire until I entered the realm of darkness where the circumference of the glow no longer reached. I turned and looked across the cemetery. In the distance I could see a white pin-point of light from a streetlight planted along Brighton Boulevard. It had the quality of a star of the third magnitude. I knew it would be my gui-don. I also knew that a ghost did not start this fire. I also knew that some-one did not want me here. Believe me, I know when I'm not wanted. I learned that in college, primarily at keggers where I drank too much beer and concluded that everyone had come to hear me imitate Bullwinkle.

I began walking sideways as I had done earlier in the day when I descended the stairs. I did this until I could no longer feel the heat of my immolating Chevy. I knew I was on the grounds of the cemetery proper when I tripped over a fallen tombstone and hit the ground. I didn't have time to get angry at the people responsible for taking care of the graves—I jumped up and began making my way toward the boulevard, watching the weedy earth carefully in the circle of my flashlight.

The chanting grew less loud the farther away I got from the house. This came as a relief. Imagine how terrible it would be if the sound re-mained just as loud no matter how far I traveled. A graveyard is a terrible place to debunk the Doppler Effect.

I passed another tombstone, passed a crucifix carved of stone, passed two headstones of the same make and model lying prone in the grass, possibly members of the same wagon train. I made it another forty feet before I began coming across headstones standing erect.

That's when I heard the first gunshot.

I hit the dirt as I had been trained to do by television. I learned it in the army, too, but I heard more gunshots on TV than I ever heard in the army.

I turned off the flashlight.

I saw that on an episode of *Combat*.

I heard a second and third gunshot, and I suddenly recognized the sounds. My tires were exploding. As I said earlier, a taxi burned up on me awhile back and the exploding tires made the same sounds: blam blam blam. It had sort of made me laugh at the time. The sounds of my Chevy tires exploding sort of made me laugh, too.

But was it a laugh of bemusement? Or was it the laugh of Renfield emerging again? Had I been driven to the edge of madness at last?

Blam!

Went the fourth tire.

I raised my head and saw a white shape directly in front of me. My thumb flipped the switch on the flashlight. The shape was a tombstone one foot away. I realized I could have broken my nose on the granite when I hit the dirt. Teeth too, but I concentrated on my nose. The thought of breaking my teeth was unbearable.

I shined the light at the inscription. I didn't see my name so I scrambled off the ground and looked back at the house. I was at least fifty yards away from it. Then I saw something move.

I shined my light to the left and thought I saw someone dash behind a tree. I swept the flashlight to the right and thought I saw another dark shape duck behind a tree.

As I said, I don't believe in ghosts, but I do believe in people. I swept the flashlight back and forth, and noted that the shadows of the tombstones wavered back and forth in unison. Maybe my imagination combined with the beam of light made me think I was seeing things move. That was damn near the definition of motion pictures, but I didn't dwell on it.

I listened hard but couldn't hear the chanting now. If it was coming from the house I was too far away. I glanced toward the boulevard and saw the streetlight, which had drifted to the second magnitude. I shined my light at the ground until I saw what I was looking for, the fragmented remains of a fallen tombstone so old that it had succumbed to erosion or vandals. I bent down and picked up a corner of the granite and held it in my right fist. I judged that it weighed three pounds. I once belonged to a health club so I had a lot of experience with three-pound dumbbells, if twenty minutes can be defined as "a lot."

I held the primitive stone weapon in my right hand, and held the monster-bullet weapon in my left hand. I began working my way toward the boulevard wondering if Thomas Edison had been involved in the invention of the flashlight—or "torch" as they say in British novels.

Suddenly I heard it again.

Chanting.

I made another 360. The chanting had a familiar ring: "Faeder ure ou oe eart on heofonum, Faeder ure ou oe eart on heofonum." I realized it was me. I clamped my mouth shut and worked my way through the center of the cemetery where the headstones were the tallest and—I assumed—the occupants were the richest. By the time I passed the middle of the boneyard the light of my burning Chevy had faded away. Ol' Betsy was gone forever and I knew it. But I didn't have time to grieve. I was in a cemetery.

I broke into a full-tilt run.

I didn't stop until I passed through the gate. I had not run that long or that far since I was in the army, according to my legs. By the time I arrived at Brighton Boulevard my lungs were heaving, my mouth was dry, and my heart was pounding. It reminded me of a date I had in college with a girl who was said to be "loose." I never found out how loose she was because Bullwinkle got tossed out of the kegger. I later heard she left with a jock but let's move on.

I stood facing the cemetery with my flashlight aimed at the tombstones and the chunk of granite gripped in my right hand. I'll admit it. I lowered myself to the dirt driveway. If I was going to die, I was going to die sitting down. Death with dignity is for amateurs.

I was breathing hard, which made sense. I was one mile above San Diego. I closed my eyes and pictured the Broncos stomping the Chargers. Small compensation, but it did relax my heartbeat.

I opened my eyes and swiveled the beam of light back and forth like a sword in hopes that my pursuers would back off out of fear that I might be able to describe their faces to the police on my deathbed. As I said, I believe in people, and one thing I firmly believed was that people are afraid of being arrested.

"What people!" Burt Reynolds shouted.

I started breathing with my mouth jacked wide open to diminish the noise of my wheezing. I listened hard.

I did not hear sounds of pursuit. I heard nothing at all. No wind. No rustling leaves. No traffic on Brighton. Nothing.

The streetlight that I had used as a guidon was a hundred feet farther south. The glow of light did not extend to the gate of the cemetery. I switched off my flashlight and let my eyes adjust to the darkness. You may not believe this, but I did it in the hopes of luring my pursuers closer so I could see their faces. I wasn't thinking very clearly. That was not unusual.

I peered into the cemetery but did not see any humanoid shapes flitting between the faint silhouettes of trees and tombstones.

I switched the flashlight back on and admitted to myself that I might have only imagined that I was being pursued. "Might" is the operative word here. The flickering and dancing of the Chevy flames might have made me think I had seen someone dash behind trees. But someone had set fire to my car, of that I was certain. I discounted the fact that my old Rocky Mountain Taxicab #127 had burned up by itself, because that particular fire had been caused by a defective air conditioner. My Chevy had no air conditioner. Someone must have torched my car. I didn't know who, and I didn't know why, but I did know one thing: I would never find out if I remained sitting comfortably on the ground.

I groaned as I worked myself to a standing position. This was not unusual. I groan every time I have to do anything. I clung to the things that were not unusual that night in order to cancel out the psychological effects of the unusual. It didn't work, but I pretended it did. That was not unusual either.

I began walking along Brighton Boulevard in the direction of Globeville. I didn't pray that a car would come along and give me a ride, but it wasn't because I'm not much of a praying man in Modern English. It was because I didn't believe that a car would stop to pick up a lone figure staggering away from a graveyard.

It didn't matter. There was no traffic on Brighton anyway. I passed beneath the streetlight that had acted as my guidon during my panic sprint. Then I did something that I immediately regretted. I shined my flashlight at the hanging bulb as a salute in gratitude for its aid. The bulb went dark.

I froze.

I stood in the darkness listening for footsteps.

Then I remembered that streetlights automatically shut off when struck by sunlight at dawn. A Denver cop had explained that to me. It was not in connection with a murder or anything. We were just shooting the breeze.

I continued walking in total darkness, wondering if I needed something beyond mere goddamn therapy. But maybe all I really needed was to pause and consider the consequences of any move I might make in the future. I filed the thought away. It might come in handy someday but I was too tired right then to embrace a crucial step in the reorganization of my entire life. I had better things to do than stop the insanity. I needed a drink of water and I needed a phone booth, and I really didn't care which came first.

As the lights of Globeville drew closer, I noted that for all the running I had done my feet did not hurt. My Keds had stood me in good stead. I buy a new pair of tennis shoes every spring, just after St. Patrick's Day, so even though they were seven months old they were like new because I use my shoes primarily to walk from my apartment to my car. But the way things had worked out that night, it appeared that I would be riding a shanks mare for a while.

"Shanks mare" is an archaic phrase that can be loosely translated as "legs horse," which simply means "walking." I assume that the phrase originated in New England where people think they are terribly witty.

You be the judge.

CHAPTER 25

I had caught my breath and my heartbeat was back to normal. All that remained was the tiredness I felt from running and the thirst that I assumed had been caused by the espresso. Caffeine is a diuretic. But mostly I felt shaken, which in turn ignited anger at the thought of someone setting my car on fire.

I interpreted the burning of my car as a warning: *stay away*. Whether I was right or wrong about that, I let the conclusion flow through me because it bolstered my determination to make it to a phone booth. It had been so long since I had walked any great distances that I began to understand the true helplessness of the human animal. A running dog would have made it to Globeville in two minutes. I felt feeble and useless. I wanted wheels and speed. I wanted to go ninety miles an hour. I peered at the glow of lights in the distance, and that's when I saw it. A tall rectangle planted at the base of a telephone pole. A streetlight cast a cone of light down on what appeared to my eyes to be a telephone booth. It was at the edge of town, which struck me as a logical place to set up a telephone booth.

I closed my eyes and whispered a prayer for absolution, begging Alexander Graham Bell's forgiveness for all the snide remarks I had ever made about his remarkable invention. What a genius. How could anybody have conceived of the idea of sending the human voice between cities using nothing more than a strand of copper wire? Of course the telegraph may have given him the idea, but let's not quibble. The man was a *visionary!*

The booth was set at the edge of a gas station parking lot. As I drew closer I saw that the windows were boarded over. Abandoned. Belly up. The victim of hard times. Location is everything. There was no traffic on Brighton Boulevard.

As I trudged the last fifty feet toward the station I was surprised to see that the booth was made of wood. It was as old-fashioned as anything gets in this country. I was stunned when I got close enough to see that it had a door, and I don't mean a door that folded in the middle like a map, but a regular door with narrow windows. The booth was painted red, but was flaked and faded. I began to grow leery. It looked an awful lot like Doctor Who's phone booth. But that's not what made me leery. I was afraid the booth was so old that the phone wouldn't work.

My heart sank as I pulled the door open and looked inside at a rotary-dial phone. I wanted to get the heart-sinking out of the way before I picked up the receiver and listened for the dial tone. I like to organize my despair into manageable blocks.

I picked up the receiver and heard a dial tone. I dropped two quarters into the slot. For some reason I expected to pay only a dime, but I guess Ma Bell doesn't suffer from chronic nostalgia.

"Rocky Cab," the dispatcher said.

"I need a taxi on Brighton Boulevard in Globeville."

"Cash or charge?"

I won't drag you through the rest of it. You know the drill. You've called taxis.

I didn't identify myself. I didn't say, "This is Murph." I wasn't psychologically prepared to be unrecognized. But I did mention that I was a Rocky driver. This was to assure the cab driver who jumped the bell that he would find me standing at a phone booth in the middle of nowhere. To be perfectly honest, I myself would never jump such a bell. People who call from phone booths frequently disappear before you arrive. But I wasn't a night driver. Night drivers sign a pact with the devil when they sign up for the graveyard shift. Night drivers walk with the zombies.

"We'll have a taxi there in twenty minutes," the dispatcher said.

That wasn't a lie, it was simply what the dispatchers always told customers. It usually takes less time for a cab to arrive because the city is blanketed with desperate Rocky hacks prowling the mean streets. It takes longer only if there is something like a championship sporting event in Denver, so I wouldn't worry too much about that if I were you.

After I hung up I leaned back against the wall and closed my eyes. I considered doing some illegal Transcendental Meditation. I had attended an introductory course in TM when I was in college but I never followed through and took the full-blown training program. I learned only enough to know that if you meditated for twenty minutes your entire physical and mental being would be energized. I realized now that I should have paid the fifty-dollar training fee, but back in college I got my bursts of energy from kegs.

On the other hand, I did know that if you mumbled a fake mantra you could "replicate" TM. I knew this because I had tried it once and it seemed to work. Keep that under your hat. I wouldn't want to cause an international incident, and India does have The Bomb.

I began whispering, "It doesn't matter, it doesn't matter, it doesn't matter …." This was also the Cab Driver's Prayer but I had found it to be an effective substitute mantra for acquiring artificial energy. I think of the prayer as the Gatorade of cosmic consciousness.

I did it for ten minutes, then abruptly opened my eyes and muttered, "It does too matter."

I felt revitalized.

I opened the door and stepped out of the booth not unlike Superman in early D.C. comics, although he eventually stopped using phone booths to change out of his Clark Kent clothes. The schtick probably got old. It was never very believable anyway since booths are so narrow, although we are talking comic books here.

I peered along the boulevard wondering if a cab might magically show up ahead of time. Most fares wonder that. Their optimism involves peeking between curtains. Been there.

I looked at the abandoned gas station. It was so old that it might properly be called a "filling" station. The pumps were like tall skinny glass lanterns. I expected Gig Young to pull up in his sports car. Out of curiosity I crossed the gravel lot and shined my flashlight at one of the rusted pumps. I nearly went into cardiac arrest. According to the meter, the price of gas was twenty-three cents a gallon when this place went bust.

I shut off my flashlight and trudged away from the pump. I had forgotten that a side-effect of nostalgia is depression.

I stood at the edge of the lot and looked down the road. I won't keep you waiting as long as the driver kept me waiting. He turned out to be a newbie. It took him twenty-five minutes to arrive. He explained that he couldn't find Brighton Boulevard on his map.

But I understood.

A newbie who walks with the zombies is a double threat: unfamiliarity with the street system combined with rank incompetence. I wrote the book.

"Rocky Cab," I said.

"What?" he said, turning to look at me as I got settled in the backseat.

"I want you to take me to the motor," I said.

"Oh," he said. He sounded disappointed. Rocky Cab is not that far from Globeville in more ways than one, i.e., most of our taxis are really old. But if the driver hopped on I-70 we would be at the motor in less than six minutes.

He made a U-turn at the gas station and headed back down the road. I had to instruct him as to which turnoffs to take. He told me he had been driving for two weeks. I would have felt sorry for him but I didn't. I never feel sorry for new guys. My attitude is that reality will weed out those who are not destined to drive taxis for a living—young men and women who would be better off with normal jobs. Reality came as somewhat of a disappointment to me. My sixteenth year as a cab driver was just around the corner.

When we got close to the motor I told him to drop me off down the block. I didn't want to cause him embarrassment by letting other Rocky drivers see a Rocky driver drop off a Rocky driver in front of Rocky Cab—I'm talking the embarrassment of circular logic.

The cost came to four-sixty. I gave him ten bucks. Maybe I lied. Maybe I do feel sorry for new guys. Keep that under your hat.

As I walked toward the motor I looked at the dirt lot where I used to park my black 1964 Chevy Impala with the red doors and the hood ornament that looked like a chrome naked lady with wings being fired out of a cannon.

Gone forever.

I walked into the on-call room and approached the cage. Stew was on duty. He was reading a model railroading magazine. He lowered it and stared at me wide-eyed.

"Murph! What are you doing here?"

"I want a weekly lease."

"Weekly!"

"I'm reorganizing my entire life," I said.

He closed the magazine and set it on the counter. "Do you want a new cab?"

Rocky accommodates drivers who commit themselves to full-time employment by leasing the newer taxis to them. But I shook my head no.

"I want number one-twenty-three," I said.

He nodded. He didn't quibble. He knew how attached drivers got to their favorite cabs. But I turned down a late-model taxi in favor of a decrepit model because I wasn't certain how this night was going to turn out, and #123 was the most obsolete junk heap in the Rocky Cab fleet. If anything happened to 123, if it was put out of commission, if it ceased to function as a registered vehicle of public transportation, it wouldn't be missed by anyone—not even the insurance company.

Stew handed me a trip-sheet and the key to 123, and I handed him fifty dollars.

You heard me right.

Fifty.

A weekly lease at Rocky comes to $350.00. On the other hand, a daily lease costs $70 per shift, which is what I normally drive. Rocky charges less for weekly leases because they want to lure drivers into the Utopian maw of perpetual labor that guarantees the company a continuous profit, since drivers are the company's sole source of income. It has the faint odor of a scam but it's just garden-variety capitalism. I would gladly pay $100.00 a day to avoid driving full-time but keep that under your hat—picking up the extra thirty dollars per day would simply mean reading fewer paperbacks and jumping a couple extra bells. That's what I call a scam.

I would have to bring the remaining $300 in if I wanted a stack of six more trip sheets, which was the normal way of going about it. A bulk deal. Or I could show up every morning and hand over another fifty, which was inconvenient to most drivers. But I always try to do things the inconvenient way. It makes people think I "know" something and ain't talkin'.

Even though Stew no longer drove a taxi I said, "See you on the asphalt." I thought of it as a form of salute that WWI pilots would make before engaging in what might turn out to be The Last Dogfight.

He nodded, I think, and picked up his toy train magazine.

I walked out of the on-call room clutching the key to 123 in my right hand as if I were clutching a magic talisman, which I was. There is no such thing as a magic talisman even though there are such things as rabbits' feet, golden rings, and monkey paws, but the only magic my key possessed was the power to awaken sleeping giants—I'm talking pistons, transmissions, and the rapid displacement of stationary objects known as automobiles. I don't know who invented internal combustion, but if it was the same genius who invented the wheel, I wanted to shake that caveman's hand.

I found 123 parked in the third row out. I checked the body for dents and dings, then climbed in and tossed the trip-sheet onto the shotgun seat. I jammed my magic icon into the steering column, brought the beast to life, and drove out of the lot. As I headed for a 7-11 to gas up, I radioed the dispatcher to let him know I was on the road.

"That's what Stew told me," he said.

The Word was out.

Murph is walking with the zombies.

"Have a nice week," the dispatcher said.

By the time I hung up the microphone, the dispatcher was yelling at a newbie who had forgotten to write down the address of a bell he had jumped. I chuckled—not with disdain but with nostalgia. I'll admit it. I hold the record at Rocky Cab for getting yelled at the most number of times during the least amount of time. I received my very first L-2 from Hogan on my second day on the job. He called me into his office to politely inquire as to what the hell was wrong with me. "I have a degree in English," I explained. He nodded with understanding and sent me back on the road. My Bachelor of Arts diploma just may have saved my meal ticket that day. What else was a man with a degree in English going to do with his life except drive a taxi? Hogan is the wisest man I know.

I stopped at the 7-11 and gassed up, then bought a large cup of coffee. You heard me right—"large." I'm talking twenty ounces.

The sides of the cup burned the tips of my fingers before I got it placed properly in the cup holder, but I ignored the pain. I had only one thing on my mind as I drove away from the pumps: Safeway. I drove there and went inside.

I came out ten minutes later with a large sack filled to the brim. You heard me right again—"large." It was so large that I had not been able to pass through the ten-items-or-less line. But that was okay. Three little old ladies were standing in the ten-items-or-less line. By the time I had made my purchases, they were still in the ten-items-or-less line. One of them was trying to talk the cashier into accepting expired coupons for cat food. The other two ladies were gripping coupons in their own fists. I'd like to grip my fists around the neck of the genius who invented coupons.

I headed for Lincoln Street.

I reached for my cup holder and lifted the hot coffee to my lips. I drank deeply. I set the cup back in the holder and blew on my fingertips. This had the additional effect of cooling my esophagus. I was barely aware of it though. My body was working on robo-matic. My mind was too busy making plans. This was unusual.

I turned onto Lincoln, drove north to Broadway, and arrived at the viaduct that hoisted me into the sky and set me down at the doorstep to Brighton Boulevard. I guided 123 onto the northeast corridor, which would take me straight to Riverside Cemetery.

CHAPTER 26

I switched on my brights as I pulled into the driveway in front of the mansion. Even though I did this for a specific reason I still felt the twinge of guilt that all Americans feel when they drive with their brights on. Brights are for unusual or emergency situations—but as far as I was concerned this was both. I wished that 123 had the hand-operated spotlight that cop cars are equipped with. That would have nicely supplemented the light show I was setting into motion.

I drove straight toward the house, right up to the edge of the steps that led to the porch. My headlights were so bright they painted the porch white. I set the gearshift in Park, laid on the horn with the palm of my hand, and raced the engine. Rocky taxis are former police interceptors. I didn't know how many cubic inches resided under the hood, but I did know that 123 had eight cylinders. It made a racket as I pressed the accelerator to the floor and eased off and pressed again. It was like keeping tempo with the ponderous bass of "You've Really Got A Hold On Me." A white shape arose like a ghost in my rearview mirror. I glanced at it. Exhaust fumes. I felt guilty as I spread a smokescreen across the front yard. It was the kind of guilt you feel when you know you're doing something bad.

Real bad.

And loving it.

I took my foot off the accelerator. The engine slowed to a quiet idle. I shoved the dashboard light switch and everything went black. I studied the house.

Nothing.

I yanked the brights back on.

I climbed out the door and shouted, "Hey Rodney! I'm back!"

With these words I felt my brain float right out of my head. This happens whenever I go ballistic, except in the past the ballistics occurred under circumstances that had angered me unexpectedly. This was the first time I had ever intentionally cut the guy-wires that kept my brain grounded—like the *Hindenburg* ought to have been before it crossed the Atlantic.

I let the burning of my Chevy and the humiliating race across the cemetery flow through me like the plans for the D-Day invasion. Unlike the Germans though, I didn't fight it. I reached in and pressed the horn a half-dozen times.

"Come on out of there and bring your bodyguards with you!"

I leaned in and reached across to the shotgun seat and dragged my paper bag onto the driver's seat, dipped my hand into the sack, and pulled out a pair of gloves, flashlight, and a crowbar that I had picked up for a song in the hardware aisle at the Safeway. It was sixteen inches long and hooked at one end.

I put on the gloves and climbed the steps to the porch and began hammering against the jamb with the crowbar.

"Rodney!"

I shined the flashlight into the house, shot the beam against the far wall of the living room, then walked down the steps and climbed into 123.

I hit Reverse and backed away, dropped the stick into Low, and began driving a slow circuit of the house. I passed the cellar door. I cruised around to the rear. The headlights swept across the cemetery as I wheeled a slow arc. I did not see any shapes dashing behind trees or ducking behind tombstones. I rolled around to the front. As I passed the porch again I laid on the horn. I had drawn a full circle with my taxi like the circle devil worshippers draw around a pentagram.

Everything within the circle was mine.

I guided my vehicle around to the rear and parked alongside the corpse of ol' Betsy. The entire car was black including the doors that had once been a hideous fire-engine red. I had never dreamed that my dream of owning an all-black Chevy would come to this. The body sat low like a grounded bat enfolded within its ebony wings. The tires were flat, melted, exploded, smoldering. The stench of burned paint, burned metal, and burned tires hovered over the body … ghostlike.

I reached for my twenty-ouncer and took a long drink. The coffee had cooled. This allowed me to drink deeper than I had ever drank deeply of unsweetened java.

You heard me right: No sugar.

I was fueled strictly by mountain-grown courage that night.

I set the half-full cup in the holder then reached for the Rocky radio. "You want chanting?" I snarled. "I'll give you chanting."

I switched it on and turned the volume up to ten. The voice of the night dispatcher broke the silence:

"Colfax and Downing!!! Blood bank!!! Union Station!!!"

It blew the roof off 123.

I dimmed the headlights as I climbed out with the paper sack in my arms. I hooked the crowbar to my belt and gripped the flashlight with my fist.

I climbed the back steps and twisted the knob, kicked the door open, and tossed the flashlight onto the floor of the kitchen.

"Rodney!"

I entered the kitchen and reached into the sack and pulled out another flashlight. I switched it on and tossed it into the dining room like a smoke-grenade. That was one of the things I touched in the army that I wasn't supposed to. It held up training for fifteen minutes.

"Rodney!"

I reached in and pulled out another flashlight, switched it on, and tossed it into the living room.

"Come out, Rodney!"

I reached in and pulled out another flashlight. This one I tossed down the hallway that led to the stairwell.

"I know you're in here!"

I was yelling louder than I had ever yelled in my life. I felt like I was yelling my soul right out of my body. I felt like I weighed nothing. The white light of the flashlights looked red to my adrenaline-shot eyes.

"Rodney!!!"

I set the sack on the floor, reached inside, and pulled out a quart bottle of ammonia.

I unscrewed the cap and stood erect holding the bottle by the plastic handle. I pocketed the bottle cap, grabbed the sack like a valise, and walked down the hallway. The chanting of the night dispatcher filtered through the back door and followed me along the hall. I stopped at the bottom of the stairs. Flashlights were shining at crazy angles all over the ground floor. Shadows that this house had never seen before were climbing the walls. I pulled out another flashlight, turned it on, and heaved it to the top of the stairs. It rattled past the balusters. I adjusted the crowbar on my belt, grabbed another flashlight, and started up the steps.

I opened my mouth as I ascended, but then I closed it.

My presence had been heralded. The time for yelling was over.

I made it up to the balcony and tossed a flashlight directly at the door of The Pentagram Room. It ricocheted to the floor and shattered. The light blinked out. I reached in and grabbed another flashlight. I switched it on and flung it low like a bowling ball. It skittered against the door and spun around shining back at my feet.

I used the beam like a sidewalk as I walked down the hallway opening doors to the small rooms. But I didn't just open them. I twisted the doorknobs and kicked at them. I heard wood splinter. With my left hand I tossed flashlights into the rooms. With my right hand I held the bottle of ammonia the way you would hold an electric knife at Thanksgiving dinner, the way you would hold a hatchet, a sack, a pool cue, depending on the business at hand: elbow cocked, muscles tensed, brain nowhere to be found.

I listened to the dispatcher's muffled chant floating up the stairwell, listened for a change of volume, listened for a sudden silence that would indicate surreptitious tampering—but the rhythmic drone continued unabated.

Go ahead—burn my taxi, I said so softly that it doesn't rate quotation marks.

I shifted the bottle of ammonia to my left hand, then lifted the crowbar from its perch on my belt and gripped it in my right fist. I stopped at the door of The Pentagram Room, raised the crowbar, and held it steady like a hatchet.

I kicked at the door. It remained closed. I stepped back and watched the knob.

Nothing rotated.

I set the ammonia on the floor, reached up and twisted the doorknob until it clicked. I kicked the door.

It swung open.

I grabbed a flashlight, lit it, and tossed it to the floor. It bounced across the pentagram and rolled into the folds of the curtain where it still laid as I last left it. No one had tampered with it as far as my eyes could judge.

I crossed the room and looked out the window. My taxi was still there, the headlights still on, the dispatcher yelling at another newbie.

I went into the hallway, grabbed the sack, carried it back into the room, and pulled out three flashlights. I lit them and set them up around the room like candles.

Then I went to work.

I reached into the sack and pulled out a tall can of spray paint. I gave it a few test hisses, then proceeded to trace the pattern of the Satanic decal on the floor, covering the black paint with white-out—not Wite-Out®. That's Mrs. Nesmith's domain.

I won't drag you all the way around the circle and across the star-shaped pattern. It took five minutes to do an effective job, and when I stood up I could barely tell what I had camouflaged. It was as though Jackson Pollock had created a white-on-white painting of something that sort of looked like something.

Then I went to work on the candles. They were still standing at the points of the stars. This took longer. Maybe ten minutes, but I wanted to do a good job. I painted the wax stubs, the liquid-looking melted parts, the metal stands. I put so much paint on the stands that they were cemented to the floor. I laid it on thick. I used two cans for the job. When I finished they looked like little white rockets stuck on their launching pads.

By now the room was filled with fumes. I could barely breathe. I liked the odor. It reminded me of model-airplane glue, which in turn reminded me of the *Bonhomme Richard*, a full-masted model sailing ship my Maw bought me for my twelfth birthday. It had 1,000 plastic parts. I glued the deck to the hull, erected three masts, and said to hell with the other 995 fo'c's'les. It looked seaworthy.

Gavin and I watched it sink in a lake the next day.

I started to feel dizzy. Strange thoughts were spiraling through my mind. Model-airplane glue did that to me in the early 1960s prior to the invention of non-prescription drugs.

I picked up my tools, backed out of the room, and gazed at the mess I had made.

I turned and walked past the balusters, went down the stairs without looking for Martin Balsam, passed through the jungle of light and shadows decorating the ground floor, and walked into the kitchen.

When I stepped outside I paused and took a deep breath and let it out slowly. I could feel the night air cooling a sheen of sweat on my face and hands. I went down the steps, tossed my sack and crowbar into 123, then reached in and shut off the dispatcher's voice.

White noise rushed to fill the vacuum.

A faint ringing blossomed in my ears, a tingling sensation that might have been there all along, but whether from the caffeine, the paint, adrenaline, or the shouting of the dispatcher, I didn't know.

I looked up at the house. Every window was lit from within. The square eyes were electric white, and not one of them blinked.

I looked at the cooling remains of my Chevy. All the paint was gone. The sheet metal was warped. The trunk was raised but that was due to the fact that it had always been kept locked by a length of twine. By "always" I mean since the night I backed into something. The hood looked like it had made a half-hearted attempt to raise itself, then gave up.

I knew the feeling. I invented it.

I peered at the blackened shape of the hood ornament on my Chevy. It looked like a lady wearing a little black dress. I walked over to the hood, pulled out a handkerchief and wiped at the statuette, revealing the gleam of untarnished chrome. It hadn't been destroyed, merely smoke-damaged. I went back to 123 and reached into the sack and pulled out a pair of four-inch pliers. I raised the hood on the Chevy and went to work on a row of nuts and bolts underneath the sheet metal.

Two minutes later I carried my chrome naked lady with wings being shot out of a cannon back to my taxi. I set her on the shotgun seat, then went back to the ruins. I unbolted the license plates from the Chevy.

I placed the blackened plates on the rubber mat beneath the shotgun seat of 123, then put all my tools away. I went back to the wreck and spent a minute scratching my footprints off the earth with the crowbar. I was trying to erase all evidence of my existence now that my Chevy no longer existed. I walked back to my cab and pulled out a pack of Kleenex from my kit and spent a minute making certain my fingers were clean even though I had been wearing gloves. As I did this I walked in circles in the dirt as if I was wearing snowshoes, wiping ash off the soles of my tennis shoes.

Two minutes later I completed another mobile circuit of the mansion, then drove down to the end of the U-shaped drive and stopped at the edge of the property. I got out of my cab and stood for a moment looking at the mansion. It was lit up like a Christmas tree at Halloween.

I glanced at my wristwatch.

11:59 p.m.

One minute away from All Saints' Day.

You can carve that on my tombstone.

CHAPTER 27

By the time I made it back to Denver, my head felt clear and my soul felt cleansed. The fact that my Chevy had been burned up by a person or persons unknown, that I had been chased through the last place on earth anybody would want to be chased, that I had been forced to sign up for a weekly lease, had driven me to perform activities so out of character that you might have thought I was normal.

I recalled the warning I had given to Shantel: the police may need to be brought in on this. I thought about the call I was going to be making when I got back to my crow's nest. Whenever my Chevy got stolen I always spoke to a dispatcher at DPD named Gladys, but she worked the day shift so I figured I would not be talking to her. Whenever I did speak to her, all I had to say was, "Hello, Gladys" and she would put out the call to the road patrols to keep an eye out for "that black Chevy with the red doors." I had gotten so used to the brevity of the calls that I was now forced to think about what I would be forced to say to the night dispatcher. It would be like starting over at Square One. The dispatcher would not know me, and as a result this would place me into the category of "an ordinary person," which I found distasteful even though I fit the description perfectly. I felt like a partygoer who knew he had no chance of getting into Studio 54—except that this was a call to the police and not to the swingingest hot-spot in The Big Apple, so I knew I would be allowed inside, but to little or no fanfare.

And anyway it wasn't to report a stolen car, it was to report that my car burned up while I was … trespassing … inside a house.

I came to a red light in more ways than one. I was at Colfax and Broadway, the heart of the heart of Denver, Colorado.

The state capitol building was off to my left. You may have heard of it. It's the place where they write *The Law*. The fact that I was guilty of trespassing twice on the same Saturday brought this fact home to me.

I began to rethink my strategy.

Just what exactly did I intend to tell the police?

It's true that my car had burned up—but had it "*been*" burned up?

Which is to say, did I know for a fact that someone had set fire to my Chevy? Had I seen the person or persons unknown set it aflame?

These are the sorts of questions that detectives ask when people like me are seated in what I like to call "small rooms."

The light turned green.

I made a left turn onto Colfax and drove past the house of law with my face averted, as usual.

I rolled along Colfax past the bars and strip joints and free clinics and began to get the feeling the police might take as much interest in me as they would take in the fact that my car was mysteriously burned up. I started to feel uneasy.

Suddenly a new tack occurred to me.

Suppose I called DPD and simply reported that my Chevy had been stolen a few hours ago? I was on record as having made dozens of such calls over the past fifteen years, so it certainly would not seem out of character. And who knows? Maybe my name was legend among the people who answered the phone. Maybe Gladys had "spread the word." Maybe the phone monitors at DPD kept their fingers crossed in the hopes that they, too, might one day receive a call from Murph and his legendary portable dump.

But there was only one small problem: I never lied to the police. The operative word there is "never." Anybody who lies to the police is living in a fool's paradise. That was the philosophy I had lived by up until I possessed "a good reason" to lie to the police.

It had never occurred to me that some people might actually have good reasons to lie to the police. I had always assumed that their reasons were terrible and were motivated by nothing more than a fear of getting charged with murder, kidnapping, bank robbery, and all the other charges that I had been cleared of because I was innocent.

But this was the first time I was guilty.

I felt like I had traveled to "the other side."

It wasn't a good feeling.

All of the sudden I was no longer driving back to my apartment—I was "on the lam." I was still headed for my apartment but the perpetual soundtrack that accompanied the movie of my life had suddenly changed from … "the hills are alive with the sound of music" … to … "running scared."

A jump-out from Andrews to Orbison is usually a soul-satisfying experience but I began to wonder if it might not be best to leave the police out of this entirely. I think it was the great Chinese philosopher Confucius who said, "Avoid the authorities."

Or was it John Dillinger?

By the time I arrived at my apartment I was a mental wreck.

I was back in my element.

I parked 123 in the choice V-spot and climbed out. I made sure all of the doors were locked, hoping that the semi-official status of a taxicab would frighten off the street punks and junkies who used to steal my Chevy. There was really nothing I could do about it, which was one of the guiding excuses of my life.

I carefully trudged up the fire escape holding onto the railing with one hand. I made it to the top without incident and entered my crow's nest. "Safe," I said aloud.

I dropped my accoutrement onto the kitchen table, went into the living room and turned on the cable. But I didn't channel-surf. I didn't even look at the picture. I turned the sound up just loud enough that I would be able to hear the drone of dialogue and commercial jingles from my bedroom. I was using the TV like a radio. Cathode Musak has the same lulling effect on me as 7-11 stores and Colfax Avenue.

I went into my bedroom and collapsed face-down onto my mattress and spent one minute thinking about nothing. This is a form of denial that I frequently engage in, and which does not always involve disasters. Thinking about nothing makes me feel as if nobody can get at me.

It didn't last long. One minute is as long as I can go without thinking about anything. Then I usually start thinking about writing a novel, which is as close to nothing as I can get before I start thinking about money, sex, or any of the other things that people think about 24/7, although I don't know what the other things are since I've never given them any thought.

I rolled over and gazed at the ceiling and tried to sort things out. The next thing I knew I was off to dreamland. I've never had much luck with sorting things out. When I was in high school I couldn't even figure out the difference between (x+y) and 0(x+y). I mean, according to the English language there is "nothing" in front of both parentheses, and yet to hear a math teacher tell it there is an invisible "1" in front of (x+y). I could deal with "whole" numbers and "negative" numbers, but when they started tossing "invisible" numbers into the mix they might as well have tied a millstone around my neck and put me to work on an assembly line.

I slept deeply that night. I slept as deeply as people do who use sleeping pills but I never go that route because pills make me feel crappy the next day. I have found that the most effective means of putting myself to sleep is to sort things out, perform algebraic equations, or embrace severe depression. The combination of all three might explain why I slept through math class.

I was in the midst of a dream where I was back in high school failing a Latin test when I felt myself being dragged to consciousness by a whining sound, so I wasn't as annoyed as I usually am when yanked bodily from sleep. As my brain rose to the surface of the real world like a glob inside a lava lamp I realized the whining sound was a siren.

My brain *lurched* to the surface with the speed of a Nike missile fired from a sub. A mushroom cloud of guilt filled my bedroom as I opened my eyes to see the years falling away from a calendar taped to the wall of my cell in Supermax.

What had I done last night?!?!?

Got *caught* that's what. The details were as irrelevant as ever.

The horror of exposed guilt worked better than three shots of espresso. I sat up straight in bed and blinked at the far wall, waiting for the sound of another S.W.A.T. team kicking down my door, although the last S.W.A.T. team knocked politely. I was holding a sandwich at the time. They told me to drop it.

The glow of red lights flickered against my living room walls, bounced through the hallway, and entered my bedroom. The hallway is really just a small foyer. My apartment is cramped. One time some firefighters pounded on my foyer door due to a bomb scare that I don't want to go into. I live a fairly exciting life for somebody who does nothing.

I looked at my clock. It was 10:01 a.m.

I looked down the length of my body and was pleased to note that I was already fully dressed. This relieved me of the anguish of having to face the police by a factor of 27 percent. I don't know if you have ever been required to put on shoes and tie them in front of impatient cops, but it makes you feel stupid.

As a consequence I only sighed instead of groaned as I got out of bed. I trudged into the living room preparing myself mentally to open the door to the sight of blue uniforms, which I had gotten rather good at over the years.

I froze.

My TV was on. The sirens were coming from the speaker. Incredulous, I hurried into the kitchen and looked out the back window. No cops. No red lights. No sirens. Renfield started laughing maniacally. I joined in as I sauntered back into the living room a free man.

I picked up the TV remote and aimed it at the Riverside mansion, which was burning on my TV screen. It was a rerun of a breaking-news story broadcast in the middle of the night. The house was surrounded by firefighters. A reporter with a microphone was standing in front of the mansion describing the flaming debacle. The reporter was a woman. Not that it mattered. What mattered was my Chevy silhouetted against the burning of Atlanta.

"… The identity of the Chevy's owner remains unknown. The license plates apparently were removed but the police speculate that whoever set fire to this historic building …"

That's enough.

You get the picture.

I found myself seated on my easy chair. My weak Irish knees had given out again. I stared at the TV. Firefighters were roaming around the house, which was lit by spotlights mounted on fire trucks. Water was cascading from hoses. Smoke billowed into the night sky. You've seen flaming debacles. They're like sex scenes in novels—predictably redundant. I don't know why writers bother. What the hell do novelists know about sex?

"And now back to the studio."

I closed my eyes and turned off the sound. I cannot stand the witty banter that takes place between newscasters because they all jabber at once and step on each other's punch lines. Is that what they teach at the Columbia School of Broadcasting?

I looked at the digital clock on the cable box. It was twelve minutes after 10:00. If I was going to earn money this week I would have to get up at 7:00 a.m. every day, which would throw my metabolism out of whack but keep my finances on an even keel. I tried not to think about it.

I began going over the events of the day before. I mentally retraced my steps through both the first and second time that I had entered the house, but at the back of my mind was the idea that neither of my break-ins mattered because all the evidence of my presence had been burned to a crisp, just like #127 awhile back—there was nothing left of that vehicle but a charcoal briquette!

The realization had the disquieting effect of comforting me. Whenever I feel comfortable, a red flag goes up in my mind. I did not see how it was possible that all the evidence of my involvement in the Riverside mansion had been eradicated. It was the sort of luck that you see only in the top one percent of the socio-economic bracket—I'm talking "both" of course. Some people are born rich, and some people are born lucky, and some people are born both.

I got out of my chair and went into the kitchen. I peeked out the window again. I knew that I would be doing that a hundred times a day for the rest of my life. A learned thing.

I felt something touch the back of my hand. I looked down and saw a droplet of liquid. It may have been melted wax but I was willing to breach the scientific method and conjecture that it was sweat. I grabbed a paper towel off the rack and wiped my forehead. I was annoyed with my skin. Sweat also happens when I'm being grilled by cops so I keep my antennae out for the slightest physical indication that I might appear guilty, reserving a small part of my brain like a radar-scanner to monitor my body for such things as trembling fingers, shifty eyes, hard swallowing, and all the other dead-giveaways that experienced criminals keep under control. I suddenly regretted that I had never been found guilty of homicide. I needed the practice.

CHAPTER 28

I trashed the paper towel and went back into the living room and began channel-surfing for other stories about the mansion. Right at the moment I wished I owned a police scanner. I had a friend in college who owned a police scanner. We listened to it in his dorm at night. It was one of the most uninteresting experiences of my matriculation. Police work generally involves minor investigations that don't come to much. Unless I'm in town.

I didn't find any more stories but I was intrigued by the reporter's description of the mansion as "historic." I wondered who owned it. Did it have official designation? Was it public property? Had I been involved in the destruction of a significant and irreplaceable part of Denver's history? I felt like a real-estate developer.

I turned off the TV.

I had to think.

Was it possible that the police could somehow link the 1964 Chevy with me? They had found it abandoned on the streets of Denver only a thousand times during the past fifteen years. "Thousand" is highballing it but I was in a state of extreme hyperbole. Would Gladys connect the dots and squeal on me? Was I the center of the universe of every lawman in Denver again?

I told myself that I should report my car stolen right now. I still had the perfect alibi—fifteen years of stolen Chevys. It would be the perfect lie if not the perfect crime. But what if the police didn't buy my story? Scribner sure as hell never bought my stories. But then Scribner never hauled me into court and demanded punishment for the manuscripts I sent them. That was before I learned that the slush pile no longer existed. I really ought to buy an updated *Writer's Market*.

I didn't know what to do. By this I mean I knew exactly what to do: if it's broke, don't fix it. This had been my guiding philosophy ever since I realized the futility of home repair, i.e., either call a pro or let fate take its course. Surprisingly I had learned over the years that if I did absolutely nothing, most problems disappeared on their own. This usually made my ego bristle because it likes to interject itself into difficult situations. My ego treats life like a *New York Times* crossword puzzle. It dives right in without regard to consequences, and I think we all know the consequences of working crossword puzzles. Does the word "czygny" ring a bell?

But there was something else that bothered me more than leaving things "well enough alone" as my Maw used to snarl. If someone had set fire to the Riverside mansion, it was probably the same person who burned my car, which meant that my involvement in this affair could be corroborated by at least one living witness, which meant that I could be implicated even if the witness was a crazed arsonist.

I finally had to admit it:

This was the worst All Saints' Day ever.

But the part of my brain that observes with condescension and disdain the things that I often fret over expressed doubt that the police would toss me into Supermax for trespassing in an abandoned house that no longer existed. On the other hand, the part of my brain that tiptoes through tulips and doesn't dare eat a peach told me that a crazed arsonist could make a false accusation that might implicate me in the felonious torching of a priceless historic building.

"Hardly likely," Mr. Disdain sneered.

"Did you ever hear of Fatty Arbuckle?!" Mr. Tulip shrieked.

I stood there astonished as the two of me traded insults. I edged over to my closet and took out my deep forest green Rocky jacket and cap and surreptitiously pulled them on. I picked up my taxi accoutrement and silently slipped out the back door leaving the Bickersons going at it. I cannot tolerate domestic disputes. It's one of the most dangerous situations that a cop can get involved in, according to police scanners.

When I got to the bottom of the fire escape I glanced at my wristwatch: 10:25 a.m. This was Sunday, which meant I normally would not be working at all. Sundays are slow for cab drivers. You have to be exceptionally desperate as well as hard working to make your nut on a Sunday.

Sunday evenings can be lucrative because businessmen are flying out of town, but I had always found it best to quit kidding myself and wait until Monday to drive. This voided the necessity of working hard because Mondays were always busy. Cab drivers refer to Monday as "Little Friday." Friday is the busiest day of the week. Any cab driver who doesn't pull a Friday shift is either insane or a hard worker, and I am neither.

Or am I?

I decided that since I had leased a cab for a week it would make sense to appear to be working on a Sunday if the police showed up and started nosing around. I wanted to "normalize" everything. I wanted the past to not be.

By "past" I mean everything that had happened since Wednesday night and everything that was going to happen in the unforeseeable future. Obviously the future hadn't happened yet but everything that was going to happen had a direct link to the past, was caused by it, and couldn't be stopped—I'm talking about the things that I knew I was destined to do in the future. I felt like an oracle.

Deciding to run by both Shantel's and Lester's houses, I was going to be a human bottle of Listerine trying to kill the millions of mental germs generating the psychological tics that were haunting me. I had gotten involved in the personal life of more than one fare, and now arson investigators were working on Sunday.

I wanted to drive out to the Riverside mansion and get the lowdown from a fireman, or a "firefighter" if it was a woman, but I fought the urge. The police sometimes referred to that tack as "returning to the scene of the crime." Having gone to "the other side" I now understood why criminals did it. They wanted to eradicate any evidence that they might have left behind. Previous to this insight I had always assumed that criminals returned to the scene of the crime because they were nuts.

As I drove to Lester's house I started thinking about the fact that I would have to buy another car. In order to distance myself from "the Chevy Connection" I would have to switch insurance companies, too. I never buy car insurance from people who advertise on TV. I buy it from people who post signs on their front lawns. You've probably seen those signs: "We'll Insure Anybody!"

Nuff said.

But the thought of taking time from my life to scout a new car made me groan as I worked my way east. Doing anything makes me groan, but dipping into my Dyna-Plex savings served only to remind me that I didn't own a golden goose. Or wait—was the goose golden or just the eggs? I didn't know, but one thing I did know was that if unforeseen circumstances drained my savings I would be forced to write a commercial novel, and the fact that I had spent twenty years trying to write commercial novels did not bode well. On the "up" side, being broke had always motivated me to sit down in front of a typewriter, but then most things motivate me to sit down. I've had jobs that forced me to stand up though, like factory jobs and janitorial jobs. That's one reason I was attracted to cab driving. You are forced to sit down—although "forced" is more of an engineering design stricture than a legal mandate. Imagine what traffic would be like if cars didn't have seats.

I knew I would soon be perusing the used car lots along east Colfax. That's where I bought my Chevy twenty years back. I cut a sweet deal with a man who owned a rent-a-wreck agency, one of those places that lease the sorts of mobile dumps that the police would pull over without just cause, beyond moral outrage. But the cars were street-legal, which was bottom-line in my book. Who the hell needed fancy-pants chrome on a bumper? I later offered the dealer fifty bucks for the pink slip and he grabbed it, which may sound unlikely but I had been renting the Chevy for six months anyway. He threw in a free spare tire, which it needed badly.

I had the feeling I would be paying more than fifty bucks now, though. I once drove a young black woman to a Safeway store, and during the trip she explained that she was forced to take a taxi that day because her own car had broken down for good. She told me she was going to buy a new car. "But I'm getting me some *decent* wheels this time! I'm not buying another one of those thousand-dollar cars! I've had it with those thousand-dollar cars! They can *keep* their thousand-dollar cars!" Up until then I was unfamiliar with the concept of the "thousand-dollar car," but as I drove toward Lester's house I felt that I was verging on the cusp of a new experience.

I arrived at the Nagle house and parked. I got out fast. I hurried through the gate and went up to the porch and rang the doorbell. I waited in a kind of cardboard-stiff stance, as if afraid to move for fear of shattering the delicate balance of my determination to learn if Lester was okay, even if it meant calling the police. Rodney's assertion that Lester's father could speak from beyond the grave was so offensive that I wanted to see Rodney hauled away in cuffs, even though I was fully aware that there was no law against insulting people's intelligence—which may have worked to my advantage in the past.

I remained in my frozen stance for one minute, then dropped the façade. I punched the doorbell again, then rapped on the glass with my knuckles, which was about as *faux pas* as a cab driver can get. Even ordinary people rarely do that. There's just something about glass that makes people reluctant to pound it with bony objects.

No reply.

I walked over to a picture window and tried to look into the house but the curtains were drawn. If anybody in the neighborhood was watching me commit *faux* #2, I hoped they would write it off as the boorish behavior typical of cab drivers. Just to punctuate the move I went back and pressed the doorbell again and waited until the neighbors wrote me off as an ordinary cabbie. Any time I do things that are legally or socially unacceptable, I go into an "act" and pretend to be doing commonplace things that hopefully appear on the surface to justify my aberrant behavior. I idly wondered if Laurence Olivier did that. I know Peter Lorre did.

I stepped down off the porch and looked up at the second story of the house. I thought about going to the back door and knocking. But I wasn't so sure that the theater critics watching from behind their curtains across the street would approve of that tack. I might appear to be a cat burglar.

I decided against it, not only because I feared a bad review but because I felt certain nobody was home. Mrs. Nagle and her son were gone, and I had the feeling they had not gone to church. At least, not my kind of church. I hadn't been to church since the last time I was home for Christmas, but don't get me started on sin, confession, and absolution. I get enough of that at Sweeney's Tavern. Sweeney once 86'd me for a murder that I want to assure you on my word of honor that I did not actually commit.

I walked back out to the sidewalk, closed the front gate, and gazed up at the house hoping I would look like a disappointed cab driver. I always jump at the opportunity to evoke sympathy from critics. The fact that I really was disappointed in no way invalidated the verisimilitude of my "act." In a way, I guess you could say that I had broken through the "fourth wall" of this melodrama by doing something real onstage—although my audience could not have known that what I was doing was real, even though they probably believed it, which gave me the eerie feeling that I might have broken through a "fifth" wall. I decided to leave before Rod Serling materialized on the porch.

I trudged around to the driver's side door and climbed in. I sat for a moment staring at the house, then became self-conscious. I picked up the microphone and pretended to talk into it. This seemed like something a cab driver might do after experiencing a no-show. I had done it plenty of times before, however, the neighbors might not have been familiar with the procedure. But they were now, the nosy bastards.

I hung the mike on the dash and picked up the trip-sheet and pretended to write something on it, but what I was really doing was wishing I could pull a stakeout. In theory I could have done that because I had a weekly lease—but again, the critics. What would they think of a cab driver who sat in front of a house for six days and nights?

What would you think?

What would the police think?

This made me think of writing a novel about a cat burglar who staked out the houses in the guise of a cabbie. I knew then that I had to get out of there, my standard approach to avoiding the typewriter.

My mental list of things to do had been growing steadily all morning and bottomed out with a visit to the police department. I felt that I would have to go there sooner or later and endure the onerous process of deciding whether to report my Chevy as stolen, or else tell the truth.

I made a feeble attempt to parse this mess.

If someone had burned my Chevy on purpose, might it not be said that—technically—it had been "stolen" insofar as I would never be able to drive it again? But experience had taught me that the police are not intrigued by intellectually satisfying conundrums. They would want to know what my Chevy was doing outside the mansion prior to its getting "fire-stolen" as they might sarcastically put it. Detectives sometimes dabble in sarcasm when all of my ducks are not lined up properly.

I decided that the time had come to go to Shantel's house and risk letting her mother know that I had gotten involved in the personal life of her daughter and her nephew.

As I drove down to 1st Avenue and headed for the Harris house I started thinking about the types of people who believed in ghosts, and seances, and even UFOs. Belief—what a concept: accepting as true something that cannot be proven through demonstrable evidence. Lester was one of those people, but he was just a kid. Kids believe all kinds of things. For instance, at Christmas I told one of my nieces that I was actually the Prince of Portugal who was kidnapped by pirates when I was a baby and brought to Colorado on their ship. I didn't think she would actually believe a ship could travel on land, but her mom got mad at me for "filling my daughter's head with nonsense." I thought that's what heads were for. You be the judge.

I can't pinpoint the year that I finally gave up believing in my belief but my introduction to the scientific method kick-started the process. As I said, I was fifteen years old and was required to describe a candle without making any judgment calls based on personal opinion. I don't know if that cured me of making baseless calls but I do know it took a long time for my faith in belief to wither away, although I will not say that I have entirely given up on belief, in the way that ex-smokers sometimes sneak a cig when they are out of town on business.

For instance I believe that someday I will sell a novel. Whenever I tell this to myself I always add "for a million dollars" but I don't really believe that. I just pretend to believe it because it's like thinking about eating a pizza piping hot from the oven. It makes me feel good. What I actually believe is that I will sell a novel and get a maximum advance of $2,000 and never see a dime in royalties. In fact, I feel uncomfortable calling that a "belief" since it is a demonstrable scientific fact—or it will be if I ever get a goddamn acceptance slip.

I turned right onto 1st, cut toward the country club, then headed north to the Harris house. I parked at the curb feeling less guilty than I had when I drove past in my Chevy the previous night. Taxicabs alleviate guilt. In this way they are like cop cars. You can go anywhere you want in a cop car as long you stay within your jurisdiction. I wonder what would happen if a Denver cop went nuts and drove to New York City in his black-and-white. By "happen" I mean jail time, book deal, TV appearances, and movie contract.

I climbed out of 123 and walked up the elongated S as if I was just a normal cab driver, which I was, although the irony was not lost on me—I wasn't really working that day even though I had paid for a lease. I was just pretending to be working, which is easy to do when you have a one-ton vehicle as demonstrable evidence. This ought to have put the kibosh on my faith in the scientific method but I was too busy ringing the Harris's doorbell to dwell on it.

Mrs. Harris opened the door. She looked at me with an expression that was both blank and familiar, in that I had seen it on the faces of countless women and quite a few men—usually when I showed up in places unexpectedly, but not always.

"Good morning, Mrs. Harris," I said. "I'm Brendan Murphy, I spoke to you on Friday, I drive for Rocky Cab." Surely she remembered me but I wasn't taking any chances. I got all that out as quickly as possible. Habit.

Her eyes flickered beyond me to 123 parked at the curb.

"Why yes, Mr. Murphy," she said with a pleasant smile.

"I just came by because I wanted to ask you a question about your nephew, Lester."

The smile faltered but did not leave her face entirely.

"Would you like to come inside?" she said.

The answer was no because I never want to go anywhere, but I went inside anyway. She led me down the hallway to the living room.

"Is your husband here?" I said. "I would like to speak to him, too."

"Jerry isn't here right now," she said. "He's playing golf down at the club."

I nodded. But I was disappointed. I wanted to discuss Mrs. Nagle and her son and I didn't feel comfortable with the idea of bringing up the subject with just Mrs. Harris. She led me into the living room and offered me a chair.

"What's this about Lester?" she said, sitting down.

"I drove him to a movie on Friday night and he told me that Shantel wanted to apologize to me in person for the problem on Wednesday but that she had been grounded."

"Oh yes, that's true" she said.

"So I thought I would come by and speak to Shantel if she's here. I drove by last night but nobody seemed to be home."

"We went to a play last night at the Denver Center for the Performing Arts," she said.

I froze.

Was I—after all—psychic?

"The play didn't happen to be *Harvey* did it?" I said.

"*The Phantom of the Opera*," she replied.

But of course—Halloween fare.

"If Shantel is home right now I'd like to let her know that everything is fine and that she didn't cause me any trouble with the taxi company."

Mrs. Harris glanced toward the green hallway, then she looked at me and offered a smile/frown. "She can't be disturbed right now."

"Oh?" I said, treading lightly.

"She's writing."

I froze.

"Writing?"

"Sunday is her day for working on her novels, and she absolutely forbids anyone to interrupt her."

My world started to spin.

Sixteen years old and writing novels—in the *plural*?

"Oh," I said again.

"She aspires to become a professional novelist."

"What sort of novels does she write?"

"Fantasy. Swords and sorcery. Kings and queens. That sort of thing."

I thought back to Wednesday. "Is that why she was dressed as a princess on Wednesday night?"

Mrs. Harris raised her chin and smiled as if she was truly delighted. "Yes. She's writing a story about a princess named Ariella."

I nodded. "Lester mentioned that name when I took the kids to the haunted house."

"Shantel went to the DCPA party dressed as Princess Ariella. That's one of her fictional characters."

It was at this point in the conversation that I completely lost my train of thought. The thought that another human being was writing a novel in my vicinity sent me into a tailspin. I could not remember why I had come there.

"You said you wanted to ask me something about Lester," Mrs. Harris said.

Was Mrs. Harris psychic or had I spoken out loud? I have been known to do that whenever my mind takes a nosedive into total blackout.

"Yes … that's right … your nephew … Lester. I spoke to his mother when I picked him up to go to the movie. After the events on Wednesday night I wanted to make certain that he had permission to take a taxi." I smiled when I said that, pardner, but she did not return the smile. "Lester's mother is your husband's sister, is that correct?"

She nodded.

I nodded back. I had taken this conversation to the edge and was not certain how much further I should go. In my experience, tailspins, nosedives, and blackouts were followed by crash landings. I thought about my Chevy burning up.

Lakehurst, New Jersey, here I come.

"Lester told me that his father died ten years ago. The reason I bring it up is because …" I took a deep breath, "… I thought his father had called for a taxi on Friday night, and to be perfectly honest I wasn't certain that Lester was telling me the truth, which is why I asked to speak to his mother."

"Lester's father died of a heart attack when Lester was six. That's one of the reasons my husband is out playing golf."

"Ma'am?"

"Lester's father was thirty-eight years old when he died. He was a smoker and never lifted a finger to exercise. My husband Jerry exercises regularly."

I myself did that once—if two sessions at a health club can be defined as "once."

"Can I ask you a question about Lester's mother?" I said.

Mrs. Harris nodded.

It was none of my business but I had long ago gotten used to asking questions that were none of my business. What the hell—in for a penny, in for a pound. I wondered why the word "penny" made it across the Atlantic while "pound" was left standing on the dock at Liverpool. Where did the word "dollar" come from anyway?

"When I took the call at Lester's house I was told that the party's name was Nagle, not Harris," I said.

Mrs. Harris closed her eyes and nodded. "My sister-in-law's married name is Nagle. Her husband, Herbert Nagle, was a financial planner. She still goes by his name. She and my … well … she and Jerry do not get along."

"I see," I said quickly. "I thought I was going to pick up a man named Nagle, so when Lester appeared at the door I didn't understand what was going on."

Mrs. Harris sighed. "Lester's mother has … disowned her brother."

A chill crept down my spine. I had blundered into the jurisdiction of a domestic dispute, about which I wanted to know nothing. In some ways I am not unlike a cop. A smart cop anyway.

Mrs. Harris shook her head sadly. "Lester does not have a male presence in the household to give him guidance," she said. "He is a troubled boy."

Tell me about it.

"Mother?"

"Yes?"

I looked around.

Shantel was standing in the doorway.

"What time will daddy be home?"

"I don't know, dear. He said he would be playing eighteen holes." Mrs. Harris looked at me. "Sunday is eighteen-hole day for Jerry." She stood up and smiled at Shantel. "Mr. Murphy came by to see you," she said.

I stood up and turned to Shantel. She looked pale. Her eyes were probing mine. I apologize for using that cliché but my eyes had been "probed" so many times in my life that I not only recognized the look, I had learned that there was no better word for it—with the possible exception of "drilled."

"Are you finished writing for the day?" Mrs. Harris said.

"No, Mom, I just came downstairs to get a soda."

"I'll get it for you, dear. Mr. Murphy has something he wants to say to you. Would you like a soda too, Mr. Murphy?"

"Oh no thanks," I said, "I have to be taking off pretty quick here."

"All right. I'll be back in a moment."

I wondered if she was going to look for a butler. I wasn't certain how rich people went about getting stuff.

"I thought I heard your voice," Shantel said abruptly after her mother disappeared down the hallway. "That's why I came downstairs. Did you *tell*?"

"Tell what?" I said.

"That I *met* you at the *mall*." She looked scared.

"No I didn't. You asked me not to tell your parents. But I have something to ask you."

"What?"

"Is your cell phone disconnected?"

She closed her eyelids hard, then opened them hard. Teenage girls are masters at that. She was communicating exasperation. "My parents took my cell phone away. That's part of my punishment for lying about Wednesday."

"Oh," I said. "The reason I asked is because I tried to call you last night."

"I couldn't have answered anyway. My parents made me go to a *play* with them. The DCPA people won't let anyone bring a cell phone into the auditorium."

My respect for live theater rose a few notches. I'll admit it. I'm pretty much a movie guy.

"Do you know if Lester is home right now?" I said, playing a little "game." "I'm going to drive over to his house. I want to talk to him about something."

She shrugged and said, "I don't know."

"What can you tell me about this Rodney guy?" I said.

Shantel glanced down the hallway at the snap of a pop-top. "Why did you *come* here?"

Nonplussed, I thought quickly, which I had gotten good at ever since I first met Shantel.

"I was originally on my way over to Lester's house and as long as I was in the neighborhood I thought I would drop by and ask why your cell phone was disconnected." I pulled out my billfold and opened it, removed the phone number that she had written down, and handed it to her. "I guess I won't be needing this anymore."

She took the slip of paper, then looked at my eyes. The word "drill" would not be inappropriate here. "That guy Rodney worries me."

"Why?"

"Lester told me Rodney suggested they hold a seance with Mrs. Nagle. He said she would be able to communicate with her departed husband. He wanted Lester to ask if she might be interested in doing that."

"Here you go, dear," Mrs. Harris said. She was walking toward us holding a can of soda.

"Thanks, Mom," Shantel said, taking it and raising it to her lips. As she sipped from the can she looked me right in the eye.

"Your mother tells me you write novels," Peter Lorre casually intoned.

Shantel almost choked.

"*Moth*-er," she said.

"I'm sorry, dear," Mrs. Harris said with a smile/frown. She looked at me. "Shantel doesn't like to talk about her writing."

"I understand," I said. "I've been trying to write novels myself since college and I never discuss it with anyone," unless I'm at Sweeney's.

"Really?" Shantel said, lowering the can and gazing at me curiously. The tenor of the conversation changed, although my scalp was still tingling from that business about the seance.

"I don't like to talk about my rejection slips either," I said.

Shantel's eyes brightened. "You've actually gotten *rejection* slips?" she said, as if a rejection slip was the most marvelous thing imaginable.

"Lots of them," I said.

She was now gazing at me the way a princess might gaze at an enchanted frog. "I've never had the nerve to send any of my books to a publisher," she said.

My heart took a nosedive. "You will someday," I said. "Rejection slips are part of the game."

A somber look came over her face. "I don't think of writing as a game," she said. "I take writing very seriously."

This was one of the reasons I didn't like to talk about my writing—I sometimes got lectures. My friend Big Al is the only cab driver at Rocky Cab that I know of who does not aspire to write novels, although I purposely don't know all of the drivers. But every driver I do know has at least one unpublished manuscript in the works. Big Al doesn't seem to have much faith in my literary aspirations, but he has never tried to dissuade me from writing novels. I think he prefers to sit back and watch fate take its course.

"Who's your favorite author?" Shantel said.

"I doubt if you've ever heard of …" Bukowski "… him."

"I mostly write fantasies," she said, "but my favorite author is Victor Hugo."

My world started to spin.

I had to get out of there. I couldn't breathe.

"I guess I better get back to work," I said. "Thank you for taking the time to talk to me."

"You're welcome, Mr. Murphy," Shantel said.

"I hope the two of you got everything settled," Mrs. Harris said, as if Shantel and I had been discussing the decorations for a high school prom.

Shantel nodded. "I'm going to walk Mr. Murphy out to his taxi."

"Okay, honey," Mrs. Harris said.

I felt sort of embarrassed listening to their affable mother/daughter exchange. My Maw never called me "honey" after cutting off my phone privileges. "Hooligan" was her word. This involved prank phone calls but let's move on.

Shantel silently escorted me down the sidewalk to the curb. She glanced back at the house, then looked at me and said, "Do you remember when you called me yesterday after you visited the mansion at that cemetery?"

I nodded. "You told me your parents came home and you had to hang up."

She nodded quickly and said, "The thing is, Mr. Murphy, I wasn't sure whether to tell you something, but I decided I should. Lester called and told me that he and Rodney used the Ouija board. He said he contacted his father again."

"Ouija boards aren't real," I said, even though you could buy them at novelty shops. You can also buy rubber chickens and throw-your-voice gadgets that don't work.

"The thing I wanted to tell you though, is that I found out Lester didn't go to that mansion at the cemetery," she said. "He went to Rodney's house out by Golden."

She was taking her time getting to the point. This troubled me. I hoped she didn't have the same problem with her novels. I did.

"Do you know the haunted house that you took us to on Wednesday night out by Golden?"

I nodded. I was trying to act casual, which I am good at. When you've driven a taxi as long as I have you get good at remaining cool under circumstances ranging from flat tires to dead customers. It's a rather wide range.

"I'm going to take a run past Lester's house and talk to him. I just wanted to …" talk about my burning taxi "… make sure he got home okay."

"I'm sorry I made you go all the way to Globeville for nothing," Shantel said. "I would still like to pay you for your time."

"I wasn't on duty yesterday," I said. "If I'm not in a taxi I do things for free." This was a lie. I never do anything when I'm not in my taxi.

The entire time I was talking to her, I was debating whether to ask if she knew that the Riverside mansion had burned down. I couldn't tell by her demeanor whether she had seen the newscasts on TV. She didn't seem rattled as I would have expected, but what did I know about the demeanor of teenage girls. I never dated in high school. I just crashed parties and hoped for the best. I didn't start dating until my first army furlough. It coincided with the first time I went off-limits and the first time I was apprehended by MPs. Three's a charm, they say.

"Did you watch the news on TV this morning?" I said.

"We don't own a TV," she replied.

I'm not going to waste your time or mine describing my psychological as well as my physiological response to her statement. Let's just say I was floored.

But this explained why she hadn't made any reference to the debacle. Should I let her know what happened? I decided not to fix it even though it wasn't broken. That would be a first.

"Good luck with your writing," I said.

For a second I thought she looked annoyed. Or was it just a psychosomatic response on my part to the guilt I felt at having said "luck" to someone who did not treat writing as a game and who did not have a TV to serve as a convenient excuse for not writing?

"Good luck to you, too," she said.

This annoyed me. If luck was all I needed to get published I would be a millionaire by now. What I really needed was talent. That's what the how-to books say anyway.

"Thanks," I said, trying to act casual as I opened the rear door, then shut it and opened the door to the driver's seat. I'm good at acting casual but I haven't perfected it yet.

I headed to Speer Boulevard and drove in the direction of downtown. Shantel hadn't enlightened me as to Lester's current whereabouts, but she had confirmed something that I had suspected. Lester had gotten further involved with this Rodney character. Then something occurred to me. Suppose Rodney was on the up-and-up. Suppose seances were real. Suppose you actually could communicate with the dead. If so, maybe I could put in a call to me ol' Dad and ask if there was ever any insanity in our family.

I could phone Maw in Wichita but I already knew what she would say: "Just look in the mirror, boy-o."

My attempt to sort things out suddenly brought on "The Fear" again. But it wasn't due to excess. It was due to something far less common.

I glanced at my wristwatch. This only increased the intensity of "The Fear" because the hour hand was telling me something that I secretly hoped it wouldn't.

The only person I was acquainted with who had the intellectual capacity to sort things out, read, figure odds, juggle races in five states simultaneously, light cigarettes, and cut to the chase without being distracted by my presence was seated in an off-track betting joint in north Denver that was now open for the day.

I began sweating bullets.

I swallowed hard.

I surreptitiously glanced left and right.

None of this helped. I knew that I had arrived at another Rubicon. The events of the past four days had given me the spiritual equivalent of "writer's block." The fact that I did not believe in writer's block held no relevance—a writer writes, even if it's only letters to his Maw begging for loans. No, I had reached a point in my life where I was blocked at every turn and did not know what to do. I do this frequently so I recognized the signs. I had no choice but to seek counsel from the one person who had less interest in my personal problems than your average IRS agent.

Big Al.

CHAPTER 29

I drove to downtown Denver and headed for the 15th Street bridge. The off-track betting joint was located on the far side of the Platte River. Passing over the bridge was like crossing the River Styx—the thing I feared most was waiting on the other side and I don't mean Death. I mean "free advice." Big Al never charged me for "consultations" but there was always a price to pay, and I'm not talking obnoxious nicknames. I had to endure dour looks, extended silences, and sarcasm so subtle that it sometimes took me a few minutes to I realize I had been insulted. But that was a price I was willing to pay because it didn't involve money.

I crossed the bridge and drove halfway up a hill where the joint was located. It was inside a four-story nineteenth-century office building that had avoided the wrecking ball of urban renewal. The place had charm, ambience, and losers. I dropped off a lot of fares there over the years. The odds of myself ever being a loser was zero because Big Al had cured me of gambling a long time ago. But I don't want to mislead you—the word "loser" does have a wider range of connotations than making legal wagers for sporting purposes.

Let's drop it.

I climbed the concrete staircase and entered the joint. It was crowded as usual. I recognized the faces of a few men who had sat in the back of my taxi during years gone by. They were as wistful as ever. Fortunately, none of them recognized the back of my head. My ponytail was a relatively recent addition to my dramatic persona. Ironically my ponytail came about as a result of a man suffering from a gambling addiction, but let's not get into that.

I scanned the tables where the bettors were ripping tickets in two, perusing tip-sheets, and examining tote-boards. Television sets were hiked on the walls near the ceiling broadcasting races from Saratoga to Pimlico.

I was grateful to Big Al for curing me of gambling. Just the sight of a television made me want to participate. I really ought to get involved in public-access TV, the methadone of failed sitcom writers.

Suddenly I saw Big Al. He was seated alone at a table in a far corner scribbling on a tip-sheet. He was figuring the odds. I hated to interrupt him. Any time anybody is doing anything, I feel guilty making my presence known. I can only speculate as to what my sudden appearance actually feels like to another person, although I have a theory that it's similar to hearing a telephone ring.

I edged behind a group of men who were discussing a mudder at Del Mar. I had no idea what a "mudder" was, which was probably for the best. I watched Big Al, hoping he would set his pencil down. I wanted to take advantage of the brief hiatus between his setting the pencil down and glancing at a tote-board to make my presence known. He might not mind being interrupted if he was engaged in the unproductive physical activity of moving his eyeballs.

But it was like waiting for a dog to stop chewing on a steak bone. I finally gave up. Giving up is always the first step in talking to Big Al.

I took a deep breath and sauntered out from behind the mudder men and casually made my way through the crowd as if I was just another loser enjoying his day off. Big Al set his pencil down and raised his eyes to a tote-board directly above my head. He glanced at me, looked at the board, then glanced at me again.

I slowed and braced myself for an onslaught of derision followed by a lecture on the evils of gambling.

"What's popping, weekly lease?" he said. "Did you drop off a fare here, or did you come here to gamble, which I know you did not."

I stopped dead in my tracks and tried to sort things out. Big Al had hit me with three questions, only one of which applied to me. I swallowed hard.

"How did you know I was on a weekly lease?" I said. I was being disingenuous of course. Like Hogan and Rollo, Big Al knew everything that went on at Rocky Cab.

He gave me a dour look. This was followed by an extended silence. The only thing left was subtle sarcasm, but I knew from experience that I would have to give him something to "chew on" before I ran that gauntlet.

Suddenly he said, "Oh no."

I nodded.

We had reached a point in our relationship where we communicated by a kind of shorthand that abrogated the necessity of him saying, "You got involved in the personal life of another fare, didn't you Greenhorn?"—at which point I would grovel obsequiously and try to withhold superfluous information from him. This worked to my advantage because Big Al always wanted to know "as few details as possible."

He took a deep breath and sighed, then pointed at the empty chair across from him.

I sat down quickly, clasped my hands, and smiled with a rictus that you see in horror films about men who die in the throws of madness. Renfield looked like this without even being dead.

"How are the horses running?" I said, violating our Code of Brevity.

"I can't win for losing," he replied

This frightened me. Big Al was not like the rest of the losers in the joint. His approach to horse racing involved the scientific method. This meant he won more often than anybody I ever met, and he also knew precisely when to quit. The same was said of Rene Descartes. So the thought of asking Big Al for advice when he was having a bad day placed a large pall of gloom on my shoulders that replaced the little pall that was always there.

"I need help," I said.

"We passed that milestone thirty seconds ago," he said. "Does this involve money?"

"No."

"Male or female?"

"Both."

He closed his eyes and sighed, then placed his pencil in his shirt pocket and pushed his tip-sheet aside.

He leaned back in his chair, folded his arms, and gazed at me with an extended silence. He then smiled a thin-lipped smile and said, "You fascinate me, Tenderfoot." He cocked his head to one side. "I have never known anyone quite like you."

I blushed with pride. That didn't last long.

"I have devoted the best years of my life trying hard not to understand you," he said. "But I think the time has come to throw in the towel. Aside from possessing a degree in English, is there any other explanation, excuse, or rationale for your seemingly chronic inability to operate a taxi-cab three days a week without driving off a cliff?"

"Probably," I said.

"That narrows it down."

"Also … I was raised Catholic."

"I fully agree," he replied. "Your familiarity with the parable of The Good Samaritan seems to have taken root to such an extent that not even the deft handiwork of a highly skilled tree surgeon could prune the tangled webwork of your unbridled altruism."

"Are you gonna help me or not?" I scowled.

He sat forward, rested his forearms on the table, and clasped his hands together "mirroring" my posture—or was it "mocking"?

He glanced one last time at the tote-board above my head, quickly cleaned a back tooth with his tongue, then looked me in the eye and said, "As you well know, I have always been averse to learning the grim details leading up to the climactic denouements of your escapades, however I believe I am going to make an exception in this case. If I interpret the look on your face correctly, you have managed to mire yourself in a land-scape of terra incognita so unprecedented that I will not be able to judge the depth of your involvement or offer a viable solution without knowing every single, tiny, molecular detail of the embarrassing predicament that you have managed to engineer through the inimitable ineptitude that is the hallmark of every Murphy Moment I have been forced to endure throughout the past fifteen years."

"Is that a yes?"

He closed his eyes and nodded.

"I think someone is out to get me," I said.

That pulled him up short.

"Why do you think that?" he said, the sarcasm suddenly evaporat-ing from his voice. It was replaced by a tone resembling that of a Denver police detective named Argyle.

"Somebody burned up my Chevy."

"When did this happen?"

"Last night."

"At your apartment building?"

"No. It happened over near Riverside Cemetery."

"What were you doing there last night?"

"Trespassing inside a house."

He studied my face for a moment. He had the same look in his eyes that always appeared one minute before a horse race was set to begin, a volatile moment which takes place at all racetracks when the odds on a tote-board rapidly change. I knew what was going on behind those eyes: he was "calculating." Big Al could place bets faster than any man alive.

He held up a palm the way people do to halt speeding trains.

"I see now that I made a mistake," he said. "My attempt to better understand the way your mind works by delving into the details of your case has gotten off to a bad start. But this can be accredited to the fact that I am somewhat of an amateur when it comes to showing the slightest interest in anything you do. The gun was jumped, as it were. Therefore I am going to ask you a series of specific questions and I want you to give me simple, straightforward, honest answers."

Now he sounded like a district attorney. Which D.A. doesn't matter—they all ask specific questions.

"I can only surmise that your illegal presence in a house near a cemetery on Halloween and the subsequent burning of your Chevy was preceded by what I shall refer to as 'events.' Therefore I would like to ask you precisely when the first 'event' took place?"

"Last Wednesday."

"Very good. We are making progress. What time on Wednesday?"

"Six-thirty p.m."

"Excellent. What was the nature of this event?"

I proceeded to describe in molecular detail the trip from DCPA to the house in Golden. Even though it was in my nature to leave things out, I didn't. I told him about my fear of having to pay a double late fee, which overrode the altruism that he had mentioned earlier. Like everything else in my life, even my altruism is flawed—or "half-assed" as Big Al quietly interjected.

Rather than drag you through my monologue I will leave out most of it since you've already been there. I'll also leave out 90 percent of the expressions that flitted across Big Al's face during my narrative. I will leave that to your imagination, which is probably better than mine, based on my rejection slips.

I described the Thursday conversation where Hogan had told me that as far as he was concerned the buck had stopped. I told Big Al about the L-2 on Friday, and the subsequent visit to the Harris house where I received absolution.

From that point on the narrative changed from a monologue to a litany: the meeting with Mrs. Nagle, chauffeuring Lester to the Flicker, the meeting with Shantel at the mall, my visit to the Riverside mansion, the discovery of the pentagram, the trip to the mansion on Halloween night, the burning of my Chevy, and my mad dash through the graveyard. I've left out some of the litany but you were there. You lived it. It bored me to relive it, too.

"So you do not know for a fact that you were actually chased through the cemetery?" Big Al said.

"No," I said. "I think I was just seeing shadows made by the flashlight."

Then I got to the hard or "trespassing" part as I hated to call it again.

"I bought a dozen flashlights at a Safeway, a quart of ammonia, some tools, and a couple cans of white spray paint."

I kept waiting for Big Al to interrupt and ask specific questions about my mind, but he seemed content to sit mesmerized like a boy in a theater watching a horror film unfold. The only thing missing from this tableau was a box of popcorn and the screaming of little gurlz.

It's a funny thing about human eyes. Except for the pupils, eyeballs themselves never change size, and yet they are the most expressive parts of the human body. They can communicate delight, disgust, fright, bafflement, amusement, and disbelief without changing shape. It is virtually impossible to put into words the "glazed look of boredom" that appears in the eyes of most people I have conversations with, aside from simply saying "glazed look of boredom." Another look that's difficult to articulate is the disbelief one sees in the eyes of people when they know you are telling a lie. You may have experienced this yourself. But what *is* it exactly? What is it about those one-inch globes of static gelatin planted in our skulls that communicate so effectively the thoughts taking place inside that three-pound pot-roast lodged between our ears?

The only explanation I have to offer is eyelids. They seem to play the same role that the setup plays in a comedic performance. Eyelids may be 90 percent of the joke. This in no way diminishes the contribution of the eyebrows, as well as frown lines, but the eyelids seem to carry most of the burden. Big Al's eyelids underwent a heavy workout that afternoon, however not once did I detect disbelief—or for that matter, delight, except when I mentioned Rollo's clown costume. We both had a good chuckle over that.

As I described my brain floating out of my head and my trip back to the mansion in #123 bent on revenge, I began to feel like lowlife scum confessing a crime—or a sin. I doubt if Big Al made a distinction. He went to a Jesuit high school. Jesuits are not big on the concept of hair-splitting your way to innocence.

His eyes remained riveted on mine as I described tossing the flash-lights into rooms like smoke-grenades. He occasionally rubbed his chin and cocked his head at various angles. But when I described spray-painting the pentagram white he froze.

"Were you wearing gloves?" he said.

"Yes."

He neither nodded with approval nor fainted with relief.

"But that wouldn't have mattered anyway," I said.

"Why not?"

"Because when I woke up this morning I saw a newscast on TV that said the Riverside mansion burned to the ground last night."

He stared at me for so long that I began to feel uncomfortable. I countered it with a feeble smile. "I guess this means that all of the evidence of my trespassing is now … gone with the wind."

His expression became dour. He likes neither *Gone With the Wind* nor puns.

"Continue the story," he said.

I then clasped my hands on the table and waited for Big Al to evaluate my predicament and advise me what to do in twenty-five words or less. He had done this many times in the past. Usually he said, "Pretend it never happened and get on with your life."

"What time did you leave the Riverside mansion last night?" he said.

"11:59."

Big Al glanced at his wristwatch, looked at the tote-board, then looked at me with an expression that I can only describe as "surrender." I had a funny feeling that he had been waiting for that race all my life.

He sat back in his chair and took a deep breath. "Well Tenderfoot, I am going to do something I've never done before. The facts in this case are not merely appalling, they are disturbing. As a consequence I am going to violate a vow that I made a long time ago, and become involved in the personal life of Brendan Murphy."

A chill ran down my spine.

CHAPTER 30

We rode in silence.

Across the Styx and over to Broadway, then up the viaduct and down to Brighton Boulevard. I drove 123 while Big Al sat in the backseat like a common fare even though the meter was not running. Most taxi drivers insist on sitting shotgun when they ride in my cab, as if the backseat was beneath them. But Big Al had climbed into the backseat without saying a word. I kept glancing at the mirror expecting to see him glaring at me, but he was looking straight ahead with a distant gaze in his eyes. I had the feeling he was thinking. I have often stated that silence in a taxi can be unnerving, but nothing can compare to silence combined with thinking, because the fare is usually thinking about hopping out and running away without paying.

When we passed Globeville he told me to take the same route through the cemetery that I had driven the first time I had visited the mansion. He, too, wanted to see the place from within the camouflaging perimeter of the boneyard. I pointed out the Doctor Who booth as I drove past. He seemed to know who Doctor Who was. I wanted desperately to discuss *Doctor Who and the Daleks* with him, but I thought it best to wait for a more appropriate time, if there really is an appropriate time to discuss low-budget British television.

I pointed out the place where I had sat on the ground with a rock and a flashlight in my hands. I did not slow down as we rolled past the ruins of the mansion on the far side of the cemetery. The fire trucks had departed and a yellow police tape had been strung across the driveway. I glanced in the mirror and saw Big Al looking directly at the ruins. He made no attempt to hide his fixed stare from anyone who might be spying on us. This made me uncomfortable. I never like anybody knowing that I can see anything because it inevitably leads to questions. Blackboards come to mind.

"That's the direction I ran," I said, pointing at the rear of the ruins and then sweeping my finger through the middle of the cemetery and on to Brighton Boulevard. "The rich people are buried where the gravestones are the tallest," I said, even though I did not know this for a fact. But it made me feel "special" to say it. I have often toyed with the idea of starting a "Tour of Denver" business where I would point out the places where Abraham Lincoln was assassinated, or Charles Lindberg built the first atomic bomb, but I would give the tour only to out-of-towners. The residents of Denver probably already know that stuff.

"Pull over here," Big Al said.

I stopped near the spot where the tombstone looked like a log cabin. Big Al stared at the smoldering ruins of the mansion. "Obviously the work of a desperate man. Rodney may have been pressed for time and needed to cover his tracks."

"Why would he cover his tracks?" I said.

"Because he fears you."

I almost fainted.

I had been waiting all my life to hear those words. When I was ten years old my dream was to stand astride the continent like a Colossus. I used to stand like that on the monkeybars at grade school until Leo Gorcey pounded me.

"What does he have to fear from me?" I said.

"Under ordinary circumstances my reply to that question would be obvious if there was such a thing as a rhetorical answer, but in this case the individual who generated the coverup may have feared that you would call the police and thus thwart his ultimate goal."

"What's his ultimate goal?"

Big Al's face turned stone-cold hard. "That's what I intend to find out. The time has come for us to connect the dots."

"Which dots?" I said. I have a lot of dots in my life.

"I'll tell you later. Right now we better leave. It may have been a mistake to return to the scene of the crime."

I couldn't believe it. I was way ahead of him on that angle. I wanted desperately to tell him how slick I was, but instead I put 123 into gear and casually drove away from the stone cabin.

"As long as we're here I want to show you something cool," I said.

I heard him sigh. It was like hearing an impatient cop watching me tie my shoes.

I circled around and drove along a dirt road that took us down a short slope that ran past a cliff-like earthen berm with doors set into the vertical face.

"Crypts," I said.

I glanced at the rearview mirror. Big Al was peering at the doors with curiosity.

"Cool huh?" I said.

"I will concede that it was almost worth the wait," he replied. "Now let us depart."

"Back to the betting joint?" I said.

"No. We will be going to my house."

A chill crept down my spine. No driver at the Rocky Mountain Taxi-cab Company had the slightest idea where Big Al lived, which is exactly how he wanted it. Hogan may have been the only person at Rocky who knew his address. It was kept under lock and key in the personnel files. Of course anybody could have simply followed Big Al home if they wanted to know where he lived, a fact that underscored the irrationality of cabbie paranoia. But knowing where a cab driver lives is not the same thing as having access to his living room. Most cabbies are loners for reasons that may not be obvious, and should remain so. I have lived in my crow's nest for more than fifteen years and have had only one unexpected visitor—aside from a fully armed S.W.A.T. team, but they don't count. My visitor was Harold. He doesn't count either.

CHAPTER 31

"Take Interstate Seventy to Sheridan and go north," Big Al said.

I drove back down Brighton Boulevard then worked my way over to the I-70 entry ramp. I didn't say anything. I obeyed orders like a cab driver indifferent to the destination of a fare. But inside I was bristling with anticipation. Big Al was directing me toward his place of residence. I felt like I was about to learn the secret of Soylent Green.

I rolled onto the interstate and accelerated to 55 m.p.h. then set my ankle on cruise-control. Sheridan Boulevard came up fast. I love interstates. As I say, they are like time machines—you can be miles away from everything in terms of space, but in terms of time you are right next to everything. I exited the off-ramp at Sheridan and slowed for traffic, but there was none. Denver is dead on Sundays. This was true of all the cities I had ever passed through with the exceptions of Frisco and La La Land. Don't ever say "Frisco" when you're in Frisco. The beatniks will think you're a hick from the stix. A learned thing.

We passed 52nd Avenue and proceeded down a long hill. I began to grow uneasy. We were headed in the direction of a suburb called "Arvada." Arvada is the Aurora of the west side. But he told me to take a right at an intersection halfway down the hill. I swung 123 onto an asphalt road that wound toward a trailer park.

Trailer park!

Was this the secret of Soylent Green? Was Big Al one of those bachelors who cut costs by renting—or perhaps even owning—a mobile home? I knew a guy in college who lived in a mobile home. He seemed so contented it was frightening. I'll admit that I once toyed with the idea of going mobile, but there was one problem: neighbors. They spent most of their time sitting outside on lawn chairs. Whenever I visited my friend I felt like I was being watched. I'd felt that way all my life but until college I never had any tangible proof. Whenever I drove up to his mobile home, climbed the steps, and knocked on his door, scores of people with slowly wavering flyswatters sat silently watching, watching, watching … and waiting. I had a pretty good idea what they were waiting for. I always brought two six-packs with me. I finally told my buddy he had to either meet me at the Campus Lounge or start living in a dorm. Our friendship eventually withered to nothing, as do most friendships based on brewski and satellite-dish TV.

I instinctively took my foot off the accelerator as we neared the entrance to the trailer park. Noting the deceleration Big Al said, "Keep driving."

Embarrassed that my ankle had "passed judgment" on him, I gave the gas some toe and kept driving toward an area covered with trees. We were rolling along a slope that bottomed out at Clear Creek a few hundred yards farther downhill. That part of Denver is relatively undeveloped. It's not unlike the landscape out toward Golden. I wasn't kidding when I said Arbor Day careened completely out of control.

The asphalt road entered a shaded area that brought to mind the word "glen." The farther I drove, the more the language changed. The road dipped slightly and we entered what I took to be a "dell." The few one-story houses that I saw back in the trees were so camouflaged that I had no way of judging their age—pre-Great Depression was my best guestimate.

There was no curb at the edges of the asphalt, just dirt shoulders. Large bushes grew close to the road. Tree branches extended over the asphalt cutting off the sunlight. We were riding in shadow. The road meandered until a broad, unkempt lawn came into view. A small house stood fifty feet back from the road, a red-shingled white clapboard structure that had Herbert Hoover written all over it.

"Pull into the driveway," Big Al said.

The driveway was a dirt two-track that led toward a small garage. I pulled in and parked, shut off the engine, and gazed at the house, which was crowded by bushes and thick-leaved overhanging branches. I couldn't believe it. Big Al lived in a *grotto*!

"Follow me inside," he said, climbing out of the backseat and walking across the dead lawn toward his front door. I felt like a presidential aide walking across the lawn at Camp David in one of those thrillers from the 1960s where the fate of the entire world pivoted on the mental health of the man in the Oval Office. But I always feel that way. I live in somewhat of a fantasy world when I'm not asleep.

I followed Big Al inside.

There was nothing particularly notable about the interior of Big Al's house with the possible exception of the baby grand piano. Also, one entire wall was hidden by what I can only describe as a home-entertainment system. I grew apoplectic with envy. I had never seen HDTV in person. But I am not going to describe the interior of the house to you in detail, although I would give my eye-teeth to describe that *rug*! Plus the lighting scheme, the video collection, and his mind-boggling library of eclectic literature. But taxi drivers are a secretive lot who jealously guard their privacy. Take me for example: absolutely nobody knows that I have a bookshelf built out of rejected manuscripts except people who drink at Sweeney's.

"Have a seat, Tenderfoot," he said, pointing at a couch. He sat on an overstuffed chair, which I noted was placed perpendicular to his media system. I was seated off to the side, which meant that the cumulative effect of the quadraphonic speakers would have been lost on me if he had been playing the stereo. A quick glance at his CD collection indicated that he owned more Stones albums than Beatles, but I forgave him.

"When I was a boy I had an aunt in Tulsa who was taken to the cleaners by a group of people who claimed to be fortune tellers," Big Al began.

"Tulsa?" I said. "Why did she live in Tulsa?"

"Enid was full," he replied patiently. "My aunt had a great deal of money. Her husband, whose name was Clyde Ambrewster, was a wildcatter. He made his oil money during the nineteen-twenties, and when he died my aunt became a wealthy widow. She passed away fifteen years ago in a nursing home. Her care was paid for by public assistance. I'm talking relief. Charity. Welfare. Taxpayers."

Was he kidding me?

Tulsa?

Why would a rich person live in Tulsa?

I was developing a psychological tic. I quickly placed it into the drawer in my mind where I keep other tics too numerous to mention, some of which I had forgotten about until I opened the drawer. It's like a goddamn Pandora's Box in there.

"I do not believe in ghosts," he said, "or astrology, palmistry, UFOs, Abominable Snowmen, the number thirteen, or any of the various categories of inexplicable paranormal or supernatural phenomena that bolstered the mythology of the human race since the first eclipse was viewed by a caveman who attributed the disappearance of the sun to the appetite of a giant invisible dragon who could be appeased only by the sacrifice of a virgin."

Virgin?

What does celibacy have to do with the alignment of orbiting planets?

"My point exactly," Big Al said, sending a shudder down my spine.

I tried to think of nothing.

"When you informed me that Mrs. Nagle is a wealthy widow, it sent up a red flag in my mind. Unless I am mistaken, Rodney Letour—if that's his real name—is out to defraud Lester's mother."

Suddenly the niggling fears and nagging mysteries of the past few days fell away like the dried skin of a dead locust. Reality had sat down on the couch next to me. It usually sits on my lap.

"If Rodney's *modus operandi* resembles that of the people who looted my aunt's bank account and forced her into poverty," Big Al continued, "then I fear he is currently worming his way into Mrs. Nagle's life and gaining her trust. He apparently has befriended her son who, with the understandable naiveté of youth, has been brought into the concept of communicating with the dead. However I do not believe that the transfer of funds necessarily will happen abruptly. I believe that he will tap into Mrs. Nagle's desire to speak to her husband and simultaneously tap into her funds until they are depleted. This is what happened to my aunt. It took six months before anybody in the family learned what was going on, but by that time the perpetrators had disappeared. They were never caught."

My heart sank deeper than the *Titanic* as I fully comprehended the depths of my responsibility for this untenable situation. If only I had not driven the kids to the haunted house without parental permission. If only … if only … if only …

"Don't blame yourself," Big Al said in a kindly tone of voice. "You were born that way."

I resented this. I was as self-made as any sap can get. I would stack my blunders up against anybody who was born in Tulsa and still lives there.

Don't get me wrong though. I have nothing against Tulsa. I've never even been there. I was just lashing out in blind anger, and Oklahoma happened to be handy.

"Let's call the police," I said.

"I'm way ahead of you," Big Al said. "People who defraud the elderly are masters at hiding their moves. We currently have no evidence that this Letour fellow is guilty of bilking Mrs. Nagle. He may not have brought up the subject of money with her at this point in the worming process."

I bristled with impatience. Of *course* Letour was guilty. There are certain people in this world who have an innate sense of who is guilty and who is innocent, and I am one of those people, along with auto mechanics, bowlers, and guys who mumble on street corners.

I know what you're thinking—what an outrageous statement! Obviously you are not one of us.

"And there is another possibility to consider," Big Al said in a somber tone of voice.

"What's that?"

"I may be wrong."

I stared at Big Al incredulously. This lasted six seconds. Then I burst out laughing.

"You? Wrong?"

I swear I wasn't feeding his hungry bee. I doubted if Big Al even had an ego. If there was anyone I had ever met who could cut right through to the sheer pointlessness of pride, gold, or the Nobel Committee, it was Big Al. His sterling record at the dog track was the result of cold-blooded arithmetical computations devoid of guesswork, hope, or sentimentalism. He was the exact opposite of people who needed some kind of goddamn therapy.

"Have you ever heard of Harry Houdini?" Big Al said.

"No," I said. "Who's that?"

It didn't work. I can't recreate the condescending tone in my voice, but he could hear right through it. Any American male who hasn't heard of Harry Houdini should be exiled to the colonies if we still have any. Big Al was just setting me up.

Little did I realize that I was the punch line.

"Houdini spent years exposing the fraud of psychic mediums."

Everybody knew this. Why was he telling me this? Why was he asking me questions that had obvious answers? Why was he describing historical facts that were common knowledge? Why was he …?

"You are going to attend a seance," he said, bringing a halt to my disingenuous internal monologue. I'll admit it. I knew the answers to those questions. I was just stalling for time, spinning my wheels, scrambling for an exit like an ordinary Joe who had gotten himself in too deep and wanted out bad.

Real bad.

"We will contact this Letour fellow and ask if he would be willing to hold a seance at his house near Golden."

"A seance that we …"

"That you will attend alone."

Damn.

"Your rich aunt from Tulsa died recently and you are willing to pay Letour almost any amount of money he demands if he can truly contact her spirit."

He was beginning to lose me there. I didn't have almost any amount of money to throw at frauds. My mind wandered.

Then a thought struck me. "Am I going to tell him that my aunt died broke?"

"Of course not. I was informed by an expert that adhering as close to the truth as possible without actually getting there was one of the most effective methods of pulling off a deception."

"Hell, I could have told you that."

"You did."

"What?"

"Fifteen years ago. You and I were having a nightcap at Sweeney's Tavern after your first day of taxi training. You made the mistake of drinking a boilermaker and subsequently telling me your innermost secrets. By the time I drove you home I was convinced that you were the walking embodiment of pure evil."

"Strange," I muttered, "I don't remember that."

"You told me things that would have frightened off an exorcist."

"All right, gimme a break, let's get on with this seance jazz." I was furious. I had always believed that the only people privy to my innermost secrets were a couple of homicide detectives. I felt like a chump.

"You will offer Letour a thousand dollars in cash in hand if he can see his way to holding a seance this evening," Big Al said.

"Is that the standard fee in the seance game?"

"I have no idea," he replied. "But I believe that when Rodney hears your offer his eyes will light up, if I may borrow a cliché from your ultimate ambition in life."

For a thousand dollars Big Al could borrow my entire body of work. I had probably spent twice that much on Wite-Out® alone.

"Hold it," I said. "Letour probably knows what I look like. I'm sure he's the one who burned up my goddamn Chevy, and for all I know he chased me across Riverside Cemetery. If I walk into his house tonight he'll recognize me."

"Not after I'm finished with you."

"What do you mean?"

"How attached are you to that ponytail?"

I froze.

I didn't need a crystal ball to see what I would look like without a ponytail: Jesse White. But I was as attached to my ponytail as I'm attached to most material things in life. Given the fact that I own nothing, his question had a comically rhetorical quality to it, although I knew he was serious. The truth is, except when I am near reflective objects such as mirrors or crystal balls, I am never aware of my ponytail. It's like the time I wore a beard in college. I felt as clean-cut as Pat Boone until I squeezed my tube of *Stripe* toothpaste in the morning and grinned at the mirror. My reflection looked like Steve McQueen in his decline.

My ponytail meant nothing to me, but there was one person in Denver who had a proprietary interest in it. His name was Gino Bombalini. It's a long story but I'll make it short. He was my barber. He invented my ponytail. He treated it the way cat ladies treat tabbies. I knew what Big Al was hinting at, but I decided to yank his chain just for fun. I was born that way.

"This?" I said fearfully, reaching back and grabbing the ponytail and raising it like a prize trout.

"Don't get coy, Tenderfoot," Big Al said dryly. "Your redemption is at stake."

I let it drop.

I was born that way, too.

"Do you own a suit?" Big Al said.

"Strange that you should ask," I replied. "Yes."

"Why is that strange?"

"Oh … no particular reason. It just strikes me as strange that I would own a suit."

"I fully agree," he said. "That's why I asked."

I swallowed hard. I was prevented from explaining to him or to anybody on earth why I happened to own a suit. I felt a noose tightening around my neck. I had to think fast. The fate of the whole world may have depended on it.

"A fare left a suit in my backseat," I lied.

"I once found a lava lamp in my backseat," Big Al said.

"I did too!"

"Jacobsen found one in his backseat three years ago."

"Why do people leave lava lamps in taxis, fer the luvva Christ?"

"Life is a mystery," Big Al said.

"It sure is."

By now we were so far from Langley that I felt safe … but … perhaps I've said too much. "If you're asking me whether I'm willing to cut off my ponytail for The Cause, the answer is yes," I said.

Big Al smiled benignly. "You are a never-ending source of wonderment to me, Brendan Murphy."

I blushed with pride. Practically everything about me is never-ending.

"Can I ask you a question?" I said.

"Yes."

"Is there an electric hair-cutting device in this house?"

"Are we talking a Vidal Sassoon hair styler?"

"Black-and-Decker Sheep 5000."

Ten minutes later I looked like Aldo Ray.

CHAPTER 32

Big Al set the shears down and handed me my ponytail. It was the best haircut I'd ever gotten from someone who had no training, and I've had plenty of those—but who hasn't?

"This is going to take some fancy explaining to Gino," I said. "He's from the old country. He was born in Sicily."

Big Al frowned. "Does Gino actually have a 'need to know'?" he said. "Perhaps the time has come for you to start paying for your haircuts."

We both had a good chuckle over that.

Big Al removed the towel from around my neck and took it into the rear of the house. When he returned he was carrying a stack of one-hundred-dollar bills. He handed the stack to me without a word. I tucked it away.

We began discussing the plan. Note that I did not put the word plan between quotation marks. That's because it was Big Al's plan and not mine. Had it been my plan I would have put it in quotes because, for reasons that are not clear to anybody, quotation marks are indicative of the false nature of the word being singled out. For instance, I sometimes refer to my novels as "novels." On the other hand I never refer to my rejection slips as "rejection" slips because there is nothing false about the rejections. They are bona fide, dyed-in-the-wool, sure as shootin', 24-carat rejections. But because the events that were going to take place that evening were conceived of by Big Al, I had complete faith in the plan. He once explained to me how to win a twin-quinella at the dog track, and later explained why I should never try it again. He was right both times.

I don't know how long we sat in his house discussing the details. I only know that I felt like a character in one of those '60s movies again. It wasn't a good feeling. The more detailed the plan became, the more I accepted the fact that I would be going in alone. I had done that often enough in the past few years to understand that the time had come to prep myself for debilitating stage fright. I once read an article that said Laurence Olivier himself experienced stage fright before stepping into the limelight and blowing the lid off the Old Met. Peter Lorre, on the other hand never got near the Old Met. He tended to blow the lid off ___________ (you'll have to fill in the blank—I was too busy throwing up in my dressing room).

We left the house. I climbed into 123, but Big Al walked around to the side of the house and entered his garage. A few moments later the door slowly arose—he had an automatic garage-door opener. I was impressed. I didn't even have a garage, although I did have an automatic opener. I called it "car thieves."

A vehicle slowly backed out from the shadow of the garage. I recognized it. Rocky Mountain Taxicab #61, the oldest cab in the Rocky fleet, the last of the two-digit cabs. Big Al owned #61. He had bought it twenty years earlier when he first started driving and had quickly admitted to himself that sitting outside the Brown Palace reading tip-sheets would be his vocation in life. Cabbies who admit things like that are called "owner/drivers." I refer to them as "realists," which is why I have never admitted that I will be spending the rest of my life twenty feet from a hotel. Why should I admit that? What if I'm wrong? What if I write a bestselling novel? I would feel like a damned fool announcing to the world that I would be a cabbie forever only to receive $100,000 advance from Scribner the next day. No way I'm gonna risk that embarrassment.

Big Al backed his cab out, then swung around the yard making a half-circle so he could pull up next to my window. He drove on his own grass. I had never seen anybody do that in my entire life.

"Stick close to me, Tenderfoot."

He rolled up his window and settled back behind the steering wheel.

In theory I could have made a circle on his grass rather than back out of the drive but I just couldn't bring myself to do it. His lawn was all dried out and yellow and looked like hell. It was the kind of lawn I always dreamed of owning. I started wondering if it wasn't time for me to move out of my crow's nest and find a nice country place to live in. It would be like the time Ricky and Lucy moved from New York to the suburbs. I remembered the knee-slapping episode where Lucy hatched a couple hundred baby chicks in the living room of their ranch house. Ricky almost had a heart attack. One would think that the logistics of having so many baby chicks running around loose inside a TV studio would infuriate the producers, except Lucy and Desi owned Desilu Productions. I wouldn't be surprised though, if a couple of camera operators went home that night and talked to their wives about getting the hell out of show biz.

Big Al drove back toward Sheridan Boulevard. I followed but tried not to anticipate his route. I'm not a mind reader and I don't play chess. By "play" I mean "win." Even if I could read minds I wouldn't play chess with Big Al. But if he did lure me into a chess game I knew exactly what I would do. I would sit down at the board, place my king horizontal, and walk away. I can read my mind like an X-ray.

We turned left onto Sheridan and headed back to I-70, hopped onto the superslab and headed west. I kept five-and-a-half car lengths between our bumpers. Safe drivers and math majors know what I'm talking about. I wasn't familiar enough with the laws of country/western music to know if two taxis traveling in the same direction qualified as a "convoy" but that's what it felt like. My mouth went dry. Being led by Big Al reminded me of a time back in college when I was required to trick a friend into going to an AA meeting at a church. His grades were on the skids. We were halfway to the church when I began to wonder if my friend had tricked *me* into going to the AA meeting.

The mountains began to loom large in my windshield. They always looked fairly low from downtown Denver but they rose up pretty fast when you were on the interstate. The pioneers who had finally decided to move on to California must have felt wretched when they realized how tall the Rocky Mountains really were. Some of them may have turned back to "Quitter's Camp." They probably felt like damned fools—a bitter yet small price to pay for permanent residence.

Big Al took the Kipling exit and headed south toward 38th Avenue. He drove into the entrance of a parking lot at a shopping center on Kipling Street and parked #61.

"You and I are going to the haunted house," he said. He glanced at his watch then looked at the sun, which was headed toward the skyline of the Rockies. It was three in the afternoon by then. I know because I looked at my own watch. I hate looking at my watch on Sundays, but this was a special case—my redemption was at stake for the fifth time this year.

"Lock up your taxi, Tenderfoot," he said. "You are going to ride in my backseat. I will need you to direct me to the house but I want you to remain out of sight. When we get close I want you to get down on the floor so that anyone in the house will not be able to see you."

He opened the trunk of his taxi, reached in and pulled out what appeared to be an olive-drab army blanket. I know my blankets, especially when they have PROPERTY OF THE U.S. ARMY stenciled on them. Was Big Al a veteran? I had never thought to ask. I try to avoid other veterans if I can. This has to do with a rather large bet I was involved in at Fort Polk that cost a number of infantrymen a month's pay. I don't want to talk about it.

"If need be, cover yourself with this," Big Al said.

"Where did you get it?" I said, since I have to know everything.

"Army surplus," he replied, his voice reeking of patience.

As I climbed into the backseat I prayed that I would not have to use the blanket. It evoked bad memories of a thing called a "blanket party" that I was also involved in at Fort Polk. If you don't know what a "blanket party" is you're probably not a veteran. It involves fists and entrenching tools but I don't want to get into that.

I sat by the right-rear door and waited as Big Al rounded the front of the cab and climbed in. "Take 38th Avenue west," I said, even though he knew this. Big Al put #61 in gear and pulled onto Kipling, drove to the intersection of 38th and turned right. I slowly slid down on the seat until the top of my head and my eyes were above the windowsill. I sometimes sat this way in the rear of cop cars. It depended on the gravity of the false accusation.

The house was approximately one mile from the intersection. I watched the tops of trees and bushes flow past but I didn't recognize any landmarks. I raised my head a bit after we traveled half a mile. The house would be on the right side of the road. There were no other buildings in the vicinity. I wondered who had built this house way the hell out here. It was too wooded and hilly to be farmland. But why anybody does anything has always been a mystery to me.

"House coming up," Big Al said.

I raised my head and saw the two pillars that guarded the entrance, saw the sign indicating that the occupant of the house gave psychic readings.

"That's it," I said.

"Stay down," he ordered.

I bristled. No big deal. I've been bristling since first grade. I spread the army blanket width-wise on the floor and slid down on top of it. The transmission hump beneath the floor made it difficult to lie flat. I felt like I was back in basic. I began to experience the ride blind, the way kidnap victims do when locked in trunks. I started thinking about writing a suspense novel, but I shut that off fast.

The cab slowed and made a slight turn. I felt the sway of momentum, the rumble of the dirt drive, heard the crunch of gravel and the squeal of brakes indicating that #61 needed maintenance.

We stopped.

"I'll be back in a bit," Big Al said quietly, just before he opened the door and climbed out.

Don't make any promises you can't keep, I thought inwardly as usual.

After a minute I decided to wrap the blanket entirely around myself. I was afraid of being seen by a passerby. What a brilliant word.

The blanket smelled like a tent. Everything in the army smelled like a tent, even the roast beef. I clutched the blanket from inside near my neck. I tried to see my wristwatch but it was too dark. I lost all sense of time. I wondered what made me think it mattered. I wondered how many people on the *Titanic* looked at their watches during the "event." Sweat began trickling down my neck. What if Big Al didn't come back? What if the police opened the door and found me wrapped like a cigar? What would I say? I chortled. This was a problem I had wrestled with all my life, i.e., seeing the funny side of serious situations, such as being interrogated by detectives for murders I could in no way imaginable have committed. I imagined Sebastian Cabot standing at the prow of the *Titanic*. He glanced at his pocket-watch and burst out laughing with bitter irony. Little did the world realize that the mystery of Jack the Ripper had gone down with the ship.

"Stay hidden until we are back on 38th," Big Al said as he slipped into the driver's seat and started the engine.

I was relieved for two reasons: Big Al had returned safely, and I now had an ending for my new suspense thriller: *Raise the Ripper*. This was turning into the best All Saints' Day ever.

CHAPTER 33

Big Al whipped a quick right into the shopping center parking lot, which shook me out of my reverie. I sat up on the seat and tugged the blanket away from my face. I quickly glanced around for cops. Habit.

Big Al parked next to a light post. Okay. I'll admit it. When I told Big Al about my run through the graveyard I left out the part about accidentally turning off the streetlight on Brighton Boulevard. It made me feel stupid.

He turned in the seat and looked at me.

"I spoke to Rodney," he said.

"How did you know it was him?"

"I asked his name. Rodney Letour. Professional psychic. I told him that a fare had asked if I knew of a psychic in the Denver area who took walk-ins. I said my fare is currently staying at the Brown Palace Hotel, that he had come in from Tulsa, and would be leaving on Monday morning, but that he would be willing to pay a thousand dollars cash up front if I could put him in touch with someone who did authentic seances. I mentioned to Rodney that I had dropped off a fare here Thursday night for the haunted house and had seen the sign in his front yard. Rodney told me he preferred to make appointments ahead of time, but when I told him that my fare was willing to pay a thousand dollars cash he said he would accommodate the man."

"What time will it be held?" I said.

"Eight o'clock this evening. That will give you adequate time to go home, put on a suit, make yourself look like an accountant from Tulsa, and rent a car."

"Oh I'm afraid I don't have enough money to rent a car," I said sadly.

"I do. You will be arriving at Rodney's in your rental a few minutes before eight. If everything goes according to plan ..." but he lost me at that point, his voice fading into the echo-chamber of my mind. That happens whenever I hear the phrase "If everything goes according to plan."

"Where will you be?" I said.

He glared at me. "I just told you."

"I wasn't listening."

"I know. I could see it in your eyes. You are the most transparent human being I have ever met."

"Thank you."

"Don't thank me. If Rodney sees through you tonight there may be trouble."

To be perfectly frank, I wish he hadn't said that. But it was good that he did. It cleared my head. Big Al was like what's-his-name giving Laurence Olivier a butt-kicking pep-talk prior to a command performance of *Hamlet*.

"Sir John Gielgud," Big Al said.

I glanced at him with fear in my eyes. And I'm not talking just a fear—I'm talking "The Fear."

"Keep your wits about you, Murph," he said. "Your job will be to expose Rodney as a phony. If he tries to con you, we should be able to go to the D.A. and rip away his mask of fraud."

"You know something, Big Al … I was just thinking," I said.

"It's too late for that."

"Why don't I call Duncan and Argyle and let them handle this?"

"Handle what?" he said. "The exoneration of Rodney Letour followed by his libel suit against you, Hogan, Mr. Hapworth and the Rocky Mountain Taxicab Company?"

"I guess I'd better get over to Capitol Hill," I sighed.

"I'll run a few bells until you return," he said.

"Are you kidding?" I said. "The west side is dead on Sunday." It felt good to take a moment to talk taxi-talk. Expertise is the last resort of the doomed.

"You never know," Big Al said, "Horace Tabor did all right on the west side."

I nodded and climbed out.

I got into 123, started the engine, and headed for Denver proper trying to ignore the knot in my stomach. You know the knot I'm talking about—the knot that appears like a noose whenever I get involved in the personal life of a fare. I had lost count of the number of times during the past fifteen years when I had found myself gearing up and going in to set straight a row of ducks that I had knocked out of kilter. But my inability to count that high is not because I'm bad at math, it's because I'm good at denial.

If I had not thought about the size of that number I might not have found myself traveling across Denver in a time machine set for twenty-five minutes into the future. That's how long I figured it would take to get to my apartment, jump into my phone booth like Doctor Who and emerge like Clark Kent. By "phone booth" I mean the closet where I keep the suit that I once bought at the Cherry Creek Shopping Center under the mistaken assumption that I had a date with … well … let's just say a date. Perhaps I've said too much. I do that frequently. I'm surprised at the number of times it hasn't gotten me into trouble.

Interstate 70 linked up with Interstate 25 and sent me south toward downtown. As I negotiated the link I glanced to the east where Globeville lay like a stale slice of pie. This may sound crazy but there was something appealing about that lifeless triangle of Denver's past. The fact that it had been removed from the timeline of Denver's economic progress since the 1920s made me sort of wish I lived there. I began to feel like Gig Young. I cannot say that this was a bad feeling, although I would say that under most circumstances. Any time anything makes me feel like anyone, I know it's time to take an accounting of my life—but I have better things to do than crawl right out of my own skin.

By the time I got onto Colfax that would take me toward my crow's nest, I was wondering how Gig Young would have handled the role of a sap from Tulsa who was foolish enough to give a thousand dollars to a con man in exchange for a bogus visit from the spirit of a dead aunt. I know what you're thinking—the role was better suited to Tim Conway. And to give honesty a second go-round here, I will admit that I looked more like Tim Conway than Gig Young, which is why I preferred to pretend to be Gig Young. He would have made a good 007 if James Bond had been born in Tulsa.

As I headed toward Capitol Hill I focused on my mission. I had to put on a monkey suit, rent a car, and be back in Golden by eight o'clock.

It was nearing four in the afternoon, which gave me four hours to get those minor chores done. If you're anything like me you know that four hours simply isn't enough time to do three things. I would have been better off if I'd had forty-five minutes to get them done because tight deadlines had the effect of making me mature. There was a direct link with Parkinson's Law here and I was fully aware of it. But I knew I could not let that jerk Parkinson get the upper hand. In spite of the sickly feeling it instilled in me, I concentrated on making certain I did not start dawdling. During a normal dawdle I would have ended up at Gandalf's looking at the pick-of-the-week shelf and wondering if I had time to drop in at Sweeney's. Me and dawdling have always seen eye-to-eye.

My intention was to run by Avis to rent a car, but I started thinking about the reason I had to rent a car, and the next thing I knew I was giving the gas a little toe and driving past the street where I lived. I rolled farther east along Colfax until I came to used-car row—or "Aurora" as it's called.

I had bought my Chevy in Aurora twenty years earlier and I hadn't rented a car since. After I passed Monaco Parkway I started looking for those flapping colored pennants that dealers string above their lots to attract people who are mesmerized by shiny objects and spinning tops. That was me twenty years ago. Now it's mostly TV. Imagine my shock when I saw the same rent-a-wreck agency still in business. It was on the north side of the street in a location where I thought there used to be a Putt-Putt golf course, but don't hold me to that. I have a free pass tacked to the cork board in my kitchen that I might have won at the Aurora course or else a course in Scranton. All Putt-Putts look alike.

I swung into the lot and parked 123. The owner stepped out of a little shack and said, "Mr. Murphy, you've come back!"

The fact that he recognized me disproved a lot of things about myself that I don't want to go into, and confirmed a lot more, mostly having to do with paranoia. Maybe he remembered me because I was the only customer who ever bought one of his wrecks. He appeared the same as I remembered him. Straw hat. Thin mustache. Sparkling grin. He looked like he had been "in the chips" for twenty years.

"The old Chevy finally gave up the ghost," I said. I was struck by my strange choice of words. But he didn't seem to notice. His eyes were too busy lighting up.

"Take a look around, friend," he said.

He was still as slick as ever. Instead of giving me the hard sell he allowed me to wander through his graveyard of discontinued models. Why a rental agent would give me a hard sell is beyond me, that's a part of the "paranoia" aspect of my existence.

Then I saw it.

It was parked in a corner of the lot and covered with spare tires. Not completely covered, but more like a table where you would toss nuts and bolts. It wasn't a 1964 Chevy though, it was a pale blue 1954 Plymouth. A buddy of mine in college drove a '54 Plymouth. The damned thing was indestructible. I couldn't have been more thrilled if it had been a 1954 Buick Special. My Maw owns one of those. She keeps it in near mint condition. My older brother Gavin stands to inherit it when Maw dies. That'll be the day.

"I'll bring it back tomorrow," I told the man.

He tried to suppress a knowing chuckling as I signed the rental agreement.

A shag boy drove the Plymouth to my apartment for me, and I gave him a free ride in 123 back to the rental agency. I pegged him as a high school graduate. The kid reminded me of myself. He had the pale, desperate, sallow-eyed, zombie-like stare of an eighteen-year-old boy working on a Sunday for the first time in his life. I thought about recommending that he try cab driving, but I felt uneasy handing out advice when I was embroiled in the midst of a chaotic situation brought on by my inability to make rational judgment calls.

I decided to wait until Monday to slip him the good word about the secret of happiness, or "cab driving" as I call it.

CHAPTER 34

There was something missing. I shot my cuffs, adjusted my tie, and pinched my cheeks, but I still looked like me. I knew why though. I couldn't see my ponytail. The image in the mirror looked like a well-dressed bland person as opposed to a hack in a T-shirt on his way to make a buck. I wondered if I should contrive a fake mustache. I gave this some thought.

Actors used makeup pencils to draw mustaches on their upper lips, but I was out of eyeliner. What do I mean by that? Simple: actors leave all kinds of things in the backseat of my taxi. Bad scripts. Bad reviews. And makeup kits. I kept the bad scripts but I always threw away the reviews and kits. "Why the hell would I ever need a makeup kit?" I always asked myself. The irony is that I kept a lava lamp. Ergo, as I stood in front of the mirror I made a personal vow that I would never again throw anything away, even if it didn't belong to me.

Then it hit me. I went into my bedroom, pulled open a dresser drawer, shoved aside my overdue library book and grabbed a pair of glasses that I had bought at an optical joint called SightCity!!!. I had also bought some disposable contact lenses that I never disposed of. When it came to 20/20 vision I was sittin' pretty.

I returned to the bathroom, removed my contacts, and put on my glasses.

I froze.

Wally Cox was staring back at me.

In order to enhance the disguise I had flattened my hair with Vaseline. I had also used Vaseline when I applied for the job at Dyna-Plex and it had flattened my hair then, too, but not in a good way. Ironically it helped me to get the job. It's a long story that ends with $20,000 but let's move on.

I stood back and looked at the black rims of my glasses, looked at the shine of the bathroom light glistening off the top of my head, looked at the pink blossoming in my cheeks from the recent pinches. I decided I should not have done that. Wally Cox never looked healthy.

I squared my shoulders, adjusted my tie, and noted that I had two options available to me that I might explore one day in the future: apply for a real job, or rob a bank—either way nobody would believe it was me.

I finally admitted it was true that clothes make the man. This depressed me. I had never fully grasped how superficial skin is. I touched the tip of my nose with a finger and raised my nostrils until I looked like Leo Gorcey. This was not unusual. I touched my upper lip with my lower teeth until I looked like my high school gym coach. We called him "Cheetah" but not to his face. He could climb twenty-foot ropes without using his legs. I shook it out. I had a job to do. Playing with my face in the mirror was as bad as getting lost in a dictionary. English majors and people with a lot of spare time on their hands know what I'm talking about.

That was that.

It was seven p.m. and darkness had fallen. It was time to climb back into the time machine. As I closed up my crow's nest and descended the fire escape it occurred to me that if I still had my beard I would look like Sebastian Cabot. I have often stated that being a cab driver is like being an actor, but a real actor didn't need makeup to create a false persona. All he needed was the sheer will and determination to pull the wool over the eyes of humanity.

I was born that way.

Ten minutes later I was back on the highway and ten minutes after that I was five minutes away from Kipling and 38th. I took the exit off Interstate 70 and headed south. I wheeled into the parking lot and drove toward the light pole where Big Al had parked 61. It was still there. It looked as if it hadn't been moved in three-and-a-half hours. I felt smug. The west side is as dead as Horace Tabor on Sundays.

I circled around so I could pull up next to Big Al, roll down my window, and speak directly to him as he had spoken to me after driving on the grass. Big Al peered curiously at the stranger parked next to him, then rolled down his window.

"I made two trips to DIA after you left," he said.

"Bull!" I shrieked before I could control myself.

He raised two fifty-dollar bills and shuffled them at me with a thumb and fingertip. "You should get involved in the personal lives of fares more often, Greenhorn," he said, as he tucked the loot into his shirt pocket.

"Nice Plymouth," he said to ameliorate my rage. "Did you buy the pink slip?"

"No!" I snapped.

"You will."

I bowed my head and mumbled, "Probably."

He nodded. He looked at his wristwatch. "Twenty minutes until H-Hour."

"What does the aitch stand for?" I said.

"I have no idea," he replied so quickly that he may have anticipated the question. He can read me like a flowchart.

I peered toward Golden then said, "I think I'll drive past the place right now and look it over." I wanted to say "case the joint" but I always felt foolish spouting jive-talk in front of Big Al. "I'll be back after the seance."

"Don't make any promises you can't keep," he said.

I frowned at him and rolled up my window.

Guiding my car out of the parking lot, I headed down the road toward Golden to case the joint. I kept to the speed limit as I drove past Rodney's place. The lights were on in the house. I eyeballed the psychic signage as I drove past. If I had continued driving I could have gone all the way to Lookout Mountain and up the winding road to the summit where Buffalo Bill Cody is buried. I had heard that the residents of Cody, Wyoming, wanted Buffalo Bill's body exhumed and buried in their own town. These are the sorts of things that obsess people who live west of the Mississippi.

I continued on down the road, whipped an illegal louie, and drove back. I passed the house again. There was no other vehicular traffic on the road. Denver is dead on Sundays in spite of Big Al's outrageous fortune. I whipped another U and pulled onto the shoulder, shut off my lights, and waited with the engine running. It suddenly occurred to me that Wichita is a darn nice town. Why did I ever leave it? What if—just for the sake of argument—I drove to my Maw's house in a stolen rental car? Would the D.A. in Wichita be as understanding as the D.A. in Denver? Did the sovereign State of Kansas still recognize the insanity plea?

I waited until five minutes to eight, then pulled back onto the road. I tried a couple of key phrases as I drove toward the house: "It's only a movie. It's only a movie." That didn't work so I switched to "It doesn't matter, it doesn't matter," but I knocked that off fast. What if I ascended into a transcendental state of consciousness and drove into a ditch? I couldn't think of anything that would please me more.

I rolled past the spot where I had parked my taxi on Wednesday night when I had dropped the kids off at the haunted house, the night I had set into motion a chain of "events." You know what chain I'm talking about. It was a chain like all the chains that shackled me to reality every time I got involved in the personal life of a fare—the chain of altruism, optimism, and ineptitude. Not even Harry Houdini could have freed himself from those forged links—it took a college student and a burst appendix to free him, and I had neither, not counting my English degree.

I turned and drove between the twin pillars and parked on the dirt driveway. I climbed out, tugged the hem of my coat, adjusted my tie, squared my shoulders, and began walking toward the house. It was the longest walk of my life.

I say that every time I screw up. It gets old.

As I approached the porch I felt a change coming over me. I'm not talking Larry Talbot though, I'm talking a purely mental condition—obviously a man who turns into a werewolf once a month does not have a mental condition, at least not at first. It sends a chill down my spine to think that Lon Chaney Junior might have become a horror actor just to gain the love of his father.

I stepped like a normal person up onto the porch and punched the doorbell. Everything was going smoothly.

"Goot evening."

I froze.

The door opened revealing a man dressed in black. I suddenly felt like Rikki-Tikki-Tavi in the presence of a cobra. The odor of black candles wafted from the house. "The Fear" began to engulf me.

"You're right on time, Mr. Ambrewster. My name is Rodney Letour."

"How do you do, Mister Letour," I said, trying to maintain my grip. I sounded exactly like Wally Cox. As small as he was in stature, Wally Cox frequently was cast in films as a man of consummate intellect who stood like a cerebral Colossus astride the sound stages of Hollywood.

I felt the old confidence returning.

CHAPTER 35

"Please step inside," Rodney said, opening the door wider and standing back.

His voice was soft and oily, and his smile held an uncanny resemblance to that of Victor Buono—pinched and affable. Rollo did that when he wanted to get my goat. He was smooth. He was good. He was like every con man ever portrayed in the movies. So was Rodney.

"I have some people I would like you to meet," Rodney said, as he escorted me from the foyer into the living room where a man and a woman were standing beside a fireplace. "Allow me to introduce Eusapia and Mister Dunninger. They will be participating in the seance."

Eusapia looked like a beatnik from the neck up, and Morticia Addams from the neck down. She was wearing a wispy, clinging black outfit. Her hair was long with black bangs, her face was pale, and her eyes were dark. She, too, had a smile like Rollo. Mr. Dunninger had no smile. His lips resembled those of E.G. Marshall: horizontal, businesslike, somber. He was wearing wire-rim glasses and a well-tailored herringbone suit. I fought the urge to feel reassured by his presence. I couldn't think of anyone I would rather have with me in a dicey situation than E.G. Marshall—preferably as defense counsel. But I knew it was all an act. This whole scene reeked of artifice. It was being staged—but not for my benefit. These frauds had their eyes on the prize: a slice of Aunt Ambrewster's fortune.

I took a quick look around the living room. The furnishings were not modern. They might have come with the house. It was the type of furniture that may have once graced the Riverside mansion. The couch was thickly padded and had fancy wooden trim on the arms and headrest. The legs resembled lion paws. I once delivered furniture for a living, ergo my mind began extrapolating on the difficulties that might be encountered when hoisting the couch through the foyer and out the front door. Once a furniture mover, always a furniture mover.

"I'm pleased to meet you," Eusapia said, gliding toward me and holding out her right hand with her fingers hanging downward. I didn't know whether to kiss it or shake it. This applied to other things in my life but I don't want to get into that.

"How do you do, ma'am?" Wally Cox said. I chortled but managed to cover it up with a hick smile and a nod. I reached out and shook her delicate ivory hand.

"Mr. Ambrewster," Dunninger stated affably, stepping away from the fireplace. He reached out and gave me a firm handshake, raising his chin slightly and peering at me through his specs as if he was sizing me up for a loan. He resembled a bank teller too, but I preferred E.G Marshall. I was once implicated in a felony bank robbery that ended in death, but I'm getting off the subject. I'll admit it. I was starting to get rattled. These three different people were crowding me, putting me at my ease, making me feel welcome, just like stereo salesmen. When anyone tries to make me feel welcome, I grab my billfold and run. Sometimes I make it. Sometimes I buy cassette tapes.

"Mr. Ambrewster is the initiate whose aunt we will be channeling tonight," Rodney said to his accomplices. He looked at me. "Eusapia and Mr. Dunninger are both mediums. The taxi driver who set up the appointment told me that you have attended other seances."

"That's correct," I lied.

"He also told me that you had not been able to contact your aunt through the other mediums."

"That's also true," I also lied. "But I'm not willing to give up, and I want you to know that I am not a skeptic even though the seances were failures. I am a scientific rationalist, and to me this means keeping an open mind. I do not believe in belief or disbelief. I believe only in my own eyes and ears."

"Excellent," Mr. Dunninger said. "The willingness of an initiate to remain receptive to the vibrations is vital to the success of a seance, just as doubt can be detrimental."

"Shall we begin?" Eusapia said.

I expected to feel a chortle well up in my esophagus. I did feel a slight pressure like a burp that didn't have the moxie, but it faded. Eusapia wanted to get right down to business. By "business" I mean money. She was like a beginning novelist who wanted to get it written, get it to Scribner, and get that big advance.

Been there.

"The cab driver told me that you charge a thousand dollars," I said. "I hope I'm not out of line here, but due to my previous experiences I would rather wait until after the seance to pay you. I do have the thousand with me though."

Does that make me sound like a rube? Big Al thought perhaps it might.

"That will not be a problem, Mr. Ambrewster," Rodney said with an oily smile. He extended an arm and pointed with his palm. Mr. Dunninger led the way. The dining room was down a short hallway. As we moved through the house, the lights behind us went out. It was very theatrical. I assumed Rodney was tripping switches as we proceeded but I didn't glance around to see him do it. I don't like people to know that I know things. There is a reason for this: if people know that I know things, they stop doing whatever it is I know, thus reducing the odds of my "getting the goods" on them. I had never "gotten the goods" on anyone so I was hoping the seance would break my forty-six-year losing streak.

A varnished mahogany table graced the center of the dining room. Heavy drapes were drawn across tall windows beyond the table. A chandelier hung above the center of the table. The chandelier had two regular white lightbulbs and four yellow bulbs that looked like candle flames. It was a sort of an upside-down Tiffany lamp. All of the bulbs were lit. The table was large enough to seat six people and a turkey dinner. I now wished I had visited the haunted house on Wednesday night. I could have gotten the entire layout, including the upstairs and maybe even the cellar. My life seemed to be one long series of interminable regrets. But that was okay. Unlike most people, when I die I plan to take as many regrets with me as possible. They will serve as reminders of the things I didn't waste my time doing on earth. That's what I call Nirvana.

"Why don't you sit right here, Mr. Ambrewster?" Rodney said, sliding a wooden chair away from the table like an efficient butler.

Sure, pal, I'll sit there. I'll sit in the "special" chair—the chair picked out for all the "initiates" who pass through your paranormal kingdom, the chair facing the window curtains, the chair that will give me a good view of the ectoplasmic apparitions that will appear above the table as the night wears on. Elwood P. Dowd liked to say, "As the night wore on." He was also fond of drink.

"I will be sitting across from you," Rodney said. "Eusapia will be seated to your right and Mr. Dunninger will be seated to your left."

Everyone took their chairs.

As soon as Rodney settled himself across from me he reached for a small box to his left, an electronic switchbox with knobs that he used to dim the white lightbulbs. The triangular glass Tiffany panels of the chandelier were streaked gray/pink. The yellow flame bulbs did nothing to improve the ambience after the white bulbs went dark. A man could have gone blind trying to play poker under those lighting conditions.

Rodney diminished the intensity of the yellow bulbs to where I could barely see the curtains of the window approximately six feet beyond his chair. I looked at Eusapia on my right and Mr. Dunninger on my left. It was as if the four of us were seated within a globe of soft yellow light surrounded by blackness. Which I guess was true.

"Before we begin I would like to describe the procedure so that nothing that takes place will come as a surprise to you," Rodney said.

Okay pal. Hit me. Lay it on me. Cover all the phony angles ahead of time.

"We will begin with a minute of silence. We will then place the palms of our hands flat on the table in such a way that the tips of our fingers will touch."

Eusapia laid her right hand on the table with her fingers splayed in demonstration, and Rodney splayed his left hand. Their little fingers touched. "Some mediums prefer that the participants hold hands," Rodney said, "but I have found that the cosmic vibrations flow best with the palms pressed against the tabletop and the fingertips completing the circuit."

I nodded.

To be honest, I was relieved to hear this. I didn't especially feel like holding hands with Dunninger. I once held hands with a hippie boy who lived near Boulder. We sang *Kumbaya.* I don't want to talk about it.

"After the vibrations have begun to flow, I will place myself into a trance that will allow me to communicate with any manifested spirits," Rodney said. "I request that you maintain complete silence until I speak. If you wish to ask questions of the spirits that I contact, try to make your questions simple and succinct. I also ask that you remain seated at all times. Do not move from your chair. Do not make any abrupt noises. If you say or do anything to interfere with my trance and bring me to consciousness, it could conceivably cause mental or physical harm to myself. If I make contact with a spirit, you might hear noises such as tapping or knocking, or you might see a glow of light that has no apparent source. Again, I ask that you stay seated, remain calm, and go with the flow."

Here's the strange part. When I took an introductory course in Transcendental Meditation the teacher said similar things, especially the part about being abruptly brought to consciousness. As far as "go with the flow," my gym coach used to say that about sports activities, such as the fast-break in basketball that required intense concentration and coordination, neither of which I possessed. I came to hate that phrase, which is why I say it so often. I am secretly mocking Cheetah.

"I am also obligated to tell you that if by any chance the table begins to move, do not be alarmed. The levitation of physical objects during a seance is not an uncommon phenomenon and should be understood as a spirit making its presence known."

I nodded again. I could smell the odor of candle wax even though I saw no candles, but beneath that was the odor of ancient wood and old furniture, the subtle smells that accumulate in a house more than a hundred years old. The part of my brain that views with utter disdain many of the things that human beings do was slowly being fragmented. I wrote it off as the essence of show biz, but that did nothing to ameliorate the eerie feeling that was beginning to creep into the scene. The creepiest thing was that I was seated in a room with people who expected me to take this seriously. Not even stereo salesmen were that creepy.

"I am now going to lower the lights so you will barely be able to see me," Rodney said. "We will maintain one minute of silence, and then we will lay our hands on the table. After that, I ask you to remain alert, open-minded, and silent. I will put myself into a transcendent state of mind. It will take a few minutes before I make contact with the spirit world and after I do, they will speak to you through me. Now before we begin, is there anything that you need clarified?"

"The infield fly rule," I almost said. I never have understood that call.

I shook my head no. "I'm ready to contact my aunt."

Rodney reached to the box and the lights began to dim. Pretty soon I could see nothing but the vague shape of Rodney sitting across from me. He was barely a silhouette. I glanced at both Eusapia and Dunninger. They were vague shapes, too. I'll admit it. I didn't like it. I was growing nervous. My only compensation was the knowledge that I was as vague as they were. For the first time in my life I didn't feel like an outsider.

Silence enveloped the room.

I gazed at the center of the table. The odor of wood and old fabric seemed to grow stronger. I became aware of the sound of air entering and leaving my nostrils. I parted my lips to cut down on my nasal racket. I felt like an oaf.

The three mediums laid their hands on the tabletop. I laid my hands down and spread my fingers until the tip of my right little finger touched Eusapia's left fingertip, and the tip of my left little finger touched Dunninger's right little fingertip. I realized that my hands were trembling, which struck me as odd because I hadn't had a drink of alcohol all day. But I knew the cure for that.

Rodney bowed his head.

Due to the fact that my arms were extended, I could see my wristwatch. Unfortunately I could not see the hands. They did not glow. It had cost me five bucks at K-Mart. It was a sweet deal, but if I had spent ten bucks I could have gotten radium hands. I now regretted that I was so goddamned cheap. I had the craving to keep track of time. I wanted to see the second-hand moving. Why I wanted to see it is beyond me, except that knowing exactly what time it was suddenly seemed important. It had seemed important to Keir Dullea, too, in a movie call *David and Lisa* where he played a manic-depressive mental patient who had deeply rooted issues with his demanding mother who smothered him with oppressive love that … well … perhaps I've said too much.

Rodney raised his head.

It was at this precise moment in time that I felt a gentle flow of cold air pass through the room. It caressed my right cheek. It was as if someone had turned on a fan and then turned it back off. The coldness faded.

I felt Eusapia's fingertip press a little harder against mine. She took a deep breath. I could hear the air enter her nostrils. She sat a bit more erect and held her posture motionless. She made a suppressed, throaty whimper, like an annoyed person mumbling something in her sleep. Then she stopped.

The four of us remained silent for maybe thirty seconds, but I'm not sure, goddamn my cheapness anyway—and then she made the noise again. I saw Rodney's head turn toward her. I wondered if she had broken his trance.

Eusapia began shaking her head no. It was like seeing someone move underwater. Rodney continued to look toward Eusapia, then he quietly said, "What is it?"

Eusapia shook her head no for seconds. The throaty noises began again and did not stop. She was like someone whimpering to wake up from an unpleasant dream.

"Who is with you?" Rodney asked softly.

I felt Eusapia's fingertip trembling in syncopation with my own. Dunninger's fingertip trembled, too.

A cold flow of air caressed my left cheek, passed across my face, and faded.

Eusapia jerked her hand away from mine and clutched her fists to her breast.

"Everybody stay calm," Rodney said so quietly that I could barely hear him. "I'm going to turn up the lights."

The yellow bulbs began to brighten until I could see Rodney's hand resting on the box where he was adjusting the knob, but he did not bring the lights up to full illumination. I looked at Eusapia. She was staring at me with her eyes wide.

"Hollister," she whispered.

I froze.

"Who is Hollister?" Rodney said softly.

Eusapia continued to stare at me. A chill crawled down my spine. I often make references to chills running up and down my spine but those are just metaphors. This, on the other hand, was an authentic frigid sensation. I recognized the name of Hollister.

Rodney raised his right palm. "I am going to bring this to an end. Everybody remain calm. Eusapia, please place your hand back on the table.

"No," she whispered.

"Okay, that's fine," Rodney said. "I am going to turn the lights up full now. Eusapia, I want you to close your eyes and relax."

I glanced at Dunninger. He was gazing at me with his shoulders hunched and his head slightly bowed. It was a querulous gaze.

I looked at Eusapia. Her eyes were closed. She slowly unclasped her hands and lowered them to her lap.

Rodney increased the illumination until the yellow light was brought to full intensity. Perspiration glistened on Eusapia's forehead. It mirrored mine. I know because I reached up and touched the lines furrowing the skin above my brows. It was a cold sweat.

Rodney glanced at Dunninger and me, then raised his palms as if to say, "Wait."

It took a full minute before Eusapia opened her eyes. She blinked twice, then said in a tremulous voice, "Do you know a man named Hollister?"

I swallowed hard and nodded. "I knew a man named Hollister who died awhile back," I said. "He was a bank robber."

CHAPTER 36

What had come over me? Why did I say that! Just because it was true? That's the worst reason in the world to say something. But the "Hollister Episode" had happened to Mr. Murphy, not to Mr. Ambrewster. As a consequence, a new dread came over me. I had tipped my hand. These people would ask questions. They would find out that Mr. Hollister had robbed a bank in Glendale and that a cabbie nicknamed "Murph" had driven the getaway car.

"Abort!" my brain barked.

Rodney reached for the switchbox and turned the white lighbulbs up to full illumination. The eerie ambience changed to the flat lighting of an ordinary middle-class dining room. Norman Rockwell couldn't have done a better job of portraying the sheer boredom of life in Denver.

Rodney licked his lips and swallowed hard. I saw his Adam's apple move. He struck me as a rank amateur when it came to camouflaging true feelings. He glanced at Eusapia, then looked at me. "Are you saying that you were once acquainted with a man who died during a bank robbery?"

"Yes," my voice said, while my brain was still trying to think of a way out of this mess. My legs were way ahead of my brain. I could feel my thigh muscles twitching to hoist me out the front door. "It happened in Tulsa a few months ago. Mr. Hollister was a businessman whose lawyer handled my aunt's estate. I met him in the lawyer's office a number of times." I was pleased with the things my vocal chords were doing. I'm usually infuriated with them.

Rodney glanced at Mr. Dunninger, then looked at me. "Did you know the man well?"

"No."

"Did he die violently?"

"He died in a hail of bullets," my voice lied.

Eusapia gasped.

Rodney looked at her. "Eusapia dear, did Mr. Hollister communicate anything to you?"

She shook her head. "No. But his spirit was terribly troubled."

Now it was my turn to swallow hard. What was going on here? How could these clowns possibly know about that robbery? I knew that fraudulent mediums sometimes surreptitiously accessed information from customers before putting them through a seance or a palm reading or whatever frauds did to get money. In this way they were not unlike taxi drivers. Cabbies do everything within their power to get people talking about their private lives. As I said earlier, the monologue is preferable to the dialogue.

A nagging worry began to grow somewhere near the base of my neck. Why would Mr. Hollister want to speak to me? I had nothing to do with his death, aside from helping him escape with one hundred thousand dollars, which brought on a heart attack. It's true that later I fingered him for the cops but …

At this point Mr. Dunninger spoke up. "Perhaps we should end the seance and move to the Ouija board. The vibrations do not feel right to me."

Rodney looked at Dunninger and then at me. He licked his lips again. He looked indecisive. "I'm sorry, Mr. Ambrewster. I've never experienced anything quite like this before. The manifestation was totally unexpected. By rights I should have channeled his spirit, but for some reason Mr. Hollister chose Eusapia. And the divination occurred much sooner than I expected. I tend to agree with Mr. Dunninger. But if you would like to begin the seance over and attempt to contact your aunt, we could give it another try. I hesitate to do that though, because I am afraid the spirit of Mr. Hollister might intervene." He looked at Eusapia. "How do you feel about this?"

She shook her head no. "There is something malevolent about the spirit of Mr. Hollister."

Rodney looked at me.

"If you prefer, we could bring this session to an end and try it again at some other date. The vibrations simply do not feel right."

Rodney had made a classic blunder. He had given me a choice. People rarely do that, but when they do, I milk it.

"What's this about a Ouija board?" I said.

Mr. Dunninger cleared his throat. "I thought it might be better to try to contact your aunt through the power of the Ouija," he said. "It's less complicated, and a less dangerous procedure, but if performed properly it can offer quite satisfactory results."

I began to feel like a customer who had stepped into a computer store to buy a Mac and the salesman was pressuring me to buy a Dell.

Five minutes later the four of us were seated around a Ouija board. You've seen Ouija boards. They can be picked up for a song at any novelty shop. I had a friend in college who owned a plastic Ouija board that he brought to keggers to hook up with women who were into Wicca. It worked like magic. He's married now.

"You and I will be touching the planchette," Rodney said, pointing at the small heart-shaped device used to point at the letters. "Eusapia will not be participating. I will first dim the lights and we will maintain a silence, after which I will place myself into a trance. I will then reach out and touch the planchette with my fingertips. That is when the divination will begin. You will then touch the planchette with your fingertips. I will indicate to you that the time has come to ask a question of your aunt. The planchette will begin to move about the board and point at the letters that will spell out the words that comprise the answer to your question."

I nodded. I wanted to tell him that I was familiar with the procedure of the Ouija board because I had seen plenty of them in the movies. I have an almost uncontrollable urge to tell people about my incredible background.

The room went dim. Rodney sat with his head bowed. He raised his hands and reached out to the planchette. I followed suit. The planchette was cold to the touch.

"You may ask your question now," Rodney said softly.

"I wanted to ask her where …" I began but Rodney interrupted me.

"Simply state your question as if speaking directly to your aunt."

"Aunt Ambrewster," I said. "Could you please tell me where the deed to the Enid oil well is? Mother misplaced it."

A cold breeze caressed my cheek.

The planchette began to move. It felt as if it was being tugged. I squinted at Rodney's hands, but his fingertips were barely touching the device. It moved across the board and stopped at the letter S.

After a moment's pause it moved to the letter H.

Then onto the letter E.

I glanced at Rodney. His eyes were half-lidded as if he were in a trance.

L.

Then T.

The planchette moved again, pointed at the letter E, backed away, and pointed at the E again.

The entire procedure took about three minutes. It would have been boring if I hadn't been so freaked out by the tugging. Was the spirit of Mr. Hollister in the room?

The planchette stopped at the letter N and the breeze passed across my face again. It faded away. The "force" that had been moving the planchette ceased. It felt like a cessation of the beating of a heart. Rodney and I sat motionless.

"Who is Shelteen?" Rodney said softly.

I froze.

He lifted his head and started to say something. A whimper came from Eusapia's throat. Rodney glanced at her.

"It's a dog," Eusapia whispered.

She was sitting erect and very rigid. Her fists were curled tightly on top of the table. Rodney took his fingers away from the planchette and sat back in his chair. He stared at her. "Are you channeling?"

She nodded.

Rodney raised his palms and began shaking his head no. "I am afraid we're going to have to bring this entire session to an end," he said. "There is something very unusual going on here. The spirits seem determined to channel through Eusapia. I have no control over this divination."

He reached to the switchbox and began to raise the lights. At that point a loud thump came from the ceiling. Rodney took his hand away from the box.

"What was that?" I said.

Rodney spread his fingers and shook his palms left and right to silence me.

Eusapia sat back in her chair. It creaked.

We waited perhaps thirty seconds, then Rodney said in a normal tone of voice, "This session has come to an end." He said it like a judge declaring a mistrial.

I realized that every muscle in my body was tense, and I mean *every* muscle. Don't even try use your imagination on that one—just look at a medical chart. There are 650 muscles in the human body and Arnold Schwarzenegger would have been proud of every one of mine.

Rodney reached for the box and turned the lights all the way up, then he took a deep breath and sighed. He looked at Mr. Dunninger and then at Eusapia. "Do either of you feel a presence in the room?"

They shook their heads no.

He looked at me. "Who is Shelteen?" he said.

"I have no idea," I replied.

Eusapia glanced at me. "She was your dog when you were a boy. A sheltie dog."

I shook my head no. "I've never owned a dog," I said. This was true. It was my Maw's dog.

Rodney frowned at me. His eyes flickered left and right to his cohorts, then he cleared his throat and raised his chin. "Forgive me for saying this, Mr. Ambrewster, but I cannot help but feel that you are not being completely honest with us." He paused and took a deep breath. "Are you absolutely certain that you had an Aunt Ambrewster who lived in Tulsa?"

"Yes."

"Shelteen told me that when you owned her you lived in Wichita, Kansas," Eusapia said.

"A dog *spoke* to you?" I said.

"Eusapia has the ability to channel animal spirits," Rodney said.

"Look … I came here to contact my aunt, not a dang dog." My legs began pushing my chair away from the table.

"Please Mr. Ambrewster, don't be upset. These sessions do not always work out the way we would like. The spirit world …"

"I'm not paying you a *dime*," I said, standing up. My voice said it actually—not me. And it was trembling. How in the hell did Eusapia know we had a dog name Shelteen? The nagging fear at the base of my neck spread like a fast-blooming flower in a Disney short. Were these people for *real*? Were there *ghosts* in the room?

"Who the hell is upstairs banging on the ceiling?" I demanded.

"This house is haunted by the original owner," Rodney said. "I assume it was his ghost who made that noise. He was murdered in his bed in 1906."

And then I heard it.

Footsteps coming down a stairwell somewhere in the house.

"Don't be alarmed by that," Rodney said. "The ghost often acts up. He is something of a poltergeist."

I heard breaking glass.

Rodney raised his palms and rubbed his face. "Oh Christ, another coffee cup."

"What in the hell are you talking about?" I said.

"I apologize, Mr. Ambrewster, but …"

"I *told* you it was not a good idea to hold a session on All Saints' Day," Dunninger said.

Rodney took his palms away from his face and nodded.

"You don't have to pay me anything, Mr. Ambrewster. I'm sorry about all this. Mr. Dunninger is quite correct. I had my doubts about the wisdom of holding a seance on this hallowed day."

My right hand slapped the breast pocket of my shirt. It was seeking something that I usually kept with me when I got involved in the personal life of a fare. I called it a "squeeze bottle." Why I called it that is not relevant because I did not have it with me.

I wanted desperately to call their bluff. I wanted to tell Rodney I knew exactly who he was and what he had done to my Chevy. I wanted to tell him I knew he had burned down the Riverside mansion and had chased me through the cemetery. I wanted to *J'Accuse!!!*

"You people are insane," I said.

I had been driving a taxi for fifteen years and one thing I knew was faces. I had seen every kind of face imaginable in my rearview mirror and a few that were unimaginable, and the expressions on the faces of Rodney and Dunninger and Eusapia revealed *naked astonishment!*

What had I gotten myself into? Was I the insane one? Were these people *honest*? Was this house *haunted*?

Another cup crashed to the floor down the hallway. Rodney arose from his chair. "Where's the dustpan?"

"In the pantry," Eusapia said.

"I'm really sorry, Mr. Ambrewster," Rodney said. "This session has been a fiasco. If you wish, we can reschedule for another night. I've got to get into the kitchen before Earl destroys every dish in the house."

He hurried past me and disappeared down the hallway.

Mr. Dunninger got up from his chair and smiled at me. "I tried to warn Rodney that All Saints' Day was a bad idea." He chuckled an apologetic chuckle. "I'm sorry that we were not able to contact your aunt. If you would like to set up another session, we can accommodate you. This is the first time we've ever had a session like this."

"You're forgetting Amelia," Eusapia said. She was sitting at the table with her arms folded across her breasts. She looked chilled.

Mr. Dunninger began slapping at his pockets. He pulled out a pipe and matchbook. "Oh yes … Amelia." He grinned and shook his head as he looked down at the matches. He fumbled with his smoking accoutrement as pipe smokers often do. "That was a pluperfect disaster. I had forgotten."

"On purpose?" Eusapia asked.

Mr Dunninger chuckled again.

"Earl's gone," a voice said.

I turned around and saw Rodney standing in the doorway holding a broom. "I'm going to start buying plastic dinnerware."

"I would advise against it," Dunninger said, sucking a flame into the bowl of his pipe. "Earl will start breaking the windows."

"You're probably right," Rodney said with a sigh, as he set the broom aside. He brushed his hands off, then frowned at me with a pained expression. "I cannot tell you how sorry I am about this, Mr. Ambrewster. If you would like to come back another time we can set up an appointment now."

I shook my head no. "I'm leaving," I said. "And I don't think I'll be back."

I turned and headed toward the living room.

"It was nice meeting you, Mr. Ambrewster," Eusapia sang out.

I raised a hand and kept walking. I heard footsteps behind me. I looked back expecting the ghost of Satchel Paige, but it was just Rodney.

"Maybe you would have better success contacting your aunt through another medium," he said. "Please don't give up on account of my failure."

"I never give up," I said as I reached for the doorknob. For the first time that night I wasn't lying, unfortunately. The only things I had ever succeeded in giving up were smoking cigarettes and seeking some kind of goddamned therapy.

I grabbed the doorknob and gave it a yank.

The door was locked.

"Nice try … Murph," a voice said.

CHAPTER 37

I turned around and looked at Rodney. He might have been Rollo. The pinched smile was the same. The only difference was the small caliber pistol gripped in his fist.

"I did everything I could to warn you off but you wouldn't take the hint," he said.

I looked at the muzzle of the pistol. I had seen muzzles before, although I am not at liberty to explain where or why, but I knew the time had come to think fast and talk faster. This was a shame because I was speechless. Muzzles do that to me.

"I knew that sooner or later you would come here, " Rodney said.

"Because you're psychic, right?" I scowled.

"Because you kept sticking your nose into places where it wasn't wanted. Busybodies always come back for more, so I took the necessary precautions."

"What precautions?"

"A man wearing a ridiculous costume enters my house under false pretenses and threatens me and my friends." He raised the pistol a few inches. "Home invasion is dangerous, Mr. Murphy."

"What made you so certain it was me?" I said, annoyed at all the trouble I had gone through to disguise myself.

"You can thank your friend Mr. Hollister for that clarification."

I frowned. Was he still playing the game? Or *was* it a game? Was Rodney real? Mr. Hollister certainly was real, if it can be said that dead men were real.

"The police take a dim view of trespassers, Mr. Murphy. And since I currently reside in the state of Colorado, you are going to make my day."

I decided it was best that I didn't have my bottle of ammonia—"make my day" trumps "spray first and ask questions later."

"The police take a dim view of murder, too," I said, gambling that I was right.

Rodney frowned, then casually handed the pistol over his shoulder to Dunninger.

"Murder?" he said. He stepped so close to me that I could smell Clorets. When you've driven a taxi as long as I have, you get to know your Clorets. I carry Clorets in my toolbox along with a small bottle of mouthwash. I pick up a lot of married men at Happy Hour. "The only criminal on the premises right at this moment is a taxi driver named Brendan Murphy who is guilty of trespassing, assault, and arson. A triple threat."

"Arson?" I said, buying time.

"You burned down the mansion next to Riverside Cemetery," he said. "The mansion where you trespassed last night. It's a pity that your automobile caught fire during your incomprehensibly juvenile act of vandalism. What could have possessed you to set fire to an abandoned house on Halloween?"

In the space of three seconds I underwent a number of attitude adjustments. I felt like I was being confronted simultaneously by a nun, a cop, and my Maw. "I don't have the slightest idea what you're talking about," I said—I think. It may have been Joanne Woodward, but it didn't really matter because Rodney smiled and said, "We have a video tape of the entire conflagration."

I looked from Rodney to Dunninger to Eusapia. "You people really are insane."

"Not as insane as the arsonist who set fire to a house and ran like a lunatic through Riverside Cemetery waving a flashlight and laughing maniacally. I will admit, Mr. Murphy, that your laughter came as somewhat of a surprise."

That made two of us.

"It imbued your performance with a verisimilitude that documentarians only dream of capturing on tape," he said. He frowned in an exaggerated, irritating, and theatrical manner. "What do you suppose the police will make of a video like that?"

"They'll probably wonder why you have a video like that."

"They will probably wonder why you interrupted a harmless

Halloween party in an abandoned house," he countered. "Your friends Lester Nagle and Shantel Harris attended a similar party on Wednesday night."

That tore it up.

It was the rip I was waiting for.

It seemed like every time I got involved in the personal life of a fare, a moment came when my personal safety took a backseat to common sense. The thought of Rodney associating with Shantel and Lester raised my blood temperature to 95° Celsius— the boiling point of water at high altitudes.

I squared my shoulders and nodded. "All right, you got me. I set fire to the Riverside mansion. I burned up my car. I ran through the cemetery. I did all those things. And before this night is over I'm going to spill it to my friends Duncan and Argyle and Ottman and Quigg and Ferguson and Boyd."

Rodney squinted. "And who might they be?"

"Just a group of ordinary Joes who spend their time hauling me in on suspicion of murder, kidnapping, bank robbery, and assault. They've got a file on me a foot thick down at DPD. It probably won't come as a surprise to them that I torched the mansion. They've been waiting years to ship me off to Supermax. But I won't be going there alone. I'm taking you birds with me, including your invisible friend Mister Earl."

Dunninger raised the pistol and wiggled it like a winning lottery ticket. "Tut tut," he said.

"You don't think I was stupid enough to come here alone, do you?" I said. "If I'm not out the door by nine o'clock the boys from the Bunko Squad will be swarming all over this joint."

Rodney's facial muscles went slack. He glanced over his shoulder at Dunninger. "Put that thing away."

He looked back at me and said, "Who in the hell *are* you?"

"I thought you knew everything, Criswell."

Another example of common sense climbing into the backseat along with my brain. Criswell was a close friend of Ed Wood—and by the startled expression on Rodney's face he knew the name, the man, and the movie.

"The only thing I know is that you have been stalking me since Saturday afternoon," he snarled, "and that you seem to be laboring under the impression that I have broken the law. So before we take this conversation any further, I would like to know precisely what crime you believe me to be guilty of."

I swallowed hard. Big Al's words rang in my ears. "We currently have no evidence that this Letour fellow is guilty of bilking Mrs. Nagle."

"Fraud," I said.

"And what is the nature of this fraud?"

"You told Lester Nagle that you contacted the spirit of his dead father."

"Mr. Murphy, for the past two years I have been running a psychic business in this location solely for entertainment purposes. I cannot be held responsible for the gullibility of customers who choose to believe that my performances are any different from that of a stage magician. The seances that I perform are not to be taken any more seriously than the films of Roger Corman."

That name was a haymaker to my gut. I was ten years old when I started taking Roger Corman seriously. There may have been a big age difference between myself and Lester Nagle but we both had one thing in common: I hate to use the word "gullibility" twice in the same scene—so I won't.

"You held a seance with Mrs. Nagle," I said.

"I have no idea what you're talking about," he said in a thin tone of voice.

I felt a turn of the screw.

"Mrs. Nagle spoke to her husband," I said. "Just like Lester spoke to his father at the Riverside mansion."

Eusapia and Dunninger glanced at Rodney. He didn't take his eyes off mine.

"Riverside was where you learned that Mrs. Nagle is a rich widow, right?"

He didn't reply. But he didn't have to reply—as I said, I knew that a man in the business of conning people out of money had ways of ferreting out "relevant" information.

"How did you know my family owned a dog named Shelteen?" I said.

The three mediums stared at me so intently that I began to wonder if I had said too much.

Me?

When it became obvious they were not going to reveal their ferreting techniques, I decided to go with Plan B as the nearest straw.

"The Bunko Squad is waiting for the clock to strike nine," I said. That may have been the most important lie I ever uttered in my life.

Rodney raised the finger of his right hand horizontally and gently rubbed the tip of his nose. He almost looked like Leo Gorcey. "I may have underestimated you, Mr. Murphy."

I couldn't decide if this was a compliment or an insult. Frankly I never did figure it out.

"I don't believe this charlatan is telling the truth," Dunninger muttered.

I chortled. I chortled even longer and louder than—Renfield!

Rodney turned to his friends and told them that he wished to speak with me alone.

They waited a moment before stepping away. Their exit was theatrical. It struck me as "haughty" although I am not thoroughly versed in theater lingo.

Rodney looked me up and down. "What's with the clown costume?" he said.

"What do you mean?"

"You weren't dressed like this when you burned down the Riverside mansion."

I bristled.

"You'll never pin that on me," I said.

"I do have a video."

We stared at each other.

My entire universe became focused solely on my eyelids. *Don't blink*, I whispered inwardly.

Rodney's eyelids began to ripple. They undulated from a squint to a probe to a determined drill. His eyebrows even got into the act, but to no avail.

He blinked.

Then he pulled his head back and offered up a conciliatory smile. "I see no reason to bring the police into this matter."

"I do," I said.

He swallowed once and nodded. "It would seem to me, Mr. Murphy, that we have reached something of an impasse. Perhaps we could cut a deal."

"No," I said. "We can't."

"What I mean to say is … if you walk out that door right now and forget that this unfortunate series of events took place, the situation might be resolved to the satisfaction of all parties."

I tried to put myself in Rodney's place. That didn't take long.

"Are you thinking about packing up and moving on down the road?" I said.

He gazed at me for a moment, then smiled. "Tell me something Mr. Murphy, have you ever considered the possibility that you might possess psychic powers?"

"I'm a professional taxi driver," I said. "We're trained to psyche people out. It's a tool we use to stay alive on the mean streets of Denver."

He nodded. "Denver is becoming a little too overcrowded for my taste. Perhaps I might look around for a less-populated burg to hang my shingle."

"Try Phoenix," I said.

Rodney started to say something else, but then he stopped. I could see it in his eyes: this was not the time or the place to duel with an asphalt warrior.

He raised his left wrist and glanced down at his watch. "What do you know about that?" he said. "My lease on this house expires at midnight."

CHAPTER 38

As I drove my rented wreck away from the haunted house I felt the same way I had felt on so many previous occasions, and not all of those occasions had taken place in Denver. Throw a dart at a map of the United States and you can bet I had fled the hole. Sometimes I drove away with a feeling of failure, sometimes I drove away shaken by the feelings that always accompanied a "pyrrhic victory"—meaning I didn't feel so much victorious as damned lucky. The operative word there is "damned." The glory of the moment was always subsumed by the fading of an adrenaline rush leaving me in a state of mild shock. Strangely enough, I had more experience with shock than failure, so I was able to drive safely away from the haunted house without swerving into a ditch.

Ditches fascinate me. As I drove along the road I wondered who had dug the ditches of Denver. According to my teachers, ditches were dug by boys who did not apply themselves assiduously to their studies.

By the time the light posts of the shopping center came into view I was feeling wistful. I was thinking about Lester and his mother, and Shantel and her parents, and how I would have to go to both of their houses and explain that Rodney Letour's psychic reading business had gone belly-up. The thing that made me most wistful was knowing that I would need to keep track of all the lies I would have to tell in order to avoid going to jail, while at the same time providing enough information to let them know that the conflict had been resolved satisfactorily.

I saw Big Al's taxi parked beneath the lamp post. A cone of light shone down on 61. Big Al had bought the taxi from a cabbie named Biff who drove it for twenty years before he retired. Biff retired the hard way. I don't want to talk about it.

As I circled around to pull up next to 61, I wondered if Big Al had jumped any bells while I was gone. I decided not to ask. In theory he could have gone to Boulder and back during my trip to hell and back.

"What's the prognosis, Tenderfoot?" Big Al said as he rolled down his window.

I gave him a thumbs-up. "Victory is ours," I said.

"That's good enough for me," he said. "I don't want to hear any of the details."

Big Al was like a first-reader at every publishing house where I had sent a manuscript over the transom. A quick look at page one and my SASE was back in the mail.

Before I could chastise him for a lack of interest in one of the most dangerous books I ever wrote, I heard a siren. At the same moment I noticed an orange glow to the west. A fire truck shot past the shopping center and turned onto 38th. No sooner did the Doppler Effect begin to fade than I heard another siren. A fire truck was coming from the north.

"A two-alarmer," Big Al said, demonstrating his uncanny ability to interpret numbers.

Suddenly our eyes locked.

It was as if my Univac and his Univac had linked up telepathically and were trading data at the speed of light, analyzing the situation, evaluating the facts, and projecting the results, rendering our vocal chords useless.

"Letour," he whispered.

The orange glow grew brighter. Sparks rose into the night sky. It was as if Golden itself was in flames.

"I have one question to ask you," Big Al said.

"Only one?"

"Is there any possibility that in the near future I shall be receiving a subpoena from the district attorney in connection with a case of arson?"

I took a deep breath and sighed. "Not in the near future," I said. "But I can't speak for next year. I don't own a crystal ball."

"In that case I think it might be best if we took different routes back to our respective hovels. I'll flip you for I-70."

"Naw," I said. "I think I'll stick around. I'm going back to the haunted house to see what happened."

"That's your call," he said with a shrug. "But just remember what Mickey Spillane says about people who return to the scene of the crime."

"What does Mickey say?"

"They're nuts."

I watched the tail lights of RMT #61 disappear down Kipling in the direction of the interstate. I then turned my attention to the orange glow. It was like a giant jack-o'-lantern rising from a pumpkin patch a dollar short and a day late. This was All Saints' Day.

In spite of my bravado at gunpoint, I already had accepted the fact that I would end up in a small room at DPD trying to explain myself to one of my "pals" with a golden badge. Naturally I would fall back on my old standby of avoiding a tight fix by telling the truth.

I know what you're thinking—what a weasel. But I had found that telling the truth to the police often resulted in exoneration followed by a silent vow to never again get involved in the personal life of a fare. The only problem in this case was the charge of "trespassing" that I was actually guilty of. I hate being guilty. The concept of Guilt combined with Truth leaves a sour taste in my mouth. But I did have one ace up my sleeve, which I mentioned earlier, to wit—the house that I had trespassed inside had burned to the ground. There was no evidence that I was guilty of the crime that I would accuse myself of committing. To the average criminal mind this might be viewed as an easy out, but historically speaking, how many criminals had been raised on Catholic guilt?

Three come to mind, two of whom were executed while in federal custody, but let's not get into that.

I waited in the parking lot for a while to see if any more fire trucks might be coming down the road. When it looked like the west side was dead, I put Blue Boy into gear. The 1954 Plymouth was a flat-blue color verging on gray. The body paint may have once been shiny but the brutality of coin washes had taken care of that. I rolled out of the parking lot and drove down 38th in the direction of the haunted house, pretending to be an ordinary Joe on his way to Golden where he lived with his wife and eight children—and who just "happened" upon the scene of the fire. Perhaps I was an accountant who would stop to ask a firefighter what had taken place. As I drove along I practiced saying "My goodness." I figured this would pull the wool over the eyes of anybody who might be wondering just why in the hell a Catholic was driving down a road at nine o'clock at night.

My greatest fear of course was that the firefighters would pull three or four corpses from the ruins of the house. Should that happen, I had an emergency plan up my sleeve. I would throw myself on the mercy of the most affable-looking prosecutor and plead insanity. My pals at DPD just might back me up on that.

I was a quarter-mile away from the scene of the fire when I saw flashing red lights, and not just from fire trucks, but from Golden police department cars. They had blocked off the road in both directions. A sense of dread enveloped me. I did not know a single Golden cop. I realized that I had made a mistake long ago of not getting involved in the personal lives of mountain folk.

A cop with a flashlight was standing in the middle of 38th. He began waving it at me as I got closer. I slowed to a stop and rolled down my window. "Good evening officer. What seems to be the problem here?"

He shined the flashlight directly in my face. I wondered if he recognized me. But he didn't look a day over thirty. He was too young to have seen *Mr. Peepers*. I very rarely got to see *Mr. Peepers* myself because it went head-to-head against *Ed Sullivan* on Sunday nights, and me ol' Dad loved to watch the death-throes of vaudeville.

"Got a house burning down here," he said, as he withdrew the blinding light from my face.

"My goodness," I said, then I braced myself for a "knowing glance" from the cop. But he just pointed the beam of light at the house, which was being sprayed with water from firehoses.

"If you're trying to get to Golden, we're rerouting traffic up to Forty-fourth Avenue," he said.

I knew 44th Avenue.

I knew it well.

It was the road I took to Golden the time I was suspected of kidnapping and murdering a homeless man by pushing him off Lookout Mountain. It was a ridiculous charge of course. I never pushed nobody off no mountain. I would swear to it on a stack of Bibles, although I do not fully comprehend the cumulative theological implications of a multiple-Bible oath.

"You can make a U-turn here and head back to Kipling," he said.

My hair almost stood on end. I was being given permission by a policeman to whip a louie on a public thoroughfare. My palms began to sweat. I swallowed hard and said, "Was anybody hurt in the fire?" but my mind wasn't really on the fire. It was fixated on the idea of whipping a legal U. How many times in a man's life is he given permission by John Law to break it? This was the stuff of legends.

"As far as we can tell the house was vacant," he said.

I began to extrapolate, to wit—as soon as I had walked out of the door Rodney & Co. grabbed their suitcases, torched the joint to cover up any evidence, and fled. I myself had pulled two out of three of those maneuvers in the past so I had no trouble extrapolating. Maybe they had "wired" the house to burn fast when it came time to evade John Law. Maybe the videotape with my "antics" was lying in a heap of liquid plastic and ashen VHS tape.

Maybe.

I was too far away from the house to see how much progress had been made by the flames. Cops and firefighters are good at keeping people away from scenes of potential injury. I once watched an abandoned building burn down. A crowd had gathered on the sidewalk in front of the red brick structure. It was at night. An angry cop came storming down the block shouting, "Get *out* of here, that wall could collapse on *top* of you people!" It was weird getting yelled at by a cop. Most cops speak softly when warning me about things.

"How did the house catch on fire?" I said, trying to look innocent.

"The fire marshal will have to figure that one out," the cop replied.

A car approached from my rear. The light from its headlights bounced off my mirror and lit up my face. Out of habit I reached up and adjusted the mirror so the cop would have less success recognizing me in a lineup.

"You better turn your car around, sir," he said. "There might be a traffic jam forming pretty soon."

I doubted it, 38th Avenue was dead on Sunday nights. But that was the taxi driver in me speculating. Another car was already coming down the road toward us, so the odds were growing thin that I could change the cop's mind through hair-splitting sophistry, my most effective method of winning bets.

He backed away from the car as I put the gearshift into Low. Calling upon my extensive knowledge of steering wheels and tight turns, combined with fifteen years of taxi driving, I wheeled a perfectly executed louie on the two-lane blacktop and began heading east. As I drove away from the scene I looked at my rearview mirror and saw the next driver in line making a fumbling attempt to pull a U-turn, wheeling left and braking and backing up and driving forward and hitting the brakes and backing up again.

I laughed out loud.

Amateurs.

What are you gonna do with 'em?

My brush with unbridled hubris began to fade as I turned left onto Kipling and made my way toward the interstate. I began to speculate. What if the fire was an accident and Rodney had not torched the place? What if Rodney and his cohorts had been killed in the fire? What if the police found an intact video tape showing me setting fire to the Riverside mansion through the clever inter-cutting of scenes depicting—for instance—someone dressed like me pouring gasoline onto the living room floor and tossing a match in the same way that I had tossed flashlights with such reckless abandon? And what if they traced the burned husk of ol' Betsy to my address?

Have I ever mentioned the fact that I am susceptible to what I call "psychological tics?" There was no doubt in my mind that this was turning out to be the worst All Saints' Day in the entire history of canonization.

"Worst #2" of course was my bus trip to Seattle after my brush with a group of illiterate parents. I sat next to a man from Little Rock who spent five hundred miles telling me everything I ever wanted to know about the Arkansas Razorbacks.

CHAPTER 39

When I crossed over Sheridan Boulevard on I-70, I glanced north and wondered what Big Al was doing right at that moment. Playing the baby grand? Suddenly I wondered if he had played into Rodney's hands earlier in the afternoon by inadvertently telling him I once owned a dog named Shelteen. I could not bring myself to believe that Eusapia could channel dogs. Just the thought of being able to talk to Shelteen again turned my blood cold. I vowed that as long as I lived I would never tell my mother about dog-channeling.

But how did Eusapia know? And what about that Hollister business? Could Big Al have let something slip? I felt guilty thinking about this. The only person in our duet capable of letting anything slip was driving a classic clunker along I-70 and marveling at how smooth the ride was. It made me squirm with annoyance to think that Big Al knew I was going to buy this baby. The seats were upholstered in cloth. It smelled like I was driving a comfy couch down the highway.

My thoughts again turned to Shantel and Lester. I would have to speak with both of them and let them know I had interfered in their personal lives without permission, which was my normal approach to interference.

Every time that happened I had a hard time tracing the golden thread that led back to my original blunder. It seemed like I would wake up one morning and find myself trying to figure out how to solve a problem that was none of my business. I rarely tried to solve my own problems but that was because I rarely had problems. I had streamlined my life down to the point where I owned virtually nothing, did virtually nothing, and drove a taxi three days a week. But maybe that was the source of my blunders. Maybe that's why I ended up getting involved in the personal lives of my fares. I was bored. This was not an original thought. Neither was the thought that I ought to get a hobby—like Stew.

The man who worked in the cage at night was obsessed with model railroading. I had been holding my breath for the past fifteen years dreading the day when he might invite me over to his house to look at his setup. More than one driver had been lured into his house to watch miniature railroad trains highballing through his living room and into his dining room. "Don't ever say 'toy train' to Stew," one of those drivers said to me with a glazed look in his eyes.

"Why not?" I said

"Just *don't.*"

On the way back to my crow's nest I stopped off at the Burger King on Colfax and ordered two. I also asked for a sack of fries because I was famished. Sticking my nose into other people's business always did this to me. I didn't ask for a soda though, because I figured the clerk wouldn't recognize me without my ponytail. Plus I was wearing a suit and glasses. My anonymity made me feel fearless. I didn't even feel like a communist. It was a peculiar feeling.

When I got back to my apartment I drove past RMT #123, which I had parked at the curb in front of the building among all the other cars that belonged to all the other people who lived on my block. I drove by just to see if it was still there. Car thieves never seemed to steal cars off the street, they always worked the parking lots. But as I said, there was something intimidating about the semi-official status of a taxi that made criminals avoid stealing them. It would be like stealing a cop car. This was only a theory though. It was possible that the resale value of a taxi on the black market was zero. I hate to give credit to car thieves for having half a brain, but they probably do.

When I pulled around to the rear and headed for the empty space of the choice V-spot where the fence-meets-fence, I felt wistful knowing that never again would I see my two-door, two-tone 1964 Chevy Impala. I felt badly that I had never taken the time to search junkyards for a pair of black doors. Me and ol' Betsy had been through a lot together. I couldn't begin to count the number of times I had driven her into the personal lives of fares. I felt as if I had let her down. If I had found a decent set of doors I could have sent her to the steelyard in style.

I parked Blue Boy in the V-spot and left the engine running for a moment in order to listen to it. Smooth as silk. The Chevy engine always had a slight tapping sound that gave me a minuscule psychological tic, which never blossomed into a full-blown visit to a garage.

But those days were gone.

I shut off the engine, grabbed my sack of grub, and climbed out. I kissed my fingertips, patted Blue Boy on the roof and whispered, "Hope you're still here in the morning." I knew he would inevitably be stolen one day. God willing, the Plymouth had no resale value at all.

Unless I was buying it.

I trudged up the fire escape, entered my crow's nest, and dropped my sack onto the kitchen table. I wanted to get out of my monkey suit. I felt like I had just returned from a wedding—or a funeral. The last time I took it off I had retuned from a date, although I am not at liberty to discuss the nature of the date. You can put your mind at ease though—there was no sex involved, like most of my dates.

A few minutes later I was wearing a T-shirt, blue jeans, and tennis shoes, and hanging the suit in my closet above my ThighMaster. I felt like Superman hanging up one of the dozen or so costumes that he owned for reasons that were never very clear to me as a boy since the costume was made of invulnerable material. It was fashioned from the baby blanket that Kal-El (Clark Kent) had been wrapped in before Jor-El (Marlon Brando) sent him to earth in a rocket ship. As a kid I always wondered how Ma Kent managed to cut and sew the clothing out of a blanket that was as hard as iron. But I didn't understand a lot of things when I was ten years old. In this way I think I was normal. Nothing has changed. I still don't understand a lot of things.

For instance, I don't understand how a producer convinced Marlon Brando to appear in *Superman*. What a coup—the kind of coup that could kill a film career.

I went to the refrigerator to grab a soda, but then decided to hell with it—I didn't care if this was Sunday night. I didn't care if I had to work in the morning. I didn't care if I had to face Shantel and Lester and their parents and maybe even the police if things went the way they usually did. I grabbed a beer and popped the top before I talked myself out of it. Boozing on a Sunday night was unheard of in Murph's Cabana, unless it was Labor Day weekend, or my birthday. Okay. I'll admit it. I seem to have a lot more birthdays than the average person, but let's move on.

I chugged the beer as I channel-surfed. This was how I often dealt with the aftermath of a traumatic experience—sometimes a brush with death, sometimes a job interview. I crushed the aluminum can with my fist of steel and tossed it in the general direction of the kitchen.

It felt good to be back in college.

I then did something I was loath to do. I shut off the cable, walked into the bathroom, and looked at my face in the mirror.

I remembered the day I got a haircut after my job interview at Dyna-Plex. A friend named Wally examined my haircut and told me I looked like my sister. I had gone to Wally's house to borrow a suit for the inter-view, however the suit did not play a pivotal role in getting the job. It was my personality. The vice president who interviewed me for the job said he had never met anyone quite like me before. I took that as a compliment because the alternative was unthinkable. Mostly he seemed fascinated by my hair. It was real long and sort of horizontal. It looked like someone had dropped a safe full of Brylcreem on my head. The other job appli-cants looked like Wally Cox.

I turned my head from side to side but couldn't see my missing ponytail. This was not unusual. But even the hair that I could see had been shortened by Big Al. I hadn't said anything during the haircut but I suspected he was enjoying the act of shearing off my hippie locks. He would have made a good army barber—or a redneck. I'm not sure what the distinction is.

I set about shampooing the Vaseline out of my hair. It took less than a minute. I had forgotten how quickly short hair could be washed. The session with my Vidal Sassoon blow-dryer took another sixty seconds. It usually took seven minutes to wash and fully dry my ponytail, not in-cluding the onerous chore of properly affixing a rubber band. It occurred to me that I ought to keep my hair short from now on. The idea of hav-ing an extra five minutes added to my life to do nothing was extremely appealing. Just think of all the things a man couldn't do in five minutes.

I replaced my disposable contact lenses, then took a long hard look at myself in the mirror. Normally when I do this I am examining the depths of my innermost being, but on that night I was trying to decide whether I looked more like Beaver Cleaver or Lumpy Rutherford.

The jury is still out.

I walked back into the kitchen and glanced at the beer can lying on the floor next to the wastebasket. It looked lonely. There were no empty pizza boxes strewn about. I sighed and picked up the can and tossed it into the trash. College was over. I decided it was time to start acting like a grownup. If you are a college student on the verge of graduation, you will eventually be forced to come to that conclusion about yourself. The first time I did it I was thirty-eight years old. I did it twice when I was forty-two, and here I was at forty-six doing it again. I really ought to get serious about that goddamn therapy deal.

Bloated on twelve ounces of brewski, three ounces of which I had surely digested by now, I switched off the lights in the front room, staggered into my bedroom and kicked off my Keds. I didn't collapse into bed though. I once made that mistake after a kegger. Carbonation and swan-dives are a bad mix.

I switched on the lamp next to my bed, then turned off the overhead light. I debated whether or not to leave the foyer light on. Aside from avoiding a calamitous burp, I had not made any critical decisions since I had gotten home, so I didn't feel it was necessary to leave it on. I switched it off, then went to bed and lay staring at the ceiling thinking about what a mess my life was.

I often use that technique for going to sleep, in the same way that actors take a quiet moment in their dressing rooms to vomit before going on stage. I began reviewing the events of the evening and I could not get out of my mind the inexplicable appearance of the ghosts of Mr. Hollister and Shelteen. Don't get me wrong though—I do not believe in ghosts, but still, how could Rodney have acquired personal information about me on such short notice?

I started thinking about the seance.

I thought about the cold breezes that caressed my cheeks after the lights went down. Theatrics of course. That's what I told myself. There were no such things as ghosts, although there were such things as shelties. When Rodney and I were touching the planchette I could have sworn his fingertips had no control over the device. I thought of Big Al's lecture on celibacy, to wit: "… a caveman who attributed the disappearance of the sun to the appetite of a giant invisible dragon who could be appeased only by the sacrifice of a virgin."

In other words, people could be easily fooled by people who were good at fooling people. By the second "people" I mean Moog, a caveman responsible for all the evil that has evolved since the moment a giant black obelisk appeared at Shepperton Studios in … England.

The third "people" was his cousin Oog, who was the first sap on earth. If you don't understand what I'm talking about, it really doesn't matter. The point I'm making is that the planchette had mysteriously moved in the same way that planchettes have moved all down through-out the history of saps. There was some sort of "trick" to it. The cool breezes too. But still …

Then there was that weird "thump" that took place during the se-ance—the ghost of Mister Earl. I'll admit it. By the time the seance had gotten to that point my defenses were just about shattered, especially by the—how can I put this?—blasé manner in which Rodney and Dun-ninger and Eusapia had spoken of Earl, the offhanded way Eusapia and Dunninger had chatted about someone named "Amelia." Could they have rehearsed that? Was there a fourth person upstairs? The answer was probably yes. Based on the things Big Al told me about frauds, they were as slick as any professionals can get, even law-abiding professionals. I had always taken a certain amount of pride in the fact that I could be a fraud when the chips were down, but I began to feel as if I was a summer-stock actor in the presence of superstars who regularly brought down the house at the Old Met. I was a bush-leaguer. A rank amateur. A nobody from Denver wallowing in delusions of grandeur. This applied to other aspects of my life but I don't want to get into that.

I thought about the pistol that Rodney had pulled on me. I will admit I was surprised because the gun had appeared in Act 3 without making an appearance in Act 1, in complete violation of the rules of stage drama. I hate it when people break "The Rules"—especially playwrights. The next thing you know you're nodding through *Waiting for Godot* and hoping the star-struck coed seated next to you doesn't have to be back at her dorm until you've washed Beckett out of her system with a few brewskis at the Campus Lounge. That was KAU in Wichita.

"The Fear" finally made its appearance in my bedroom. It usually does after a hard night of getting involved in the personal lives of my fares, whether holding hands with hippies, bursting into rooms at the Y, or crashing beach parties at Malibu. It's a miracle that The Mob hasn't broken my legs just to keep me off the street for my own good.

I could have gotten shot. I could have gotten shot one rainy night at Union Station, but I've probably said too much about that already. A word to the wise: don't ever invest me with top-secret classified government information.

Nuff said.

I thought about Shantel and Lester again. I was especially worried about Lester because evidence indicated that I had run his mother's psychic out of town. I hate evidence. Me and evidence have had a running battle ever since I spoke my first word, which I assume was "Mama." There is a dull predictability to babies.

I lay in the darkness thinking about ghosts and guns and talking dogs, and then I did something I hate to admit. I got out of bed and crossed to the foyer and turned the light back on. I didn't do it because I had made a decision though. I did it because I was afraid that if I didn't do it, I would hear the maniacal laughter of Renfield coming from the general area of my pillow as the night wore on, and I hated it whenever I found myself running blindly across my bedroom in the dark. Sometimes I stubbed my toes.

CHAPTER 40

That night I dreamed I was walking down a street. I've had that dream a thousand times. I don't know what it means. Hopefully nothing. I woke up Monday morning, November 2, and wondered what day it was. By "day" I meant did it have an official name like "Halloween" or "All Saints" or was it just a regular day? Then I remembered: it was All Souls' Day. I remembered because I got the answer wrong on a test in religion class during the sixth grade. More proof that learning comes from making mistakes and not from memorizing books? You be the judge.

My favorite calendrical name is St. Swithin's Day, but I am not familiar with its background. I just like the sound of it. The only thing I do know about Swithin is that he was a counselor to Egbert, the king of the West Saxons, but everybody knows that.

I must have had a good night's sleep because I drifted awake at 5:30 a.m. I normally wake up at 6:00 on work days. I wanted to roll over and go back to sleep but I was afraid I would find myself walking down *the street*!!! It didn't matter though. I was fully refreshed and totally awake, two of my least-favorite adverbial phrases.

Since I had some time on my hands I decided to make a cup of coffee and eat breakfast while seated at the kitchen table rather than driving ol' Bets …

I had momentarily forgotten that ol' Betsy was a goner and that my taxi was parked at the curb out front waiting for me to suit up and get back on the road. For some reason this made me feel organized. It wasn't a good feeling. To paraphrase Ratso Rizzo: "You know what they do to you when they find out you're competent." I've avoided competence most of my life, although it didn't take much effort—if it did I would probably be CEO of Microsoft by now. I pondered the fact that both *The Graduate* and *Midnight Cowboy* ended with Dustin Hoffman sitting at the back of a bus. He was dead in one of the movies and on his way to get married in the other, but I couldn't remember which was which. Too early in the morning to think straight. I needed that cup of joe.

The first thing I did when I got into the kitchen was peek out a window. I was looking for cops. Habit I'm sorry to say. The next thing I did was fill a cup with hot water from the spigot, then I dumped a teaspoonful of instant coffee into the water. Frankly I do not know what the difference is between my java and a Starbucks brew, aside from the cost and flavor.

It was ten minutes to seven when I left my crow's nest and climbed down the fire escape to the parking lot. In the past I had sometimes felt I was on an underground multiple-listing service distributed freely to car thieves, so the presence of Blue Boy boded well.

I knew I was going to buy the pink slip. But I took a moment to walk around the car and examine it closely before committing myself. I sometimes did that with women even though it made them skittish.

I finally went to the front of my building and climbed into #123. I had a weekly lease for which I owed $300, and so far I had not earned dime one. This did not bode well, and was one of the reasons I rarely pulled weekly leases. Having a taxi available twenty-four hours a day was like having a shelf full of VHS tapes that I never watched. I needed the motivation of a tight deadline, whether it involved a taxi lease or a movie rental—just get it viewed and get it back by 7:00.

I started the engine, turned on the radio, and contacted the dispatcher to let him know I was on the road. I then braced myself to hear the magic words "el-two." That was another habit I had gotten into not long after I began getting involved in the personal lives of my fares. Bracing myself I mean. I received my first L-2 on my second day on the job, but we've had that conversation.

It was too early to go knocking on doors so I figured I would save my visits to the Harris and Nagle households until 11:00 a.m. Unfortunately that gave me four hours to fret about what I would be facing when it came time to unburden my soul and confess to whatever I would end up confessing. As I said, I did not know exactly how much appalling information I would to have to reveal to the respective families. I was just going to "wing it," which is not only the best but the only way I know how to do anything. I'm not in jail and I hardly ever work, so the method has a sound precedent.

The prospect of driving every day for the rest of the week affected me the way real jobs affect normal people: I turned off my brain. I drove downtown to position myself in the assembly line, or "the cabstand at the Brown Palace Hotel" as it is known internationally. Since Monday was referred to as "Little Friday" by cab drivers, I knew business would be hopping to the extent that people would be going to DIA.

I parked fifth in line at the Brown, and within thirty minutes I was first in line. A man came out of the hotel carrying a briefcase and climbed into my backseat. "DIA," he said. I felt so smug it would have made you sick. When he handed me sixty bucks at the terminal and told me to keep the change, I became insufferably blasé. I made myself sick. I don't know why I waste my time buying scratch tickets. I drive one.

By ten o'clock I had grossed one hundred and ten dollars. This was not unusual. It was Monday. Wait until Tuesday, the most innocuous day of the week. By ten o'clock on a Tuesday I'm lucky if I've grossed thirty bucks. That really makes me sick.

I cruised the mean streets of Capitol Hill picking up decent money and trying not to be smug about it until ten-thirty. And then suddenly …

"One twenty-three, el-two."

I was driving past City Park when that shot crossed my bow. I was in the process of turning my brain back on and preparing myself spiritually to drive over to Shantel's house to face the music. Part of my prepping consisted of divesting myself of the hope that nobody would be home. If you've ever done anything that you didn't want to do, you may have experienced that yourself. It's a holdover from my childhood—specifically "homework." My motto these days is "Just get it done and get it out of the way," whereas my inner-child's motto is "Turn on the TV *now*!"

I picked up the microphone and said "Check" then I swung over to University Boulevard and drove to the motor while "Murph Jr.," as I call my inner-child, pouted and sulked. But then I had taught him every-thing he knows.

Or did I?

It was the old chicken-and-egg conundrum, the-child-is-the-father-of-the-man, etc. I spend a lot of time trying to blame kids for things. I win 14 percent of the time.

I parked outside the on-call room and went inside. I gave Rollo a cursory nod as I walked past the cage. He knew I had been called in on an L-2. I didn't have to explain it to him. He knew everything that went on in his petty little kingdom. It made me feel like a medieval serf. As I trudged up the stairway to Hogan's office I was battling an uncontrollable grin. Hogan ignored it. He probably thought I was trying to suck up to him. I abandoned that during my third year as a cab driver.

Hogan nodded and said, "Thanks for coming in, Murph," the serf.

I clamped my lips shut.

Hogan paused and peered at me … then went on with what he had to say. "Have a seat."

My smile evaporated. Hogan never offers me a seat unless the news is unpleasant. A learned thing.

I sat down on "my" chair in front of his desk.

"I got a phone call a half-hour ago from that woman Missus Harris, whose daughter you drove to the haunted house last Wednesday night," he said. "She told me she wanted you to come to her house today but she did not tell me why. So I asked you to come in to the motor because I would like to know what the situation is here."

He paused and looked down at the desk, pursed his lips, and moved a pencil approximately three inches from left to right. My heart sank. When Hogan starts toying with inanimate objects, things have taken a dark turn.

He glanced up at me and said, "The last time I spoke to you I made it clear that the buck stopped here. But apparently the situation has not been resolved satisfactorily, and I am concerned that Rocky Cab might be drawn into an untenable situation. You know as well as I do that your job has been dangling by a thread ever since … well … ever since …"

"Since my second day as a taxi driver," I interjected.

Hogan does not normally tolerate being interrupted while speaking, but in this case he nodded—sadly I felt, although I may have been reading too much into his affirmation.

"I can't have these phone calls coming into my office, Murph. So I just want to ask you right up front. Are you involved in a situation that might cause legal action to be taken against the Rocky Mountain Taxicab Company?"

"No," I said. "This is personal. In fact I was just getting ready to drive over to the Harris house when I got your el-two."

He gave me a modified version of the fish-eye—he squinted—but I didn't blame him. Liars often pretend to be in the process of correcting a situation as soon as they are cornered and forced to admit they have been "found out." Sometimes they say, "The check is in the mail." You may have experienced this yourself.

"I've lost count of the number of times that I have gone to bat for you, Murph," Hogan said. "But the one thing I always knew was that I could count on you to tell me the truth. So I just want to ask you one question. If you go talk to Mrs. Harris today, will this be the end of it? Will I be getting any more phone calls from the woman?"

I was tempted to point out that he had asked me two questions, but I squelched it. This wasn't high school English class, this was reality, and the problem with reality is that you can't peek at the back of the book for the answers, which was how I managed to pass algebra with a good solid D.

"I'm going to take care of it today, sir," I said.

The look of shock on his face matched the surprise in my heart. I had never called Hogan "sir" before.

I started to apologize, but then remembered that he wasn't a sergeant. If you are a young man or woman thinking of joining the army, don't ever refer to a sergeant as "sir."

Just *don't*.

"That's good enough for me, Murph," he said, smoothing over my social gaffe. "Right now there are only two people at RMTC who know about this situation: you and me." Then he did something strange. He pulled out his wallet and removed a one-dollar bill and slapped it down on the desk. "This greenback stays right here until you tell me I can put it away."

I finally realized the enormity of what I had done. I had caused Hogan to perform a ritual. I hate rituals. I hate the ceremonial repetition of rites that are imbued with symbolism that means nothing to me. If you have ever been required to do anything twice, you probably know how I felt.

"You won't be getting any more phone calls from Missus Harris," I said with steel in my voice. Little did he realize that I would simply tell Mrs. Harris to stop phoning him. This was one of the reasons I hated ritual. If I can outfox it, it isn't real, and if something isn't real, why am I pretending to take it seriously?

The answer is simple: survival.

I survived a week at Boy Scout camp when I was ten years old by pretending to be trustworthy, loyal, and honest. I don't remember the rest of the ritual, I only remember the ten bucks I stole from an Eagle Scout.

Meeting over.

I stood up and walked out of Hogan's office knowing that my job was dangling by a thread. This had always been true but an L-2 from Hogan served as a gentle reminder—like the postcards I keep getting about the overdue library book in my chest of drawers.

I trudged downstairs and passed through the on-call room without pausing to genuflect to King Rollo, even though I knew I would pay the price one day for my lack of servility. But I had an ace up my sleeve. I could always exile myself to the kingdom of Yellow Cab. They'll hire anybody.

CHAPTER 41

It was high noon when I stepped outside the on-call room. I hate it when situations deteriorate at high noon. That's one of the three things I have in common with classic western sheriffs.

I climbed into 123, started the engine, and made sure that both the AM radio and the Rocky radio were turned off. I didn't want any distractions as I drove to the Harris house. I didn't even plan to stop at a phone booth to inform Shantel's mother that I was coming over. I knew Murph Jr. well enough to know that the slightest distraction would prevent me from following through on the job at hand. Whenever I sit down to write a novel I hide my TV remote so the sight of it won't distract me. It rarely works.

I drove straight down University Boulevard. I was focused. I was in "The Zone." I was determined to make Hogan put that dollar bill back into his wallet.

But I managed to turn right on Speer Boulevard and drive to the Harris's street without glancing at the golfers on the fairways of the Denver Country Club. That was easy enough. There was no motion to distract me. Golfers don't move. They just stand there. It occurred to me that there might be a pretty penny in the invention of a chair designed for golfers. "Drive While Sitting Down!" That had a familiar ring but I turned right before I could develop the concept any further, thank God.

I approached the Harris house as I had done so many times during the past few days. Golden leaves were still fluttering to the ground. I was far enough away from the house that I was able to glance to the top of the trees in front of it without being seen by the rich people peeking through their windows. They were mighty tall. The trees I mean. I didn't know what species. They looked sort of like aspen, but at that point in my life I just didn't care anymore.

I parked in front of the house, climbed out and made my way up the elongated S trying hard not to think about James Joyce. That was not so easy. Practically everything makes me think of James Joyce. I really should have majored in botany.

"… Ding-dong …"

This was it. The curtain was going up. The only question that remained was whether the audience would be thrilled by the sight of Laurence Olivier, Peter Lorre, or me. I chose Door #2. Peter Lorre was a performer nonpareil when it came to fawning, groveling, and obsequious toadying. He taught me everything I know.

"Mr. Murphy, good to see you!" a man's voice piped. It was Mr. Harris.

I swallowed hard. Why do I always feel guilty when husbands answer doors? I squared my shoulders and braced myself for a haymaker to the gut.

"Hello, Mr. Harris," I said. "My supervisor Mr. Hogan down at Rocky Cab told me that your wife called and asked that I come over."

"Yes, we called the taxi company earlier and your boss told us you were on duty, so we asked if it would be possible for you to come by today."

I started to tell him that anything is possible in this three-ring circus we call cab driving, but I squelched it. I often play word-association games when people talk to me because it helps me to not hear what they are saying. But I stuffed that bauble back into my toy box and paid close attention. I felt so mature it would have made you sick.

"Come on in, Mr. Murphy, Beth is in the living room."

I walked down the long green hallway and heard the door close at my back. I felt trapped. I was back in my element.

I made a slow right turn into the living room—and stopped dead in my tracks.

Beth Harris was there—but so was Mrs. Nagle. Seated on the couch were Shantel and Lester. They all looked up at me but nobody spoke. A chill gripped my heart. I felt like I had been tricked into another AA meeting.

But then something occurred to me. Was this a different sort of setup? Was it possible that Rodney and his cohorts would step into the room and hold a pentagram devil-worship daylight seance in the home of a millionaire? As I often stated, I wished my imagination would take off like that when I was trying to write a novel.

"Thank you so much for coming over, Mr. Murphy," Beth Harris said, standing up from her chair and approaching me. She was wearing a light-blue pantsuit. I have no idea what relevance that has to anything.

"You're welcome," I said.

"Hello, Mr. Murphy," Shantel and Lester both said as they stood up from their chairs.

The only person who remained seated was Mrs. Nagle, thank goodness. I was starting to feel "crowded."

"I believe you've met my sister, Constance," Mr. Harris said, crossing the living room and placing a hand affectionately on Mrs. Nagle's shoulder.

"Yes, we have met," I said, remembering to remove my Rocky cap. I had gotten out of the habit of removing my cap indoors after I was booted out of the army. The military is virtually psychotic on the subject of headgear worn indoors. It turned me into a rebel.

"Why Mr. Murphy, you've cut your ponytail!" Mrs. Harris said with a musical note of delight in her voice.

"Oh … uh … yeah … well … I'm always trying out new looks," I said with the cool aplomb of David Niven.

"You look like Gollum," Shantel said.

That tore it.

In six months I would look like Francis the Talking Mule, but let's move on.

"Thank you for taking the time out from your job to drop by, Mr. Murphy," Mr. Harris said. "This is a school day for Shantel and Lester but we kept them home so they could be present when you arrived."

"Why don't you call me Murph?" I said.

"Well thank you, Murph. And why don't you call me Jeff?"

"All right … Jeff."

I knew I had made a tactical error. I don't really like to get chummy with anybody—not millionaires and not nobody. They usually end up borrowing money. Not the millionaires, just the nobodies.

"Would you like something to drink?" Mrs. Harris said.

Would I? Got any Cutty?

"No thank you, ma'am, I'm fine."

"Why don't you have a seat there, Murph," Jeff said, pointing me toward a fancy chair. I once sat on a chair upholstered in silk, but that was long ago and in another disaster.

I sat down and waited for the bad news. It wasn't long in coming. From my perspective all news is bad news.

"Shantel?" Mrs. Harris said. "Would you like to say something to Murph?"

Shantel nodded and took a few steps toward me. She clasped her hands in front of her waist and smiled. She had the regal bearing of a young lady who had been educated in a fine finishing school. It made my skin crawl.

"First of all, Mr. Murphy, I want to apologize to you for all the trouble I caused you during the past week, and I want to let you know that I told my parents everything."

Everything?

Fer the luvva Christ. I felt like dashing down the hall and diving through a window—but then I told myself that Shantel couldn't possibly know about the "incident" in Albuquerque.

At this point Jeff stepped forward and put his arm around Shantel's shoulder.

"Shantel told us that you were concerned enough about both her and Lester's welfare that you voluntarily took it upon yourself to drive out to that mansion near Riverside Cemetery to see if Lester had gone there with that man who held the seance on Wednesday night."

By now my skin was no longer crawling. It was getting up on its feet. It made me think of writing a horror novel with a grotesque premise, but I shut that down fast. What the hell—I'll tell you the title: *The Skin Creature.*

"I have to admit I was upset when I learned that Shantel had involved you in this situation," Jeff said. "But I quickly realized that she could not have picked a better man to ask for help. So I want you to know that I deeply appreciate the things you've done for both my daughter and nephew."

I glanced at Lester. He wasn't wearing any costumes that day, unless being well groomed was a form of "costume." In my world it is.

Lester smiled and nodded, but he didn't say anything. I liked that. I wished everybody on earth acted like well-groomed teenagers.

"And there's something else," Jeff said. "After Shantel told us everything, I took it upon myself to go to my sister's house for the first time in a long time and find out what's been going on." He turned and looked at his wife. "Beth told me that she mentioned to you the fact that we have been estranged for a long time. That was a deplorable situation and I blame myself for letting it go on so long. But thanks to your intervention, Constance and I have settled our differences. It would never have happened if you hadn't shown your concern for the welfare of these two young people."

Intervention?

That word rang a bell but I couldn't place it.

Or could I?

Maybe I just didn't want to.

"I'm happy I was able to help out," I said.

"You did more than just help out, Murph. You may have saved my sister from losing a lot of money. Apparently that so-called psychic was taking an inordinate interest in my sister's financial situation. He claimed to be able to communicate with the spirit of my brother-in-law Herbert who passed away ten years ago."

Rodney!

I was *right*.

Or perhaps it would be better to say that Big Al was right.

"He was a fraud," Mrs. Nagle said.

We all looked at her.

I started to correct her, then realized she was not talking about Big Al.

"That man was interested only in my money," Mrs. Nagle said. She spoke as slowly as she had spoken to me on the night I went to her house in search of Lester. "My brother Jeffrey prevented me from making a terrible mistake."

"Mr. Murphy deserves all the credit, Constance," Jeff said. "Without his help, things may have taken a bad turn."

Mrs. Nagle looked at me and smiled a wistful smile. "Thank you so much for returning my brother to me, Mr. Murphy."

I realized at that point that Mrs. Nagle may have been suffering from a slight mental affliction. There was something peculiar about her manner, but let's don't go too far down that road. Bursting into Malibu beach houses was one thing, but diagnosing mental conditions was not my area of expertise. I don't have an area of expertise—with one possible exception: I was born to drive while sitting down.

The specifics of the situation concerning Rodney's worming were none of my business and I did not ask for any, but I knew Rodney well enough from our brief encounter to know that the Nagle family was now in good hands. Jeffrey Harris was no longer estranged from his sister, and Lester had a father figure to look out for his best interests—and isn't this what every boy needs? A millionaire who likes him.

Been there twice.

As I sat in my chair I began to wonder whether I ought to break down and tell them everything else that had happened, or if I should keep my mouth shut and my fingers crossed, two techniques that had served me so well in the past that you might expect I would have known the answer. But I had to think about it. That didn't take long. I never spend much time thinking. I simply reminded myself of something Big Al said to me once—or twice—I tend to lose count. "Just pretend none of this ever happened, Tenderfoot." I felt as if a giant invisible pooka was standing over my left shoulder.

"Lester, would you like to say something to Mr. Murphy?" Jeff said.

Now it was Lester's turn to demonstrate regal bearing. He walked up to me and smiled. "I'm sorry about all the trouble I caused you this week, Mr. Murphy." He glanced at Shantel then looked back at me. "I know that I said some things that might have annoyed you when you were driving us to the haunted house that night so I just wanted to apologize for that, too."

If I had been wearing a starched collar I would have tugged at it with a forefinger and fidgeted anxiously. Instead I stood up and shook hands with Lester, and told him that he was forgiven. I didn't actually say "forgiven." I said something like, "That's okay, pal," but I don't really remember. I was so overwhelmed by all the forgiveness, gratitude, and genteel behavior floating around the room that I was losing contact with reality, thank goodness.

"Well I expect we've taken up enough of your work time," Jeff said with a smile. "We'd better let you get back to your job. And I would like to pay you something for your time."

"No thanks, Jeff," I said. "This ride's on me."

It worked.

I walked out of the house broke.

CHAPTER 42

Jeff followed me outside and accompanied me down to my taxi. I got that pooka feeling again. Sometimes Harvey looks like Big Al, and sometimes he looks like Maw.

"If you have a moment, Murph, I want to tell you something else," Jeff said. "I didn't want to say anything in front of the family but I called the police and made some inquiries about this Rodney character. I learned a couple of disturbing things."

I knew it. It looked like I was going to end up making the confession that I had dreaded all along. I almost dropped to my knees and began reciting the Act of Contrition. For those of you non-Catholics out there, that's a prayer Catholics recite when they are contrite.

Jeff folded his arms and frowned. "It seems that the mansion where the seance was held on Wednesday night burned down."

I froze.

"It happened on Saturday night but they don't know who did it. They figure it was probably teenagers playing around inside the abandoned house. One of the policemen I spoke with said the burning had the earmarks of Devil's Night. Apparently that was an abhorrent custom that used to take place in Detroit on Halloween, mostly involving young people." He shook his head sadly. "It makes my blood run cold to think that Shantel and Lester might have been mixed up with the sort of people who do things like that. This situation could have turned out much worse."

"It did," I wanted to say, but kept my mouth shut.

"The other thing I wanted to tell you is that the police phoned me this morning and told me that the house where Rodney Letour lived burned down last night. It might have been arson. The final report won't be coming in for a while, but it looks like that Letour fellow may have burned down the house himself and then left town. God only knows what he may have been trying to hide."

"God and Murph," I almost said.

"So I just wanted to thank you again from the bottom of my heart for intervening," Jeff said. "It's difficult to be a father. It can be darn hard to keep track of what teenagers are up to. I owe you a lot."

"You don't owe me anything, Jeff," I said. "The fact that Shantel and Lester are okay is payment enough."

He reached out and shook my hand. It seemed like every time I got involved in the personal life of a fare my hand got a real workout. It reminded me of my family. Irish-Catholics tend to shake hands a lot when they get together. Mine do anyway. I keep a small bottle of Corn Huskers Lotion handy whenever I go home every twenty years.

"Say, Murph, do you play golf?"

That sentence scarred my brain permanently.

"No."

"Well I think it's about time you learned," Jeff said. "I would like to invite you to be my guest to play eighteen holes whenever you have time."

"I'm not much of an athlete," I said obsequiously. "My handicap alone would probably set a course record."

"I don't really think of golf in terms of athletic activity," he said. "The game has a Zen quality that seeks perfect balance between the mind and body. In fact, the effort involved is more cerebral than muscular. It demands intense concentration in order to maneuver a ball hundreds of yards into a tiny hole. In the final analysis, golf is a game of inches."

He might have been describing cab driving—but he wasn't.

I knew how to get out of this horrifying prospect though. The other millionaire I knew once offered to teach me how to ski. Let's just say that I have never looked down the twin-barrels of a snow-covered slope. "I would be glad to join you on the links sometime, Jeff. I'll let you know when I feel up to the challenge of balancing my mind."

"Good enough, Murph. I look forward to it. I probably should mention that I like to play in the morning."

"I like to do things in the morning, too," like sleep.

We shook hands again. It was becoming intolerable.

"All right!" he chirped. "Back to the ol' grind, eh?"

Grind?

What grind?

I drive a taxi for a living.

I opened the door to 123 and climbed in, settled myself behind the steering wheel, and took a deep breath of the kind of air that you find inside vehicles of public transportation. I felt revitalized.

That didn't last long.

I glanced at the house and saw Jeff opening the front door. At that moment Shantel came outside. She stopped to say something to her dad, then began hurrying down the sidewalk toward me.

I'll admit it.

I fumbled my key and it fell to the floor mat. I could not help but think that Harvey had something to do with my failed escape attempt.

Shantel came up to my window and leaned down to speak. "I have a favor I would like to ask of you, Mr. Murphy."

I stifled an internal sigh and said, "Only if you promise to call me 'Murph' in the future."

"Okay, Murph," she said with a smile. It was a Pepsodent smile. Mary Ann has one of those, too. "I know I said I told my parents everything, but that was just me. Lester has something he would like to tell you but he didn't want to say anything inside the house." She turned and looked at the front porch where Lester had appeared, although I assumed he had walked out the door.

"Lester and I are going to the Cherry Creek Shopping Center in a little while, and we would like to know if you could meet us at the snack bar. It won't take long, but he wants to tell you something in private."

If I recall correctly, it was that fine character actor Ned Beatty who once said, "There's no end to it."

"How about if I meet you in an hour?" I said.

"That will work." She glanced back at Lester and then turned to me. "He's a lot sorrier than he looks. But it's really hard for Lester to express his emotions."

"I understand," I said. Lester just might make a good cab driver some day.

Let's cut to the chase:

An hour later I parked 123 in a slot near the cabstand in front of the mall. I climbed out and walked past three taxis that were waiting for fares. It made me feel smug to walk away from my cab while the working classes were chained to the assembly line.

I made my way down to the snack bar and saw Shantel and Lester sitting at the exact same table where all of this had begun. The bad part anyway. When they saw me coming they both stood up. Most people cross the street when they see me coming. I still do a pretty good Bullwinkle.

"Can I buy you kids a soft drink?" I said.

"Oh, no thank you Murph," Shantel said. "We won't keep you long. Lester just wants to say something to you. I'm going to do some window-shopping."

With that she walked away leaving me and Lester standing alone at the table. The situation would have made me feel awkward but I was thinking about the fact that I had not heard the phrase "window-shopping" in years. I don't get out much.

"Thanks for doing this, Mr. Murphy," Lester said.

I let it pass. I had the feeling he needed to call me "Mister Murphy" until he said everything he had to say. The formality seemed requisite. He looked nervous.

"Let's sit down," I said.

We sat on opposite sides of the plastic table. There weren't any squealing kids running around in Halloween costumes. Halloween was over and the decorations had been replaced with silhouettes of pumpkins and turkeys. The squealing kids were dressed like pilgrims.

"I guess Shantel and I caused you a lot of problems this week," he said in his slightly adenoidal voice. "Or I guess mostly it was just me."

I liked that. He was accepting blame for the situation. He would make a terrible taxi driver.

"The reason I wanted to talk to you is to tell you some stuff that I think you would want to know."

He had me figured wrong, but I let it pass. He was just a kid. He would eventually learn that nobody ever wants to know anything, except priests. I have a lot in common with priests. I used to spend my Saturday nights in confessionals, too.

"I'm listening," I said.

Lester got a pained look on his face, then tugged at his shirt collar and fidgeted slightly on his chair. I wondered if he was Catholic.

"You know that guy Rodney Letour?" he said.

"Yes."

"Well … a couple days ago he started asking me questions about you. It was after I showed him the taxi receipt you gave to me. He wanted to know why you gave it to me." He swallowed hard. I'll admit it. I felt like I was looking at a mirror—a *time* mirror. Lester reminded me of myself when I was his age. This made me think of writing a novel about a time mirror. I'll let you take it from there.

"What kind of things did he ask?" I said.

"Well… he wanted to know who you were, and how I met you, and things like that. But he acted real friendly, you know, like he was just curious. But I think I might have told him some things I shouldn't have."

"Like what?"

"For one thing I told him about the police investigations you said you were involved with. I also told him your phone number."

?!?!?!

"How did you know my phone number?"

"I got it from Shantel. Only she doesn't know I told Rodney. Please don't tell her I did that. She's been sort of mad at me for the past couple of days. I feel really bad about this because I didn't even think about what I was doing. Rodney had this way of … you know … finding out stuff without acting like he was trying to find out."

"Let me ask you something," I said. "After I dropped you off at the theater, did you go with Rodney to another seance?"

He nodded and looked down at the tabletop.

"Did he try to contact the spirit of your father?"

He nodded again.

"Did your father's spirit ask to talk to your mother?"

He nodded more slowly.

"Did you and your mother take part in a seance?"

He spoke quietly: "We went out to the house by Golden yesterday for a seance."

"Around noon?" I said.

Okay. I want to get this part out of the way real quick. A teardrop landed on the table beneath Lester's bowed head.

He looked up at me and said, "I really messed up."

"Listen, man, I'm going to buy you a soda," I said. "I need a coffee anyway."

He nodded. I stood up and made myself as scarce as the nearest concession that sold espresso. It was thirty feet away. By the time I got back to the table Lester had pulled himself together. I handed him the soda and sat down. I looked at my latte and was surprised to see that I had already drank half of it. I began to get the feeling I would be walking with the zombies that night.

"Rodney Letour was a fraud," I said. "It's impossible to contact the spirits of the dead. Your mother was exactly right. Rodney is just a con man, and con men are good at getting information out of people. Don't feel bad, Lester. I've been conned plenty of times in my life. If he hadn't gotten that information out of you he would have gotten it from somebody else. You just happened to be handy. You're not to blame for this. You don't have anything to feel sorry for. Rodney is just a ..." I tried to think of a synonym for "bastard" because I didn't want to spout off like a remedial G.I. in front of this kid. I did come up with some pretty funny synonyms though—but I'll let you dogfaces use your imaginations on that one. "... jerk. The police are going to catch him someday."

"I hope so," he said. "My mom really believed she was talking to my dad during the seance."

Life.

What are you gonna do?

"Can I ask you a question?" I said.

"Yes."

"By any chance did you mention to Rodney that I once owned a dog named Shelteen?"

He frowned at me. Then he raised his eyes and looked above my head. I wondered if he was seeing Harvey.

"That's funny," he said. "I do remember telling him that."

How in the hell ... "How did you know that?" I said.

He frowned again. It was a "thinking" frown. I used to see straight-A students do that in high school. I myself never did it though. I was too embarrassed to let the other kids know I was thinking—not to mention my teachers. My teachers always got angry if I paused one millisecond to think things through. They wanted the answers *right now!!!!!* I personally feel that speed plays an inordinately important role in our educational system when it should be irrelevant. But I guess I'm just one of those rebels who believes that correct answers are more important than fast answers.

"Shantel told me," he said.

"How did Shantel know?"

He shrugged his shoulders and shook his head no. But I was already ahead of him. I remembered my first meeting with Mrs. Harris. Her dog Peanut charged me with his fangs bared. Admittedly they were tiny fangs, but they could have played havoc with my shoelaces. "I once had a sheltie named Shelteen," I had said to her. She may have mentioned this to Shantel. Dog owners are incurable gossips.

I also realized that Rodney could have nosed around, asked a few questions, and dug up the information about the Hollister Case from the Denver Public Library newspaper archive. Or he could have called DPD and inquired about a cabbie named Brendan Murphy who had been involved in one or more police investigations. He might have passed himself off as a journalist. Anybody could do that. What's a journalist anyway? Just a nosey parker with a college degree. Rodney could have even talked to a Rocky driver, or a Yellow driver, or a Checker, or a Metro, or … I guess it's like my teachers used to say—research is everything. I failed everything by the way.

As I sat there at the table I suddenly began to feel a psychological tic evaporating from my brain. That was a new one on me. It felt kind of good. It made me want to seek some kind of goddamn therapy and give my brain a real "latrine party." That's the euphemism we dogfaces used in reference to thoroughly cleaning and mopping a barracks for inspection. In many ways my brain is like an army barracks. I hear a lot of snoring in there.

"As long as we're on the subject, there's something important I want to ask you," I said.

"Okay."

"Were you with Rodney Letour on Saturday night?"

"You mean on Halloween night?"

"Yes."

"No. Me and Conrad and the other guys went to a costume party."

I took a long pull at my espresso and set it down. "The reason I asked is because the house at Riverside Cemetery burned down on Saturday night."

The muscles of his face went slack and his eyes got wide. I knew I was revealing new information to him. Faces don't lie, although the people behind the faces often try to get their eyelids and certain sections of their jowls to take part in fraudulent reactions. But I'm a face expert. I've seen thousands of them in my rearview mirror. I'm *The Mirror Creature*.

"The burning of the house was reported on TV," I said. "I take it you didn't happen to catch that story."

"No I didn't," he said. "My mom and I don't own a TV."

I grabbed my espresso and drank deeply. I needed it bad.

Real bad.

What the hell do people do who don't own TVs? Play harpsichords? Paint pictures? *Talk* to each other, fer the luvva Christ?

"I spend most of my time reading books," Lester said. "Shantel has been trying to get me to write a novel but I'm not much interested in being a writer."

My jowls went slack. "What are you interested in?"

"The behavior of people," he said. "When I get to college I want to major in psychology."

I blanched. The conversation was spinning completely out of control. Was this Future Shrink of America messing with my gourd—or was it just the espresso?

"So you didn't hear anything about the house burning down?"

"No—what happened?"

"They don't know. The police think it was arson."

"Gosh," he said. He said something else, too, but I don't remember what. I was too busy thinking about the fact that I rarely heard anyone say "Gosh." I wonder what the derivation of the word is. Astonishment, I suppose.

"Shantel is a good writer," he was saying when my mind got back on track. "You should ask her if she would let you read her book about Princess Ariella."

"All right, I'll do that," I said. To this day I'm not sure if I was lying, but I will say that I never read Shantel's manuscript. I'm waiting for Scribner's hardback to come out next month.

"Is there anything else you want to tell me?" I said.

"No. I guess that's all. Except to say I'm sorry."

"That's okay, pal. And I want to let you know that I think it was very mature of you to have this conversation with me. I appreciate how difficult it must have been. I don't hold any hard feelings against you, and I want to thank you for telling me all these things. I also want to tell you that you don't have to worry about Rodney Letour bothering you or your mother. I believe he left town."

"That's what Uncle Jeff told me this morning."

End of conversation.

"How are you two gentlemen doing?"

I glanced around and saw Shantel standing over my left shoulder. She was clutching a hardback copy of *Les Misèrables*. I turned back, grabbed my espresso, and finished it off. I heard the echoing laughter of zombies.

"Mr. Murphy and I are finished," Lester said.

"That's good," Shantel said, holding up the book. "Look at the novel I bought."

"You can call me 'Murph' from now on," I said to Lester, as I stood up in order to set into motion the onerous process of pretending to be interested in Victor Hugo's latest best seller. It was an illustrated edition. I don't want to talk about it anymore.

Let's end the chase right here.

Unlike the time I went out to Hollywood to rescue the girl that everybody was convinced I murdered, Shantel did not kiss me on the cheek when we parted. She did shake my hand though. So did Lester, who called me "Murph" as he thanked me for the last time.

Leaving them to do whatever teenagers do at the malls when their parents are rich, I trudged out of the cul-de-sac and made my way toward the supersonic see-through elevator that would take me back up to the real world—or my "taxi" as I call it.

CHAPTER 43

Does this story have a happy ending? That depends on whether you've ever owned a 1954 Plymouth.

Buzzed on espresso and high on the joyous feeling that always comes from not having ruined the life of everybody who was in my taxi recently, I aimed the hood of 123 toward the enchanted suburb of Aurora. Destination: flapping pennants. I made a couple of feeble efforts at kidding myself but I knew I wasn't. It made me wistful to think that the corpse of ol' Betsy had been carted away to an unknown destination—but a destination is everybody's destiny. It seemed fitting.

That's the kind of logic I use when I'm trying to avoid guilt. Why I should feel guilty about the fate of one ton of Detroit steel might make a good article in *Psychology Today*, although Lester could conceivably write up a groundbreaking graduate thesis based on the inner workings of my gourd—but who couldn't?

I crossed Monaco Parkway and began eyeballing the wonders of east Colfax in search of the rent-a-wreck agency. It may have been the espresso because I arrived at Havana Street before I realized I had bypassed the site entirely. This was not unusual, so I whipped a coward's louie by going around the block and aiming my grille west.

I was halfway back to Monaco when I began to get an eerie feeling. Was that a Putt-Putt golf course I had passed a few blocks back? Where the hell was the rent-a-wreck?

I circled the block and put my mind into what I call the "methodical" mode for lack of a better misnomer, and drove slowly along Colfax studying the north side of the street looking for the flying pennants that had attracted my eyes twenty years earlier like bright and shiny spinning tops. I didn't see them anywhere.

A feeling of dread began to crawl down my spine. As a professional taxi driver I had always taken pride in my ability to negotiate the mean streets of Denver, discovering hitherto unknown shortcuts, memorizing obscure landmarks, and negotiating side streets where angels feared to tread. Like Dan'l Boone ranging confidently through the woods of ol' Kentuck, I felt right at home in the urban wilderness of the Denver metro area. Yet suddenly I felt lost.

I circled around and drove west again, and began to experience the creeping fear that is said to filter into the minds of people who suspect that they are going completely and totally insane.

But I knew a cure for that.

I pulled into a gas station to ask directions.

A mechanic was repairing a tire in the garage. I climbed out and approached him. I asked if there was a rent-a-wreck agency somewhere around here.

He squinted at me, then picked up a rag and began wiping his hands the way bartenders do. He stepped out of the garage and looked up and down Colfax. "Rent-a-wreck," he mused.

I nodded.

"Ya know, I did see a rent-a-wreck a couple blocks west of here."

My heart soared like an eagle. I realized that I was not insane. That didn't last long.

"In fact there were about ten of them," he said. "They went out of business pretty quick. That was one of those what'cha call 'fad concepts' that work for a while and then stop working."

For some reason this made me think of writing, but I shut that off. "I thought there was a rent-a-wreck place where the old Putt-Putt golf course used to be," I said.

"Naw, the Putt-Putt's still there. The greens are there anyway, but it went out of business a long time ago. Never was no rent-a-wreck in that location."

He stopped wiping his hands with the rag and peered at me. "Why do you ask?" he said.

Because I'm insane. "I got a call over the radio to pick up a customer there." I don't know why I lied, but it was certainly not unusual.

He nodded, then shook his head no. His body language killed the conversation. I liked that.

"Thanks anyway," I said.

I climbed back into 123 and pulled out of the station heading west. I looked at my rearview mirror and saw the mechanic wiping his hands with the rag and staring after me. I had a funny feeling he knew I lied to him. Again, not unusual. Par for the course.

All of the sudden I began to get another eerie feeling. When I arrived at Colorado Boulevard I turned left and headed for 13th Avenue. I turned right on 13th and drove west. As I passed one particular street the phrase "penny lady" welled up in my mind. It's a long story.

I kept driving until I came in sight of my apartment building. By then I was starting to sweat. I will even go so far as to admit that I was afraid. I was afraid I would pull into the parking lot behind my building and see an empty space where I used to park ol' Betsy. I slowed as I approached the entrance to the lot. I almost closed my eyes as I made a right turn into the drive but my years as a cabbie had taught me not to do what I normally do when I am confronted by almost everything. Blue Boy was still there.

I drove right up to the rear bumper, parked, and climbed out.

I approached the Plymouth with trepidation. I glanced around at the neighborhood to see if anybody was watching me, then I reached out and placed a sweaty palm on the trunk lid. The car didn't disappear with the muffled pop that you often hear in cartoons. I was relieved not only to discover that the car was real but that the trunk lid was firmly locked in place. As I said, the trunk of ol' Betsy had a broken latch so I kept it shut with a bit of twine. It tended to bounce when I drove around. The thumping got to be annoying, but not so annoying that I tried to repair it. You may have experienced this yourself.

I stood in the choice V-spot touching Blue Boy and wondering what the hell I was supposed to do. I had possession of a car that I had not paid for. This was unusual, I swear. Should I call the cops? Should I contact the Bureau of Missing Persons and tell Duncan and Argyle that I misplaced the owner of a rent-a-wreck agency?

Renfield started laughing, but he actually seemed amused. I visualized the interview between myself and the detectives in a small room down at DPD. I saw myself spilling my guts and confessing involvement in the burning of an historic building in Globeville and the mysterious immolation of a house near Golden. By now Renfield's laughter was echoing off the walls of the condo next door, so I shut it off fast. I noted a few heads peering out of the windows, thus confirming my long-held suspicion that people sometimes look at me.

To cover up my abnormal behavior I pretended to examine the body of Blue Boy, looking for dents and dings. To further enhance the verisimilitude of my performance I opened the shotgun door and leaned in like a normal person might do. To put a final cap on my "act" and bring down the curtain I popped open the glove compartment as if I was looking for the sorts of things that people keep in glove compartments. That's when I saw it:

The pink slip.

I froze.

I glanced around the neighborhood, then reached in and grabbed the piece of paper. I stood up and examined it.

I started thinking then. I started thinking how odd it was that the same rent-a-wreck agency where I had gotten ol' Betsy had been in business after twenty years. Like the mechanic said, "… one of those 'fad concepts' that work for a while and then stop working."

I thought about the fact that the rental agent had looked exactly the same as he had looked twenty years earlier. Same straw boater. Same thin mustache. Same smile. Same oily personality. Same glint in his eye. I had written off the glint as the glint you see in the eyes of all salesmen who see me coming a mile away. But now I wasn't so sure.

As I stood there in the lot peering at the piece of paper, which for all practical purposes gave me legal title to the Plymouth, I noted the date in one corner: October 31.

Halloween.

But didn't I rent this on …?

I swallowed hard.

I almost crumpled the paper into a ball, then remembered not to do that.

I put it into my T-shirt pocket and subsequently made one of the biggest decisions of my life: I decided to quit work.

I had already earned my standard fifty bucks, and I still had five days left to earn back my lease plus profits. Ergo, I had no rational reason whatsoever to continue driving. I'll admit it. My reasons for not doing things are not always rational, but let's just leave it at that.

I climbed back into 123 and drove it around the block and parked it in front of my building.

I grabbed my accoutrement, locked the vehicle, and walked around to the back lot, noting that Blue Boy was still resting in the choice V-spot like a faithful mutt. That's when it occurred to me to attach my naked chrome lady to the hood. I was willing to bet I could find a skilled person somewhere in the Denver metro area who would do that for me if I gave him enough money. People will do almost anything for money. I don't know why I say "almost." I'll let you take it from there.

I headed for the fire escape knowing that in the days to come I would peek out the window of my crow's nest to see if the Plymouth still existed, and then, after awhile, I would stop peeking. Standard operating procedure after developing a psychological tic. I also knew that the day would come when I would step outside and discover Blue Boy missing. But I knew the cure for that. A quick call to Gladys and everything would be copacetic.

As I trudged up the steps toward my back door I made an attitude adjustment and decided to embrace the piece of advice that Big Al had given to me so long ago that it didn't matter because he gives it to me a dozen times a year anyway. "Just pretend none of this ever happened, Tenderfoot."

As I unlocked the back door I reminded myself to speak with Mr. Hogan at the first opportunity and tell him the time had come to remove the greenback from the top of his desk. That was one ritual I was willing to perform, and not only out of respect for Mr. Hogan but because I wanted to ask him if I might be allowed to have the dollar. It would be a souvenir of one of the worst weeks of my life, and would remind me to never again get involved in the personal life of a fare. I needed that reminder.

I needed it bad.

Real bad.

But mostly I wanted the dollar to buy a scratch ticket.

Like I say: I have absolutely no ethics.

The End